The Da Vinci Legacy

The
Da Vinci
Legacy

LEWIS
PERDUE

TOR®

A TOM DOHERTY ASSOCIATES BOOK
NEW YORK

This is a work of fiction. All the characters, organizations, and events portrayed in this novel are either products of the author's imagination or are used fictitiously.

THE DA VINCI LEGACY

This book was originally published in 1983 by Pinnacle Books.

A Tor Book
Published by Tom Doherty Associates, LLC
175 Fifth Avenue
New York, NY 10010

www.tor-forge.com

Tor® is a registered trademark of Tom Doherty Associates, LLC.

ISBN   978-0-7653-3305-6

First Tor Mass Market Edition: January 2004

Printed in the United States of America

P1

To Papa who gave me my love of words
from which all my writing springs

About half of this book is true, so I'd like to thank some of the many people who helped me with the research.

I am particularly indebted to Dr. Carlo Pedretti of UCLA and Bologna, one of the world's most renowned experts on Leonardo, and Lella Smith of the Armand Hammer Foundation for access to much of this book's information on the Codex Hammer that was purchased by Dr. Armand Hammer, chairman of Occidental Petroleum.

Doctors Rich Morrison and Andrew Cassadenti of the UCLA Medical Center were instrumental in helping me research toxic agents and their antidotes.

I am also grateful to a number of others who helped me but need to remain anonymous to protect their careers and reputation.

I also owe a debt of gratitude to my wife, Megan, who continues to put up with me and my writing. *(This is even more so given the twenty years that have passed since I wrote this for the first edition published in 1983.)*

As I said, about half of this book is true. It's up to the reader to figure out which half.

The Da Vinci Legacy

Book One

Chapter 1

Killing made him happy. Waiting to kill was the only thing that made him anxious. He was anxious now as he sat in the rocky cool that shielded him from the broiling heat outside.

With the back of his hand he wiped away the tiny beads of sweat that had formed on his upper lip despite the cool of this cave, this man-made cave. Stealthily he looked about him, careful to pretend an interest in the mass. Yes, he thought, it was a cave made by man—of marble from Elba and gold from Africa and lavishments from the world at large. He loathed churches—all churches—but especially ones like this that had extravagantly demanded the life's labors of thousands. Churches and caves. They were all Stone Age abodes for Stone Age thinking.

"Lord God of Hosts," the congregation chanted in unison. "Heaven and Earth are filled with Your glory." Trying to remain unobtrusive, he mumbled along with them in his journeyman Italian.

He looked about him at the elaborate paintings of saints and angels and seraphim and cherubim covering the cavernous walls. And in marked contrast to the grandeur, he saw the people—poor and lower-middle-class folk sitting stiffly, unaccustomed to the formal clothes they wore only to mass. The men, with much callused hands, hair obviously cut by their wives. The wives, corpulent yet somehow dignified by their sheer bulk. And among them all, squirming ill-at-ease youngsters who'd rather be almost anywhere else at all.

Standing out from this drab and ordinary crowd like gems in some plowed field were tourists—mostly American he figured—well dressed, well coiffed, well fed, just like him. Although at six-three he was a bit taller than the others, he could still be mistaken for an American tourist. That had been the fatal mistake of more than a few people.

"Hosanna in the Highest." He looked at the prayer book, reading along.

"Blessed is he who comes in the name of the Lord."

In front of him a small boy of about nine twisted restlessly from side to side, bored with the service, and apparently unimpressed with the cathedral, the Duomo at Pisa, with its famous Leaning Tower nearby.

"Hosanna in the Highest."

The congregation fell silent and the priest, robed in red silk vestments—for this was July 2, the Feast of Precious Blood—continued the mass in Italian.

The man wiped away the new sweat that had formed on his lip, and nervously combed his fingers through his sandy blond hair. As the words of the mass washed over him, he scanned the nave. Unlike most cathedrals, this one was well illuminated with huge windows at its apex that bathed the interior with light. Gently, almost imperceptibly, the massive bronze lantern they called Galileo's lamp oscillated with the air.

The man glanced anxiously up at the railed walkway perched almost at the ceiling of the massive cathedral and at the single door to which it led. His eyes floated slowly down from the door, across the gold-encrusted image of Christ, and down to the altar with its imposing crucifix, six feet tall, bronze, and designed by . . . he searched his memory . . . by Giambologna. Yes, he thought, that was it, Giambologna. Christ, what this civilization could have done if its finest minds hadn't wasted all their time carving, casting, and painting crosses.

"Yet on that very night," the priest intoned, "He gave the greatest proof of His love. He took the bread in His hands." The priest took the bread and raised his eyes to heaven. The man looked up too, sneaking one more glance at the railing, the door.

"He thanked you, blessed"—the priest made the sign of the cross over the bread— "and He broke the bread and gave it to His friends." Watching intensely, the man's hard, cold blue eyes did not waver from the altar as he reached into his French tailored coat and touched the ivory handle of the Sescepita with his fingertips. Reassured, he returned his hand to his thigh. In front of him, the nine-year-old tapped the floor restlessly with the toes of cheap shoes. The noise played a jittery pitter-pat on the man's nerves.

The smell of incense grew stronger and the colors of the cathedral intensified. He could feel each layer of clothing that rested damply on his skin. His senses always grew more sensitive at times like this. He loved killing; it made him feel so alive.

"When the supper was ended," the priest continued, picking up the chalice in both hands, "He took the cup, gave thanks, and shared it with them, saying: *This is the cup of My Blood—*"

The man's muscles tensed like strained ropes.

"The Blood of the New Covenant."

The man looked up at the door above the altar.

"This Blood shall be shed for you, and—"

A shriek of blinding terror filled the cathedral. A thin man, bound hands and feet, hurtled toward the floor, his neck tethered to a stout nylon climber's rope.

"No-o-o-o-o," the man yelled in German as he fell. "Oh. Jesus! No-o-o-o!"

As the screaming body plunged through the Sunday morning silence, the blond man stood and made his way toward the door; the nine-year-old stopped tapping his feet. The priest dropped the jewel-encrusted chalice; it clattered down the steps of the altar, spilling the consecrated wine as it did.

The nylon climbing rope suddenly ran out of slack and throttled the thin man's screams as the noose closed about his neck. But still the body fell as the elastic rope stretched tight. The body smashed into the marble floor with the muffled thuds of breaking bones.

The blond man was halfway to the exit when the rope jerked back to its original length, yanking the broken body upward, where it tumbled toward the altar. The congregation held its breath in a silence that seemed to suspend time and gravity. For one short awesome instant, the body seemed suspended above the altar. Then the next moment, the thin man's abdomen impaled itself on the top of Giambologna's cross.

Blood flowed freely down the image of Christ and across the altar, curdling as it mixed with the wine from the overturned chalice. The priest crossed himself and fell to his knees begging forgiveness.

Horrified screams filled the cathedral as a few worshipers went to the aid of the priest, and the rest surged for the exit just behind the blond man.

Outside, the blond man turned briskly to the left and pursued the figure of a large man walking briskly from the cathedral, toward the round, marble baptistry that stood in the shadow of the tower. Screams grew louder now as the terrified congregation flooded the grounds of the cathedral, calling for the police.

The baptistry quickly emptied as people rushed outside to see what the commotion was about.

"Wonderful work," the blond man said warmly as soon as he was alone with the hulking man he had followed inside. "Even I didn't see you throw him over the rail and I was looking."

"Danke, mein Herr," the hulk responded respectfully. He had a heavy Germanic face and the build of a Bremen steelworker, which he had once been. And though the same height as the blond man, the German easily weighed fifty pounds more.

"I'm quite sincere," the blond man continued in faultless German. "It was quite a performance. The lesson will not go unnoticed. I particularly liked the bungee rope tied around his neck."

The German beamed. They called him "The Schoolmaster" not for his education, but for all the "lessons" he had taught others. "Thank you again, *mein Herr,* but you flatter me too much. I am only doing my job." He smiled expectantly.

The blond man slipped a well-manicured hand into his coat. What he withdrew, however, was not money, but a long knife with a round ivory handle, ornamented with gold, silver, and jewels. In the Middle Ages, the Sescepita had been used by pagan priests to perform sacrifices. It was priceless.

The Schoolmaster was quick for a big man, but he failed to react in time. The first slash spilled his intestines across the cool marble of the baptistry. The second left him with a hideous red grin below his chin. He slid to the floor, his back against the font.

"Ah, Schoolmaster," the blond man whispered in German to the fading light in the big man's eyes. "A little knowledge is a dangerous thing. A lot is even more dangerous." He paused as the large man's eyelids flickered. "And too much? Well, too much can get you killed." There was a flicker of comprehension in the eyes before they hid forever behind the man's heavy eyelids.

The blond man quickly wiped off the ancient weapon on the German's shirt and resheathed it. As he strode from the baptistry, he wondered briefly how long it would be before someone else thought he knew too much.

Chapter 2

Wednesday, July 5

The day dazzled. Sunlight glinted off sand and water, and poured from the cloudless sky, as Vance Erikson sped south along the Pacific Coast Highway, hunched over the handlebars of his restored 1948 Indian motorcycle. The powerful engine growled between his legs as he passed car after car. It felt good to be back in touch with civilization, even if it meant having to deal with the sycophants and lizard-faced accountants who worked for the oil company.

Less than an hour before, Erikson had rolled into the rugged Ventura County exploration camp, and the administrator—the most reptilian of lizard-faced accountants—rushed from the trailer.

"Kingsbury wants to see you," Lizard Face said breathlessly. "Where have you been? Why didn't you take your radio with you? Where are your monthly reports?" The sentences rolled out without punctuation and filled with undisguised contempt. Lizard Face hated him, would have gotten him fired if not for two reasons: Vance's unorthodox methods had made him the number-one exploration geologist Continental Pacific Oil had ever had, and besides that, the company's owner, Harrison Kingsbury, had all but legally adopted Vance as a son.

The intersection of Sunset Boulevard grew near very quickly at ninety miles per hour, and Erikson began slowing. The traffic would pick up here. No matter—he consulted the diver's watch on his wrist—he had plenty of time.

At the turnoff to his house—a little two-bedroom stucco beach bungalow only two blocks from the Con-PacCo Building—he hesitated. Maybe he should swing by there and change his clothes. The plaid shirt and dungarees he wore now were dirty and beat-up from a week in the bush. He sighed heavily. No, not yet. He wasn't ready to face those ghosts.

As he approached the ConPacCo Building he saw a collection of vans and sedans, bearing the logos of L.A. television stations, parked at the curb in front of the building. One of Kingsbury's media events, obviously. Vance maneuvered the bike between two of the vans that blocked the wheelchair ramp, drove the bike up on the sidewalk, and killed the engine.

As soon as he stepped through the doors, he was accosted by an athletic, conservatively dressed man in his early thirties. Nelson Bailey, ConPacCo's vice president in charge of exploration logistics, and a Harvard MBA, looked as if he'd just stepped from the pages of *GQ*.

"I heard you were coming," Bailey said flatly. His face,

though not outwardly hostile, betrayed nothing resembling a smile.

"I didn't expect a welcoming committee," Vance replied sarcastically. "Especially not one of your rank." Vance kept walking and swept past the man. Reversing his path, Bailey caught up with Vance as they reached the elevators that went to the top floor. Vance pressed the call button.

"He's in a hurry," Vance said, turning to smile at the vice president whose annoyance played so clearly on his face. "I don't think it is in either of our best interests to keep the founder waiting."

The dark mood on Bailey's face deepened. "You think you're so smart, don't you, mister? Well, you're going to get yours one of these days."

"What's wrong this time?" Vance retorted. "Didn't I use the right typeface on my monthly projection reports?"

"You damn well know what's wrong. You sent me the same goddamned report this month as you did last month."

"Correct," Vance replied. The elevator arrived.

"Well, you can't do that," Bailey said as they boarded the elevator.

"Why not? The figures are the same."

"We have systems and regulations in this company and they're there for a reason—"

"Yeah, it's a freaking full-employment act for brown-nosing bureaucrats."

"Goddamn it, Erikson!" Bailey exploded. "You can't just continue to flout our system. The old man can't live forever, he can't protect your eccentric ways after he's gone. We're going to get you!"

The elevator glided to a halt and the doors slid open.

"We know what you and the old man are up to with this Da Vinci thing," Bailey said quietly, but not so quietly that Vance could miss the cold hatred in his voice. "We know all about it, and if you're not careful, you could find yourself in a situation you can't handle."

Vance stepped out of the elevator and turned to face the other man. He was smiling as the elevator doors closed.

What could he know? Vance wondered. Even *he* didn't know what significance his Da Vinci report could have had. Besides, it was an esoteric item of interest more to historians and art collectors than to anyone else.

We know what you and the old man are up to . . .

What the hell, Vance decided as he headed for the auditorium. Inside the auditorium, he stood for a moment in the back of the room to get his bearings. The television klieg lights illuminated the podium; the small conference auditorium was packed with reporters and ConPacCo personnel, including, to Vance's surprise, virtually the entire staff of the Kingsbury Foundation, the philanthropic end of the corporation and Kingsbury's vehicle for supporting the arts.

He stood there in his faded jeans, muddy hiking boots, and plaid shirt and combed his dark brown hair with the fingers of both hands, trying to bring to it some semblance of order. His muscular body, hardened by a rugged life in the outdoors, gave shape to his grubby clothes and to the cracked brown leather air force flight jacket he always wore when he rode his bike. Vance squinted against the television lights as his eyes focused on Kingsbury.

Kingsbury stood on the podium, trying to quiet the

crowd and bring them to order. His white hair, as always neatly combed back exposing his perfect widow's peak, shone under the television lights almost like a halo. Beneath the thick shock of hair was a patrician's face, lined with the honorable lines of a man who had known adversity and overcome it in style.

What a man, Vance thought admiringly. The son of a Welsh mine worker, Kingsbury had immigrated to the United States in 1920 as a teenager. Within five years after arriving in New York, Kingsbury had parlayed a nearly bankrupt fuel oil distributorship into a chain that covered five states in the Northeast. Two days before the bottom dropped out of the stock market in 1929, he was a millionaire. Because he had not speculated in the market, his business survived the Depression handsomely, and he'd used the profits to open up trade concessions in China, expanding those to oil drilling and exploration. He had earned a seat in history alongside the great oil entrepreneurs Jean Paul Getty and Armand Hammer. His was the largest independently owned oil company in the world, kept large and successful through his unflagging energy and unorthodox thinking. Vance shuddered to think what would happen to the company when Kingsbury died and the android MBA clones got their hands on it—they'd probably sell out to some multinational.

"We may as well begin," commanded Harrison Kingsbury, and the room quickly grew quiet. "Mr. Erikson will be along shortly and I'll want him to do most of the talking. After all, this is really his discovery. But I'll tell you now that the Kingsbury Foundation is about to begin a piece of investigative reporting into one of the first recorded cover-ups in history."

Still unseen in the shadows at the back of the room, Vance groaned inwardly at Kingsbury's overdone sense of the theatric. Still, the television newspeople loved the old man for it; they were eating it up. Vance was considering a quick escape and had in fact turned toward the exit when Kingsbury suddenly spotted him.

"Here he is now."

Like well-cued Rockettes, the entire assemblage swiveled to face Vance. "Come on up here, Mr. Erikson, and speak to the gentlemen and ladies of the press." Vance gave them all a wan smile and headed for the podium noting that the meat puppets—those well-coiffed, sartorially splendid television announcers with their capped teeth and well-coached voices—all gave him frowns of disapproval for his rough and dusty clothes.

"Straight from the oil fields, I see," Kingsbury commented after Vance arrived at his side. The audience laughed indulgently.

"As you all know," Kingsbury continued, his voice suddenly businesslike, "Vance Erikson leads a double life. He is not only the best exploration geologist in the world . . ."

Vance winced at the compliment. ". . . but he is also the finest amateur Da Vinci scholar in modern times. He assisted me and my consultant, Dr. Geoffrey Martini, in the recent purchase of a rare codex—one of the most beautiful collections of writing by Leonardo da Vinci. Through their excellent guidance and advice, I obtained that magnificent codex from an old and venerable Italian family who had never before allowed the public to inspect it.

"In examining the codex, Mr. Erikson made a startling

discovery: Two of the pages were actually a clever forgery, dating from shortly after Leonardo's death. The forgery was obviously designed to cover up a missing section. I have decided to throw the financial muscle of the Kingsbury Foundation and Continental Pacific Oil Company behind a search, to be headed by Mr. Erikson, to unearth the reason behind this Renaissance cover-up, and to trace and recover, if possible, the missing pages themselves. And now, I'll turn things over to Mr. Erikson."

". . . and he's announcing it at a news conference at this very minute." Nelson Bailey leaned forward in his leather executive's chair and tugged nervously at his pin-striped vest as he spoke. "That asshole Erikson is with him. The old man is turning this into a genuine media show."

"Don't get so excited," a low voice from halfway around the world said soothingly. "The missing pages are so buried in history there's no chance they can trace them now—at least not before we obtain them."

"But you don't know this guy Erikson," Bailey whined.

"Don't *worry*. The time is so close now, we could carry this off even if the old man and his helper knew what was in those papers."

"But you don't *know* Erikson," Bailey persisted. "At least let's take care of him before he can do any damage."

"No, Nelson, and that's final." The voice was stern now. "I think you're letting your personal dislike for Erikson cloud your judgment. That is not what the Bremen Legation is paying you for. We pay you to observe and to report. You've done a good job of that, and I suggest you keep on doing it. We will decide what action is going to be taken and when. Do you understand?"

"Yes," Bailey said anxiously. "But you—"

"No buts. The transaction is entering its most delicate stage, and I want to make sure nothing upsets our liturgical friends."

Why was he dealing with idiots like this Bailey? the man in Germany asked himself as he ran his free hand over the top of his immaculate blond hair. An insignificant stooge, that's all the man was, hired to keep an eye on the Da Vinci Codex until the transaction was concluded. It was unfortunate that the codex had gone to a buyer like Kingsbury, with his unorthodox manner and his own Da Vinci scholar. For someone whose full-time profession was geology, Erikson was surprisingly good. Bremen Legation's dossier on Vance Erikson ranked him, in fact, the second-best Da Vinci scholar in the world, behind only Professor Geoffrey Martini. No matter, the blond man decided. Even with both experts working full-time on locating the missing papers, Kingsbury still couldn't stop the Legation from concluding the transaction. And once the transaction was complete—he smiled to himself—then nothing and no one would stop the Legation from doing anything. Anything at all.

"Don't worry, Bailey," the blond man said, modulating his voice again. "Just keep me informed on what's taking place with Erikson, and we'll make sure the situation doesn't get out of hand. If we have to, we'll teach your friend a little lesson. Does that make you feel better?"

"I guess so," Bailey said hesitantly. "For now."

"Good. Good-bye." Quickly leaving his elegant office, the blond man strode down a short hallway and into another room. Slipping on a glove, he grabbed a large brown Norway rat from a cage, holding it by its tail to avoid being bitten. Then, still holding the rat, he returned to his office and flung the rat into a far corner. Before the rodent could strike the floor, a sleek falcon sprang from its perch and caught it between sharpened talons. With a quick crack, the rat's neck broke in the bird's powerful beak.

"Herrman," the blond man said in German into the intercom. "Please clean up for Mephistopheles when he's through."

Vance Erikson looked up to stare into the klieg lights. "I'm not really prepared for all this," he told the assemblage of reporters frankly. "I've been out of the office for some time—"

"As have I," Kingsbury interrupted, patting Vance's shoulder in a fatherly gesture. "But when I got back last night and read Mr. Erikson's report on the codex, which was waiting for me, I grew quite excited.

"Normally I would have given this my immediate attention, but as you all know, I was defending us against that well-publicized hostile takeover battle. In any event, I believe this is the most exciting thing to happen in the art world in decades. Vance," he said, turning to the younger man with an apologetic shrug and a please-forgive-me smile, "I know it's been weeks since you prepared the report, but I'm sure you can remember enough. Why don't you just wing it for the reporters?"

Vance threw up his hands in surrender and grinned. "Okay," he said, turning back to the crowd. "I'll do my best.

"Those of you who covered the purchase of the Codex Kingsbury may remember that in addition to being one of the few Da Vinci codices never translated from Italian—and never shown to the public—it is also one of the few that Leonardo, or his close friend Francesco Melzi, bound while he was still alive.

"Leonardo worked on large sheets of parchment," Vance explained, warming to the discussion, "and covered each sheet with a bewildering variety of drawings, inventions, funny stories, and even pornographic doodles. Most of these pages bore no relationship to each other, and seemed like the ramblings of an eccentric genius. After Leonardo's death in 1519, his drawings were left to his friend Melzi, who—"

"We all know most of that already." It was an auburn-haired woman in one of the first rows who stood up and interrupted Erikson. "That's history. We can look it up in our clips if we need to. Why don't you get to the point?"

Vance recognized her immediately. She was Suzanne Storm, associate editor of *Haute Culture* magazine, and probably the bitchiest woman he had ever met. He couldn't seem to get away from her. Every time he delivered a paper on Leonardo, every time he accompanied Kingsbury to a museum opening, she was there, with her sarcastic comments. She resented Erikson as an interloper with a scientific degree intruding on the world of art and culture—her world. She never passed an opportunity to belittle him as a dilettante who was out of his league. Chagrined, he glanced quickly over at Kingsbury, who had seated himself in a folding chair to one side of the podium. The older man merely smiled benignly.

"Well, if everyone here has all the background material they need—" Vance searched the faces of the press, looking for a clue. Well, if any of them needed background, they would get it later. Apparently no one wanted to tangle with Suzanne Storm. "So be it. Very well, Ms. Storm, what would you like to know?"

"For a start, *Mister* Erikson, how about telling us just how you discovered the forgery when the best Da Vinci scholars of the past four hundred years overlooked it. And just what was in the missing pages." She paused. "And why someone would want to cover up the missing pages." The reporter looked around at her fellow media representatives, then back at Vance. "Would you have us believe," she asked provocatively, "that this was a Renaissance Watergate—starring the original Machiavelli?"

Vance ignored the sarcasm. "I'll take your questions in order," he said evenly. "I discovered the forgery shortly after Mr. Kingsbury purchased his codex—known then as the Codex Caizzi, after the Caizzi family. I was browsing through the collection of the national library in Madrid looking for Da Vinci connections, when I found the diary of one Antonio de Beatis, secretary to the Cardinal of Aragon in the early 1500s. It seems that de Beatis convinced Leonardo to let him take a look at his collected writings."

"You're digressing, Mr. Erikson."

"Thank you for keeping me on track, Ms. Storm." Vance eyed her steadily.

"At any rate, de Beatis spent several years reading Leonardo's notebooks and cataloging them. De Beatis's diary contained a complete index of Leonardo's writing including the only collection which had actually been bound at the time—the codex Mr. Kingsbury purchased from the Caizzis. In comparing de Beatis's index with the purchased codex, I noticed a discrepancy in the contents—"

"Which was? Mr. Erikson, please get to the point." As Vance turned involuntarily to look at Suzanne Storm again, he was gratified to see the arts reporter for the *L.A. Times* lean over to her and say distinctly: "Give him a chance, will you?" Several other members of the audience murmured their concurrence.

"Two pages of the codex purchased by Mr. Kingsbury had been forged," Vance continued. "The watermarks on the paper were of a type which Leonardo did not have access to. They were of a type found on paper made some time after Leonardo's death. The subject matter of the forged materials is inconsequential and seeks to serve as a transition over the missing pages. The missing pages, according to the diary of the cardinal's secretary, concerned Leonardo's observation on weather, storms, and lightning."

"Why would anyone want to cover up the theft of those pages?" Storm asked. "And who would want to do that?"

"I don't know the answer to that, Ms. Storm. Perhaps our investigation in coming weeks will shed some light on that."

"I doubt it," she said. "And how is it that *you*—an amateur—found this diary when recognized scholars missed it?"

"Because I was just browsing in the stacks. The diary was apparently forgotten or miscataloged."

"You found it by accident?" Her voice was skeptical.

"Yes," he said, "and if you remember your history, there were quite a number of Leonardo's writings that were lost at the same library because they had been miscataloged."

"Mr. Erikson did the unusual, Ms. Storm." Harrison Kingsbury's commanding voice filled the auditorium now. He'd stood up and was walking toward the podium. "He took the unexpected route and he found what no one else knew existed. That's how he finds oil for ConPacCo, Ms. Storm, and that's why he's been so successful. It's called looking beyond your own nose." He smiled at Vance. "I think that's enough for today," he told the reporters. "If you need any further information please contact my public information people. Thank you for coming."

Chapter 3

Friday, August 4, Amsterdam

Someone was following him. Buttoning his overcoat against the probing splashes of the wind-driven rain, Vance Erikson pressed on, head against the wind. It was ludicrous: Who could be following him? If *anyone* was, he chided himself. It was just his imagination playing tricks on him.

He stopped to look up at the street marker on the side of a red brick building. Keizergracht: Yes, that was the street he wanted. The bell in the tower struck seven. He had half an hour to kill before his dinner appointment. Vance turned left, catching as he did a fuzzy glimpse of a figure gloomily obscured in the rain a block away. The streetlights had just come on, but the illumination was blanketed in the downpour that sent raindrops the size of marbles careening into the old cobblestone street, and occasionally down the back of his raincoat.

Vance moved quickly along the new path. When he looked back, he saw the figure materialize around the corner and head slowly toward him. Vance stopped. The figure stopped. Vance resumed his walk; the figure followed suit.

It didn't make sense. But then, none of the past month had made any sense at all.

First there was the surrealistic trip to his house in Santa Monica. Most of his Da Vinci notes and library were there. He'd walked in and the place was full of holes, places where Patty's things had been.

What had it been, three months? Just about. Three months ago Patty had confronted him with her list. Maybe it wouldn't have been so bad if it hadn't been for the list. They had been married for two years. True, they'd had some problems, but every couple does. She wanted security, he wanted adventure. That was where the big division came. And she wanted *things,* lots of them, and a big place to put them all. He thought things began to own people after a while.

He hadn't realized things were so bad. Maybe he hadn't wanted to see them. Time and again he asked himself how things could have gone that far without him seeing it. But it had, and on that cool Sunday afternoon in May, she had interrupted his reading of the Sunday papers and matter-of-factly told him, "I want a divorce."

That hurt. Was there someone else? he had asked. Yes. That had hurt, too. Trust had become an expendable commodity. That all hurt, but what did the most damage was the list. It was neatly outlined on the crisp white paper with Excel's neat orderly columns and rows in Patty's compulsively orderly style. It was a list of everything she had bought, how much it cost, and when it was acquired. He remembered the latest entry, a huge home entertainment system with a massive flat screen that had cost more than $10,000, bought just that January. She didn't use the system very much, but she liked *having* it. These things, she announced, she was taking with her. The rest, she said, they could split.

Ever since they had been married, she had been keeping the list. It was as if she had looked at the marriage as a temporary thing from the start, and that was what hurt the most. Whatever happened to thinking about forever? When you believed in forever, you didn't need lists.

Yes, Vance thought now as he walked through Amsterdam, that had been one hellish trip back home. But he'd survived. He managed to get his Da Vinci notes and enough clothes out of the house before the demons put any more holes in his soul. He'd wondered then if burning it all down would incinerate the demons inside him.

But he hadn't had much time to sulk.

Harrison Kingsbury had been anxious to get the search going and sent him back to Madrid three days after the press conference. Kingsbury personally drove him to the airport. The old man never had liked chauffeurs.

The trouble started in Madrid. The director of the Vinciana collection at the Biblioteca Nacional met him at the airport with profuse apologies.

"We had no idea the man was a fraud, no idea," the little man kept saying. "He had all the right credentials, all the right identification, even a letter on the papal stationery."

What, Vance had asked impatiently, was he talking about?

It took Vance nearly an hour to get the story out of the distraught director.

"It was almost a month ago," the man said. "July 5, a man who said he was an aide to the Pope had come with a request to borrow the de Beatis diary. He had a letter, signed by the Pope's principal assistant, requesting that the book be loaned to the Vatican Library for study.

"Of course we were delighted to help the Holy Father," the director blubbered. "How were we to know? When the diary had not been returned as promised we contacted the Vatican Library. They had never heard of the man! Never heard of him! The office of the Pope himself had never heard of him. The man was an imposter!"

Yes, the director said, the theft had been reported to the police, but to be brutally frank, there was little hope the diary would ever be seen again. It was probably in the private collection of a wealthy crook. Art thefts were like that, the director philosophized.

Vance left Madrid the same afternoon with the names of three people who had examined the diary before it was stolen and a description of the thief. The man who had "borrowed" the valuable book was lean and tall, with shiny black hair, a liturgical air, and a red birthmark shaped like a bird on the right side of his neck.

The rain beat harder now, marching along the canal in opaque curtains and thudding off Vance's sodden Irish tweed hat. Where was the Amsterdam he loved? Vance wondered, the *gezellig*—warmth, coziness, and outgoing sociability of its people. Inside somewhere being warm, cozy, and sociably outgoing, he thought. Although his shadower's footsteps were muffled in the rain's anarchy,

Vance knew the other man was still there; he could feel his presence.

The lights of a neighborhood bar/café glowed bright ahead, and Vance headed toward it with relief.

Inside, the warm, humid air felt good even if it was smoggy with tobacco smoke. He stood there for a moment letting some of the water drip off him, and then pushed his way through the after-work crowd and found a narrow slot at which to stand at the bar.

In his halting Dutch he ordered *oude genever*—aged Dutch gin—and then turned to face the door, hoping he'd see the man following him pass by and disappear into the night. But the man never passed the window. His drink arrived and he took a heavy swallow. The alcohol burned its way down and puddled in his stomach. He closed his eyes, took a deep breath, and slowly let it escape, making room for calm to take its place. For the first time since leaving the airport, his heart ceased its urgent tattoo.

The peace made room in his mind to allow the events of the past few days to assemble themselves in his thoughts.

He had learned that the first of the three men to examine the de Beatis diary recently had died of heart failure. That's what his widow had told Vance when he visited her in Vienna. The professor was old—nearly seventy-six— she told him, and it was best he went quickly in the night.

Traveling to Strasbourg, the tale repeated itself. A professor emeritus at the University of Strasbourg who had traveled to Madrid to look at the de Beatis diary had suffered heart failure just seven days before his sixty-eighth birthday. Two men who had read the diary, two men dead. Vance had nearly convinced himself it was a coincidence, until just a few hours ago when he noticed the man following him. He was unremarkable-looking, about five feet ten, medium build, wearing a dark, undistinguished gray suit with a forgettable tie and shirt. The only unusual physical characteristic—and what made Vance notice him—was the way the tuft of hair over each ear stuck up over the man's bald head, making him look like an owl.

Vance had first seen the man at the airport. He saw him again at the KLM bus terminal near the Rikjsmuseum. Then again at his hotel. And even after the summer storm blew in off the Zuider Zee and snuffed out the bucolic summer's day in Amsterdam, the man was still behind him.

How could it possibly be coincidence? Yet the man looked so harmless—dumpling-shaped, in his late fifties, and definitely no match for Vance.

If he'd been in the United States, he'd have confronted the man hours ago, but in a foreign city, he didn't want to cause a scene—perhaps the man spoke a language Vance didn't speak—and he especially didn't want to cause a scene over vague misapprehensions that might not be grounded at all in reality.

After another *oude genever,* Vance decided that he'd collar the man if he was waiting when he left the bar.

The third man on the list of diary readers, Vance knew, was still alive. As he sipped the sharp spicy gin, Vance recalled the conversation he'd had earlier in the day with the slightly absentminded but nevertheless brilliant Da Vinci scholar Geoffrey Martini.

Martini was spending the summer in Amsterdam studying the isolated leaves of Leonardo's notebooks that had found their way to the archives of the Dutch national library. Martini invited Vance over for the evening and Vance had eagerly accepted, relieved that his old friend and former professor at Cambridge was unharmed. Vance couldn't wait to tell him of the theft of the de Beatis diary. Vance looked at his watch; he was due at Martini's momentarily, so he paid his tab and pushed his way back into the dusk.

The rain had ended. House lights and streetlamps and the signs on stores reflected golden light off the random curved stones.

At the first two street corners, Vance turned around to look for his little owl-headed man. But the man was nowhere to be seen and Vance promptly forgot about him as his thoughts returned to the Da Vinci forgery and his visit with Martini.

Vance held Professor Martini in the greatest affection; the man had believed in him when no one else would.

He'd met Martini in 1966, in a small pub just off the Cambridge campus in England. The university officials had just finished telling Vance why they were not going to accept him. It was the matter, they had said, of the dishonorable discharge and of the considerable reputation he had made for himself in the world of gambling. Why Martini picked him out of the crowd at the Lamb and Flag that day he'd no idea, but it changed his life.

Martini listened to him explain that the dishonorable discharge had come when the army had caught him diverting supplies to build a small hospital for wounded children near Basra in the first Persian Gulf War. Though he'd been barely out of high school then, he masterminded the project, whose coconspirators included more than a dozen doctors, medica, a major in the Corps of Engineers, and others. He was the only non-officer, and when Washington found out about it all, they made him the example; the others walked without a slap on the wrist. Martini had listened sympathetically when Vance described how, desperate for money, he developed a blackjack counting method that was so successful that he had been banned from every major casino in the world, but not before he spent a year traveling from one to another amassing a small fortune.

As he made his way through the darkening gloom, Vance remembered Martini's face, the unruly shock of white hair, the droopy mustache, and the tall, thin bent frame of an aging but spry old man who would be seventy-nine in another month. A man who had thrown his weight around at the university and persuaded the administrators to admit Vance. Martini had nurtured the young man's interest in Leonardo, chided him for going into another field, and had worked side by side with him over the past decade as Vance fed his insatiable curiosity and love for Leonardo.

The prospect of seeing Martini now, for the first time in the months since Kingsbury had bought the codex, lifted Vance's spirits and invigorated him. Fifteen minutes later he yanked the old-fashioned bellpull outside the professor's narrow, four-story town house overlooking the Prinsengracht Canal.

As Vance stood by the door, he heard faint movement inside, but still the door didn't open. Vance rang the bell again. Scraping noises and thumps inside were the only response. Vance leaned over the step railing to peer into the lighted window, and through sheer curtains made out the hazy outlines of a tall man standing over one seated in an armchair.

His pulse quickened. The standing figure was definitely not the professor.

"Professor!" Vance shouted as he tried the doorknob. It was locked. "Professor Martini, are you all right?" he shouted again, pounding on the varnished mahogany door with his fist. "Open up the door, open up or I'll go for the police!" Vance leaned on the door and tried to force it open. He applied his brawny shoulder time and again, but the massive door, having withstood the rigors of five centuries, wouldn't budge now for one man.

His wild antics had attracted a half-dozen curious onlookers in the street.

"Police," he said urgently in English. "Call the police," he repeated in broken Dutch. A middle-aged man seemed to understand and pulled out a cell phone and dialed.

Vance walked down the stairs again to the front window. He was about to try to open it when the front door flew open, spilling pale yellow light on a tall, thin, dark-haired man who lunged past.

"Stop!" Vance yelled. Ignoring him, the man sprinted over the broken and uneven sidewalk. Vance shot off in pursuit.

Cars parked haphazardly on the sidewalk—as was the custom here—made the going tough. Finally, the man found a break in traffic and ran down the middle of the narrow one-way street. Vance followed him, across a bridge over the canal and then left, running with the traffic. Vance was gaining, grateful now for all of those miles he usually ran along the beach. The man's footsteps slowed as he ducked right, into an alleyway. Vance heard the man's shoes scrape on the pavement and then a thud as if the man had fallen down.

As Vance rounded the alley corner the man was but ten yards away and running with a limp. Suddenly Vance hesitated. In Iraq, he'd spent most of his time stealing cinder blocks and generators. He found himself wishing now that he'd stuck with the martial arts lessons he'd dropped a year ago after only a dozen sessions. Well, he wasn't going to let the man go, that was for sure. Gathering speed, he tackled the man from behind.

The tall man let out a cry and then gasped as Vance landed on top of him. He tried to roll away, but Vance was all over him, throwing quick wild punches, one after another, some landing, others glancing harmlessly off. The professor's assailant stood up unsteadily, favoring his right knee. Even in the dim light, Vance could see blood through a gash in the man's trousers where he'd slipped on the sidewalk.

Then the tall man loosed a left hook that snapped Vance's head back and opened up a gash over his left eye. While Vance reeled backward, the tall man took off again, limping badly. Blinded in his left eye from the blood that ran profusely from the cut, Vance stumbled forward, hitting his leg against a metal trash can. A wine bottle fell to the ground. Vance grabbed it up, wiping blood from his eye with one hand and wielding the bottle with the other. When he drew close enough, he swung the bottle as hard as he could. Vance heard the man exhale sharply and watched him tumble face first onto the pavement, where he lay, crumpled and still.

Breathing heavily, Vance wiped his eye on the sleeve of his raincoat, leaving a brilliant crimson smear across the tan poplin. The pain above his left eye became a cannon throb as he bent over the prostrate figure in the alley and rolled him over onto his back. On the right side of the man's neck, nearly hidden beneath the collar of a turtleneck sweater, was a strange red mark. Vance held his breath as he pulled the collar down. In the dim light he made out the shape. A bird, a soaring hawk.

"Jesus," Vance said out loud. Exactly the description of the man who absconded with the de Beatis diary. Squatting on his haunches, Vance searched the man's coat pockets. No identification. The man groaned, regaining consciousness. The police, Vance thought. Got to get the police. As he stood up, unsteadily, Vance heard a scuffling behind him. He spun around just in time to see the owl-headed man swinging the same wine bottle. Vance ducked but the bottle glanced off the side of his head, stunning him; he dropped to all fours. The man swung again and this time caught him squarely on the crown. Vance went down heavily, marveling at the galaxy of brilliant pinpointed colored stars.

As he felt the musty wet odor of the pavement, he wondered if this was the part where the man was supposed to put the bullet in his head.

Chapter 4

The world returned reluctantly with a desultory accretion of time and light, bringing with it the relentless throb of pain. When Vance opened his eyes, he saw only a blur. Gradually, he realized he couldn't focus his eyes because he was lying facedown in an alley. He struggled to remember where, what . . .

He pushed himself up on one elbow. With his free hand he gingerly explored the cut over his eye. It had stopped bleeding. He ran his hand over the rapidly growing hen's egg on the base of his skull; the finger came back without blood.

Laboring to his feet, Vance leaned against the alley wall, trying to make the world stop spinning. Vance started to walk and his knees buckled. Moments later he stood up again, and cautiously walked toward the mouth of the alley, clutching the rough brick wall for support. Nearby church bells struck eight. He'd not been unconscious for very long.

As he approached Professor Martini's house, he saw the police cars and an ambulance. Fear for Martini's safety cleared his head in a moment. He broke into a jog, ignoring the growing hammering in his head. A large crowd mobbed the narrow lane between the canal and the row houses.

"Let me through!" he demanded. "Let me through, please." A few annoyed heads turned to confront him, but at the sight of this bloody man with the crazed eyes, people quickly stood aside.

A blue-uniformed constable at the front door took a drag from a filterless cigarette and watched Vance make his way up the steps.

"How is he?" Vance asked. "I'm a friend."

The constable took another drag on his cigarette before dropping it on the stone step leading to Martini's house and grinding it out with the toe of a stolid, trustworthy shoe.

"What happened to you?" the constable asked.

"I think I got hit by the same man."

The constable nodded.

"And you would be?"

"Vance Erikson. Professor Martini and I—"

Recognition spread over the constable's face. "I've read about you in the newspaper. You have something to do with Da Vinci."

Vance nodded.

"Your friend is dead, I'm afraid."

Vance stared with gaping mouth.

"Come." The detective took Vance's elbow and tried to steer him toward a platoon of Amsterdam police cars. "Come with me, let's talk."

"No!" Vance twisted out of the detective's grip. "I don't believe you." He headed toward the open doorway. "I want to see."

"Look here," the detective said. "I don't think you want to see, not if he was your friend."

But Vance was already through the door. In the front sitting room, uniformed and plainclothes officers huddled around an armchair. A crime-scene technician took photos. Vance felt his heart collapse when he walked closer to the object of their attention.

Tied to the armchair, Professor Martini's body hung limply at the ropes around his arms and chest. The beige rug beneath the chair in the modest living room glistened red. The professor's white hair was matted with blood, his face puffy and bruised. His head hung loose, chin on chest, his wisdom, all that knowledge, all that goodness tied up in the mysterious neural connections of his brain now lost, gone with the last synaptic spark.

The Dutch constable nodded to the others, then, along with them, watched in silence as Vance walked slowly over to Martini's body and tenderly grasped the hand.

"Good-bye," Vance said, and turned slowly away.

After a heavy silence the constable spoke: "You know we'll need to talk with you, don't you?" Vance nodded. "Where are you staying?" Vance told him, and the constable assigned one of his squad to take Vance back to get himself cleaned up. This time, Vance went without a complaint.

*   *   *

After the doctor had left his room and he'd showered, Vance sat on the edge of his bed, two detectives arrived with a bottle of *half om half,* a once traditional but now increasingly rare Dutch liqueur. He drank the spicy, orange-hinted drink and answered questions as the detective asked them. He described his relationship with Martini, the reason for tonight's visit, and the man with the hawklike birthmark.

The next question shocked Vance.

"Do you know what or who Tosi is?"

"No," Vance lied quickly without quite thinking about the deception. "Why?"

"Your friend managed to write that name on his trousers with his own blood."

Chapter 5

James Elliott Kimball IV squinted through the haze of cigarette and hashish smoke, trying to ignore his middle-aged dining partner. Across the capacious room, a fleshy, bald-headed man lay on his back on a velvet divan while an amply furnished woman, naked save for nylons and a black lace garter belt, covered his completely nude body with kisses. Around the room, at least two dozen more people in pairs, trios, or other combinations lasciviously ministrated to each other's bodies and sexual fantasies.

The food at the Caligula Club was not much better than average. Still, the ambiance, Kimball reflected, definitely placed it in a category of its own. A members-only establishment in a wealthy suburb of Amsterdam, it catered to every human appetite, for food, drink, and sexual pleasure. The group sex area was illuminated with a computer-driven light show. The Caligula also provided private rooms for private sex, and a set of sex boutiques to satisfy even the most bizarre fetish and perversion. As a charter member, Kimball had access to the membership list and was perpetually astonished that the club had about ten percent more women than men.

Reluctantly, Kimball brought his attention back to his dining partner, forty-eight-year-old Denise Carothers, the founder and chief executive officer of Carothers Aerospace, a top multinational manufacturer of advanced military weapons and technology.

"Come again?" Kimball asked, irritated at having to turn from the Bacchanalian vision.

"I said, I think that it maybe necessary to remove Erikson at some later point, but I don't think it wise now."

Kimball's glacial blue eyes flickered dangerously in the dim light. He combed his fingers through his sandy blond hair as he always did when annoyed.

"Why not?" Kimball asked in a guarded voice.

"Because I know the old man. He loves Erikson like a son. If we took Erikson out of the action, Harrison Kingsbury would just spend millions trying to find out what happened. We don't need that sort of interference this close to the transaction.

"Besides," Carothers continued, "I think Martini's death will scare him off. Erikson might have wondered about the first two, but he can't fail to notice this warning. I think he'll back off, at least long enough for us to consummate the transaction."

Kimball stared silently at the remains of his steak tartare and wondered angrily how he would ever get rid of that man Erikson. From his earliest childhood memory, people had done his bidding. It seemed right. The only people who didn't obey—his parents—soon got used to leaving him alone. It was one thing for him to tell his stooge Bailey at ConPacCo to leave Erikson alone. It was yet another for someone to tell him, Elliott Kimball, to do the same thing, even if that person was the chairwoman of the Bremen Legation. He seethed. The sour taste of indigestion burned in the back of his throat. He wanted revenge against Erikson, and he wanted the proper respect from this woman who wouldn't allow him to take that revenge.

"My dear, you don't know Erikson as I do," Kimball said indulgently. "You have no idea how cunning the man is . . . he doesn't play by the rules."

"He doesn't play by the rules? What do you mean by that? Why should it matter? We don't play by the rules either, unless we make them up."

He looked at her for a moment. There had been a time, when he was younger, that he had told her everything. "Well," he began slowly, "it was my junior year at Harvard. We had a rugby scrum with a group from MIT. He was their captain, and—"

"I thought you told me you had never met Vance Erikson."

"It wasn't really a meeting," he said and looked at her, annoyed. It was his experience. She had no right to chastise him for not telling her. He wasn't her nineteen-year-old gigolo anymore. "It wasn't a meeting, but it was important.

"He was their captain," Kimball continued as his eyes focused on the event in the unpleasant past. He told the story more to himself than her.

"The game tied up and there couldn't have been more than five minutes left in the game. We were the best, but Erikson . . . Erikson just came up with strange plays and unorthodox ways to run the old plays. It . . . it just wasn't proper. And in the last five minutes we had the game won when . . . when Erikson got the ball and suddenly reversed field and left all his blockers and headed for the goal line. It was . . . it was stupid; nobody can leave all their blockers behind like that. And I saw him first. I had him. I was bigger, taller . . ." his voice trailed off.

Now, in the dim light of the Caligula Club, his face flushed with anger and humiliation as he remembered the pain in his stomach as Erikson had leaned low and plowed into him, and he remembered how blue the sky was when Erikson came back to help him up after crossing the goal line. He hated Erikson even more now. His reemergence, his meddling in the Da Vinci Codex, was nothing less than an undeserved victor coming back to rub in the shame.

"I know how you feel about Vance Erikson," Carothers said soothingly. "I understand your desire to right the wrongs he represents to you, but you must wait."

No, Elliott, not yet," Carothers said firmly as she placed her hand on his thigh and gave him a familiar caress. She had known Elliott Kimball for years. His father's stock brokerage firm, Kimball, Smith and Farber, had handled the first public offering of Carothers Aerospace. She knew about Elliott's escapades as a child; how he'd burglarized the homes of his father's wealthy friends for thrills; how he'd kidnapped a young friend and held him for ransom; and how, at age sixteen, he'd deliberately run down a pedestrian with his Corvette "to feel what it was like to kill someone." The elder Kimball spent thousands on Elliott's defense—the best of criminal lawyers—and hundreds of thousands of dollars in campaign contributions. It had been the best justice money could buy, yet the judge had still given the juvenile Kimball a six-month jail sentence, "to show that even the rich are not immune to the penalties of justice."

Kimball's father and Boston society in general were relieved when, after getting out of prison, Kimball made a public repentance and expressed sorrow and contrition for his wayward life, promising in an interview with the *Boston Globe* "to do my best to live up to my obligations to society and to be a responsible member of society." To make good on his promise, he graduated cum laude at Rutgers and made the law review at Harvard.

Only Carothers had known it was a smokescreen to distract the authorities from the new Elliott Kimball. Carothers knew because since the time she'd helped relieve him of his virginity when he was eleven, Elliott had confided his most intimate experiences, even reenacting with her sexual experiences with other women, boys, and men. He also told her about the joy that killing brought to him, about the metaphysical itches that only death could soothe.

"There are people who kill for a living," Elliott told Carothers after he'd been paroled. "I want to do that, Denise. I want to very much because I never felt so alive inside, I never felt so good, so important as I did the day I smashed that old guy. But I don't want to be like those people in prison. They killed out of anger or because they got caught in a robbery. I want to kill for the fun of it. I want it to be a class act and . . . I want to kill them with my hands and watch their eyes as they die." Carothers had seen that Elliott Kimball got his wish, for even then, twelve years earlier, when the boy was only eighteen years old, the newly formed Bremen Legation was making enemies who needed to be taught lessons. She and Elliott agreed that no one would be killed unless she had first approved the person, time, and place. It had been a marvelous arrangement for more than a decade, although she was disappointed that in those years the young man's tastes in sex had turned to younger women.

"I truly sympathize with how you feel about Vance Erikson," Carothers said as she moved her hand to his groin. "After the transaction, then you can do anything you want to. But not before."

He shifted suddenly in his seat as her hand massaged his growing erection through the fabric of his trousers.

Reluctantly, Elliott nodded.

The two locked eyes. Neither blinked. Then Elliott broke the silence. "You're the boss." To himself, he added: "For now."

She nodded. Then: "Shall we do it here? Or would you rather go take our usual room?"

Chapter 6

The red tile roofs of tiny medieval Lombard villages drifted below as the huge Alitalia 747 droned its way south toward Milan on the last half hour of the long flight from Amsterdam. Looking down at the tiny speckled flecks of humanity scattered through the olive-green countryside, Vance Erikson wondered again why he had lied to the detective in Amsterdam. It would be easy enough for the man to find out that he knew Umberto Tosi, professor of Renaissance history at the University of Bologna and an authority on Leonardo.

Why? he wondered. And for the millionth time his mind told him why: It was personal. It was personal because it was his fault.

If only—the clot of guilt tightened in his chest. If only he'd gotten to Martini's house sooner. If only he hadn't wasted so much time drinking gin, then Martini would still be alive.

It was no mystery why he'd lied to the policeman. It was his fault that Martini had died and it was up to him to see that the killer was found. And fueling the powerful engine of guilt was an anger that burned inside his chest, an anger that someone could have done such a thing to a man like Martini. And that anger glowed so white-hot that Vance was not going to take a chance that the killer might live out a comfortable life sentence in a warm dry jail. That would never happen as long as Vance Erikson was alive.

Whoever had killed Martini was going to pay.

The Amsterdam police had been kind—much kinder than American police would have been to an Amsterdammer—but the tension of their suspicions that he had played a role in the murder hung over the entire meeting.

Over and over they had questioned him, and each time he told them everything he wanted to tell them . . . leaving out just enough of the key details so that they would not soon be following the trail he was now on.

He told them about the assailant, and gave them an accurate description of the man in the alley. But he didn't tell them about Tosi, and he didn't tell them his suspicions about the deaths of the Leonardo scholars in Strasbourg and Vienna. He saved that information for himself, for he had a score to settle, and only the death of the killer by the hand of Vance Erikson could remove the guilt.

Deep under the roiling emotional matrix of anger and guilt was an as yet unheard voice, the voice of fear. For there was clearly some sort of murder plot aimed at a small and select group of people: those who had read the diaries by Antonio de Beatis. He was the only other person in the world who had read them. He didn't like the feeling that he was next.

What did Tosi know? Vance wondered as the 747 began its descent into Milan's Malpensa airport. Whatever Tosi knew, Vance prayed that he'd know soon enough.

A huge exhibition and symposium on Leonardo was being held tonight at the Castello Sforza in the old part of Milan. For more than six months now, Vance had planned to go. He'd looked forward to listening to a paper on Leonardo as a military engineer that was supposed to have been presented by Martini. The symposium was an annual event at various sites in Europe associated with Leonardo.

Six months. It seemed like a decade, another lifetime. Six months . . . before Patty, before Martini, before . . .

He shook his head as if to shake away the unwanted thoughts. Below him outside the window Milan grew steadily larger.

Vance cleared customs easily and an hour later arrived at the tiny pensione on the Via Dante about halfway between the Duomo and the Castello Sforza, and within walking distance of both. While he could certainly afford five-star luxury, Vance prefered the authentic ambience at the pensione, its high ceilings, the original frescoes by unknown Renaissance artists adorning the walls of its breakfast rooms, the way no one spoke any other language but Italian, and the neighborhood, which catered to Italians rather than tourists. He had stayed here since his days as a student.

Bidding the taxi driver *ciao,* he slung his single soft-sided bag over his shoulder and marched through the huge gates into the courtyard and up five flights of stairs, eschewing the venerable old elevator that creaked up and down in its black wire cage in the middle of the stairwell.

He rang the bell, and the concierge came to the door.

"Signore Erikson!" she exclaimed, exuberantly hugging him to her massive bosom. "So wonderful to see you again," she said in Italian. "It has been too long since your last visit."

Warmed by the friendliness, Vance sat and chatted with her while admiring the photograph she showed him of her youngest son, eighteen years old, who had just entered the university, and sipped on cappuccino while she brought him up-to-date on all the events in her family. Signora Orsini came from a family whose members had been liberated by the Americans in World War II, and who still had a special fondness for the United States. They had let none of the *comunista* propaganda change their minds. After several minutes, her face suddenly clouded over.

"Ah, signore, I almost forgot," she said. "There was a man here early this morning. He came so early the gates weren't open, and he pounded and yelled so long he woke me up and I went down to see him." Her face lost its jovial smoothness as she wrinkled her brow. "He was a middle-aged man. He claimed to know you. But he seemed so . . . so disturbed. I didn't dare open the gate. But through the Judas gate, he handed me an envelope and said I should give it to you."

Vance replaced his cup on the table so hard that he spilled some of the sweet warm coffee.

Signora Orsini didn't seem to notice. "He was very agitated," she continued. "He looked frightened, he was as pale as he could be, and he said that I must give this to you. He said it was a matter of life and death." She rummaged around in her apron and withdrew a crumpled envelope, beaten but still sealed.

She watched Vance silently as he ripped open the envelope and read the message inside. It said. "It is urgent that I see you. They are going to get me, too. Meet me at 7 P.M. tonight, Santa Maria delle Grazie."

It was signed "Tosi."

Back in his room—the usual one facing the courtyard—Vance paced and unpacked, and then paced some more.

They are going to get me, too. Who were they? Did Tosi know who killed Martini? Tosi was a mediocre Da Vinci scholar, but a superb scientist. He had once been a physicist specializing in nuclear power until he became a critic of the atomic power industry and found himself without an income. He was a tough man; whoever had frightened him had done a hell of a job.

By the time he'd hung up his other suit and two extra shirts, hoping the wrinkles would grow less severe before tomorrow's symposium, his stomach began to growl and he headed back down to the Via Dante to find a place to eat. It was one P.M. when he finally found a small *ristorante* just off the Via Mazzini.

Desultorily, he ate an antipasto and a plate of *spaghetti alla carbonara,* and washed it down with a half bottle of the house white. The panic in Tosi's brief note gnawed at him.

Vance pushed an errant strand of hair out of his eyes.

He tried to imagine what someone could care so much about in a diary that was nearly six hundred years old—care enough to kill those who'd read it.

He poured himself another glass of wine from the carafe, then reached for his shoulder bag and withdrew a sheaf of photocopied pages, now starting to wrinkle and discolor from use. This was his copy of the de Beatis diary; the museum had allowed only one other to be made, for fear of the bright light damaging the delicate leaves.

He sipped the wine and paged through the diary. Occasionally, he turned the pages sideways to read a footnote he'd added and, less frequently, one that had been placed by Martini when the elder scholar had read it months before.

The world shrank to the size of one man reading at a table. No light, no sound, no visions intruded into his world of concentration. Perhaps there was a hidden meaning in the de Beatis words, something Vance had missed before. But he could unearth nothing. It couldn't be the diary itself, he decided finally, laying the pages aside. It had to be in the missing pages themselves and the diary.

Both the diary and the Codex Kingsbury had lain—unread and thought lost—in the archives of the library in Madrid, the victim of careless cataloging and of too many books and too little space. Both had been discovered by researchers who took an unorthodox approach to the library's collection and just went browsing as Vance had when he discovered the diary.

No one had read either work for centuries. And now, someone—who?—feared that a reader might, by reading the diary, be able to deduce . . . what? . . . the location of the pages missing from the Codex Kingsbury and replaced by the forgery? He nodded to himself, his eyes staring vacantly through the curtains of the restaurant at the afternoon sidewalk traffic. Yes, that had to be why the diary's readers were killed.

The entire concept of secrets more than five hundred years old still being a threat to twentieth-century people seemed preposterous. Yet there were three dead men, and they could not be ignored.

With the question lingering in his mind, Vance left sixteen euros on the table to cover his meal and departed, pushing his way into the thronging crowds on the sidewalk outside.

He squinted against the daylight as he made his way back up the Via Dante toward the Castello Sforza. A huge banner with a likeness of Leonardo hung from the castle's massive brick tower. Below in the circular drive in front of the Castello, he watched lines of cabs picking up and dropping passengers. These would be tourists, he decided. The conference attendees would enter from the opposite end of the huge castle and pass directly into a modern conference room hollowed out inside this Renaissance fortress.

The thought of the conference brought him back to Martini. The professor had been scheduled to deliver an address on Leonardo as a military architect and engineer, a subject that was also one of Vance's favorites. What might the conference organizers do? he wondered. Martini's address was to have been the keynote.

In search of an answer to that question, Vance found himself a quarter of an hour later sitting in the conference coordinator's anteroom. Activity was frantic, almost desperate, he noted, as aides and secretaries—many of them priests and nuns—richocheted from one place to another speaking in rapid-fire Italian, their voices edged with anxiety.

It was a big conference and things were going wrong.

The door to the director's office exploded open, and like a half ton of obese armament, the director shot out, firing two more sentences over his shoulder at an aide still in the office.

"My God!" He smiled at Vance and quickly embraced him. "Am I glad to see you! I've been desperately trying to get in touch with you! You—" His face fell suddenly. "You've heard about—"

"Professor Martini," Vance said.

"Yes . . . horrible, horrible," the director said, looking down as if he could see his shoes, hidden as they were by an enormous belly.

"It was—"

"Let's not talk about it now," the director interrupted him, holding up his hand like a traffic cop. "I can't bear to hear any more. After this . . . this circus"—he waved his arm to indicate the chaos of his office—"is all over, then I'll cry a long time but now . . . now life must go on at its own pace. Which"—taking Vance's elbow and directing him toward the door—"is as frantic a pace as could be. That is why I'm so glad to see you now. Not," the director said, thinking he'd made an error, "that I'm not glad to see you at other times but, well, I need your help.

"You were Martini's best pupil, no?" the director asked once they'd left the bedlam of the office for the relative quiet of the corridor. "So I would like you to take his session for him tomorrow," said the director without waiting for Vance to reply. "You can either deliver your own talk, or deliver the one which he had prepared."

"I'd be—"

"Wonderful!" the director said. But before he could add another word, he was dragged off by agitated employees who needed his help on a crisis.

"Have you seen Dr. Tosi?" Vance called after him.

The director shook his head. "Try the Excelsior. I think he is staying there," he managed before the door of the office slammed.

Vance looked at his watch; it was only 3:30 P.M. He had some time to kill and he decided to spend part of it visiting Tosi at his hotel. Perhaps they could clear up everything without the melodramatic evening meeting at the church.

Three hours later, Vance was more confused than ever. He'd taken a taxi to the Excelsior, a luxurious modern high-rise hotel with all the amenities that Americans were known for liking, such as private bathrooms and room service, that upper-class Europeans were only now beginning to agree made sense.

"Signore Tosi checked out this afternoon." The desk man's reticence had dissolved when Vance waved a hundred-euro note under his lushly bearded but immaculately clipped chin. "Yes, I remember it better," the man had said as if he'd been watching too many American "B" movies. "Signore Tosi regretted his early departure"—the man smiled unctuously—"and left"—he consulted a receipt—"about noon. He departed with two priests."

Priests? Despite Tosi's Italian heritage and his love of Renaissance art, most of which was found in churches, Tosi was a thoroughly irreverent man whose distaste for religion and the people who practiced it was vocal and perpetually close to the surface. Something, he said, about Catholic school and nuns with rulers.

Vance Erikson walked along the Corso Magenta, his head spinning in the late afternoon sun. The world was turning into a kaleidoscope, more like a surreal painting by Dali than a masterpiece by Da Vinci. The commercial hum of daytime was yielding to a softer, more human tone of playing children, television sets, and supper preparations, all clearly heard through the large open windows on the second and third floors along the street. When the familiar columned turret of the church of Santa Maria delle Grazie came into view, Vance was fifteen minutes early. He decided to use that quarter of an hour to greet the elaborate restoration of Da Vinci's *The Last Supper*. Although Leonardo's masterpiece had miraculously survived the Allied bombing in August 1943, it had nearly succumbed to a less dramatic but far more virulent enemy: time. The paint had faded and started to peel in places. It was a treasure that would have slowly and cruelly been eroded to nothing had it not been for a restoration effort that, itself, was nothing short of miraculous.

At the door of the refectory, Vance paid a bored and sleepy attendant and walked into the cool damp room. Facing him, illuminated by several dim floodlights, was Christ and his stunned disciples, all responding to the words of their master: "One of you shall betray me." It was the oldest of human dramas, played out a million times a day and a million times in a lifetime. Trust misplaced—once destroyed, never repaired.

Vance didn't know what he really believed about Jesus, but he knew truth when he saw it, and it didn't matter a damn whether this man was God incarnate. What held significance was the truth revealed: truth that trust will always be betrayed by those we love. Vance saw the truth in the man Jesus: Here was a man who trusted and loved and died for his faith in God and in other human beings.

A shoe scraped on the dirty concrete floor behind him and Vance nervously whirled to face the noise.

"We close now, signore," the attendant said in Italian, stifling a yawn with a grimy hand.

At the door Vance took one last look, then stepped outside. Over the small piazza, a single lightbulb in a metal reflector, hung over the square on a thin cable, bobbed gently in the evening breeze. Overhead, gathering shadows chased the light of a retreating day.

Vance checked his watch. Time to meet Tosi in the church. The single lightbulb cast harsh shadows in the gathering darkness, and cast elastic shadows from his legs as he covered the twenty yards to the church entrance at an easy gait.

He pushed the heavy wooden door open and stepped into the sanctuary. The gloom inside matched the gathering night. Vance saw only one other person there, a bent old woman in a dark shapeless dress with a shawl over her head. He watched as she placed a votive candle in a stand on the right side of the ornately decorated hall and departed. Vance shivered involuntarily. He was alone in the dimly lighted sanctuary. He took a seat next to the aisle in the pew nearest to the door and waited.

Fifteen minutes later, Tosi had still not arrived. *They're going to get me, too.* The loudest sound inside the church was Vance's own breathing, and it grew shorter and faster as the minutes slipped away.

At 7:30 he began to question his decision to handle everything himself. I should have notified the police, he realized guiltily, as soon as I left Tosi's hotel. He resolved to do that now as he stood up to leave. As he reached the door, it swung slowly, dramatically open. Then from the darkness materialized the white face and whiter clerical collar of a priest. The rest of the man's body, save for the glinting cross at his side, blended in artfully with the shadows.

"Mr. Erikson?" the priest asked in English.

Vance stared at him, speechless. "Yes. Do I know you?"

"No," the priest said, making no move to step out of the shadows, "but we have a mutual friend who asked that I convey his deepest regrets for his inability to keep his appointment with you."

Then Vance saw the man fumble in a deep pocket of his robes, expecting him to hand over a message from Tosi. Instead, the priest produced a pistol and aimed it at him.

Chapter 7

The priest held the gun steady, aimed unwaveringly at Vance's face.

"I don't want to hurt you, Mr. Erikson," the cleric said. He took a step toward Vance, moving from the inky shadows into the dim illumination of the sanctuary. He was short, no more than five feet five, middle-aged, with close-cropped salt-and-pepper hair that lay against his head in tight waves. He wore heavy black-rimmed glasses.

Vance found his voice with difficulty. "Well—" he cleared his throat nervously. "If you don't want to harm me, why don't you just put that thing away?" He paused, then, "Is that something you use in the new mass or something?" He tried to manage a smile, but stopped when he saw the man's face harden. This priest took his religion seriously.

"You will come with me," the priest said. Vance stood rooted, in fear and rebellion. He didn't like people telling him where to go, especially at the point of a gun. But, he thought, at least that means he isn't planning to kill me . . . yet.

"Where do you want me to go?"

"That's hardly your choice, is it?" The priest gestured toward the door. "Now, move." He stood to one side to let Vance pass.

Vance hesitated.

"Hurry up!"

Vance walked past the priest toward the door. As he entered the small anteroom, Vance felt the cold firmness of a pistol in the small of his back. "Don't try yelling for help."

Vance made his way to the front door, pushed it open, and stepped outside into the night. An instant later Vance heard a thud and scrape behind him. He turned as the priest tried to recover his balance, having obviously stumbled on the threshold. Vance ran.

Behind him, the priest cursed blasphemously. A gunshot echoed. Vance ducked around the corner of the entrance and flew past the front of the church, heading for the Corso Magenta. He ran wildly, trying to keep the shoulder bag he carried from flapping against his thigh. Another shot cracked through the darkness as he reached the street. He felt the slug thud into the papers in the shoulder bag. Wide-eyed, he looked back and saw the amorphous black mass of the priest's robes flowing in the shadows. He saw the muzzle flash of another shot, whose report reached his ears just as the slug smashed harmlessly into the building across the street. For someone who didn't want to hurt me, Vance muttered to himself, you're cutting things awfully close, mister.

The two near hits had dumped more adrenaline into Vance's system. He grabbed his bag with one arm and sprinted down the Corso Magenta yelling in Italian, "Help, police, murder!" All along the street people rushed, exclaiming, from their dinner tables and peered cautiously from their open windows.

Another shot rang out, but Vance had no idea where the slug went. Suddenly his thumping footsteps were the only ones he heard. He ducked into a doorway and chanced a glance back at the church. To his relief, he saw the priest standing at the corner of the Santa Maria delle Grazie, motionless, as if he were undecided whether or not to take up the pursuit. Then as the shouts from neighborhood residents grew louder, the man abruptly turned and ran in the other direction.

Trembling with fear, Vance huddled in the doorway for a few seconds on shaky legs, gulping ragged breaths, his bladder suddenly demanding attention. Then, fearful that the priest might return, Vance stepped out of the doorway and, at a dead run, headed back toward his room. Only when he'd let himself in through the locked gate of the pensione and secured the lock behind him did he allow himself to rest.

The elevator was waiting at the ground floor. For the first time, he stepped in and let the antique lift carry him upstairs.

He took a taxi to the police station—he didn't want them disturbing the peace of Mrs. Orsini's pensione—and spent an hour and a half talking to a detective, going over and over again the description of the priest.

"You are sure, absolutely sure, the man was a priest?" the detective, obviously a devout Catholic, kept asking him. And Vance kept telling him that yes, the man had worn a priest's robes, though of course there was no proof the man was actually a priest.

"Terrorists," the detective said, "or perhaps the Mafia."

The police looked at the hole in his shoulder bag, took his report, then let him go with the admonition that he should not leave Italy without notifying them. Terrific, Vance thought.

Vance took a cab toward his room, stopping nearby at the state-owned Poste-Telegraph office at the Piazza Vittorio Emanuele II. It was a little after 9:30 when he walked through the magnificent cross-shaped arcade with its intricate dome of iron and glass. In less than ten minutes, the operator had connected him with Harrison Kingsbury at the ConPacCo headquarters in Santa Monica. When Vance had called the day before to tell him about Martini's death, Kingsbury had not been in town, so he was relieved when he heard the oil tycoon's voice on the other end.

"Vance?" the voice asked. "Is that you?"

"Yes," Vance answered. "I—"

"Horrible about Martini," Kingsbury cut in. "You have any idea why someone might have wanted to kill him? Could there be any connection to your visit there?"

"Yes," Vance said. "It sounds crazy, but I think there is a connection." He paused. "You have my earlier reports about the deaths in Vienna and Strasbourg—"

"And you believe the deaths are connected?"

"At first I thought it was just coincidence, but with Martini and—"

"I've made a few telephone calls to Amsterdam and The Hague," Kingsbury interrupted again before Vance could relate his experiences of that night. "I've stirred up the Dutch police and their antiterrorism intelligence service. They owe me a couple of favors, and I'm calling in one of them."

Vance listened quietly to Kingsbury, once again in awe of his elderly boss's energy. At seventy-three, the man showed no signs of slowing down. Yes, he would have someone in just about every country in the world owing him favors.

". . . Dutch police have extra people assigned full-time to doing nothing but solving the mystery of Martini's death," Kingsbury was saying.

"Boss?" Vance managed finally to interrupt Kingsbury's soliloquy. "Boss, I've got something important to tell you." Vance related the violence of that evening, and the events earlier in the day leading to his being placed on the speaker's agenda of the Da Vinci symposium.

"It's wonderful that you've been asked to speak, Vance, but I want you to get your ass home tonight. I want you alive, you scoundrel," he said affectionately. "After all, you are my most valuable exploration geologist. I can't afford to have you killed."

"Boss," Vance said, "I understand your concern. And I appreciate it. But I can't just run away from this thing. After all, it would be an insult to Martini for me to fail to deliver his paper tomorrow." Vance waited for a response and heard only silence.

"True," Kingsbury said after a while. "But tonight I

want you out of that grimy little place you always stay and somewhere else you've never stayed before, somewhere people wouldn't think of looking for you."

"All right," Vance replied. "I'll change rooms, but I'm going to have to do some thinking about leaving Milan until I know more about what's going on." It would be a battle of the wills, both of them knew that. They were both stubborn. "Although I'm not much closer to finding the missing pages than I was a month ago, somehow, it seems a lot more important now to find them. If I don't, the lives of three good people, maybe four if Tosi is dead, will be lost for nothing."

"All right," Kingsbury agreed reluctantly.

"You know it's true," Vance said. "Don't tell me that you don't want those pages now more than ever."

"Sure I'm intrigued," Kingsbury admitted. "But I'm not sure I want the answer badly enough to get you—or anyone else, for that matter—killed. Besides, what can you do that the authorities in Holland and Italy can't?"

"I think you know that answer, sir," Vance said. "Are they really going to believe that someone is killing to cover up the contents of some papers that are centuries old? And if they did, could they really track those missing papers better than I can?"

"Damn it, Vance," the old man exclaimed. "I sure as hell hate it when you're right . . . especially with this. You could get hurt, you know."

"I don't think I need to be reminded of that," Vance said, fingering the healing cut over his left eye and thinking of the hole in his shoulder bag. "But so could the person who killed Professor Martini, and I intend to find whoever that was." In his mind's eye, Vance could see

Kingsbury sitting at his massive desk in his office overlooking the Pacific. The old man would be doodling on a sheet of memo paper in his ornate calligraphy, nodding his head: Yes, Vance, you're right. I wish you weren't.

"I understand," Kingsbury said. "I agree. But I want you to accept some help from me. The deputy chief of Italian intelligence is an old friend. I'm going to give him a call. I want you to accept any help he gives you. Is that clear?"

Later that evening, Vance bought a half bottle of Barolo and took a taxi to the Hilton. He'd come back to the pensione tomorrow to get his things. He sat and drank the wine in his new hotel room with the lights off, watching the traffic on the street below. Finally, he pulled down the sheets and slipped into bed.

The night passed fitfully. The same nightmare played over and over until dawn: Always he found himself back at the Santa Maria delle Grazie, facing the priest's gun. The last time, the priest grinned a hideous death-mask smile and pulled the trigger again and again. Vance awoke as the slugs ripped through his body.

Chapter 8

Sunday, August 6

The bleaching Mediterranean sun glared relentlessly down on the roofs of Milan and on the heads of its citizens. It stole every spare drop of water, turning the clay-baking heat into a steaming humid ordeal. Even the air-conditioning system that soothed the conference room with quiet murmurs of cool air suffered from temperatures beyond its abilities.

Cursing silently, Suzanne Storm dabbed at her face with tissues, trying to stop the sweat before it gathered into streaming droplets and ruined her artfully applied makeup. The director of the Da Vinci conference sat stoically in front of the podium with his suitcoat properly buttoned. The rest of the audience, however, had shed coats and ties and had rolled up sleeves.

Give me the dry heat of Florence—or Los Angeles—anytime, Suzanne thought. For the millionth time that day, she shifted in her seat and smoothed out the wrinkles in her skirt. It had been a waste of time and money for *Haute Culture* to send her to cover the conference. Stultifying, boring, she thought. Was it possible for someone to die of terminal ennui? The people at this conference were even less interesting than the stuffed-shirt cookie pushers she'd had to entertain for her father when he'd been ambassador to France.

She stifled a yawn and patted at a drop of perspiration as it trickled down the back of her neck. She should have worn her hair up today. But the cool morning had held no promise of being the scorcher the afternoon had become.

She reached back and gathered her bright auburn hair and lifted it off her neck for a moment, and then dropped it, shaking her head to let it settle evenly again. She glanced at the Piaget on her wrist: nearly 3:30. One more speaker after this one, and then the cocktail reception. What she wouldn't give at this very moment for a chilled martini.

She looked around and found that she was not the only person nodding off, anesthetized by the potent narcotic of the current speaker's monotone drone. Her eyes dropped to her program. The next speaker scheduled at least didn't suffer from blandness. If anything, she thought, he was a bit too interesting, a bit too flamboyant to be real life, and certainly not bland enough for her to take him seriously as a Da Vinci scholar.

Damn, Suzanne, she reproached herself. There you go again.

Her thoughts went back to a month before. She had been watching the evening news when they aired a story filmed at the press conference where Harrison Kingsbury announced that Erikson had discovered a forgery in the newly purchased codex. They'd run the portion where she challenged Erikson on his conclusions. She'd looked like such a witch. Was she really like that? Could that really have been her? She thought of the way she interviewed and questioned people, and she thought, again, of Vance Erikson.

No, she decided, she didn't question other people as harshly as him. For the past two years, since she'd been working as a writer for *Haute Culture,* she had run into him time and again. The art world was a small incestuous one and the same people were constantly involved with one another. It was as small and incestuous as the world of Ivy League and other top Eastern schools. She had first run into Vance Erikson at a party during homecoming at Skidmore during her freshman year. He had just entered graduate school at MIT and all of her friends found him terribly exciting—not like the typical MIT bookworm. His date for the evening, an alumna of Skidmore, wore him like a jewel, he of less-than-savory gambling fortunes.

"Imagine being kicked out of the casino at Monte Carlo for being too good!" they had fawned. All but Suzanne. While they had melted from his intense blue eyes and mischievous smile, she held back. She found him too self-confident, too irreverent. Who did he think he was to flout the conventions of society? How did he think he could get away with all that? *She* hadn't. She did her duty at her father's political parties. Maybe she didn't enjoy them, but she did her duty. This cocky young man with his nonconformist ways insulted her sense of duty.

But on this hot Sunday afternoon in Milan, her thoughts

troubled her. The television show, and her conduct, came back to haunt her. Could she be wrong about Erikson? It was all so confusing.

Up at the podium, the speaker, a frail old man from the University of Padua, shuffled off the stage, assisted by one of the director's staff. The director took the podium and began to introduce Vance Erikson, reading his credentials from a typed sheet of paper. They were impressive, she admitted to herself for the first time.

She watched as the director finished his introduction, and Erikson strode across the platform to assume the podium. There was a noticeable increase in activity in the room as people suddenly came to life, sitting at attention. New arrivals filled seats that had been mostly vacant all day.

There was that self-assured walk—confidence. No, something more than confidence. He doesn't give a damn, she realized. He really doesn't give a damn what people think about him. And from her seat, twelve rows from the front, she watched his eyes while he stood at the podium, animated, captivating, waiting for the applause to die. Suzanne Storm hated to admit she'd been wrong, but now she allowed as how she might have been. At least, she thought as Erikson began his introduction, at least I ought to give him another chance, a fair chance.

Vance smiled as he waited for the applause to diminish. He looked around the room and found scores of familiar faces. Then, down in the first row was the baby-sitter Kingsbury's police friend had arranged for him. The man was huge, intimidating, and completely out of place. The man had been waiting outside his door this morning and followed him around like a lost puppy . . . that is, if lost puppies carried Uzi machine guns.

Abruptly Vance spotted Suzanne Storm. His stomach tightened.

"Damn," he muttered to himself.

Reluctantly he brought his attention to the pages of Martini's paper, the margins covered with his own hastily scrawled footnotes. Since that first time they'd met at Skidmore . . . what was it he could have said? What could he have done? Whatever it was, he decided, it had surely come back to haunt him now.

The applause trickled to silence and Vance began his speech.

"This was to have been Geoff Martini's presentation, not mine," he began. "I'm just the messenger here today and so I hope as I speak you will honor him by seeing him here today rather than me, for there is nothing I know about Leonardo that doesn't owe something to him, his generosity and his genius."

Vance continued his tribute to Martini, describing the professor's immense contributions to the study of Leonardo, and relating how Martini had found him in a small pub near the Cambridge University campus and altered the course of his life. When Vance finished, his eyes were moist and his voice had grown softer. He saw that many members of the audience, too, felt his sense of loss.

"But it's fitting that we continue with Professor Martini's work," Vance said as he turned to the pages before him on the podium, "and keep his work alive even though he will write no more.

"Like other Renaissance artists," Vance began in an easy way, "Leonardo was expected to be more than just an artist. Indeed, like his contemporary Michelangelo, Leonardo was a superb military architect and planner. While Michelangelo redesigned the fortifications of the walled city of Florence, Leonardo took his talents farther north, where he served as a military engineer under Cesare Borgia and under Count Ludovico Sforza, the Duke of Milan who constructed this magnificent castle we are in today.

"Indeed, this is the area in which Professor Martini has invested . . . had invested the greatest portion of his time."

Speaking with only an occasional reference to his notes, Vance set the stage by briefly touching upon some of the modern-day military inventions first conceived by Leonardo: the submarine, the armored tank, parachutes, scuba gear, the helicopter, and crude forms of guided missiles and cannon ordnance. He did not linger on any of these for they were well known to those assembled.

"Of course, the technology of 1499 could not begin to keep up with Leonardo's mind. His concepts were impractical for that era, because advances in metallurgy, electronics, and chemistry had to be made before his inventions could be put into use. It's important to realize that his inventions were workable concepts which had to wait for the centuries to catch up with them.

"No one knows this better than the Krupp industrial works," Vance said as he walked from behind the podium and stood next to it, casually leaning on his right elbow as he spoke. "Although the Krupp family had been making weapons and armor since the sixteenth century, they fell on hard times in the nineteenth century, and were nearly bankrupt in 1870 when Alfred Krupp discovered a drawing by Leonardo of a breech-loading cannon.

"The concept of a breech-loading cannon was a radical one. No longer would artillery crews have to expose themselves to enemy fire by loading their weapons from the muzzle. So, Krupp decided to build Leonardo's cannon. The rest is history: Leonardo's cannon design revitalized the Krupp arms works and the company went on to be the largest military weapons producer in the world, supplying the heavy armor and powerful artillery for Hitler's Blitzkrieg.

"Think of it," he said, lowering his voice. "A concept from a genius of the fifteenth century nearly defeated the combined armies in a twentieth-century war." He paused. The room was silent, save for the murmuring of the air conditioner." It's staggering to realize that this man's genius lives on to affect us even today.

"And it's even more intriguing when you consider that Leonardo detested war. He called it *bestialissima pazzia*—the most bestial madness. Yet he continued to invent weapons because he knew that the only thing worse than fighting a war was losing it. So he continued to invent cannon and fantastic arrangements of catapults and crossbows for his contemporaries and submarines and helicopters for our contemporaries. In fact, one of his inventions, a bearing arrangement, had to be reinvented by the Sperry Gyroscope Corporation to use in navigation aides for high-altitude bombers. Yet Leonardo's codices contain drawings of the precise bearing structures which modern scientists and engineers struggled for years to duplicate."

The atmosphere in the lecture hall was electric. All eyes were on Vance, seemingly charged with his enthusiasm. Even Suzanne Storm gazed wide-eyed at the figure on the podium, her features frozen as if in a trance.

"And those are only among those codices which have *not* been lost. We know that *thousands of pages of* Leonardo's writings have been lost or destroyed over the centuries. What surprises might we find in those? What lessons—or dangers—might those contain?

"Remember, in his letter to Duke Sforza, Leonardo stressed his military skills and told the duke that he had invented a weapon so horrible that he hesitated to put it on paper for fear it would fall into the hands of evil men! Some scholars believe that refers to the submarine; others, however, feel it refers to an as-yet-undiscovered invention described in some of the papers which have been lost.

"Whether or not these assumptions are true—or can ever be proved definitively," Vance said, "the lasting lesson we can carry with us about the man Leonardo is that he was a visionary, a pragmatic visionary. He hated war, but at the same time realized it was inevitable. And in recognizing the inevitability of war, he saw the necessity of inventing weapons of war so that his side could be victorious. In his own words, Leonardo explained: 'When besieged by ambitious tyrants, I find a means of offense and defense in order to preserve the chief gift of Nature, which is Liberty.'

"And so it remains today," Vance concluded.

The applause rolled through the hall. Smiling, Vance gathered his papers and said thank you, but his words drowned beneath the sea of clapping. But as he stepped down from the platform, Vance's smile vanished as his bodyguard politely but firmly made his way to his side. He nodded professionally to Vance as he approached, and then scanned the audience, his head constantly moving looking for danger before it could happen.

The delivery of the Martini paper was the conference's last scheduled event of the afternoon and was to be followed by a cocktail reception afterward. By the time Vance had finished talking to well-wishers in the lecture hall and made his way outside to the cocktail party in the courtyard, it was nearly six o'clock. To his dismay, the first person who pushed through the crowd to greet him was Suzanne Storm. He steeled himself.

She walked up to Vance as he took his drink from the bartender. "You really wowed them in there," she said warmly.

"I suppose that merits another black mark in your book," Vance replied. He eyed her over the rim of his glass of cold white wine, waiting. He caught the brief glint of anger in her green eyes.

"Well, only if you want to make it that way," Suzanne replied evenly. "Actually I came over here to give you a compliment."

"A compliment? From you?" He shook his head skeptically. "For two years you've been—" Then he caught himself, suddenly aware that something in her manner was different today.

"Go on," she urged, "you started to say something."

He stared at her. Was she baiting him? Playing coy, setting him up so she could knock his feet out from under him?

"I was about to say"—he paused, mastering his anxiety, stifling the urge to launch an offensive to protect himself—"that considering the past couple of years, a compliment is the last thing I would expect to come from you."

"Yes . . . well." She looked at him, wanted to but couldn't bring herself to say she was sorry. There was nothing yet to prove that she had been wrong. Still . . .

"Well?" he asked to break the silence.

"Well . . ." She searched for the right words, something to get the conversation on an amiable plane, but something short of capitulation. ". . . my magazine has certain standards and—"

"I don't meet those, is that what you're trying to say? Well, you've said it every time I've ever seen you, and in every article you've ever written which concerned me. I know all that,"—his words spilled out rapidly,—"so it's really not necessary to repeat it." He scowled at her. This confrontation had been a long time in coming, and he welcomed it now. At first he'd let her criticism roll off his back, but after a while . . . Well, damn it, he was entitled to a blow or two in his own defense.

They stared at each other.

"Would you get me a drink?" she asked politely, struggling with her temper, trying to say something neutral, playing for a little time to compose herself.

"I think you're perfectly capable of doing that yourself, Ms. Storm," Vance replied and then turned to talk to a museum curator from Antwerp who'd appeared at his elbow and was obviously waiting to talk to him.

"*Magnifique,*" the man said, clasping Vance's hand. "Although we deeply regret the passing of Professor Martini, we are grateful to have you carry on his work. Isn't that correct, Jan?" he said, turning to a younger man at his side.

With murder burning in her eyes, Suzanne Storm whirled away from the group and ordered a martini. She positioned herself near a table of canapés and sipped at the drink with a vengeance as she observed Vance and his circle of admirers. She quaffed her cocktail, got a refill, then drifted to the edge of the group surrounding Vance. As people departed, she gradually edged her way closer.

Vance made a studied effort to ignore her, avoiding eye contact and going out of his way to avoid talking to her. "*Mister* Erikson," she said loudly. Everyone around Vance turned to look at her, and then back at him. "May I have a word with you for a moment?"

Vance opened his mouth to say something and then noticed the eyes on him. He shut his mouth and let her lead him to a quieter corner of the courtyard.

"What the hell was *that* for?" he said irritably. "Haven't you done enough damage to me and my reputation? Why do you—"

"Damn it! Just give me a chance to speak," she said sharply. "If you will be polite enough to keep your mouth shut for one minute, you'll find that I am trying to see if there isn't some way we can come to a truce in all this."

"A truce?" Vance frowned. "You're the one who's doing all the attacking, not me."

Suzanne swallowed hard.

"You're right," she said.

At that moment Vance looked as if someone had slapped him; a blank look of incomprehension spread across his face.

"I'm right?" he said tentatively. "You said I was right? Did I hear you correctly?"

She nodded. "About the truce," she said. "About the truce."

Vance tilted his head and screwed up his mouth, thinking. She looked at him tilting his head first one way, then the other, unbelieving.

"I don't understand," he said finally.

"Understand what?"

"Why?"

"Why what?" she asked. "You're not making sense."

"Why all of the sudden are you making peace offerings?"

"Because I'm . . . Because I'm reassessing—no, that's not right. I'm trying to figure out if I really have been treating you as badly as you seem to think I have."

"So why now?" he persisted. "Why here, in Milan, at this conference?"

"I don't know," she replied honestly.

"Well, that's the first time I've ever seen you without an answer."

She drew in a sharp breath and exhaled audibly.

"Okay," he said. "Truce." Her face lost some of its frown lines. "I'll watch my tongue and you watch your writing. Is it a deal?"

She nodded. "A deal."

"So where do you want this to go?" he asked. "I know you don't want to interview me. What do you want? I can give you a tour of Milan . . . you know, a feature for your magazine on Leonardo's Milan or something like that?"

"No, that's not really what I had in mind—though it's a good idea, it really is. What I would like to find out . . ."

She searched for the diplomatic words. "What I would really like to find out is how you can hold down another full-time job, and still maintain your reputation in Vinciana." Not bad, she decided. At least she hadn't said what she was thinking: I'd like to know if you deserve your reputation, or if it's just a function of your ability to snow people, like you did in the lecture hall today.

"I'm not sure if that's what you really have on your mind," he said perceptively. "But I'll take it on face value. In exchange, I want to know why you've been on my case for two years."

"Okay," she agreed after a moment and held out her hand. He took it to shake and noticed that it was cold and wet. The three-balled man-eater who had been chewing on his ass in print for two years was nervous. Maybe, he thought, she really was sincere.

"So where do we begin?" he asked.

"What's convenient?"

"Well, I won't be back in the States for a while," he explained.

"Ah," she said. "Kingsbury's quest. Sir Gawain in search of the Holy Grail?" She didn't sound sarcastic.

"Right," he replied equably. "So we'll have to do it over here if you want to do it soon."

"Sounds all right to me." She smiled. "How about dinner? You know, neutral territory, breaking bread and all that?"

"Sounds good. When—tonight?"

"Not tonight," she said apologetically. "I've got a prior commitment." He shrugged. "But tomorrow night's open or the day after that. We could do lunch, if you feel better about that."

"No, no. Dinner's fine. I prefer to just catch a quick bite at noon, but . . ." He gazed upward, and changed his mind. "How about lunch tomorrow . . . at one of the café/trattorias at the Galleria Vittorio Emanuele? We could have a light lunch?"

"Fine, where?"

"I'll meet you by the British Airways office at noon."

She agreed and then turned her head as she spotted someone at the edge of the cocktail crowd.

"There's my previous engagement," she said matter-of-factly, pointing at a tall blond man who looked vaguely familiar to Vance. He heard Suzanne call the man's name as she wove her way gracefully through the crowd. Elliott, it sounded like. Or Edward. The pair quickly disappeared into the swirl of cocktail-party guests.

Chapter 9

A gentle breeze wafted through the towering vaulted arches of the Galleria Vittorio Emanuele II, offering a soothing apology for the oppressive heat that had gripped Milan for the past two days.

But Vance Erikson felt neither comfort nor relief as he leaned, irritable and restless, against the closed, shuttered entrance to the British Airways office. Across the gallery, some thirty yards away, the stylishly dressed but unmistakably massive form of his bodyguard gathered admiring glances from women as they passed. Although feigning interest in a display of books, the man was in fact watching the reflection in the window; Vance suspected that nothing escaped his attention.

Tosi was missing.

Nobody knew where he was. The Milan police had called him into the office just that morning to question him further about the assailant at the Santa Maria delle Grazie. Tosi had not shown up for the conference and he had failed to contact his office at the University of Bologna.

The detective who'd questioned Vance that morning had almost acted as if Vance himself was responsible for Tosi's disappearance. Not-so-subtle hints: Drugs? Mafia? Involvement in "undesirable" political elements? Are you *quite* sure, Mr. Erikson? He had returned to the conference afterward to listen to the other speakers, but a lead ingot of anxiety crushed his chest, made him unable to concentrate or even sit still. For the rest of the morning he'd wandered up one street and down the next. Walking helped him move through his thoughts. He feared that whoever had killed Martini and attacked him would try again. And that the Milan police seemed to think he was responsible for Tosi's disappearance. If things got worse, he decided, he'd have to call Kingsbury and get a lawyer.

He looked at his watch. Suzanne Storm was late, by thirteen minutes now. Confusion over that woman's motives was also pressing on him. Why, after all these years of antagonism, had she become suddenly so conciliatory? What was she up to? He couldn't bring himself to trust her. Since his ordeal with Patty, trust was in short supply. Too bad, he thought. He'd tried to get to know her that first evening they'd met at Skidmore, but there had been instant fireworks. Still, he had been attracted. But then, what man wouldn't be? It had been his little head talking, not his big one.

The sharp rapid reports of heels rat-tatting off concrete broke his reverie, and he turned to see Suzanne hurrying toward him, elegantly outfitted in a clingy green silk creation.

"Sorry to be late," she called.

For a moment Vance forgot that this was the woman who had taken every opportunity to stab him in the back, who, until yesterday afternoon, had never said a kind word to him. He stared at her, at her fine high cheekbones, at the way the silk molded itself to her. For an instant he was caught in her sensuality, taken aback by sheer physical attraction. Then, with an almost imperceptible nod of his head, he returned to his senses. She became again the shrill art critic for whom he could do no right.

"Sorry," she was saying for the second time, at his side now, "I'm not in the habit of being late, but—"

"That's all right," Vance said shortly. "It gave me some time to do a bit of thinking. I thought we might eat here," he said, indicating the sidewalk restaurant across the arcade. "But . . ."

She tilted her head to one side, questioningly.

"Well, you took like royalty today." Oh, hell, he thought, he'd meant it lightly, but it came out sounding like an obsequious compliment. "What I meant to say is that we ought to go somewhere where they can appreciate your elegance."

"My goodness, Mr. Erikson," Suzanne shot back archly, "*you are* on your good behavior today. So gentlemanly. Even for an oil engineer."

Fifteen minutes later they were seated at a comfortable banquette in Chez Jules on the Via Montenapoleone, with the muted strains of a Verdi opera playing in the background. Barely above the opera bubbled the tastefully hushed conversation, *sotto voce* laughter, and the delicately suppressed dining sounds of people whose manners forbade the clinking of silverware against china.

Suzanne seemed comfortable in the surroundings, taking in the room without obvious stares or unnecessary movements. It was quite a room, too, Vance reflected, the sheen and glitter of crystal chandeliers, real silver, dark wood paneling, and fine bone china merely serving to set off the genuine Renaissance masters that hung on the walls. Vance leaned forward and spoke softly to Suzanne, pointing out the paintings he was familiar with. "A Botticelli"—he indicated delicately with his head, for this was the sort of place where polite people did not point with their fingers—"Bramante." The walls were like a coffee-table picture book of the Renaissance.

"Vance!" The resonant voice shattered the carefully cultivated calm of the restaurant. Heads turned first to the caller, a distinguished, elegantly tall man, dressed fashionably though not foppishly, his black hair and mustache impeccably cut and combed. "Vance. Is it really you?"

The man glided across the restaurant floor, dancing gracefully among the tables, waiters busboys, and diners. Jules Graziano had the olive skin of the Mediterranean and the fine high cheekbones of France. A mouthful of straight white teeth smiled broadly as he drew closer. Silence was broken only by a Verdi aria as the diners, many of them the people who moved and shook Milan, stared as tastefully as they dared. Who was this guest so special that Graziano had broken the carefully orchestrated peace of his own restaurant?

Graziano hugged Vance, then turned his attention to Suzanne. "You are too beautiful for this scoundrel," Graziano told her, clutching her hand dramatically to his lips. "Why don't you tell him to leave and we will have lunch together? I will have my chef prepare the cuisine of the century."

"Suzanne," Vance interrupted with a grin, "meet Jules Graziano, the most ingratiating gigolo in all of Milan, and the owner of this greasy-spoon diner."

"I'm honored," she said.

They chatted for a few more moments, and then Graziano rushed off to order some special dishes for them, stopping first to gaze again at Suzanne. "It is I who am honored," he said, sighing and then grinning broadly before he departed.

Vance's bodyguard had been seated discreetly at a small table in the front by the window. The table was nearly hidden from view by a brace of palms, and the man sat there motionless except for his eyes. Vance wondered if the man was really human. He didn't seem to eat or go to the bathroom; at least Vance had never seen him do so.

"I ought to kill you," Suzanne told Vance in a voice that said she was only half joking. "I thought I'd die when everyone turned around to stare at us."

He laughed. "Why me? It was Jules who made all the noise."

"I suppose so," she said. Then, trying to change the subject, she asked, "Do you come here often? You seem to know the owner so well. What is his last name again?"

"Graziano," he helped her. "Like the boxer. But"—he grinned mischievously—"you won't find Jules around when the fists start flying. He was a pit boss at the casino in Monte Carlo the night they kicked me out—"

"For what?" She'd heard stories, but they'd all seemed too incredible.

"For winning too much."

"Can they do that?"

"Sure. Any casino in the world can kick you out if they think you're going to win too much." He saw her look. "I know that seems unfair, but remember they're in the business of making sure you walk out with less money than you walked in with."

"Did you cheat?"

"Cheat? I didn't have to. Just had a good system and a good memory. Blackjack. That was my game." He paused a moment to talk with the wine steward. A Pinot Grigio? Yes, signore, on the wine list . . . No, Vance wanted a special one, from the Collio region, Felluga if possible. The wine steward said he would try and, after a hasty conference with the maître d', produced the desired wine.

"You seem to know a lot about wine," Suzanne ventured after the man had left. "I'm impressed."

"Oh, I don't know that much," Vance demurred. "Just a little about what I like. The rest . . . I forget," he added with an infectious smile. Suzanne found herself smiling too, and suddenly feeling a bit foolish. An out-of-control feeling she didn't like. To steady herself, she spoke.

"Blackjack," she said evenly. "Tell me how do you beat the house without cheating?"

"It's really pretty simple. I kept a running count of all the cards that were played and compared them to a special strategy chart I developed and memorized. The chart pretty well determined just about every conceivable situation that could be played.

"It took about fifty hours of memorization," he said, "to master the system once. Then, besides that, all you need are steady nerves, discipline, and adequate financing. Casinos call it 'counting.' After they spot you, they'll generally surround you and suggest that you leave—a suggestion backed up by some of the most incredible muscle-slabbed apes this side of the Neanderthal."

"And this happened to you? I'd be mortified . . . all those people watching as you're led away. Weren't you embarrassed?"

"The first couple of times."

"The first couple of times? This happened more than once?"

"Well, yes. In just about every major casino in the world. And Graziano over there"—Vance indicated the maître d' with a tilt of his head—"was the guy who had to throw me out in Monte Carlo.

"Look, it's really not such a big deal," Vance said, laughing at her expression. "The only people who really care about the casino losing money are the owners. The rest? Well, they like to see the customer have a good time. And they respect the person who can come into a gaming parlor and outwit it. According to Graziano, there are maybe nineteen people in the world who could have done what I did there. And most of them have been banned like I have. One guy took more than $27,500 in forty-five minutes at the Fremont Casino in Las Vegas. He's won more than five million bucks overall. But he has to wear disguises now. I quit because I'd made enough money and I didn't want to fool around with the horseshit of stage makeup and all that."

The wine arrived, presented by a highly respectful

wine steward. After the ritual of label inspection, cork sniffing, tasting, and pouring, Vance pronounced the wine delicious and sent the wine steward away cooing unctuously.

As the level of the Pinot Grigio approached the bottom of the bottle, conversation grew easier. Suzanne described her studies in Paris and related how she had hated playing hostess for her father's diplomatic bashes.

"He's got some big corporate job now, doesn't he?" Vance asked tactfully. A new administration had not taken kindly to Ambassador Storm's divergent views.

"Lobbyist," Suzanne replied so disdainfully that Vance decided not to pursue the subject.

While the waiter was clearing away their appetizers, Suzanne asked Vance how he'd met Kingsbury and how they'd developed such a close personal relationship.

"It happened at Christie's," Vance explained. "Kingsbury was trying to buy a set of Da Vinci notebooks. Meanwhile, I'd been advising another wealthy bidder on the same items. We won. So the old man decided he'd rather have me on his side. But we hit it off personally too. He was a real heller in his youth—he still is. Gave everybody fits. Every time the competition thought they had Kingsbury boxed in, he'd find an out, something unorthodox, something that defied all of the careful principles the right Ivy League business schools taught." Vance told her about the time during the gas glut of the 1950s when Kingsbury had gone to a crude oil supplier and offered to pay the going rate for oil.

" 'You're crazy,' the man told him. Yeah, he was crazy, all right, crazy like a fox. Kingsbury said, 'I want to make sure that when the shoe is on the other foot and a shortage develops, I'll get all the oil I want. That's why I'm buying from you now.' The supplier made a fortune with oil that would otherwise have bankrupted him; and later, when the oil embargo hit in 1973, Kingsbury's refineries never stopped. It drove the major oil companies berserk. All they wanted was to bankrupt the competition and take over the entire market. I guess Kingsbury's crazy deal produced double-time work for a lot of oil company psychiatrists."

He chuckled. "I've always done things the 'wrong way.' I even find oil in a way that everybody tells me can't work—but it does work, and Kingsbury likes that; maybe he sees a little of himself in my particular brand of insanity. Hell, even I don't know why my method works. I just pack up my bike, head for the hills with a few geological maps, and the land just seems to talk to me. Then I come back and tell people where to drill. I have the lowest percentage of dry holes in the entire oil industry," he added proudly. Then, suddenly self-conscious, he looked at Suzanne and reddened slightly. "I hope I haven't bored you with all my talk about oil."

"Not at all," she replied hastily. "I mean it. There's more to it than I ever realized." And more to you, too, Vance Erikson, she thought to herself in surprise. "You seem a bit of a renegade," she went on. "To tell you the truth, I admire you for it. I guess I've led a rather cloistered life, in a way. My one act of rebellion was to become a journalist. My family wanted me to get married to some nice, acceptable, wealthy young man and become a society matron. Instead, I studied journalism at Skidmore. I wanted to start working for the newspaper in Saratoga. I had it all set up, then my father pulled some strings." She stared down at the tablecloth. "He got the job offer withdrawn. Without that money, I couldn't afford to continue at school. So"—she stabbed at the white linen with her fork—"I took my father's suggestion and studied fine art at the Sorbonne. Finally I finagled a measly paying job with the *International Herald Tribune* covering the arts in Europe, a sneaky return to my journalism, I guess. Before long, I'd gotten a job at *Haute Culture*."

Vance smiled. "It sounds like you did an end run around your father," he offered. "Went along with him and somehow ended up where you wanted to be."

She nodded, then laughed. Funny she'd never considered her family a laughing matter before. But today, now it just didn't seem so—weighty. She was enjoying herself. "He accepted it gracefully after all," she went on. "I suppose he decided that the field of high culture was an acceptable one in which to exhaust my rebelliousness. Thought I'd retire while still desirable and get married—preferably before the age of twenty-five. Well, I'm past that now and I have no intention of retiring. But the suggestions from my father and the rest of the family are coming fast and furious now. Time to stop the playing, they say, and find a husband. Before I'm a shriveled-up old maid!"

"Not much chance of that happening, Ms. Storm," Vance Erikson said, with an odd expression on his face.

"Might as well order lunch while we can still see straight enough to see the menu," he offered. She agreed.

They split an antipasto of prosciutto and melon, and then each ordered fettuccini with slivers of truffles on top. This was followed by veal Milanese.

Between mouthfuls, they continued the small talk, each grateful for the lack of hostility that had plagued them both. The wine buzzed pleasantly in their heads. The conversation repeatedly came back to the conference, to Leonardo, and finally, after the dishes had been cleared and each had taken a sip from their cups of espresso, Suzanne brought up the de Beatis diary and the startling announcement Kingsbury had made at the news conference in Santa Monica a week ago.

"What are you going to do now that the de Beatis diary is missing?" she asked.

Vance's face hardened. Until that moment, he'd actually forgotten for a few minutes about Martini, the theft of the diary, the missing Tosi, and the need for the bodyguard. He saw Suzanne's look of concern.

"Don't worry," he assured her. "I'm not mad at you for asking, it's just that . . . I've been able to forget—for the past few minutes—all of that."

"I'm sorry," she said sincerely. "Look, we don't have to talk about it now . . ."

"No, that's all right. I have to deal with it sometime." Vance stared blankly out the front window. His bodyguard's outline was gently visible as a shadow on the delicate white curtains that protected the restaurant's patrons from the trespassing glances of passersby on the sidewalk.

"I still have a copy," Vance told Suzanne. "It is resting in the Hilton's safe-deposit box right now. Martini had the only other copy, but the Amsterdam police who searched his office found no trace of it." Vance felt an odd sense of relief as he revealed this all to Suzanne.

"Interesting," she commented. "But the only thing with any monetary value is the original. Why would someone want to steal a copy? Anyway, didn't the Amsterdam police say they thought Martini's murder was just an act of random terror?"

Vance ignored her last question. "They'd steal it for the information," he said flatly. He then described a theory that had only just come together for him: Martini's death, and the deaths of the professors in Strasbourg and Vienna, had been caused by someone who either wanted the information in the diary, or wanted to keep those men from revealing what they knew about it.

Suzanne brushed her auburn hair back from her face. "That's a helluva story," she said. "One incredible tale."

"Nothing can be proven yet," he said. "That's one reason I haven't even told the police what I think about Vienna and Strasbourg."

"I'll have to admit it does seem far-fetched. Couldn't it just be coincidence?"

He sighed. "I wish I thought it were. But too many things have happened." He related the tale of his aborted meeting with Tosi.

"It was Tosi's handwriting?" she asked.

"I don't really know," he said. "I suppose that the police will have checked that out by now; they have the note. What is your point? Are you saying that someone might have killed him and then tried to set me up? No, no," he said quickly, answering his own question. "It had to be Tosi. I remember the concierge at the pensione describing the man who brought it. Her description fit Tosi and he was alone."

"I think he's dead," Suzanne said with a sudden firmness. "I don't really know why I might think that. My instincts tell me so."

"Unfortunately, I think you may be right. But why?"

"Why? Why would someone want the information kept secret badly enough to kill for it? What did Tosi know?"

"As far as I can tell," Vance offered, "Tosi never looked at the diary and didn't have a copy. I have no idea what he could possibly know that would get him in trouble."

For some moments they sat silently, sipping at their thick milky coffee and pondering the problem. Suzanne gazed intently into her coffee cup, as if some vision would appear with the answer, not about Tosi, for that was a story she didn't entirely believe right now, but about Vance Erikson. He was the question.

Across the street, Elliott Kimball pondered the same question. Slouched on the seat of his Jaguar XJ-12, he fixed the restaurant and its immediate surroundings with an unwavering scrutiny. They had been in there for nearly three hours. What the devil were they talking about? If in fact they still *were* there; maybe they'd somehow slipped out the back. Only the light shadow of the hulk as he sat by the window kept Kimball from going into the restaurant to check.

Kimball drank the last of the Perrier he'd brought along with him, painfully aware that it would only make the ache in his bladder worse. But he was so thirsty. He hadn't time to get someone else to cover Erikson, not at least until that night. Things were not going well. He hated being off balance like this. He was not in control yet, and that worried him.

Tosi hadn't shown up at the conference. Suzanne Storm had told him that yesterday. Then there had been the call from Carothers.

"They had a go at Erikson last night," Carothers had

told him. "Watch him, take him if you have to. But don't let *them* get him. He's better off dead than in their hands."

"Maybe that's our solution," Kimball had suggested.

"No," she'd answered firmly. "That would upset Kingsbury. He'd start an inquisition. We can't afford that quite yet."

But why Como?" Suzanne asked as she finished off her coffee. "What do you expect to find there?"

Vance shook his head. "I don't know. Perhaps there's a clue at the villa."

"The villa?" Vance had become remote again; she couldn't seem to pierce his thoughts.

"What?" he said, startled. "Oh, yes . . . sorry, I guess I was wandering. At the Villa di Caizzi."

"That's the family that sold the codex to Kingsbury, right?" He nodded. "But I thought they lived in Switzerland."

"They do; actually, they have several domiciles. The one on the eastern shore of Lake Como, near Bellagio, is their least known, and it's where their rare-book collection is kept. The Da Vinci Codex they sold was just the tip of the iceberg. I wouldn't be surprised if they've got more Da Vinci materials there, or"—he paused, looking distantly into his coffee—"or if they've got the missing pages."

"Where—" she was about to ask him where he would be staying in Como, but was interrupted by a tall, gaunt gray-haired man who had materialized behind Vance.

"Pardon me for interrupting," the gentleman apologized. He held a bowler hat in one hand and an umbrella in the other. He looked as if he'd just stepped from a Savile Row tailor shop. "But I did want to say how marvelous your talk was, Mr. Erikson." Vance recognized the voice, frowned, and turned toward the sound.

"Dean Weber," Vance acknowledged, his voice sharp and edged with anger.

"I didn't have time to commend you on your talk yesterday, but I want you to know that we at Cambridge are proud, very, very proud of your accomplishments."

"No thanks to you, Dean Weber," Vance snapped. "Or have you taken more kindly these days to gamblers and other such unsavory characters as me?"

The older man's face tightened. "I see . . ." Dean Weber said curtly.

"No, Dean Weber," Vance continued. "I don't think you'll ever see. You tried to keep me out of Cambridge and you did everything in your power to make my four years there as unpleasant as possible. And now you expect me to graciously accept a compliment which comes not from an appreciation of my work but because you missed the chance to—"

"Vance!" Suzanne said reproachfully.

Without another word the elder Cambridge dean whirled on his heel and stalked angrily from the restaurant.

"Why did you do that? You were rude, that . . . that," she sputtered. "That was one of the most disgusting displays I have ever seen!"

"You expect me to be gracious and tell him, 'Thank you, Dean Weber, for stabbing me in my back? The wounds don't bleed anymore and the scars hardly show.' You expect me to be gracious like that when I know the only reason he came by now is because he wants to suck up to someone who succeeded despite his best efforts and now he wants to take credit for it?"

"But you antagonize people needlessly," she persisted. "You could have just let him say his piece and leave. It's like you live your life so you can deliberately offend people."

"Like the way I paid for my education with gambling money?" he asked. "Like I offended the sensibilities of the army by building a hospital that reminded them of the babies and children they had maimed? I offended Dean Weber the first time I met him because I *existed*. *I* was not his kind of person and he did his best to stop me. He even went as far as calling the president of MIT in an attempt to keep me out. 'Morally unfit,' that's what he said I was."

"Maybe he was right," Suzanne shot at him. Their voices were growing louder, but the restaurant had nearly cleared, and there was only one couple, amorously involved in a far corner. Graziano had diplomatically absented himself.

"That's a cheap shot from someone who's been baiting me for two years now. You ought to go back and take a good hard look at your performances at some news conferences before you start getting on my case about needlessly offending people!"

She raised her hand to slap him, then stopped. Instead she got up gracefully in her chair and leaned over to whisper in his ear.

"Grow up."

Then she turned and made her way to the entrance where she disappeared into the afternoon sunlight.

Christ, she looks mad! Elliott Kimball thought, swiftly turning his face away to avoid being recognized by Suzanne. He angled the rearview mirror to get a better

look, but a yellow Fiat taxi quickly pulled over to the curb
and took her away.

She's a beautiful woman my friend," Jules Graziano said
sympathetically as he slipped into Suzanne's still-warm
chair.

"Yes," Vance agreed. "Beautiful woman on the outside,
but I don't know about her once you scratch the surface."
He gave the sympathetic restaurateur a brief summary of
Suzanne Storm's coverage of him. He clucked, shook his
head.

"I'll say one thing for you," Jules said. "I never in my
life saw a man with as much icy cold determination and
pure nerve as you at the blackjack table," Graziano began.
"You were in some tighter-than-a-virgin's-asshole situations and I never once saw you lose your cool: But it's too
bad you lose control when you sit next to a woman." The
restaurateur laughed and slapped him on the shoulder.
After finishing off a bottle of Brut Spumante for old
times' sake, they said their good-byes and Vance left.
There's no friend, he thought, like a person whose life
you have saved.

Outside, the Via Montenapoleone bustled with late-
afternoon shoppers, chic women with chauffeurs following, their hands laden with boxes from the elegant ateliers
of Milan's best.

Traffic on the narrow, gently curving street flowed
sluggishly among the illegally parked limos. Behind
Vance, the hulk waited dutifully while Graziano's door-
man tried to hail them a cab. The bodyguard was beginning to make Vance nervous. He rarely spoke, beyond

telling Vance that his name was Jacobo (pronounced *Ya-co-po*). Vance decided that he would call Kingsbury that night and ask if the hulk could be dispensed with.

Taxi after taxi passed, full, not that Vance minded. He enjoyed watching the faces along this most chic of streets with its dusty sand-colored buildings and richly ornamented awnings and lavishly attired doormen. It not only smelled of money, it looked and sounded like money. Suddenly impatient, Vance strode to the corner and caught a cab where the traffic was freer.

The hulk closed the door after them and the taxi driver gunned the engine. The car leaped forward two car lengths, then lurched to a stop as the driver stabbed on the brakes.

"Hilton," Vance told the driver who took that as a mission from hell. He drove, much as any other Italian cabbie, like the possessed on his way to an exorcism. Start, stop. Lurch, accelerate. The taxi bucked its way along in half-car-length steps, first on the curb, then back on the street. When they turned left, the traffic spread out into a four-lane boulevard and the driver drove like a normal test pilot.

His head ached from the confrontation with Suzanne Storm. Perhaps she was correct about his treatment of Weber. Perhaps he should have let the old man pontificate and blather. She'd made him feel guilty and he didn't like that. He hadn't done anything to feet guilty about.

Weber was one of the few grudges he held. The man hadn't screwed him accidentally; he had malevolently and determinedly tried to thwart Vance's career.

Still, the contretemps at the restaurant swirled in his

head. And the eye of this storm was Suzanne Storm. He wanted her approval. He shook his head at the thought. Seeking approval wasn't his style.

Had he not been so wrapped in thought, oblivious to reality, Vance might have seen the hulk suddenly grow more alert, his face frowning on a traffic jam ahead. Vance might have seen the man reach inside his jacket and unsnap the leather holster that held the Uzi machine gun. There was the faintest of breaks in the traffic pattern. The cabdriver noticed it, too, but then the driver was never surprised at what the traffic could produce in Milan.

Surreptitiously, the hulk withdrew his gun and held it ready, just covered by the hem of his suitcoat.

The windshield disappeared in a fusillade of automatic weapons fire, the slugs ripping into the seat in front of Vance.

"Down!" was the bodyguard's only command. He slammed a hand the size of a pot roast into Vance's back, slamming him to the floor of the tiny car.

More slugs ripped into the seat; Vance heard the driver gasp just before the taxi swerved abruptly to the right and smashed head-on into something very hard. Gunshots came from every direction. Rock-salt-sized particles of glass from the rear window pelted Vance's back as he struggled to turn over in the confined space.

Squirming over so he could finally see, Vance watched the hulk fire a short burst through what had once been the windshield. In the intermittent lulls between firing, Vance heard the frightened screams of bystanders and the angry shouts of those who hadn't run. People were yelling for the police.

"Stay down!" The bodyguard's voice left no room for dissent. In amazement Vance watched as his massive protector fired in first one direction and then another, ducking low to dodge incoming rounds as if he knew beforehand exactly when and from where they'd be coming.

Then an explosion rocked the car from behind. The trunk end lifted, then slammed back to the pavement, snatching Vance's breath from his lungs and apparently enraging his bodyguard. Again the hulk fired, furiously now. Like a dervish he whirled and shot. Abruptly he froze, his eyes wide with surprise. The Uzi fell from his hands into the front seat of the taxi and clattered to the floor. With his fingers the bodyguard reached around to search for the wound in his back, as another slug slammed into his chest, hurling him against the rear seat. His apologetic eyes found Vance's, and before they closed, he managed to mouth one word: "Run."

Run. Run, that's what the man said. A million times in a millisecond, Vance told his body to obey, but stubbornly it remained fetally curled in fear. Another burst of slugs ripped into the hulk's shoulders and toppled him forward; Vance watched mutely as the bleeding torso of the man tipped and then fell across his own body. He gasped as the weight of the body hit him, then lay still.

For a moment Vance didn't move. Then, with an enormous effort of will, he straightened up and heaved the man's inert form off him, simultaneously tripping the rear door catch with his foot. He kicked open the door and rolled out of the cab, scrambling on all fours like a crab. A line of machine-gun slugs followed him, kicking up tiny geysers of dust. Vance lunged forward and rolled. The geysers followed him but swept wide.

Behind him, he heard voices yelling and somewhere in the distance the rise-and-fall wail of police sirens. They'd never reach him in time, Vance thought desperately, his face into the sidewalk. It was like being face-to-face with an armed burglar in your home and having the police put you on hold.

Panting, Vance sprang to his feet and made for the edge of an alleyway about twenty yards away. Only inches in front of his head, a single shot from a revolver blasted at the brick. A brace of automatic weapons fire pulverized a ragged pattern of periods in the bricks ahead of him and then reversed to try it again. Breathing wildly, Vance dropped again to his knees as the slugs cut an angry swath across the space just recently occupied by his chest. Ten yards. The bullets pursued him. He headed for the shelter of a rubbish container, but it danced with the palsy of gunfire as he approached it.

Urgently he sprinted through the alley, avoiding the small stream of wash water, then ran down its gently sloped middle.

"There he is," a man's voice shouted in Italian. Vance made for the safety of the alley wall as a single shot resounded in the narrow passage. Other voices followed. Wildly he tore along the twisting alley, saved from the probing slugs of his assailants' guns by the winding passage. Afraid his pursuers might attempt to head him off at the other end of the alley, Vance slipped and skidded as he turned tight into the first side street. Behind him he heard their footsteps.

As he ran, his mind began to clear itself of the sticky paralysis that had gripped him. Be creative, he thought, cold and creative. He reached a main street and spotted a brilliant red subway marker. Traffic was still backed up. Breathing heavily, he pushed his way into a clot of workers on their way home, their arms filled with every manner of packages, briefcases, and bags. The noise of a thousand babbling voices filled the sparsely decorated and dimly lit station. He purchased a ticket and oozed through the turnstile, looking about for any sign of his assailants. Then he realized it would do no good: He'd never gotten a good look at any of them.

The thought preyed on his paranoia. Who was trying to kill him? The old woman over on the bench with a mole the size and color of a raisin on her cheek? The businessman perusing the day's issue of the *Wall Street Journal*? He shook his head, trying to clear his thoughts. No, they couldn't be. Get serious, he thought. Look for someone in a hurry. Look for someone who looks like me. Maybe he'd shaken them off. Perhaps he'd gotten far enough out of their sight before descending to the subway. He felt safer here, he thought, there were too many people around. He looked gratefully at a pair of policemen who stood casually by a riveted girder, talking to each other.

Then, suddenly, he knew he couldn't ask them for help. They'd take him back to the station, and sooner or later, he'd have to face the same detective who had been so accusing this morning, the detective who'd insinuated that the violence Vance was involved in had to be part of a drug ring or a terrorist organization. Then he'd have to explain the dead man and they'd ask him more questions he couldn't answer. A nauseating thought gripped him: Maybe then they'd consider locking him up as a suspect.

He turned away from the policemen and threaded his way toward the platform. He didn't care which train he took in which direction. All he knew was that he wanted to be as far away as possible right now from the men up above who were hunting for him.

"Hey! Watch it!" Vance heard angry voices behind him. Turning, Vance saw a well-dressed man some thirty yards back elbowing his way through the rush-hour crowd. Their eyes locked. It was predator and prey, and Vance had no doubt which he was. The man was just shoving his way through the turnstile, but he'd neglected to buy a ticket. A subway employee questioned him. Vance used the delay to forge his way toward the edge of the platform.

A cool breeze, faint at first, but growing stronger, blew from one end of the platform. A train was coming. Vance stood in the second tier of people; only one broad-hipped woman in a cotton print dress stood between him and the edge of the platform. Vance looked back. The man had bought a ticket and closed the gap to twenty yards. They watched each other intently above the heads of most of the crowd. The man looked to be an inch or so taller than Vance—six feet tall, maybe six-one.

The distant rumble of heavy machinery came to him faintly, then grew louder. The breeze of dust and oil and the ozone of sparking electricity and the pulverized cigarette butts and detritus of human habitation pushed harder now, tugging at eyelids and whooshing with a voice of its own. The man was ten yards away. Vance could see his face clearly now: middle-aged man, perhaps forty-five, silvery hair, and wire-rimmed glasses with gold frames. The man's face was long and wore a sad expression like a hound's. The effect was magnified by the drooping wrinkles that ran vertically up and down the sides and cheeks of the man's face, from his high cheekbones to the end of his long pointed chin. There was a malevolence in the dark burning eyes.

With a shriek of bare metal against bare metal, the subway train braked to a gentle halt. The crowd surged forward as the doors opened. Over the protests of the woman in front of him, Vance wedged himself through the crowd to the red and white car. Behind him the crowd angrily objected as the hound-faced man shoved his way through. With his back to the car, Vance sidled his way between the car and the crowd, making better distance there than his pursuer was through the crowd. There was perhaps fifteen yards between them now as the doors of the train opened to disgorge its occupants. A rapid stream of humanity cut off the man's progress as Vance continued his sideways flight along the car until he, too, was stymied at the next door.

But when Vance reached the door, the flood of departing passengers ebbed and then reversed itself as the vacancies were filled with people from the platform. But the man with the hound's face took advantage of the flow also. He jammed himself in the flood tide and had nearly reached the door at the other end of the same car when Vance lost sight of him. Frantically, he looked for the man who hounded him. Then he saw him. The assassin had managed to get on the car in one last surge of crushed bodies anxious to get home. The doors closed once and then jumped back automatically as they closed on an elbow or a briefcase somewhere. Summoning all his strength, Vance

bent low like a fullback ready to meet the defensive line
and then lunged for the door as it closed. He slipped
between two people then body-checked a businessman
facing the door. Vance and the businessman tumbled out
of the car and crashed into the startled crowd at the
edge of the platform.

Vance mumbled his apologies and scrambled to his
feet. He would always remember the evil fury burning
in the hound-faced man's eyes as he glared from behind
the window glass as the train pulled out of the station.
Vance helped the angry businessman to his feet, mumbled something about having been pushed, then took the
next train from the station.

Half an hour after Suzanne Storm left Chez Jules, Vance
Erikson strode purposefully from the restaurant and headed
down the street. Kimball hadn't expected the sudden departure on foot. Hastily, he left the Jaguar at the curb and set
off on foot behind Erikson.

It hadn't taken Kimball's practiced eye very long to
determine that he wasn't the only person following Erikson. Ahead of him two men, one on either side of the
street, kept a casual but wary eye on the American as he
walked up the boulevard searching for a taxi. Kimball
beat them to the next taxi after Erikson's. But, he noticed
as he confronted the two men, they carried two-way radios
with small flesh-colored earphones plugged into their ears
and their jackets bulged with something other than thick
wallets. They were undoubtedly in touch with someone
who would intercept the taxi and its occupants.

It hadn't taken long for events to prove him right. As
Erikson's taxi approached the Via Monte Rosa, a trio of

men, who could have been brothers of the other two thugs, materialized on the sidewalk and opened fire on the taxi carrying Erikson and his bodyguard. Swiftly Kimball instructed the driver to drop him off, and then headed toward the confrontation at a dead run. He was conspicuous if only because he was running against the tide of panicked bystanders.

By the time he'd reached the scene—it had taken barely half a minute—the gunmen had killed the driver and the bodyguard and were cautiously approaching the battered and bullet-ridden taxi that had piled itself up against the side of one of Milan's bright orange electrical trams.

They must be desperate, Kimball thought as he approached them, slowing a little to draw less attention to himself. No one would attack this openly, with this many witnesses, if they weren't scared. The Brothers wouldn't do it this way. It had to be—a body tumbled out of the far comer of the cab and scrambled away toward an alley on the other side of the street.

With a silky smooth motion, Kimball removed his Walther PK38 from the hand-tooled holster under his left armpit and held the gun motionless at his side, its deadly black burnished finish blending in with his suit. He ran swiftly to the column of a portico across from the gunmen and crouched between it and a massive rubbish bin. As the gunmen transferred their attention from the cab to the fleeing figure, he brought the Walther to bear. You, Vance Erikson, I'd like you, he thought. But just as swiftly, he altered his aim and loosed two deadly shots into the temple of the first gunman just as the man fired his automatic machine pistol at Erikson. The shots punched two small red holes in the man's head. But his fall went unnoticed by his companions, who had headed off in pursuit of Erikson. As he watched Erikson disappear, Kimball returned the Walther to its cradle. They wouldn't catch him now, he thought with some disappointment.

Chapter 10

The green waters of Lake Como lapped gently at the stone foundations of the ancient monastery of the Elect Brothers of St. Peter. The farmers who plied the narrow twisting road along the eastern boundary of the massive villa simply called it *"il Monastero,"* and they said it with hushed voices, even hushed thoughts, if that was possible, for no one from the countryside had ever penetrated its mysterious walls. The monks rarely ventured into the village some five miles to the north, and when they did, they spoke of nothing but their purpose in coming: "Some nails, signore, five kilos please," or "A shipment of heating oil . . . we'll send our vehicle to take delivery."

Over the generations, stories about the monastery multiplied, fed on the secrecy that surrounded it: The monks were priests banished for heresy by the Pope; they were tortured in the villa by Vatican hangmen for refusing to repent; the monastery was the papal storehouse for gold and jewels, containing vast vaults filled by the boats that docked and conducted their business there during the night. Local lore filled the five-hundred-acre forested villa with werewolves and vampires and every manner of Antichrist transmogrified into the hideous reptilian bodies of nightmares.

Brother Gregory had no objections to those legends. They made the inhabitants of the area around the monastery defer to him, speak to him with awe. He liked the rumors, too, because there was a particle of truth in all of them, however magnified. But mostly Brother Gregory, the rector of the monastery and the highest-ranking member of the Elect Brothers of St. Peter, liked the rumors because the fear they inspired kept away prying eyes and curious juveniles more effectively even than the thousand-year-old stone walls twenty feet high with their twentieth-century detection devices and razor-edged coils.

Some thirty feet above the lake, Brother Gregory leaned thoughtfully against the stone balustrade of the porticoed veranda that jutted out over the water of the villa's main building. He rearranged his black robes under him to make himself more comfortable as he turned to scan the lake below. Normally he felt secure here. But the events of the past six weeks had been unsettling.

Indeed, the unfortunate turn of circumstances in the past seventy-two hours burned at his entrails even more. It was his fault, his mistake. He had been a fool to believe they could have brought Vance Erikson here. But he had yearned for the younger man's expertise, his vast store-house of information about the magnificent Leonardo. He pushed his heavy black-rimmed glasses back on his nose and thought covetously of the thousands of leaves of Leonardo's codices that rested in the bowels of *il Monastero*'s vast archives, codices to which only he had access. He pushed back his hood and ran his fingers through his wavy, close-cropped salt-and-pepper hair. Erikson could have unlocked the secrets to those long locked mysteries of Leonardo's genius.

Their secrets had remained concealed since Antonides de Beatis had transferred them to the Elect Brothers in the mid-1500s. Oh, how the cardinal's secretary had worked to possess the entire works of the genius! His cleverly arranged visit to the dying Leonardo had nearly succeeded; he took possession of many of the works then. But Melzi, Leonardo's friend, forcibly prevented the removal of them all, even when de Beatis had shown up with a papal order of seizure.

Could Melzi have known about the secretary's involvement with the Elect Brothers? Had he refused in the face of a papal proclamation because he knew it came not from the Pope, but from a select group of papal aides loyal not to the Pope, but to the Elect Brothers of St. Peter? Brother Gregory grew angry at the thought of that Antichrist and the whole line of Antichrists who inhabited the Vatican. Abruptly he left his seat and stood up to his full five-foot-five height and headed for the path that led to the formal gardens.

The Elect Brothers needed all of Leonardo's inventions—especially his weapons—if they were to over-throw the prince of darkness who masqueraded as the pontiff. They had nearly all of them now. Over the centuries, they had stolen and killed for the Leonardo notebooks they needed, using de Beatis's diary as a catalog. The writings and inventions of Leonardo that now rested in museums or in private hands such as that of the oilman Kingsbury contained nothing of importance to them. Those publicly known writings contained, for the most part, the benign and harmless, the eccentric and esoteric. The only significant document that had fallen into public hands was Leonardo's cannon drawings; they had made Alfred Krupp rich. Yet even that, he mused now as he paced the rolled pea-gravel walk, even that weapon paled in comparison to the ones locked in the monastery's archives. And those dwindled to insignificance compared with the secrets that would be unlocked by the upcoming transaction.

The transaction would reunite missing pages of Leonardo's notes, which had been stolen two hundred years ago by a traitor among the Elect Brothers and given to the Vatican. Together those missing pages formed the complete drawings and notes on the most powerful weapon ever invented by Leonardo, or indeed by man of any age.

The Brothers had dealt with that traitor in a ghastly way that was vividly remembered at the monastery to this day: Small portions of flesh were cut from the man's body, then roasted, and the unfortunate individual forced to consume them until he finally died. The Vatican had invented that torture, had used it during the Inquisition, and thus it was fitting that the Pope's tool should die in a way sanctioned by popes that had come before.

That horror that hung over the order served to deter any

who might consider transferring their allegiance from the Elect Brothers to Rome. For that early punishment had become the model for punishment of traitors ever since.

Gregory stopped his walk and leaned over to remove a small pebble that had wedged itself in his sandal. His brow furrowed.

There was a traitor among them now, he knew. Finding the man would not be easy. The Vatican had grown sophisticated and cunning in its long war against the Brothers, a war dating from the eighth century. The Church had grown fat in that time and had lost direction, substituting icons and sacred images for the true faith. The Brothers had spearheaded the drive of the Iconoclasts— icon smashers—and had lost. For their efforts, the Brothers were excommunicated in 1378 after the Great Schism and it was then, financed by powerful political foes of the Church, that they moved to Como in the foothills of the Italian Alps to this villa. They had to fight both physically and spiritually.

Only the rugged mountainous terrain and the safety of the lake's water saved the brothers from the depredations of the Vatican's satanic barbarians. But the Great Satan himself, the Pope, had not been able to extinguish them. They had people loyal to them as spies in the courts of every major kingdom and even in the Pope's household itself. It was the Brothers who overthrew Sylvester II and installed Pope Gregory, the patron of the Brothers. He had almost been the perfect pope, but he reneged on the promises he had made to the Brothers. He was installed in Rome on the shoulders of the Brothers and then he turned against them, so they allied with Henry IV and overthrew him, but they got Clement III.

On and on it went, Gregory reflected bitterly, starting to pace again along the walk. Popes climbing to the top on the Brothers' shoulders and then trying to destroy them later because they had too much power. It was true, he conceded as he approached the guest house, they had the power to make popes and to break them. But they were never able to hang on to the power long enough to alter the course of the Church, to set it back on its true course. That, he thought with a faint smile, would change after the transaction. It would relegate the Great Schism to a minor footnote in church history.

At the foot of the stone steps leading up to the guest house, Gregory turned to face the brilliant clear sky over the lake and watched the sunlight and shadows play across the precipitous, glacially carved slopes. There would be fewer days like this soon. As summer passed into fall, the lake would get hazier and foggier.

Once he cleared up the issue of Vance Erikson there would be no clouds over his life, no enemy who could resist him. No, Mr. Erikson, he thought to himself as he searched for the keys that would open the locked iron gate to the guest house, I was wrong about you. I should not have tried to bring you here. I should have killed you on the spot. I underestimated you then, and my brothers underestimated you yesterday. But I'll take care of you. You'll see. You can't run from me forever.

He found the correct key and inserted it in the new, shiny bronze deadbolt laid into the original black iron grillwork. Once inside the massive wooden door, he stood quietly in the entryway, listening for sounds. Upstairs a keyboard clacked.

"Professor Tosi," Gregory called. The keyboard stopped. "May I bother you a moment?"

Vance rested his head against the cool glass pane of the first-class compartment window as the train climbed from the humid lowlands around Milan to the cooler climate of the alpine foothills. Como was a delight this time of the year, a favorite destination of the heat-oppressed Lombards.

Vance closed his eyes as the car plunged into the darkness of one of the dozens of tunnels on the hour-long ride from Milan to Como. A vacation would be delightful. Yet here he was, running, a fugitive from—he didn't know whom. Someone had tried to kill him yesterday, and had nearly succeeded. Were it not for the professionalism of his bodyguard, he, too—like the hulk—would be dead. As the last person alive to read the de Beatis diary, Vance Erikson was marked.

He opened his eyes as the train once again burst into the sunlight. Lush green foliage rushed by the window, blurring with speed. If the train was on time, they'd be in Como in fifteen minutes, at 3:45. The trip from Milan was only an hour, but it seemed to Vance that he had been on trains continuously since the day before. Not wanting to risk a return to his hotel, he'd taken the subway to the central station in Milan, where he'd bought a ticket for the first train scheduled to depart. It had taken him to Rome. There he bought a ticket to Imperia on the Ligurian coast. From there he traveled to Genoa and back to Milan, sleeping fitfully on the train, changing cars frequently to see if anyone followed him. It was harder to hit a moving target, he kept telling himself. Until that target got so tired from moving that it began to make mistakes.

During a stopover in Genoa, Vance placed four telephone calls: First, he left word with the Milan police that he had decided to get out of the city and see the countryside; then he called his hotel to inform them that he would be keeping his room longer than expected, and to please have it serviced daily. The third call took longer. It was to Harrison Kingsbury. The oilman's secretary told Vance that Kingsbury was out of town on another long trip, which would culminate in Turin, Italy, in two weeks, so he could sign the papers with an Italian refinery company that had been bought by ConPacCo. Was there any message? she asked. Disappointed, Vance said no, he'd call again. The fourth call had been to Suzanne Storm's hotel room. She was not in. He left a message with the desk: "Please tell Ms. Storm I apologize."

Apologize? That acrimonious scene at Chez Jules played again in his mind. Yes, he thought. Perhaps I owe her an apology. No, he decided. Not perhaps: definitely.

Sure, Jules, I'm a cool customer. He laughed ironically and closed his eyes and tilted his head up, trying to clear the fatigue from his brain, to banish the dull gnawing tension that gripped the back of his neck. Como was the only logical next step, he had decided. The Caizzi family villa, where the Codex Kingsbury had been kept, perched at the edge of the lake about three miles from Bellagio. A confusing passage in de Beatis's diary had mentioned Como too, but was too vague to decipher. Since the cardinal's secretary had written the diary two centuries before the Caizzis built their villa and three hundred years before they bought the codex, there couldn't be any connection there. Vance wished he had his copy of the diary with him—his memory of the specifics was not perfect—but he hadn't wanted to risk returning to the hotel to retrieve the diary from the safe-deposit box there. Probably de Beatis came to Como for a vacation, Vance reflected, just like everyone from Leonardo to Napoleon I, Bramante, Maximilian, and the rest of Europe's elite had. Just for a vacation; no other reason. The passage in the diary about Como had not been a particularly lengthy or significant one, and try as he might, Vance couldn't pull it up from his memory.

When the train finally pulled into Como, a handful of passengers disembarked with Vance: an elderly couple with armloads of colorfully wrapped packages, a couple of men whose crisp suits fingered them as businessmen, and a straggly assortment of students with duffel bags, pack frames, and sleeping bags. The businessmen headed straight for taxis; the elderly couple was met by a younger man and woman; and the students made for the tourist information booth. As Vance lingered by the bus stop in front of the station, he looked about him cautiously, sizing up passersby. Was anyone paying too much attention to him? Was there a gun under that suitcoat, in that handbag? Part of him mocked this new caution, but another more dominant part had begun to play the prey, realizing that this was a lethal game he played, one with severe penalties for losing.

Vance boarded the orange bus and, after purchasing a ticket from the machine in the rear, sat down near the back and scrutinized each passenger who boarded. Then, just as the doors started to close, he jumped off. He'd remembered that one from *The French Connection;* maybe it would work here. Grabbing a taxi, Vance instructed the driver to take him to the Metropole e Suisse on the Piazza Cavour. The old luxury hotel was right on the waterfront at the heart of the city. Normally Vance stayed at a less expensive Class-III hotel farther from the shore, but he needed the anonymity of the Metropole. Besides, he knew he'd have to start doing things a bit outside his ordinary habits if he was to elude those who wanted to kill him.

Vance left the cab on the Lungo Lario Trento, about a block from the hotel. He walked the rest of the way by the water, along the broken stone sidewalk under an archway of trees that gracefully draped their limbs from both sides, forming a perfect green tunnel through which the sun glinted brightly. A late-afternoon breeze swept down the lake, scattering scraps of paper and wrappers into little swirling dust devils in the gutter. Weary tourists who had opted for long boat treks up the lake were now trooping happily down the gangplanks from their boats, cameras dangling from their necks.

Couples of every age sat on the green wooden-slatted benches that faced the lake, and watched the tour boat crowds and the boats and water taxis and, farther out, the sailboats on their moorings, all gently bobbing, nodding their assent that, yes, this was certainly a pleasant time and a pleasant place to be.

Vance watched them all, enviously, painfully aware of their uncomplicated enjoyment of life. Nobody was trying to kill *them*. He went past the Metropole, crossed the street at the light at Via Luini, and headed for a leather-goods shop. There he used his ConPacCo American Express card to buy an overnight bag. At a huge department store near the Via Cinque Giornate, he bought toilet articles; and at a men's store a block from his hotel, shirts, socks, underwear, and two sweaters. He had a story all prepared to tell any curious clerks about the airline losing his luggage, but no one questioned him. He placed all his new purchases inside his luggage.

Now well equipped to face a hotel desk clerk who would wonder at a new guest without luggage, Vance walked to the Metropole and checked in after slipping the clerk fifty euros to get a reservation on such short notice. He bought a copy of Il Giorno in the lobby and followed the bellman to his room. The room, on the third floor, overlooked the lake and the awesomely steep forested slopes of the hills, and provided a teasing distant glimpse of the snowcapped Alps. The view captivated Vance, as it always had; probably it was the reason why the rich and famous had always been drawn here. The sun had begun its descent toward the hills to the west. Deep olive-black shadows crept slowly from the hills on his left, plunging that side into obscurity, but the warm amber light painted the hills on his left with comfortable warmth that made the buildings and villas there shine with gold.

But there was no comfort here tonight for Vance; only fear and melancholy. Fear for his life; fear he had done the wrong thing in coming here instead of going directly to the police in Milan. And why on earth had he chosen this place? The last time he had visited Como had been with Patty.

How long do we stay vulnerable? he wondered as he turned from the window and began to unpack the bag he had packed only minutes before. How long can human beings ache before their hearts close off the wound? He and Patty had taken a moonlight cruise in one of the old-style water taxis; he remembered how she'd snuggled close and warm in his arms and told him she loved him. He remembered her sleeping face in the morning when the frown lines had smoothed themselves out, and with her hair carefully arranged by chance, shining in the day's first rays.

And, too, as he mechanically spread out his toilet articles in the bathroom and placed his folded clothes carefully in the bureau, he remembered the empty closets when she had left. Forlorn bent wire coat hangers where her clothes had once hung. Only memories of love remained. He shook his head slowly and then dressed for dinner.

Downstairs, the formal dining room was barely filled; it was only 7:30 and the dinner trade had just begun to filter in. The maître d' seated Vance at a well-lighted table that overlooked the lake through sheer curtains. The Metropole's dining room was one of the better, if more expensive, places to eat in Como.

But on this evening, the wine tasted like water, the prosciutto like cardboard. The tortellini felt like lumpy paste in his mouth, and the veal made no impression at all. The food was good; he knew that intellectually. But nothing meant anything to him right now except crushing the ache in his chest, filling that vacuum that threatened to suck his entire life into it. He picked and sipped listlessly at the meal, and returned morosely to his room. He dropped into a fitful steep, dreaming that Patty was trying to shoot him.

In the morning Vance felt better. The night's sleep had chased away his depression as it always did, and he plunged into the early morning sunlight with a new lightness to his gait. The little sidewalk extension of the Metropole's dining room consisted of a couple dozen glass and wrought-iron tables with umbrellas arranged within a rectangle in front of the hotel demarcated by shoulder-high shrubs growing in concrete planters. He took a seat in the corner facing the lake and scanned the menu.

Though he usually liked to go native when he traveled, this morning he was grateful he was staying at a hotel that catered to appetites that demanded more than brioche and jam for a meal. He ordered three eggs over medium, breakfast sausage rolls, and American coffee, and then settled back to comfort the now audible rumblings in his stomach. Coffee arrived in a silver pot. Vance poured a cup and unfolded a copy of *Il Giorno,* which came with breakfast.

He scanned the headlines for any report of the shoot-out, and saw nothing. He read about protests against stationing American warships in Italy, an antinuclear march, resignations of four more Italian cabinet members whose membership in a secret society had been exposed, a report from a convocation examining the shroud of Turin that said once again that it was almost sure the shroud was that of Jesus Christ, announcements that inflation had risen to forty-seven percent and air pollution was getting bad all over Italy.

A breeze blew off the lake and ruffled the pages of the paper. Vance waited until the wind died, then turned some more pages. At the top of page four, a headline leaped out at him: **TERRORIST ATTACK KILLS FOUR IN MILAN.**

Vance folded the pages back and read:

An agent working for the Italian government antiterrorism bureau and a defrocked priest were among four people killed in a guerrilla shoot-out in Northeast Milan Monday afternoon. . . .

Vance read the list of the dead: the taxi driver with four children and a wife to feed; a bystander, a high school student only sixteen years old; a large armed man who worked for an executive security company; and a priest. A priest!

> Police investigators said that the defrocked priest had been relieved of his clerical duties and excommunicated from the church in 1969 for his participation in a protest. In that protest he led a mob of demonstrators into a church in Empoli where they destroyed statues, icons, and other sacred images. Police said the man, who was apparently one of those who attacked the cab, had no other criminal record.

This is getting more than a little weird, Vance thought as he finished the article. No mention of him—to his relief and perplexity—and no comment from the Italian anti-terrorism bureau on why the hulk had been where he was.

Relieved, Vance found that his appetite had returned with the arrival of his breakfast. The day was looking up. He read the story again to make sure he had missed nothing. He was about to lay the paper on the table when another small story caught his eye: **BOMB BLAST KILLS MAID AT HILTON.**

The knots in Vance's stomach raveled themselves back into an emotional monkey's fist. The knots drew tighter as he read on.

> Mrs. Anna Sandro, 47, a chambermaid at the Milan Hilton, died Monday night when a bomb exploded as she opened the door to bring fresh towels to a hotel guest. Milan

police said the bomb was wired to the doorknob of the room and that it may have been intended to kill the room's occupant. Milan police refused to name the room's occupant, but identified him as an American oil-company employee here for a conference.

"Damn!" Vance muttered to himself.

Instantly he was more afraid than he'd ever been in his life. More afraid than he'd been in Iraq, more afraid than—as his heart pounded, he tried to remember when he'd ever known this profound terror. Unknown people he couldn't recognize were really trying to kill him, but they had killed innocent people instead. Those people had died because they had been too close to him at the wrong time. And then he thought of the deaths in Vienna and Strasbourg, Tosi missing, Martini brutally murdered. Vance grimaced and held his head in his hands. Death cut a broad swath and it seemed determined to add him to its list. He shook his head and stood up; his decision was made.

He owed Martini justice, and he owed something to those poor people in Milan who'd gotten caught between him and death. The answer, he knew, was somewhere in the de Beatis diary. The police would laugh at him. Who'd ever believe a five-hundred-year-old diary could kill so many people? He himself would have laughed at the idea if so many people hadn't been killed already. He could laugh at the concept, but he couldn't laugh at the corpses.

What are you trying to do?" Elliott Kimball shouted, the veins popping out on his temples. "Are you trying to sabotage everything? Would you ruin everything we've so carefully arranged?" He stormed back across the plain terracotta floor, breathing heavily, the hissing of his breath like jets of steam from an overheated boiler.

"How can you just sit there, damn it!" Kimball towered over a spartan desk, staring at the man who sat calmly in the chair behind it. Over the sounds of Kimball's heavy breathing came the gentle slap-slaps of waves at the foundation pillars.

Brother Gregory looked indulgently up at Elliott Kimball's boxed-in rage. The tall, sandy-haired man clenched and unclenched his fists, his face muscles twitching and trembling.

"Of course not," Brother Gregory breathed in a voice so quiet that the other man had to hold his breath to hear him. "You forget that we have been working toward this for more than half a millennium, and your organization for less than a century."

"Look, Gregory," Kimball said harshly. "I'm just about fed up with all of your 'we've been trying harder' shit. The fact is that you've been a bunch of fucking losers for centuries, and you've finally been given a chance to cure that and you're right on the edge of fucking it up again, and by God"—Kimball saw the monk wince as he took the name in vain—"I'm not going to let you screw up the Legation in the process."

Only the hard set of his jaw betrayed Brother Gregory's placid facade. To show anger, he often told his novitiates, was to lose control. "I believe you're a bit overwrought, Mr. Kimball. I can't see that any harm has been done."

"No thanks to your little escapades," Kimball spat, turning from the desk and walking across the dimly lit room toward a plain wooden cross hung on the bare stone wall. He closed his eyes and took a ragged deep breath and held it, trying to exorcise his rage. "First of all," Kimball recommenced in a lower, more controlled tone, "you should not have approached Erikson without informing us. You know how close he is to Kingsbury and you know damn well that Kingsbury could be a formidable obstacle if he wanted to be. And then Monday . . . how the hell did you—" Kimball broke off, trying to regain control of his rising fury. "What did you think you would accomplish with your ambush, even if it had succeeded?"

"I do not justify my actions to you or anyone else, Mr. Kimball," Brother Gregory stated, his voice low and cold. "We are the people to whom kings and prelates for centuries have had to justify themselves. I'll not have you or anyone else questioning the motives or authority of the will of God."

Kimball opened his mouth to speak and swiftly shut it. There was no arguing with the true believer, no compromise with those who slaughtered all in the name of Jesus or Allah or Yahweh.

"Yes," Kimball said smoothly, his swallowed bile bitter in his throat. "You are quite right." The corners of Brother Gregory's thin cruel lips began to snake upward. Push the right buttons, Kimball reflected sardonically; just push the right buttons.

"I forgive you," Brother Gregory said mellifluously. "And having heard your confession, absolve you of your sin and blasphemy."

Kimball struggled to avoid rolling his eyes in disgust.

"Thank you," Kimball said in the most penitent manner he could muster. "As you have told me yourself on a number of occasions, you believe that the Bremen Legation is God's instrument for you to use in realizing God's work for you and the Elect Brothers." Brother Gregory was nodding imperceptibly now. Christ, Kimball thought, how can he really take this seriously?

"The Bremen Legation," Kimball went on, "wants only to assist you in doing God's work and, to that end, to counsel you as you work with us. I urge you, respectfully, to avoid any confrontation with Vance Erikson, at least until the transaction is completed. I—"

"I see no reason to accept that advice, Mr. Kimball," Brother Gregory interrupted. "It is God's will that the transaction be completed. No one—not you, not me, not Mr. Erikson or his powerful ally Harrison Kingsbury— can thwart the will of God."

Kimball opened his mouth in anger, then quickly rolled his eyes toward the ceiling and crossed himself. Well, hail Mary, full of crap! Kimball thought. Here goes, it's worked a hundred times before; Jesus won't fail me now. Out loud he said.

"Yes, yes, you're quite right. But as the instruments of God, we must determine how God wishes us to treat Mr. Erikson and how that treatment supports his overall will of successfully concluding the transaction." Brother Gregory's brows wrinkled. "To that end," Kimball continued, "I'd request that you in your holiness pray and advise me how we should proceed."

An expectant silence fell upon the room. Would it work yet another time? Kimball wondered nervously.

Finally the monk in his black robes spoke. "For a secular person not of the faith, you frequently surprise me. Perhaps I have done too little praying about this; it is easy to find oneself so wrapped up in the end result that one pays too little attention to the small steps it takes to arrive there." Kimball stifled his sigh of relief. "Of course, you must realize that I cannot commit myself to any decision on your advice right now." Kimball inclined his head reverently. "I must wait for the word of God"—he crossed himself—"to make itself known."

He'd won! One small step for the Bremen Legation, Kimball exulted silently; one giant leap to getting rid of you and your macabre empire, Brother Gregory.

With a characteristic wave of his head, Brother Gregory indicated the audience was at an end. Kimball was escorted to his room by one of the brothers, who would remain outside to make sure that Kimball remained there until it was dark and time to leave and return to Como.

Vance Erikson crossed the lobby of the Metropole Hotel with his head down and his hands plunged to the bottoms of his pockets, the folded copy of *Il Giorno* wedged firmly between his waist and his elbow. Lost in thought, he failed to see a young woman spring from her chair at the sight of him and walk swiftly and gracefully across the lobby to intercept him. Quickly she closed the distance between them, reaching him as he got to the stairway. She extended a well-manicured hand and tapped his shoulder. "Vance."

The newspaper fell to the floor as he withdrew his hands from his trouser pockets and spun around. His face was ashen.

"Vance, it's just me." Suzanne smiled reassuringly.

He stood face-to-face with her now and swallowed hard. "Geez, you scared the hell out of me," he said apologetically.

"Can we have a cup of coffee?" Without waiting for an answer she took his elbow, steering him back toward the café. "I just got here and I'm starved.

"I got your apology," she said when they were seated and Suzanne had ordered a continental breakfast. "Thank you very much."

"I think you owe me one now. An apology."

She frowned. "What for?"

"Nearly scaring me to death!" He grinned now and they both laughed. She smiled back at him, liking what she saw: a robust handsome face with a winning smile and an indestructible sense of humor, especially for a man who'd been through what he had in the past few days. She watched as the breeze parted the leaves on one of the shrubs, and the sunlight poured through and played across his face, his eyes turned deep, deep blue, the color of oceans when the water gets deep.

"All right," she said equably. "I apologize."

"Accepted."

Where was the wariness? Suzanne wondered. Maybe she'd ceased to be a threat, at least when compared to people who were trying to kill him.

"How did you find me?" Vance asked.

"Remember at dinner, before things got rough, you said that you were probably going to Como, to call on the castle of the Swiss heirs who had sold Kingsbury the codex?"

"That seems like a million years ago," he said, trying to remember. It wasn't clear in his mind, but then nothing from that day had remained unscathed from the events that had overtaken him. "Yes," he lied, "I remember it clearly. But that doesn't answer how you found me *here.*"

"Have you ever counted the hotels in Como?" she asked. "There are twenty-five of them, according to the regional tourism authority. I started with the list they gave me," she said, pulling it out of a fine, hand-tooled purse of reddish brown leather, "and started at the top of the list." He took the list from her. The list began alphabetically by class. There were only three Class-I hotels in Como and the Metropole was the second of those. He was dismayed at how easily she had found him. If she could, then others might also.

"Clever," he said honestly. "But you're just lucky I don't have a taste for Class-IV hotels."

She laughed.

"But coming here wasn't the most intelligent thing for you to do. You may have noticed there are a number of unhealthy things following me around."

"I know," Suzanne agreed. "That's why I came."

"That's why . . .?"

"Absolutely," Suzanne said enthusiastically. "It's a helluva story. Do you think I want to go home and let someone else cover it?"

They looked at each other silently for several minutes, each trying to figure out what the other was thinking. Two prototype people, finally encountering someone who had no ready handles they could grasp.

Her breakfast arrived. They were silent as Suzanne hungrily consumed the food.

Vance sipped at his coffee silently, watching her eat.

"So when did you come up?" he asked after a minute. "On the train this morning?"

She finished chewing a bite and washed it down with coffee. "Last night," she said, taking another swallow and replacing the cup delicately in its saucer, making only the faintest of sounds as the two pieces of china touched. "I rode up with Elliott Kimball."

"Who?" Vance said. The name sounded vaguely familiar.

"You know him," she said noncommittally, "rich, Harvard Law. I think you played rugby against his team once."

Vance searched back in his memory. He saw a blond-haired man she had met after the conference reception. "Blond hair, tall?" he asked. She nodded as she took another bite of brioche.

"Yes," Vance said absently, his thoughts still in the past. "Vaguely."

"Well, he certainly seems to remember you well," she declared.

"How do you know him?"

"From college."

"Is he here?" Vance asked cautiously.

"I don't know," she said. "He dropped me off at my hotel—I'm staying at the Villa d'Este up in Cernobbio—and left. He said he'd leave a message for me."

"Villa d'Este," Vance whistled. "That's a pretty ritzy place. Makes the Metropole here look like a Motel Six."

"Expense account, remember? The magazine's paying for it."

Vance shook his head. The Villa was probably the most exclusive and expensive place to stay on Lake Como. It had been a private villa for royalty of half a dozen nations and still offered the ultimate in luxury and beauty.

"Well, despite your royal tastes, I guess you're in for a story. I suspect it would be more trouble to try and get rid of you than to let you come along," he said, smiling at her.

"Very perceptive of you," she said. "I can be a lot of trouble when I put my mind to it."

"I know," he said, thinking of the past two years. "This wouldn't be the first time you made trouble for me."

"True, but from what I can tell, you've got your hands full with a lot more serious trouble than I've ever caused you."

He nodded grimly as the body count of the several days flooded through his mind. The body count, the killers who had sighted in on him and everyone near him. That was real trouble and it wasn't going away with an apology.

Chapter 11

I still don't understand why you're doing this." Suzanne Storm raised her voice so Vance could hear it over the throb of the hydrofoil boat's powerful engines. He acknowledged her question with a nod as the boat swiftly left behind the graceful amber image of the Villa Carlotta and the lakeside village of Tremezzo.

"You're outraged that all this could have happened in the gentle world of Vinciana, aren't you?" she asked.

Vance searched her intelligent green eyes, reluctant to admit that she was right.

"Of course I'm right," she went on. "Don't forget I've been studying you for some years now. For an eccentric person, you've got a strong sense of propriety. You get very defensive about your sacred cows. People *you* think don't belong in the world of Leonardo are stealing codices, killing scholars, and are after you."

"Yeah, well . . . that's enough to upset most anyone," Vance said defensively. "Besides, conspiracies and intrigue were an everyday part of Leonardo's time. Remember, he and Machiavelli often worked together."

"I know, I know," she said, plunging ahead. "But that's not part of the way you think the world ought to work today." She paused and fixed his eyes with a penetrating stare. "In fact, I think you're more offended that someone has dared to violate your standards than you are about specific people being killed."

He fixed her eyes with a hard look of his own. "That's not true," he said.

She'd touched something private, and it made him angry. Vance burned inside, but he hid it.

"Well, it doesn't really matter," he said. "Because I'm doing it anyway."

"I think you don't see what could happen," she interrupted. "What makes you think you can do something the police can't?"

"Hell, I don't know," Vance admitted. "You're right, I'm not a cop. I—"

"You're conceited," she interrupted again. "It takes one super *grande* ego for someone to think they have a chance of surviving, much less prevailing, in the mess you've gotten into."

"You sound like you're trying to talk me out of doing anything."

"I think you ought to leave this to people who know what they're doing. You just haven't thought about what could happen if you don't."

"It doesn't do to let your imagination go too far in wondering what might happen in anything," Vance said.

"If you really thought of what could happen to you on a freeway, you'd never get in a car. If you really considered all of the horrible things that could happen to you in your lifetime, the only sane thing to do would be to blow your brains out."

She shook her head ruefully. It was a long shot but he was bright and resourceful. He just might succeed where a professional would fail, if only because he didn't know it couldn't be done.

The hydrofoil's powerful engines slowed. They were approaching the dock in Bellagio, the tiled roofs of its aged buildings shining bright pink with the late-morning sun. A church tower wearing a bluish green copper hemisphere like a skull cap stood alone over the village. Vance watched as the boat's captain reversed the hydrofoil's engines and brought them gently against the pilings. To his right, waiters were clearing away the remnants of breakfast dishes at an outdoor café set under a bower of bougainvillea. On the other side of the pier, three priests tied up their twenty-five-foot motorboat and tilted the outboard motor out of the water.

It was nearly noon when they stepped off the boat, surrounded by tourists and swarms of small children.

Bellagio had once been an exclusive resort, a favorite of wealthy Englishmen. But it had not aged gracefully, and today it was a dowdy and somewhat sleazy old matron. Surliness and mediocre food had replaced quality in the *ristorantes*. Quaint streets where diamonds and precious metals once reigned were dominated by cheap gimcrack souvenir stands. Only the opulent private estates outside the town still maintained their elegance. Bellagio had become a tourist trap and a convenient supply depot for the people who lived or vacationed at their villas.

Vance took Suzanne's elbow and steered her away from an arcade of sidewalk vendors selling costume jewelry and mementos of Italy made in China, and headed toward a steep, narrow set of stairs that ran toward the top of the hill. The stairs wound through the old part of Bellagio, past the entrances of tiny shops and restaurants, and the gates to private residences with offices underneath.

As they climbed, the sounds of the tourist infestation faded. Vance began to fill Suzanne in on some of the details of his acquisition of the Codex Caizzi for Harrison Kingsbury.

"Bernard Southworth serves as the attorney and agent for the Caizzi family," he explained. "All of the negotiations for the sale of the Codex Kingsbury took place through him. Count Caizzi only showed up for the actual transfer of the codex, which took place in the library of the Castello Caizzi, on the very top of the hill, outside of town."

"That was the huge white palazzo that we saw on the way in."

"Right. It has a view of all three branches of the lake. It's stunning. I couldn't believe it."

"Southworth doesn't sound like an Italian name," Suzanne commented.

At that moment, a deliveryman laden with racks filled with straw-covered fiascoes of Chianti stepped nimbly down the steps. To let the deliveryman pass, Vance and Suzanne stepped into the doorway of a small shop that apparently repaired electrical appliances. Inside he noticed out of the corner of his eye that two of the priests were stressing the importance of repairing some device quickly that day. The shopkeeper looked terrified.

The Chianti deliveryman made his way past them and as Vance and Suzanne resumed their climb, she spoke softly. "Did you hear that poor man in there? He was frightened out of his wits."

"Priests can sometimes do that to the faithful."

"No"—she shook her head—"I mean, he was truly afraid. It was more than just respect or something."

"They're probably the monastery," he said. "Around here, they have a reputation as baby eaters or something. I think it's a carryover from the Inquisition. Nothing to concern us."

They reached a small, well-kept entrance with a brightly polished engraved brass plaque. Bernard Southworth, Esq. II

"Oh, right," he said, remembering her earlier question. "Southworth was an Englishman who came here in the thirties, fell in love with Bellagio, and stayed." Vance reached for the shiny brass door knocker and rapped sharply four times. The dark mahogany door swung open, revealing a dumpling woman in a domestic's uniform.

"Signore Southworth, *per favore,*" Vance asked.

"Momento." The woman closed the door and returned a minute later. "Mr. Southworth is extremely busy at the present moment. Can you come back tomorrow?"

Vance and Suzanne exchanged a quick glance. "But I called this morning," Vance protested. "He said he would see me."

"He has gotten very, very busy," the woman said doggedly.

"I must see him. It is very important."

"And I tell you he is too busy right now." The woman's voice was angry now. She started to close the door. Vance stepped quickly forward, and held it open with his foot.

"I'm going to stand here," Vance said. "And if Mr. Southworth is so busy that he can't see me until tomorrow, I'll stand here until then." The woman glowered at him. "Go ahead," he went on. "Call the police."

"Vance!" Suzanne said sharply. "You're causing a scene."

"Glad you noticed," Vance said, smiling. "I hope Southworth will notice too. Like most well-bred Englishmen, he hates a scene." Two old women with loads of wash stopped to stare at him openly.

"I want to know why he changed his mind," Vance told Suzanne. "It's been only about two hours since we called him. What could have happened?"

"I don't know. But this is embarrassing."

"I know." Vance smiled. "It's supposed to be."

"Signore, signore!" The servant had returned.

From behind her came a deep bass voice with rounded vowels.

"Let him in," Southworth said wearily, "let him in or I shall have no rest at all." The woman shot Vance an assassinating glance and swung wide the door. Vance and Suzanne stepped in. The room was dimly lit and filled with the overstuffed furniture and dark woods of a private English men's club. It smelled of expensive pipe tobacco.

"Good morning, Mr. Erikson," Southworth said, his voice cold and controlled. He was lean, almost gaunt, dressed in a gray pin-striped three-piece suit with a gold chain spanning the vest pockets. His silver hair was combed with not a single hair out of place, but his carefully trimmed silver mustache twitched almost imperceptibly with anger.

"Aw, you didn't have to put on such a warm welcome for us," Vance said sarcastically. He indicated Suzanne. "Mr. Southworth, this is my . . . associate, Ms. Suzanne Storm."

Southworth nodded his head. "A pleasure. Now, Mr. Erikson, what is so very important that you must come barging into my office when I am with a client?"

"I want to visit Signore Caizzi," Vance said. "I'd like—"

"Quite impossible," Southworth interrupted.

"Could you telephone him on my behalf?" Vance asked.

"Out of the question," Southworth said. "Mr. Caizzi has left the strictest instructions he is not to be disturbed. He has had a terribly trying time for the past two weeks and then the shock of last night."

"The shock of last night?"

"His only surviving brother died of a heart attack."

"His only surviving brother?" Vance asked incredulously. "What happened to the other two?"

"That is what I am trying to tell you," Southworth said.

"I thought you were trying not to tell me anything," Vance mumbled to himself. "Two weeks ago, Enrico and Amerigo were killed when the airplane Enrico was piloting crashed."

"Who died last night?"

"Pietro," Southworth said.

"So that leaves only Guglielmo," Vance said. The silver-haired attorney nodded silently. "My God," Vance said as he thought. Another heart attack, another Da Vinci connection broken. Enrico was a fabulous pilot, meticulous with the mechanical care of his airplane. "Do they know what caused the crash?"

"He ran out of fuel," Southworth replied.

"Then I guess I'll just have to pay Guglielmo a visit," Vance announced.

"No!" Southworth said quickly, too loudly. The lawyer cleared his throat. "No, you mustn't do that."

Vance studied his face. The belligerence had given way to fear. What was this man afraid of?

Abruptly, another man appeared at the door of Southworth's office.

"You would not want your conscience to bear the burden of causing more grief and sorrow to a fellow human being, would you?" The question came from a tall, broad-shouldered priest whose presence seemed to fill the room. In his right hand the priest held a revolver. Behind them Southworth's servant stifled a cry. She had been standing beside the door, completely forgotten.

"Is that part of some new sacrament?" Vance asked. The tall priest took a measured step forward and stood beside Southworth. The lawyer saw the gun for the first time and paled visibly.

"I don't think that's called for," Southworth told the priest. "Not here. Not in my offices."

The priest's eyes barely flickered. "Shut up," he said.

Vance stared at the muzzle of the gun. "I'm getting a feeling of déjà vu," he said. "But I just can't seem to get used to priests pointing guns at me." Out of the corner of his eye he could see Suzanne; she looked poised.

"You are a most persistent nuisance, Mr. Erikson," the priest said, pulling back on the hammer of the revolver. Vance and Suzanne dropped to the floor as the room resounded with the revolver's booming reports. On all fours, Vance followed Suzanne to the cover of a brocade-upholstered sofa.

"Oh, God. Oh, God. Oh, God!" It was Southworth's servant. She had been hit by the first bullet.

The room exploded again: a slug ripped through the back of the sofa and gouged a short trench in the hardwood floor.

"Damn it all, man!" It was Southworth. "Give that to me. You have no right!" Suzanne and Vance huddled behind the sofa and listened to the scuffle.

"Let go, you crazy Brit!" the priest shouted.

Vance leaped to his feet, slipping at first on the waxed floor, and then plunged into the fray. Southworth had both his hands on the revolver; the priest was struggling to regain control, while striking the lawyer with his free hand. Vance's first punch caught the priest on the side of his head, staggering him, and his second landed squarely on the cleric's nose. There was a loud pop of tearing cartilage.

"Bastard!" the priest screamed, loosening his grip on the gun. Southworth tugged with all his might, pulling the revolver toward him, but the priest had recovered and, with an extraordinary display of strength, twisted the revolver so it pointed at the lawyer's face. He pulled the trigger.

Southworth's scream electrified the air for a split second before it vanished in the shock of the blast. The lawyer's grip on the gun loosened with a spasm, and his gray pinstripe-clad body fell to the floor, twitching for an instant.

Vance leaped for the gun. He had almost gotten one hand on it when the priest lashed out with a powerful backhand that caught Vance under his chin and snapped his head back. Through a multicolored galaxy of pin-pointed lights that burned in his eyes, Vance saw the priest point the gun. Quickly he rolled away as the gun exploded again. The muzzle flash singed the hair at the back of his neck. Dimly, he could hear Southworth's wounded servant whimpering, and outside, the sounds of excited voices muffled by the closed door. Someone was banging frantically with the door knocker.

The priest whirled, and Vance reached for a brass lamp. The priest grinned demonically as Vance grabbed the lamp; he raised the gun. Vance yanked the cord from the socket, the clatter of the flailing plug melded with the clicks of the revolver's hammer being cocked. Vance's entire body tin-gled with fear. Then a subdued shot rang out, sharper, not as booming as the priest's revolver. Then another shot and another and another all in rapid succession. Vance stared in amazement as first a small red hole appeared under the priest's right eye, then one in his temple and two in his neck. The revolver whirled around his trigger finger and clattered to the floor, discharging its round into the base-boards. The priest seemed to sink into the floor as his legs collapsed under him. He fell first to his knees with a wrenching thud and then toppled face first to the floor. Vance dropped the lamp and turned slowly. Kneeling beside the sofa was Suzanne Storm. Grasped profession-ally in both hands was a tiny, snub-nosed automatic pistol. Vance looked from her to Southworth's dead servant by the door, to Southworth who lay spread-eagled faceup on the floor with a gaping hole where his face should have been, to the priest and back to Suzanne.

"This is not a very healthy thing we got into," he said shakily.

Suzanne rose to her feet and walked slowly to him. He could feel her faint fast breaths of fear on his face as she faced him.

"Where did you get that?" Vance asked, pointing to the gun.

Suzanne ignored his question. "Come on, we've got to get out of here," she said brusquely. She grabbed her purse and stuffed the gun into it. Outside, the sounds of the crowd had grown louder, and someone was turning the locked doorknob. "It's only a matter of time before someone breaks in," she added quickly—"probably with the police."

"You're right on that," Vance said grimly, shoving the priest's revolver into his waistband. "Look. This way." He led Suzanne through the first floor of Southworth's offices, through the kitchen at the rear, and out into an alley that snaked up and down the hill with steps like those at the front. They headed up, taking the stairs casually, two innocent tourists off the beaten path.

Run! Suzanne's body told her; walk said her mind. Run! commanded her instincts; walk said her training. She took Vance's arm to make sure he'd walk too, but when she did, she found the warmth comforting, the hard firm muscles reassuring.

They climbed the stairs for another five minutes before reaching the top.

Suzanne turned to him. "Okay, what now?" she asked wryly.

"I don't know." Vance grinned feebly. "I'm making it all up as we go along. Left would be best. We could head to the Grand Hotel; it's just a short walk from here. We can get lost in the crowds. And then . . . then we rent a car and take a trip to the Castello Caizzi. I've got a feeling Guglielmo Caizzi may be awfully glad to see us." He turned, heading north with long, quick strides.

"I was afraid that's what you were thinking," she said wearily and ran to catch up with him.

No, signore, we have no cars for hire," the concierge at the Grand informed them. "Only for hotel guests. I'm sorry."

They left the elegant lobby and stepped from the marble steps to the sidewalk, in the direction of the main part of Bellagio.

"It's a long walk," Vance said.

"I still think you ought to let the police deal with it."

From the distance came an angry blast from an auto's horn. "What would we tell the police? That three of the Caizzi brothers have been murdered and that I think that Guglielmo will be next . . . if he isn't already dead? Who's going to believe that?"

Suzanne nodded. "Still . . . I don't think we ought to go poking around up there."

"You can go back to Como, if you want," Vance said, "or you can wait for me at a café here in Bellagio. But I'm going up there to see Guglielmo Caizzi."

With a scream of tortured tires, a black Mercedes 450SL burst around the curve, its engine racing. Vance and Suzanne watched, horrified, as an old workman riding a beat-up red bicycle with fat tires and a rusty wire basket full of eggs and milk leaped from his bike as the Mercedes careened straight for him. There was a metallic thud when the bumper of the Mercedes clipped the bike's basket, throwing the bicycle off balance. The bike careened over the curb, slinging a mesh bag of broken eggs across the sidewalk and two cartons of milk into the stucco walls of an adjacent building where they broke open with an explosion of white foam.

Dazed, the old man struggled to a sitting position as the driver of the Mercedes slammed on his brakes.

"Stay out of my way, you toothless old bag of shit; you're lucky I didn't kill you!"

Then the driver punched the accelerator and sped away, leaving behind black stripes on the pavement and the sulfurous stench of burning rubber in the air.

Vance stared at him, roiling with rage, as the Mercedes pulled up to the parking lot of the Grand Hotel and disappeared inside it.

"Bastard," Vance mumbled, and went to help Suzanne. She now had the old man sitting up; he was shaking his head.

"I'm fine, just fine," the old man kept saying as he got to his feet and walked over to his bike, wheeled it into the street and pedaled out of sight.

"Tough old rooster," Vance remarked. "He'll probably outlive us both."

"That's not going to be too hard, considering the past couple of days."

"Come on," he interrupted her, taking her arm. They headed back toward the Grand Hotel.

"Where are we going?" she asked.

"I have an idea."

"Oh, hell, not again."

"Oh, yeah," Vance said. "Watch this." They approached the 450SL belonging to the young Italian man. The hood ticked and clicked as the engine cooled. "Walk with me like you own the car. If the parking valet comes out, don't make eye contact."

"Vance, what are we—"

"Just get in like it was yours," he ordered.

"But this is against the law."

"So is assaulting little old men," he retorted. "Just trust me. Act like you own the car and nobody's gonna look at us twice."

They got in, and as Vance expected, the keys were in the ignition.

"This is not legal at all," Suzanne said, staring into the side mirror as they drove up the winding road that led to the Castello Caizzi.

"I heard you the first time."

The raggedly paved asphalt road wound its way up to the hills above Bellagio in a series of snaking switch-backs, passing among terraced olive groves, small farm-houses set close to the road, and through vineyards heavy with ripening grapes. There was little traffic.

There was a change in Vance, Suzanne thought as she watched him drive. He'd lost the edginess he'd had a couple of days ago. Then, she thought, he'd seemed insecure, tentative and . . . overly sensitive. Now, she thought as she looked at his keenly intelligent face, with its muscular square jaw and penetrating blue eyes, he was in control of himself again.

She liked those eyes, the way they radiated life. I could read his every thought, she told herself, if I could only understand the language of his eyes; they're that expressive.

Ahead, the white stone of the Castello Caizzi loomed larger and larger, a proud symbol of a proud family. Vance downshifted for a tight 180-degree turn, and then accelerated slowly into third gear. He searched his memory for details of the castle, cursing himself for not having been more alert on the day he, Kingsbury, Martini, and a phalanx of attorneys had trooped up here to sign the final papers, render a mammoth check, and take possession of the Codex Caizzi, now the Codex Kingsbury.

"The castle is a cross between a medieval castle and an eighteenth-century villa like those by the lake," he told her. "In 1427 Count Caizzi had been awarded an old castle dating from about A.D. 1100, ravaged by numerous battles and sieges. The count, and his descendants, gradually renovated, altered, and added to the structure over the centuries. To the massive stone walls that surrounded the 175-acre estate, successive occupants added a moat, fed by an aqueduct, and addition after addition to the living quarters."

Out of the corner of his eye, he watched as she reloaded the clip of her automatic and checked a spare clip in her purse.

"That was some fancy shooting back there," Vance said. "Where did you learn to do that?"

"I took a course," she answered.

"You took a course," Vance repeated flatly, "and it taught you how to shoot that straight, that, uh . . . professionally?"

Suzanne jerked her head at the word "professional" and fixed him with a suspicious glance. He didn't mean anything by it, she decided. "I was very good in the course. I did my homework."

"No kidding," Vance agreed. "In fact, I'll bet the priest

back there would have given you an 'A' on your final exam."

"How can you joke like that?" Suzanne said reproachfully as Vance slowed the car, looking for a spot to pull over. "There were people killed back there."

"What else are we going to do, cry?" Vance retorted. "This whole thing is so absurd that we both ought to be laughing so hard we can't see straight: A geologist who thinks he's a Leonardo expert joins forces with a hoity-toity culture magazine writer to go off and track down a conspiracy that's killing people left and right. Here we go, armed with a couple of graduate degrees between us, a revolver with one bullet in it, your little popgun, and a lot of chutzpah."

"And more than a little stupidity," she added.

"Yeah, a lot of that," he agreed.

The smooth road deteriorated as Vance angled the Mercedes off the asphalt and onto a gravel path into the forest that quickly turned to bare earth ruts. They were beneath a ridge and still out of sight of the castle. Once they were hidden in a stand of young poplars, he turned off the ignition. The throb of the Mercedes's exhaust died smoothly, replaced by silence. Below them, a seaplane skimmed the water near Tremezzo and alighted gracefully at the dock. In the distance dogs barked, but mostly there was the conversation of the wind with the poplars as the heart-shaped leaves with their saw-toothed edges whispered some unintelligible gossip.

Dried leaves and grasses crackled gently as Vance and Suzanne made their way wordlessly along a narrow twisting game path among the poplars. It paralleled the asphalt road for about half a mile and then headed uphill toward the alabaster-white castle. Glimpses of the castle grew rare as the undergrowth thickened through a field that had once been cleared, but now was being reclaimed by nature. Trees gave way to brambles and shrubs that grew taller than their heads.

Abruptly the brush gave way to lovingly tended rows of vines and carefully tilled soil. He motioned with his hands for them to stop. He squatted, and Suzanne followed suit.

"Where are we?" she asked, leaning on his shoulder.

"The Caizzi family vineyards," Vance whispered. He turned his head and found himself very close to Suzanne's face. The aroma of her perfume filled the intimate space between them. "The Caizzi have always made wine," he explained. "Those are his vineyards, all champagne grapes. His cellars make nothing but champagne and it is never sold, only enjoyed at his parties, receptions, and celebrations."

They looked at the vines, heavy with ripening grapes, skins frosty with the natural yeasts of fermentation. They waited, listening for sounds of others, looking for signs they had been spotted. Maybe, Vance thought, he was wrong. Maybe there was nothing wrong here and there were no guards. Maybe he had once again let his imagination run away from him.

They waited for five more minutes. Finally Vance's knees began to ache from the squatting position.

"Let's go," he said, standing up. The castle walls were about two hundred yards away. A gamekeeper's and general service entrance had been knocked through the old castle walls at the south end. They'd try there.

Keeping beyond the last row of vines, which ran chest

high, Suzanne and Vance made their way around to the
south side of the walls.

The slope grew too steep here for vines and was given
over to trees and brush. A mountain of garbage terraced
its way down the slope. Even the grandest of us all still
have assholes, Vance thought. From the shade of the
trees, Vance scanned the walls, more than forty feet high,
white and impenetrable save for the single opening at its
base. A neatly maintained wood lean-to room huddled
against the wall.

"That's where we go in," Vance said, indicating the
lean-to. The gentle breeze died for an instant, and they
heard voices and the sounds of a television coming from
the lean-to.

"There're people in there," Suzanne said.

"I didn't say this was going to be easy, did I," Vance
replied. "Come on!"

They covered the 150 yards to the entrance to the lean-
to at a dead run. The voices inside were louder now;
almost intelligible. There were two voices, one with the
rough dialect of the hills, and the other a mellifluous cul-
tured tone that betrayed education—the sort of voice one
might hear in church. When Suzanne and Vance reached
the lean-to, they wedged themselves in a corner formed
by its side and the massive stone wall.

"Okay, what now?" she asked.

"Wait here," he said. She nodded and pulled her automatic out of her purse.

Vance sprinted across the open ground to the trees and
made his way slowly to the garbage dump. There he
noticed a small tractor with a scraper blade and bulldozer
treads parked at one edge. The unmistakable odor of

methane gas grabbed at his nostrils, the inevitable result of decomposing garbage. Good, he thought, this is going to make my job even easier.

He turned to the tractor, opened the fuel cap, and sniffed; it was diesel fuel. Plenty to start a fire.

What in hell was he doing, Suzanne wondered. Her position here was too vulnerable: anyone walking around the wall or coming out of the door would see her; maybe she should go join Vance. She transferred her pistol to her left hand and wiped the cold sweat from her right palm. She looked around her: only an oil drum and several cardboard cartons for cover. And then as if some demon had read her worst fears, she heard footsteps in the lean-to, and the hinges of the screen door squeaked open. A third man had joined the first two. As they walked through the door, their voices all grew noticeably louder.

Suzanne dropped quickly to her knees to hide herself from their view. Above the rim of the oil drum, she saw the back of a head of black shiny hair, and she ducked as it turned to face her. She clicked the safety off the automatic. A smoldering cigarette came flying toward her, hit the wall, and bounced to the ground beside her.

The men were laughing, and joking—not the voices of men on their guard. Soon she could make out some of what they were saying. One man, apparently a custodian, was hauling a bin full of trash. The other two—one of them addressed as "Father" by the others—were laughing about some joke told inside.

At his own vantage point, Vance ducked behind the tractor as the men's voices grew louder. From a space beneath the tractor he watched them emerge from the lean-to. Suzanne! They would see her, for sure. Heart pounding, he watched as an older man with a bald head and very bushy mustache walked into the sunlight, pushing a large garbage can on a hand cart. Laughing, the man stopped to turn around to talk with a young man in overalls—perhaps someone who tended the vines—and a tall man dressed in black vestments, another priest.

The men finished their conversation. The priest and the younger man in overalls walked back inside, leaving the older man to empty the load of household and kitchen debris at the landfill.

Wasting no time, Vance crawled under the tractor and found the petcock used for draining water from the diesel fuel. It was stubborn, but yielded when he tapped lightly on it with the heel of his shoe. Finally, the fuel poured its oily aromatic way to the ground, darkening the soil and then running downhill toward the garbage. He took the book of matches Suzanne had given him and touched it to the still running stream of diesel fuel. There was a gentle Fwoomp! and black smoke and flames climbed skyward.

Vance had sprinted back across the open space to Suzanne before the men in the lean-to, still engrossed in telling jokes, noticed the flames. Suddenly the joke-telling ceased, and both men stepped tentatively to the door. The next instant they were running across the open space, the priest's robes flying behind him like a black contrail.

"Now!" Vance commanded as he and Suzanne leaped to their feet and raced into the little shack.

From the dimly lit interior of the lean-to, they passed swiftly into an even more dimly lit corridor that ran along

the interior of the wall. The damp stone walls, lit irregu-
larly by low-wattage bulbs, curved out of sight at both
sides. From the right came sounds of voices in the distance. They went left.

They walked cautiously and passed a stone stairway
leading up to the rampart level. A faint splash of bluish
light spilled from the top. They pushed on in the yellow
dingy light of the corridor, stepping from the pool of light
to almost total darkness, back to light where they reached
a padlocked wooden door with rusty iron hinges and fas-
tenings. Daylight knifed through a crack between the
ancient weather-beaten planks. Vance placed his eye to
the cool, rough wood and peered through.

"Here, take a look." Through the slit, she saw a moat,
now filled with lilies and other aquatic plants, and yet
another wall. The doorway through which they looked
opened out onto a footpath that ran the circumference. To
her right, she saw a covered bridge spanning the moat,
leading into the castle from the entrance leading to the
lean-to. To the left was a small railed footbridge.

Using the barrel of the priest's gun, Vance pried at the
rusty old padlock on the door, and it yielded quickly,
groaning as it did.

"Damn!" Suzanne whispered.

"What's done is done," Vance said as the door swung
wide enough for them to slip through sideways. "If someone heard us, it's too late to do anything about it now."

They raced along the footpath, crossed the bridge, and
ran through an arched doorway on the other side. Above
the outer wall, heavy black smoke roiled lazily into the
sky. Beyond the wall, they heard men shouting at each
other.

"When I came here for the negotiations, I got a tour," Vance said. "There are three entryways like this one from the moat gardens that had been punched through the castle's sixteen-foot-thick walls in order to allow its guests access to the moat. Each entrance has its own garden in a small courtyard on the opposite side. These courtyards pen onto a central courtyard like that found in most large castles."

Suzanne nodded as they exited the passageway and skirted the courtyard gardens. They made their way around the perimeter and under the overhanging balconies held up by salmon-colored marble pillars. Suzanne's eyes darted from one feature of the castle to another, from the ornate carvings to the frescoes on the walls protected by the balconies. "That's a Brunini," she said. They walked another half-dozen paces and she stopped again. "That statue"—she pointed toward the figure of a nude man and woman in a marble embrace—"that's a Canova. I didn't know it was *here*."

Suddenly shouts from the outer courtyard brought her back to reality. They pressed themselves into a doorway and waited for the men to leave. The voices passed, talking loudly and excitedly about the fire. Vance wiped the perspiration from his upper lip, and wished that he had more than one bullet in the gun he had taken from the priest.

When the men's voices receded, Vance and Suzanne stepped from the doorway and made for a set of stairs.

"All of the bedrooms and living rooms open out onto the balcony which overlooks the main courtyard," he told her hurriedly as they dashed up the wide marble stairs. "Caizzi has got to be in one of them if he's still alive."

At the top of the stairs they were met with the sight of porticoes and columns marching away in a circle from both sides. Vance and Suzanne walked clockwise around the circumference, peering into every room. Where was the lord of the manor, Count Guglielmo Caizzi?

Outside, near the fire, the shouting grew louder and louder. Vance guessed that the methane gas from the dump would turn the fire into an inferno that would occupy just about every able-bodied person in the count's employ. They heard sirens in the distance, obviously fire engines making their tedious way up the hazardous switch-back road.

About a third of the way around the courtyard, they came upon a room with all of its drapes closed. They looked at each other and nodded: This would be it.

Through a thin parting between the heavy silk tapestry-like drapes, they could see the still supine figure of a pale elderly man, his body covered from toes to chest by linen sheets. At the top, the man's pajama-clad arms and shoulders stuck out. Count Caizzi did not look healthy.

By the side of the bed stood a short priest, talking furiously on the telephone. The well-glazed and tightly closed windows muffled all the sound. The man was agitated and paced back and forth as he talked. They would have to act quickly. If the fire's origin was discovered—once someone found the open petcock on the tractor's tank—a search would be on for intruders.

"Okay, this way," Vance whispered. They scurried back to a portal leading to the interior corridor.

They stopped before they reached the corridor and pressed against the wall, listening.

A scraping. That's what they heard first. Someone was in

the hallway. Over the sounds of the scraping came the muffled, anxious voice of the priest talking on the telephone.

How would they neutralize the sentry without alerting the castle?

"I have an idea," Suzanne whispered softly in Vance's ear. "Be prepared."

And before he could stop her, she had walked boldly into the corridor and up to the guard.

"Quick!" she said urgently. "This way; we need your help! Please hurry!" She stood and waved her arms anxiously. Men are men, she thought, even priests; she'd played that for all it was worth on too many occasions to count.

"Oh, please, it's important; won't you hurry?" Suzanne gave it her best damsel in distress act. The guard moved toward her warily. She took two tentative steps toward him.

"Oh, I'm glad so you were here," she said breathlessly and took the priest's right arm as he approached. "They said you could help."

"Come on, now. We haven't got much time." She pulled the man toward the entrance, tugging at his arm.

Vance listened to her performance with admiration. A remarkable woman, he thought as he flattened himself against the wall, trying desperately to silence the sounds of his ragged breathing. Suzanne came around the corner first, followed a split second later by a pudgy red-faced priest with a shiny bald pate and red eyebrows.

As she rounded the corner, she pretended to slip, and fell to the floor, gripping the priest's arm as she did.

While the priest reached for her with his other arm, Vance arced the butt of his pistol down, putting all his shoulder and back muscles into the swing.

"Oohmph!" The bald priest exhaled sharply as the

blow connected with the back of his head. He collapsed to the floor with a muffled thud and lay still.

Vance extended his hand to Suzanne to help her up.

"I'm glad I'm on your side," he said, grinning.

On tiptoes they ran to Caizzi's room. Vance tested the knob; the door was locked. Back Vance went to the unconscious sentry, but the man had no keys. They listened carefully at the door, but the priest inside was saying little now, mostly grunting yeses and nos. Then, finally, he said good-bye and slammed the receiver down. Vance knocked on the door. An old-fashioned key rattled in the lock and finally the door opened to reveal a tall, angry priest, and beyond him on a bed, a still man that Vance recognized as Count Caizzi.

"Say one fucking word and I'll blow your brains out," Vance said as he brandished the revolver. The priest's eyes grew large as surprise replaced the anger on his face, and he opened his mouth to scream. Before the priest could sound the alarm, Vance hit him in the Adam's apple with the side of his left hand, turning the scream for help into a strangled gurgle. While the priest's hands went to his damaged throat, Vance slammed his right fist into the man's solar plexus; with an audible exhalation he fell to his knees, gasping for a breath that would not come.

Vance stood over the man, hot blood coursing through his brain. "Don't try to call for help again," he warned. "Things *can* get worse." Grabbing a handful of tissues from Caizzi's bedside, Vance stuffed them into the priest's mouth. He looked around for something to keep the man's mouth closed with. Finally, he untied the rope-like belt from the priest's robes and passed it through the man's mouth like a gag.

The priest glared up at him, pain from his injuries mixing with hatred. He gagged for a moment, then recovered, breathing loudly through his nose. Vance took off his own leather belt, and looped it around the priest's hands at the small of his back, tying off the belt so the man's hands couldn't slip out.

"Now, get up," Vance commanded. "Come over here." Vance led him to a blank wall, stood the priest about three feet from it, and made him lean over until his head touched. "Spread your legs," Vance ordered and when the priest hesitated, kicked them into a wide stance. "Don't move." By the time Vance had finished, Suzanne had dragged the unconscious sentry's body into the room and shut the door and locked it.

Through all the commotion, Caizzi had hardly stirred. Once Suzanne and Vance had searched both of the priests for weapons, and found none, they turned to the waxy pale man in the bed.

"Count Caizzi," Vance said softly, shaking the old man gently. "Christ, he's all skin and bones. Count Caizzi," Vance repeated. The old man on the bed stirred, grimacing and licking his lips. "It's Vance Erikson, Count. Remember me? I work for Harrison Kingsbury."

"Erikson," the old man said dreamily without opening his eyes. "Yes, yes, I remember." The man rolled his shrunken head from side to side, struggling to open his eyes. "Erikson, I didn't know you were one of them." Vance and Suzanne leaned close to hear his words. "I never . . . never would have . . . sold the codex if I had known."

Slowly the old man's crinkled tissue-paper lids opened to reveal rheumy, dull eyes that labored to focus.

"Part of who?" Vance asked.

"Them," Caizzi said, raising his hand painfully from the covers for an instant, waving it feebly around the room. "The brothers."

Vance's eyes fell on the bedside table. An assortment of hypodermic needles and drug ampoules lay scattered on a white enameled tray. He plucked one from the clutter.

"Morphine," Vance said tonelessly. "The man's zonked out.

"No. I'm not part of them. We're here to help you," Vance said.

"Too late," the count said, his eyes anxiously trying to focus on Vance's face. "Yes . . . too late for my brothers . . . too late for me. . . . Let me alone, let me die." He closed his eyes.

"No!" Vance said urgently, and shook Caizzi's bony shoulder. "We're going to get you out of here."

"Won't work," Caizzi said, coming back to life. "The Brothers are everywhere. They'll find me."

"Who are the brothers?" Vance asked.

"All around . . ." Caizzi said. "The Elect Brothers of"—his voice faded—"St. Peter. All his bastard spawn."

"All these priests?" Vance asked. "From the monastery?"

"Yes . . . yes," Caizzi answered. "Tried to stop them for years . . . tried to . . . tried. . . . Couldn't . . . they've finally won."

Suzanne left the bedside and checked on the unconscious priest. She knelt over him, took his pulse. It was fluttery. She looked over at the priest who still stood against the wall. Pigs, she thought. Dirty filthy pigs, to do this to an old man.

"The codex," Caizzi was saying when she returned to the bedside.

"They did this because of the codex?" Vance repeated incredulously. "Why?"

"Because I sold it," Caizzi said proudly. "For centuries the Brothers wanted it, but we always kept control."

Caizzi was rallying, his voice stronger, clearer. "Everything was fine as long as the codex remained in the castle. When I sold it to you, the Brothers . . . Brother Gregory told me I'd pay . . . This is my payment."

"My God!" Vance exclaimed. "Why? Why?"

"Because it will destroy them," Caizzi said vehemently. "It brought you and it will bring others." He coughed a deep phlegmy hack. "I'll die for it, but it was my one act." He coughed again violently. "I'll die with my self-respect." He coughed again, closed his eyes, and breathed heavily, raspily through his mouth.

"What are they doing that must be stopped?" Vance asked.

"The answer is across the lake," Caizzi said wearily. "They—"

The French windows exploded then in a blizzard of glass fragments driven by slugs from a silenced automatic weapon that ripped through the white curtains, sending them into a frenzied dance. The slugs slammed into the mattress and into the old man's frail body. Vance dove for cover under the bed as something hot sliced through his arm.

Damn, damn, damn! Brother Gregory cursed silently as the old gray Fiat pulled up to the drawbridge of the Castello Caizzi. The sweet smell of burning diesel fuel reached his nose when the driver opened his window to speak with Brother Anthony, who guarded the front entrance.

"Go with God, Brother Piero," the muscular priest said to the driver, then bowed to Brother Gregory in the rear seat.

As the car lurched forward over the wooden drawbridge, Brother Gregory's ulcer flared. The past three hours had been a trial. First there had been that twit Kimball from the Legation. Gregory's insides seethed as he thought about sharing power with infidels like him and his masters. But that was the mistake made by the Brother Gregorys in the past. They had refused to share power with the temporal authorities and thus never remained in power long enough to accomplish their ultimate goals. Lord Jesus Christ, Gregory prayed silently as the car pulled into the main courtyard, please forgive me, Your humble servant, for the sin of consorting with infidels, and may You give me the strength to crush them when they have served their purpose.

Kimball was the epitome of all that he hated about the infidels: Protestant, wealthy, confident in his damnation. But Kimball had only begun the tribulations of the day. There had also been the telephone call informing him that Brother Annunzio had been killed while visiting the Caizzi lawyer, Southworth. From the description, Gregory knew Vance Erikson was the killer.

And now this fire. It had to be Erikson. What did the man think he was trying to accomplish? He would get nothing from Caizzi. The Brothers had broken the man's mind with a brain-rotting array of drugs. The count had paid. Gregory smiled. Yes, the man had paid. One more day's worth of . . . treatment, and he would sign the deed to grant the Brotherhood possession of Castello Caizzi. After that, there would be no need to keep the man alive.

Curse Brother Annunzio for getting killed! Damn the brothers guarding the castle for letting Erikson wreak havoc like this. The Fiat pulled to a stop next to a staircase. Brother Gregory sat still in the back, struggling to control his rage. He was angry at himself for allowing Vance Erikson to live. It had been a serious lapse of judgment and must be corrected.

"May I have the Ingram with a silencer?" Brother Gregory asked his driver. "Erikson was my mistake, and I must correct it." The driver expeditiously removed the machine pistol from its case, screwed in the silencer, folded back the stock, and inserted a long clip of ammunition.

Shitgoddamngoddamnthathurts," Vance said through clenched teeth as he clutched his arm. Slugs continued to rip through the count's bedroom.

"Here," Suzanne said, prying at his fingers, "let me take a look." Vance winced but allowed her fingers to peel away his own and pull back the fabric of his shirt for a better look at his wound. "Ow!"

"You're being a baby," she said. "You've just got a small cut here on the surface."

"Small?" Vance grimaced. "How small is that?"

"About three inches long across the back of your arm. It looks a little deep, but the blood has already started to clot."

"Right," he said, picking up the revolver he'd stuck in his waistband. "Let's get out of here before we collect some wounds that are real serious." Outside on the balcony, they heard footsteps cautiously crunching through the broken glass, but they couldn't see anyone through the tattered curtains, fluttering sorrowfully in a light breeze. Suzanne fired. The steps stopped.

They bolted from the room and ran to the right, away from the corridor where they'd knocked the sentry unconscious.

"Inside, inside," they heard the other priest yelling from the room. "They're heading north!" Behind them they heard the footsteps break into a run.

Heels clattering wildly on the marble floor, Vance and Suzanne sprinted down the corridor.

"There!" a voice behind them cried in Italian. As they rounded a bend in the corridor, a slug shattered a diamond-shaped pane of lead glass next to Suzanne's head. Surfing pure adrenaline, they bolted past door after door until they neared a stairway leading down.

"I figure we've run about another third of the way around the castle." Vance's words came sandwiched between his heavy breathing. "I'll bet that this stairway leads down into one of those little courtyard gardens."

They slowed their pace to make the turn when they spotted a man running up the stairs toward them.

"Oh, shit," Vance said. They tried to stop, in order to use the corner as cover, but their heels couldn't find traction on the hard marble floor; their feet slid out from under them. Like baseball runners sliding into home plate, Vance and Suzanne glided across the meticulously polished floor. A regularly spaced line of pockmarks exploded white and puffy at waist level on the cream-colored plaster wall behind them. If they hadn't slipped, they would have been dead by now. All around, the footsteps of their pursuers grew louder.

A solid rail ran around the three sides of the stairwell as it exited the floor. They scrambled toward it, rolling to safety as the man with the automatic weapon recovered his aim and brought the gun to bear on them. Marble chips spouted from the floor. Blindly, Suzanne fired a shot around the corner.

"They're armed!" someone yelled. Cautious steps proceeded up the stairwell. Then a chorus of shouts exploded from the corridor behind them. Vance whipped the revolver from his waistband and fired the one remaining shot in his gun. Suzanne followed suit, emptying the clip into the host of charging men. Vance's revolver slug thumped loudly into the lead man's left breast, staggering him and knocking him back into two other men. Suzanne had managed to hit the fourth man three times, but he was a big man and still came at them.

They crawled around the corner of the railing, momentarily out of the line of fire. Cautiously, the man on the steps poked his head around the far corner of the rail.

Lacking any other weapon, Vance threw the empty revolver at him; he ducked.

Things were not looking good for the home team, Vance reflected grimly. But a few split seconds was all that Suzanne Storm needed to eject the spent ammunition clip from her automatic and slam another one in. Vance huddled in awe as she efficiently reloaded the gun, fired another shot blindly around the corner toward the band of four men and then another at the man on the stairs. There was a yelp of pain.

"Got him!" Suzanne cried. Then they crawled toward the edge of the railing, hoping to make a dash down the stairs. Edging in front of Vance, Suzanne fired around the corner of the rail, and then down the stairs toward the man she'd just wounded. There was another cry of pain.

On hands and knees, they scrambled to the stairs. A

short, fair-haired man was strewn along the steps, his limbs askew, his head pointing downward. His eyes stared blankly out, oblivious to the trickle of red that poured from a hole in his forehead, through his fair hair and down the cool marble steps. Vance lunged for the dead man's weapon, a stubby, boxy-looking weapon. Vance had seen it in the movies: It was an Ingram.

He grabbed the Ingram as the big man Suzanne had wounded appeared over the railing, accompanied by the two others. Vance pulled the trigger and sprayed the railing, struggling to maintain control as the automatic weapon danced around. The three men ducked; the Ingram ran out of ammunition. Vance dropped the useless weapon. It clattered down the stairs. Quickly he and Suzanne followed. At the bottom, they stood still for a second, bewildered. This was not the staircase Vance had remembered. There was no courtyard, no opening to the outside at all. Instead, the corridor ran in two directions, and another flight of stairs led down. Which way should they go to get out? There were only two openings in the castle walls; those were sure to be well guarded. Suzanne fired up the stairs again, and then inserted a fresh clip.

"How many of those do you have?" Vance asked, amazed. "For a journalist, you walk around with quite an arsenal in your purse."

"This is the last one," was all she said. "Nine shots."

"Wonderful," Vance said glumly. Slugs began to clatter down the stairs. "Let's get out of here." They headed down the next flight of stairs, but it ended, to their frustration, in another corridor. "No good," Vance mumbled. "Just more of the same." He started for a heavy wooden door with a small iron-grilled window. He pulled it; it swung back slowly but smoothly. They stepped quickly inside and found themselves in a circular well with stone steps spiraling downward.

"Go first," Suzanne said. "I've got the gun. I can cover us." There was a look in her eyes Vance decided not to argue with. They ran quickly down the counterclockwise spirals.

Far above them, they heard a voice, carried perfectly down the tube of stone. "Where does this lead?" the voice asked. With a shiver, Vance recognized the priest at Santa Maria delle Grazie.

"I don't know, Your Excellency," someone else replied. Three other voices all admitted they had no idea where the stairway went.

"What the hell have you been doing here for the past three weeks if you don't know where things go?"

There was a wild chatter, then, "Oh, never mind!" he yelled impatiently. "Go after them."

Suzanne and Vance continued their downward climb. When they reached the landing at the bottom of the stairwell, they heard their pursuers cursing at each other as they stumbled madly down the narrow twisting steps.

Water vapor rose visibly from their sweating skin in the suddenly cool air. In the dim light, Vance looked at Suzanne. She was flushed with the exercise, but her breath came with the easy manner of a well-conditioned athlete catching her breath. Warily she watched the stairwell, holding the automatic pistol loosely at her side.

There were two exits out of the small landing, one without a door leading off into an unlit corridor, and another with a heavy wooden door; Vance pulled it open. On the other side of the door was yet another spiral staircase, this one unlit. It disappeared into a blackness like the blackness in nightmares from which the only escape is to wake up.

"Suzanne." She left her position and stood by him, just inside the stairwell. Vance was about to speak when he heard the sound. The footsteps had stopped, and through the veil of silence came the metallic thunk, thud of something bouncing down the upper stairwell followed by a massive blast that shuddered through the confines of the small room.

For an instant the room exploded with the light of a hundred suns and then the shock wave, confined by the heavy stone walls, slammed into them like a steel fist. Suzanne felt the blast of the hand grenade fill the room and press her between the heavy oak door and Vance's body.

The heavy oak door had absorbed the brunt of the blast, Vance thought as he plummeted into the darkness. He grabbed wildly in the dark and plucked an iron railing out of the blackness. For a second he held it, until the impact of Suzanne's body hurtling into his broke his grasp. Pain shot from his ankle as it twisted cruelly on the edge of a step, and then he rediscovered the railing, and this time his grip held.

Vance stood shakily on the steps and helped Suzanne to her feet. He heard his own voice from underwater ask her where her pistol was. She didn't seem to hear. When he reached for her hands, he realized the gun was gone. They had lost their only remaining protection. He pulled on Suzanne's hand, and she followed him into the darkness of the stairwell. As their hearing gradually recovered, they heard the sounds of their pursuers grow louder.

The flight to the bottom was clumsy and painful. Vance

twisted his ankle again, and Suzanne kept falling into him. After two eternities, Vance stepped off the last step and nearly fell down as his legs tried to take a step that wasn't there. Suzanne bumped into his back. This door, like its twin at the top, had a small opening covered with iron bars. Through the bars Vance saw the settling rooms for Caizzi's champagne.

"Can you hear me now?" he asked Suzanne.

"Yes"—she nodded—"better."

"Good," he said as he pushed open the door and led her into the cavernous room with its vaulted ceilings. "I have an idea."

The dimly lit room contained row after row of dark green champagne bottles, sitting at an angle, bottoms up with their necks resting in a wooden *pupitre* rack. The count had always been obsessive about making his champagne the traditional—and very expensive—way. Where most commercial vintners had mechanized the *methode champenoise,* Caizzi had retained the old methods.

After the grapes were pressed and fermented once, they were bottled, capped, and set in the *pupitres* to ferment again. Every day, a special cellar worker known as a riddler came into the caves, tapped each bottle lightly, and turned it slightly. The light tapping, performed over a period of weeks, would gently force the sediment to the neck of the bottle, from which it could later be removed.

The life of a riddler would be remarkably boring were it not the element of danger involved. The tremendous pressure that develops during secondary fermentation makes each bottle a potential bomb. One tap too heavy, one flawed bottle, one dropped bottle, would send glass fragments flying in every direction, propelled by the powerful pressure inside. Riddlers over the centuries have been blinded and killed in the pursuit of their delicate job.

Vance knew from his earlier visits that Caizzi bought his bottles from a small regional maker who made painted and etched bottles that made them elegant objects of art much prized for their beauty even when the champagne was gone. The special glass and the etching, however, made the bottles less robust than commercial champagne bottles.

Up an open metal stairs Vance and Suzanne climbed, to a catwalk that gave the cellarmen access to the upper tiers of bottles. Positioning Suzanne at the end of the row, at the opposite side of the cave from their entrance, Vance then swiftly returned to the other end of the huge room—easily fifty yards wide and twice that long—and crouched down on a metal catwalk between two racks. Gently he lifted a bottle from its *pupitre,* willing his hands to be steady, and quelling the urge to run. Moments later, the short priest with the heavy black glasses emerged from the shadow of the staircase, looking about warily and scanning the room with the muzzle of an Ingram MAC-10 with a huge sausage-shaped silencer on the end.

The priest stood in the doorway for a long time, the dim bulbs glinting off the lenses of his eyeglasses as his eyes started to work their way up.

Come on! Come on! Vance silently urged the other men on. Get out here. One man arrived and stood by his leader, and then another. The priest's eyes carefully scanned the racks opposite Vance. In a few more seconds, they would spot him.

A flickering movement caught Suzanne's eye. She looked down and spotted the form of a man moving stealthily in the aisle below. He had seen Vance and was angling for a better shot. Suzanne looked first at the man, then at Vance, and again at the single man down in the aisle. He must have come through another door. Vance! She wanted to yell.

She saw the priest, and then three other men, spill out into the dim light of the secondary fermentation room. The lone man moved closer. She pulled a bottle from the rack. It was heavy. Could she throw it as far as the man? He was a good thirty yards away. Taking the neck in her hand, like a juggler with an Indian club, she stood up quickly and hurled the bottle end over end as the man, now in position, trained the muzzle on Vance's head.

At that moment, Vance silently urged his bottle into the air and reached for another as a thundering boom echoed behind him. Vance whirled his head and saw a man drop his weapon and clutch his face, screaming; blood trickled through his fingers. Then another explosion and more screams—Vance's bottle had reached its target. Vance whirled back around and threw another bottle, and another and yet another at the cowering group of men who had retreated into the doorway. Blood streamed down the priest's face and filled his eyes. Vance threw another bottle at the man, which exploded against the wall beside the door, forcing the priest inside the stairwell, where he closed the door.

"Oh, Mother of God, help me," the man who had tried to shoot Vance was pleading. The man, dressed in rough workman's clothes, was on his knees in a widening puddle of champagne stained pink with his blood. His hands covered his face as he weaved from side to side, crying. "My eyes, my eyes. Oh, Mother of Christ, stop the pain!"

Vance climbed down the metal steps and motioned to Suzanne to join him.

He raced over to retrieve the man's gun, another Ingram.

"Where did he come from?" Vance asked Suzanne when she arrived.

She pointed to the other side of the room. "There's another door there." The sound of running feet came dimly to their ears. Vance started for the door, pushing Suzanne before him. A burst of automatic weapons fire raked the spot they had been standing on, and struck instead a row of bottles. The bottles struck by the slugs exploded, but the explosions didn't cease as bottle after bottle adjacent to those struck went up in a chain reaction with massive explosions and showers of glass and foam.

A bottle nearby exploded and suddenly there was more danger from the room than from the priest and his soldiers. They ran through the entrance and up the stairs, as their attackers were forced to retreat before a barrage of exploding bottles.

"I've read about this," Vance said between gasps. "Instances where one exploding bottle had touched off a chain reaction which destroyed most of the contents of a champagne cellar."

The sounds of the explosions diminished as they climbed upward, into a long corridor and up two more flights of steps. They blinked rapidly when they finally emerged into the brilliant sunlight. No more than ten yards in front of them was a gray Fiat and a lone priest, lounging on one of the fenders like a limo driver waiting for his boss.

"Move away from the car and don't say anything or you're a dead priest," Vance said as he ran swiftly toward the man, the Ingram leveled at him. Almost at the same instant, the short priest with the glasses emerged from a doorway some seventy yards away, accompanied by two men. Vance and Suzanne leaped into the Fiat as slugs thudded into the car's fenders.

"Take this and see what you can do with it." He handed her the gun as he struggled with the Fiat's engine. It wouldn't start. The engine turned over lethargically, and would not kick over. Suzanne fired the Ingram at the attackers and they scattered.

"The portcullis!" the short priest yelled. "Lower the portcullis!" Vance found the choke and pulled it as a guard by the gate hit a large industrial push button and sent the massive iron gate sliding slowly toward the roadway. Suzanne shot at another guard and he fell in a heap in the roadway as the old gate with its vertical bars clanked slowly downward, a medieval relic powered by modern machinery. Vance slammed the gearshift of the Fiat into first and the car leaped forward. The rear window exploded as slugs ripped through it.

"Get down!" he said to Suzanne, but she ignored him as she faced the rear kneeling defiantly on the front seat, firing the Ingram out the hole left by the back window.

The gate continued to close, its vertical bars lancelike, tipped at the bottom with ornamental spear points. "Brace yourself," Vance yelled. "This is going to be close." He accelerated as fast as the Fiat's miniature lawnmower engine could stand. Vance saw the prone figure of the man Suzanne had wounded lying in the roadway to one side; reflexively, Vance swerved to miss him. The hood of the Fiat passed under the falling phalanx of the gate's lances; the spear tips scraped across the front of the roof and penetrated. They were hitting the metric equivalent of forty miles per hour now, and the Fiat suddenly slowed. The roof began to cave in and a hideous screech of metal against metal filled the air. One of the spear points protruded through the roof, and the Fiat's engine groaned like a steer at the end of its rope. The spear sheared off. With a grateful whine, the Fiat freed itself and leaped forward, free of the gate. As they raced over the drawbridge and through the wall, the gate came to rest, impaling the wounded man Vance had tried to avoid. Suzanne closed her eyes.

Chapter 12

I t was all coming together so well now, Hashemi Rafiqdoost reflected with satisfaction. He pulled hard on the
water pipe, filling his lungs with the potent hashish.
Preparations were complete; it was now necessary only to
wait. Anger welled up in Hashemi's chest at the image of
the blond American, that arrogant bastard, daring to tell
me how to conduct my business; suggesting that I might
need help to accomplish this job. No, Hashemi thought,
smiling at the thought of his revenge, I've fixed Kimball
and his little gang of amateurs for good. This one will be
mine alone; the risk and the credit.

The anger passed, and Hashemi opened his eyes. From
his seat in the second floor of his rented house on the Via
Germanico, he watched the sun set over the little gardens
in this old residential section of Rome.

He leaned back in the comfortable overstuffed armchair

he had dragged over to the windows. What a curious pair Kimball and Brother Gregory were, he thought: Kimball working for a fascist group of multinational corporations, Gregory for his infidel crusader religious goals. Hashemi shook his head in wonder and slowly released the lungful of smoke. And what was an even bigger mystery than Brother Gregory's monastery itself was what he and the American could possibly have in common. What was it that bound the unbridled greed of the multinationals with a religious goal? Why did a fascist organization like the Bremen Legation want to hire an assassin like Hashemi Rafiqdoost? Not that Hashemi really cared. He'd killed left-wing journalists in Istanbul for right-wing generals, and right-wing generals in Ankara for the left-wing TPLA, the Turkish Peoples Liberation Army. He thought they were both crazy. The strictest of Islamic republics governed by the mullahs was the only correct way for people to live.

He smiled as he reached for the pipe again, rubbed his thick wirelike eyebrows, and again closed his lids over dark brooding eyes; eyes that one member of his Hezbollah militia cell had described as "the eyes of Satan." They were a distinguishing feature that made it necessary for him to wear dark glasses most of the time. Customs officials could overlook his slight five-foot eight-inch frame, his closely cropped hair, and the respectable businessman's attire he customarily wore when traveling. But none of them, he knew, would ever forget his eyes. Even as a small child, he'd been able to frighten and intimidate with his eyes.

The setting sun played against his closed eyelids and lent road-map images of their veins to his vision. One by

one he visualized his caches of hidden weapons, all carefully concealed, each one easily adaptable to the schedule
of his quarry. If his prey varied schedule and travel to
thwart attempts on his life, it wouldn't matter a damn.
When the word came from Kimball and Gregory, the man
would be dead.

As sleep stealthfully crept through his head, Hashemi
pondered what to call himself. Carlos had been the
Jackal. Hashemi would be . . . "the sword of Allah." Yes,
he thought as the pipe's mouthpiece slipped from his fingers, that was it. The world would tremble when they
heard of the Sword of Allah.

The sun had set by the time Suzanne and Vance returned
to Como. Darkness came as a relief, at least now they
wouldn't attract the curious stares of other motorists, who
invariably had gaped at the wrecked Fiat with its shattered windows and gnarled mangled roof. As they neared
Como, Vance discovered something even more miraculous than their escape from the Castello Caizzi: a parking
space. He pulled the Fiat into the space. It was a no-
parking zone. Vance decided to act Italian; he left it there.

Silently, they both got out of the car and made their
way down to the tree-lined walk of the Lungo Lario Tri-
este. When they reached the broad sidewalk that overlooked the breakwater and small harbor, Suzanne moved
closer.

"We might as well blend in," she said, slipping her arm
around his elbow. They were surrounded by strolling couples, young and old. Her hand was warm and firm on his
arm. Suzanne and Vance stopped by the railing, pretending to look at the boats, while scanning the crowd for a

tail. Vance sighed. This foreign land of intrigue and violence was growing familiar to him. He was adapting to the violence and deceit; growing wary, and aware, noticing the significance in things that before had gone unnoticed.

But more was developing inside him than just the development of this new survival instinct. He was, by the hour, becoming more aware of Suzanne Storm. Now, as they stood silent at the black iron rail overlooking the lake, he marveled at the way she had so forcefully entrapped the sentry outside Caizzi's door, and in fact her cool demeanor through the rest of the afternoon. A remarkable woman.

He felt her hand and the gentle touch of her hip as she stood close. Was she really just giving others an impression—blending in, as she had put it? He found himself hoping it was more, maybe even something to fill his emotional desolation.

She squeezed his elbow gently and moved closer. A cool evening breeze blew off the lake and toyed with her hair. It felt good. Lights from the town danced lively on the crest of each wave, sweeping light along until it splashed dazzling against the breakwater and disappeared in a gently whispering foam.

"I've thought about it," he repeated softly; a whisper. "You were right to begin with. It was crazy for me to think I could do this by myself. I'd go to the police tonight if I weren't so damned tired."

She looked at him. Beyond the fatigue, his eyes had a strong, determined set to them, a look she was coming to know well. Yes, earlier she had been sure that going to the police was the best thing. Best to let professionals handle this all; best to let *them* get hurt, not amateurs. But something nagged at her now, though she couldn't put her finger on it. While Vance had decided she was right, she had changed her mind. She knew now that going to the police was the wrong move.

Still arm in arm, Vance and Suzanne headed toward the brightly lit Piazza Cavour. Sidewalk cafés faced each other along two sides of the street, with broadsides of lights and tables and shrubbery in concrete planters.

They crossed the street to the northern corner of the piazza, to the outdoor café of the Metropole, pausing to let a mob of children and parents pass on their way to stand where gelato was sold. One stout, elegant matron could be heard protesting, in Italian: "But, *cara,* it will spoil your appetite! You haven't had dinner yet."

Suzanne and Vance looked at each other in surprise, and laughed. "It seems like a million years since we had breakfast, doesn't it?" Vance said, shaking his head in wonder.

"At least," Suzanne agreed. "And I'm starving." They stepped off the curb toward the Metropole.

"Wait!" Suzanne said sharply, pulling back on Vance's arm and momentarily throwing him off balance. "Over there, between the Metropole and the tourism office. What do you see?"

Vance squinted. It was hard to see anything that wasn't brightly lit, such was the profusion of lights.

"A police car," he said finally. "No, two police cars. So what?"

"Are there usually police cars parked in front of the Metropole?"

"Damn."

"Come on." She pulled him across the street to a bus stop.

"Where are we going?"

"To my hotel."

Vance mumbled his assent and followed her in silence.

One of the orange buses picked them up after less than ten minutes of waiting, and they sat silently side by side as the bus ground along the western shore of the lake, past the Villa Olmo, through little settlements of dusty red-tile-roofed houses scattered alongside the road, squeezed between the lake and the steep slopes. Massive villas, their grounds hidden from public view by artful landscaping, slid by in the night. For centuries Lake Como had attracted wealthy like a magnet. The wealthy built their villas on the lake and came to live in them because their privacy was assured. The authorities asked no questions. The stories of debauchery and mystery, of powerful political deals, of continents divided among the powerful, were legion. Many of them were true.

Finally, the bus coughed up the short incline into Cernobbio and clattered to a stop. Vance and Suzanne stepped off quickly.

Again Suzanne took his elbow and they started north along the main street, passing a ramshackle gasoline station that looked like a prop from *The Grapes of Wrath,* and then continued down a slight incline, past shops and the rapidly aging elegance of the Regina Hotel.

Gradually, the streetlights spaced themselves farther and farther apart, and the buildings of the village gave way to trees and a tall stone wall on one side. Soon they turned right, along the road leading to the Villa d'Este.

Now a hotel, the villa had been built in the second half of the sixteenth century for Tolomep Gallio, the immensely rich Cardinal of Como and powerful secretary of

State to Pope Gregory XIII. Over the centuries it had passed through the hands of the rich and powerful including Caroline of Brunswick, the estranged wife of King George IV of Great Britain, whose libertine ways sparked legends of her Falstaffian sexual appetites. The last private owner had been Empress Fedorowna, the mother of Czar Alexander II.

It had been converted into a grand luxury hotel in 1873 and remained one of the last on the lake to retain an air of elegance and royal sumptuousness, albeit with a royal and sumptuous price tag.

"How the hell are you going to get me in?" Vance demanded. They had walked past the putting greens through a tunnel of magnificent trees cleverly lit to preserve privacy. "Someone is bound to notice my clothes." The day had taken its toll: dirt and small specks of blood stained his white shirt. His khaki pants were torn at one knee where he had slipped. "You can get past because you're staying here; besides, you don't look much worse for wear. I seem to have attracted most of the lightning today."

She laughed lightly, told him not to worry, and proceeded to reveal her solution.

Twenty minutes later, Vance stepped from the metal grating of the villa's fire escape into her room. While Suzanne closed and locked the windows behind him, and drew the drapes, Vance brushed himself off.

The room was elegant in the English tradition: dark wood furniture, leather upholstery on overstuffed chairs, heavy silks and satins and brocades and a plush carpet that appeared thick enough to devour small dogs or children. The wallpaper below the wainscoting was a conservative print, and the walls were almond-colored with ornate moldings painted to match. A broad king-sized bed occupied most of the room with a sofa and two sitting chairs clustered around a lamp with a base of cherubs. A Manet reproduction faced the bed, while a Pissarro stared down from the wall behind the sofa. Vance gazed about him, taking in the luxury. He started toward Suzanne, who still stood facing the closed drapes, then stopped abruptly when he heard a muffled sob; then her shoulders hunched and she covered her face with her hands.

"Damn!" she said angrily through her tears. "I always do this. I'm fine as long as things are sparking, but just as soon as things cool off, I . . . I . . ." She turned and looked up at him, tears streaking down her face. Automatically, Vance opened his arms and held her. She pressed her face into his chest and sobbed lavishly, crying through little gasps of breath.

He stood there stroking her hair, trying to soothe her, knowing she needed to cry. He'd known people like her in his life. In a crisis, they were all tempered steel—cool thinkers, quick, accurate decision makers; people to depend on when a life was at stake. But when the pressure vanished, they fell to pieces.

She sniffed and looked up at him, her eyes red, her lips quivering as she struggled to control herself. "You probably just think I'm another silly woman," she said, biting her lip.

"No," Vance answered firmly, gently, "I don't think you're silly. Just normal." Inside him, unfamiliar feelings were brewing. Here was someone who needed him, if only for a few minutes. It made him feel warm and useful inside, a way he hadn't felt for months. It was a feeling he was glad he was still capable of feeling. And yet, this woman in his arms was quite capable of taking care of him. He thought of the day they'd been through and of the times he might have been killed save for her courage and good judgment. He'd never had that: someone who could take care of him. Certainly not with Patty. Suzanne slipped her arms around his waist; he pulled her tightly to him. Her sobs were less frequent now.

Here we are, Vance thought, two survivors who have shared the experience of cheating death, bound for life by a common experience neither of us will ever forget. Suzanne looked up, her face only inches from his; he gazed into her eyes.

She closed her eyes. Feeling, she thought; there was so much feeling in his eyes, so much . . . love. A second later she felt his lips on hers.

She pressed him tightly against her as his body found hers and he hugged her so tightly that for an instant she couldn't breathe. She parted her lips. Then the very air caught fire and consumed them as she led him to the bed and pulled him down beside her.

He felt her hands searching, probing, caressing as he kissed her lips, her neck. She moaned as he kissed the sensitive skin under her chin and left a trail of kisses to her breasts. In that subtle way in which gradual changes seem to manifest themselves in a flash, things were suddenly clear.

"I—" Vance hesitated.

"I know," she said. "I love you, too."

Chapter 13

Harrison Kingsbury's thoughts were jagged and broken as he eased the hired Mercedes sedan out of the snarled traffic of Fiumicino Airport. He'd often wondered why the locals called it that rather than by its formal name: Leonardo da Vinci Airport.

But on this Roman summer day, that was the least of his worries. The chairman of the board of the largest oil company in the world, a man with whom he'd engaged in mortal combat for more than three decades, had politely, almost deferentially, called him and invited him to a private meeting at the oil company's villa on Lake Albano, southeast of Rome. The man had never shown him even basic courtesy since Kingsbury had aced the world's largest out of the oil concessions in Libya, Peru, and half a dozen other countries, all within a six-month period. He was a poor loser, and to Kingsbury that meant he was a weak, insecure man.

Kingsbury chuckled to himself while he sped swiftly but efficiently through the traffic. Others in his position were chauffeured around in limos, surrounded by bodyguards. Fools, he thought, shifting his wiry six-foot six-inch frame in the seat to make himself more comfortable. Luxuries like that made men—and, he supposed, women—soft. They grew dependent on other people to do their work for them, and soon they became pathetic weaklings, hungering for the trappings and the luxuries and the perquisites of the job rather than for the challenge of the job itself.

Look at Merriam Larsen, Kingsbury reflected, leaning on his horn to warn a slower vehicle out of his way. What has Larsen accomplished in his three decades as chairman of the world's largest oil company? He's grown fat and boringly noninventive. His company has made obscene profits, not because profits are obscene, but because they were made through price gouging, political bribery, murder, extortion, price fixing, and influence peddling. The flabby intellects of gargantuan corporations had to use that type of muscle when their creativity, inventiveness, and sense of adventure withered beneath a glutton's paradise of luxury.

Kingsbury had made his profits—dollar for dollar better than Larsen's company—with pride, by finding oil where the giants had been too lazy to explore; risking his money on new technology where the big oil companies feared to tread. His profits, Kingsbury thought proudly, came from productivity; Larsen's came from extortion.

He frowned: It was almost as if Larsen and his brigade of bandits in the Bremen Legation were actively inviting governments to punish them. They paid practically no income tax; they raped and pillaged and looted the economies of the world and blundered blithely onward like a huge welfare case, supported by the honest labor of the poor and middle class. It had to stop somewhere. What worried Kingsbury most was that his company, which paid its honest share of taxes and still made profits, would inevitably get caught up in the whirlwind of punishment that would crush these multinationals.

Kingsbury shook his head. The big oil companies seemed to grow more and more blatant in their defiance, waving their windfall profits in the faces of legislators around the world, crying for more and more tax breaks, while they greedily used their billions in excess cash to gobble up smaller companies.

A spark of anger glinted in his silvery gray eyes as he remembered the bid Larsen's company had made for ConPacCo only six months before. Kingsbury had fought in the courts and in the board room and on the floor of the stock markets. Only the public announcement of a major new discovery of natural gas by ConPacCo that drove his stock up dramatically had thwarted the takeover. Kingsbury smiled; they had won because suddenly they were too big a mouthful for the oil giant to handle. Kingsbury and a handful of other large independent oil companies were all that kept the giants even a little honest. He'd always embarrassed the giants by refuting the lies they told Congress and the American people. "We can't pay taxes and drill for oil," they said. "I pay taxes and find more oil than they do," Kingsbury would counter. Those fat slugs who run the majors wouldn't know free enterprise if they stumbled over it and fell on their well-padded arses.

The turnoff for Lake Albano chased his angry thoughts from his mind. Skillfully he maneuvered the Mercedes off the multilane Autostrada and onto the narrower two-lane highway heading south. What was waiting in Albano? And why had they dropped Vance Erikson's name so mysteriously? Vance had tried to contact him, two or three days ago. But the message his secretary gave him did not convey any particular urgency. And the lack of a number where Kingsbury could reach Vance was not unusual. The younger man frequently went off onto expeditions where there were no telephones at all. Yet the anxiety continued to nag at Kingsbury.

The sun was nearly overhead when he passed through Gandolfo. There, high above the lake, was the Castel Gandolfo, the summer residence of the Pope. Kingsbury glanced at the directions Larsen had sent him, and motored on through to Albano, where he turned the Mercedes to the northeast and wound his way up a serpentine road toward Colli Albani, the most prominent peak overlooking the lake.

Larsen met him personally. He was waiting inside the villa's massive iron gates. Behind the Mercedes two armed guards closed the iron gate, then returned to their white stone blockhouse beside the villa walls. Smiling, Kingsbury reached over to unlock the passenger-side door.

"Would you like a ride?"

Larsen returned the smile with a painfully forced one of his own. "Yes, thank you," Larsen replied. "I was just taking a walk as you drove up."

Still can't admit that you ever might condescend to greet someone, can you, Merriam? Kingsbury wanted to say. "Healthy . . . walks are," Kingsbury said instead.

"Yes, it is healthy," Larsen agreed, playing the game.

"Especially with a place like this to walk."

Kingsbury groaned to himself. He'd heard it all before, but Larsen began to explain it again: Lawns six hundred years old; chapel blessed by the Pope himself, villa with fifty-nine rooms, constructed in 1602. "Cost the oil company forty million dollars—all tax deductible," Larsen added.

Almost before Kingsbury had brought the Mercedes to a halt in the circular drive in front of the gray stone mansion with its cherub urns and obligatory fountain, young men rushed down the marble steps to open the car doors. Young brown-nosing MBAs, Kingsbury reflected derisively; they'll hitch their chances of success to being good court eunuchs rather than to business acumen.

"Good afternoon, Mr. Kingsbury. Good afternoon, Mr. Larsen," the eager young men chirped.

The interior of the villa looked just like what most Americans imagined for oil magnates, and what oil companies tried to tell them didn't exist. If only, Kingsbury thought wryly, if only struggling middle-class homeowners who couldn't afford their mortgages could see firsthand what their taxes had paid for there might be blood in the suites. Figurative would be good, Kingsbury thought, but literally was alright as well.

The foyer was a massive archway with an intricate tile mosaic floor. There were no coats to take, so the butler faded unobtrusively behind a beige-and-brown marble column after he'd closed the door behind them.

"This way," Larsen said tersely. Kingsbury followed him down a long hallway lined with a gold and royal blue carpet in an intricate pattern. Kingsbury slowed for a moment to scrutinize the pattern and found that it was the oil company's corporate seal. In the center of the corridor, four arches merged in a dramatic vaulted ceiling, and from the center hung a massive crystal chandelier.

"Waterford," Larsen commented as they passed under it. They walked through rooms with statuary and friezes, artwork that Kingsbury recognized as by Mifliara and Hayez, priceless works by lesser known artists. Finally, after walking for more than a hundred yards, they came to a set of double walnut doors stained dark brown with brightly polished brass hardware. A stolid man in a gray suit, who looked like a badly cast CIA agent, opened the door for them. As the man leaned over to turn the doorknob, Kingsbury caught sight of a shoulder holster in his armpit.

The doors closed. Kingsbury stood in the middle of the room, gazing first at the neoclassical furnishings, all genuine antiques. He stared incredulously at a fresco that bore the unmistakable marks of Leonardo, but it was a completely unknown work. Oblivious of Larsen's amused regard; Kingsbury stepped reverently over to the fresco and examined it closely. It had been cut from some other wall and inlaid in this room, he noticed. But where had it come from? he wondered. Historians frequently remarked at the paucity of artworks by Leonardo. Where were they all; and, specifically, where had this one come from?

"Please be seated, Harrison."

Kingsbury flinched at Larsen's familiar use of his first

name, but he nevertheless dragged his attention reluctantly away from the fresco and chose a straight-backed, brocade armchair. Larsen seated himself on a small divan with matching gold and burgundy brocade. The fresco, boldly and beautifully displayed above the aquamarine wainscoting, dominated the room.

"Yes, it's genuine," Larsen said, following Kingsbury's eyes. "But," he added conspiratorially, "we wouldn't want the congressional committees to hear about our owning it, now would we?"

"You know how I feel about that," Kingsbury said sharply.

Larsen nodded his head indulgently. "Yes, I'm sorry to say, I do know your position . . . on that and a hundred other things."

The two men stared at each other silently, eyes locked in a starting hold, two wrestlers awaiting the referee's signal to begin.

Kingsbury spoke first. "But we didn't come here to talk about art, did we?"

"In a sense, though, we did," said a third voice.

Startled, Kingsbury turned in his chair and looked behind him toward the corner of the huge room. So taken had he been with the Leonardo fresco that he had failed to notice the young man with the sandy blond hair, who now drew close and took a seat on the opposite end of Larsen's divan.

"Kimball, isn't it?" Kingsbury said, recovering his aplomb.

The man smiled thinly. "I didn't think you'd remember."

"How could I not? What was it"—Kingsbury paused and pursed his lips in thought—"five years ago when you and your boss here dragged me against my will into your little den of thieves. The Bremen Legation." He spoke the last words with pointed irony.

"I hardly think that's fair, Harrison." There it was again, Kingsbury thought: Why is he being so familiar? "I have never known you to do something against your will," Larsen continued. "Although God knows I've tried often enough."

True, Kingsbury thought. He had accepted the invitation to join the Legation with grave reservations, only because he thought it would help him keep a better eye on what his enemies were up to. The ploy hadn't worked out well, and aside from a few profitable contacts with government officials in Japan and Europe, he saw little benefit to the membership. Frightened by his bold and populist views, the Legation excluded him from the inner circle. He never could figure out why they had invited him in the first place.

"Yes . . . well," Kingsbury responded. "My membership in the Legation is hardly the point of this cloak-and-dagger exercise, now, is it?" He frowned as Kimball shifted his legs; there was some sort of knife resting in a sheath in the man's coat. This is getting stranger by the moment, Kingsbury thought. There was a long pregnant pause.

"Mr. Larsen," Kingsbury said finally. "I know we are not here to discuss frescoes. I have a company to run. So can we please get to the point." The point, Kingsbury had deduced, must be a merger proposal. In seconds, Kingsbury would realize how wrong he really was.

"It's about your . . . employee, *Harrison*," Larsen said irritatingly. "Mr. Vance Erikson."

"It seems," Kimball interjected, "that he has been engaged in a rather unusual activity for an exploration geologist. He's been spending large amounts of money over the past weeks, poking his way through the circles of Vinciana."

"I'm quite aware of that, Mr. Kimball. Leonardo is part of his charter," Kingsbury snapped.

"But did you know that some . . . unfortunate events seem to have followed him!" Kimball continued. "Some events which have raised more than just eyebrows?"

"Vance is an unconventional person," Kingsbury said evenly. "Most of his success, like mine, has come because he does not allow himself to degenerate into the ruts which trap most people."

"Oh?" Larsen smiled nastily. "Do you consider *murder* an acceptable way to pull oneself out of a rut?"

Kingsbury recoiled as if slapped in the face. "I hardly think that—"

"Murder, Harrison, murder."

"I don't believe it!"

Kimball leaned over and handed Kingsbury a folded-back newspaper. It was that day's *Il Giorno*, from Milan, with a small article circled in heavy red pen. Kingsbury took the paper. After a moment he handed the paper back.

"This says nothing about Vance being wanted for murder. Merely that the Milan police want to question him concerning the murder of three other Da Vinci experts, a natural enough thing. Vance was a close associate of those men, and his life could also be in danger."

Larsen gave Kindsbury a jackal's smile. "Did you know

that Vance was involved in a shooting which left three people dead?" Kingsbury shook his head, thinking, with a sudden pang of guilt: Was that what Vance had called him about? Larsen was still talking. "Did you know a maid was killed by a bomb planted in his room? That Vance visited a lawyer in Bellagio and moments later the lawyer and a priest were shot dead? That the lawyer's maid identified Vance as the killer? And did you also know that Vance broke into and entered the Castello Caizzi, and that when he'd left, the count was found shot to death?"

"What are you trying to say?" Kingsbury replied angrily. "That Vance Erikson was responsible for all that? Come on, Larsen, what do you take me for?"

Larsen shook his head in mock sadness. "I've never taken you at all, Harrison. In thirty years, you've always been the one taking me."

Kingsbury ignored this. "What are you trying to tell me, Larsen? Quit your weaseling and for once just say something without being devious about it."

"The Milan police have come by some information implicating your boy in all that. He skipped town after the shoot-out, which, by the way, left the bodyguard you assigned to him dead." Noting with satisfaction Kingsbury's look of alarm, he went on.

"Let me tell you a little story, Harrison. I think it may open your eyes a little."

An hour later, Harrison Kingsbury left the neoclassically furnished room without even a glance at the Da Vinci fresco. The spring had vanished from his step, and his heart felt like an endless void. *He had done* it, was Kingsbury's only thought; Larsen had finally done it. A man he despised had him checkmated. Humiliated, Kingsbury sat behind the wheel of the rented Mercedes and drove slowly back to Rome. For the first time in his life, he felt like an old man.

Chapter 14

Morning came on breezes of dreams, pleasure more fleeting than dew as the Italian summer sun rose slowly in the sky.

Vance Erikson felt the morning before he recognized it; from beyond the closed windows came the sounds of people talking, working, living. The sounds laced themselves among his dreams, finally drew tight their fragile strands of reality, and pulled him gently from sleep.

He cracked his eyelids a slit, and then blinked wide as he tried to remember where he was. He looked at Suzanne lying beside him and confusion turned to relief. He knew now why his recurring nightmares hadn't visited last night.

Propping himself up on his left elbow, Vance gazed at her face: Her auburn hair burned with red where a slat of morning sunlight spilled through the curtains. She smiled faintly in her sleep.

Had he really said he loved her? Could she have said she loved him? It was too fantastic for his head to understand, but his heart knew better. But I don't believe in love at first sight, he told himself and then smiled as he remembered that it had been hate at first sight . . . or had it? And did it matter? Time and a lot of tomorrows would tell.

He got up and padded quietly across the room and used the telephone in the bathroom to call for breakfast. He was starving. Vance walked softly to the bed, and looked down on Suzanne. Suddenly she opened her eyes, and startled Vance out of his reverie.

"Don't look so surprised," Suzanne said. "Besides, I'm the one who ought to be shocked." She looked at him appraisingly. Suddenly Vance was aware of his nakedness.

"My mother used to warn me about being in strange hotel rooms with naked men," she said, reaching for him. "She warned me never to let them get away; come here."

"But I just ordered breakfast," he protested without conviction.

"I've always adored cold eggs," she said as she slipped her arms around his neck.

Suzanne was sipping tea from a bone china cup from the room-service tray. "And the reason I got such poor grades at the Sorbonne," she said, "was that I kept leaving to search for that story which would make the *New York Times* hire me as a foreign correspondent. I was so naive then." She laughed.

Vance looked at her, amazed. "Somehow I can't imagine you naive," he said, reaching out to stroke her arm as they sat side by side on the edge of the bed.

She smiled ruefully. "I guess I wised up the last time I went to Beirut."

"You went to Beirut and came back alive?" Vance asked incredulously.

"Oh, yes . . . three times," she answered nonchalantly. "But the last time was the kicker. I was trying to interview one of the leaders on the Muslim side and got caught in a mortar attack. Scared the hell out of me. Suddenly a nice quiet job looked very appealing."

"Is Beirut where you learned to shoot a gun?"

She nodded. She didn't offer any more information and Vance decided not to ask.

They looked at each other for a long moment. Then Suzanne took his hand and gave it a squeeze, her eyes dreamy.

"You're so far away," he said. "Where are you?"

"Saratoga. A party at Skidmore, when I first met you, and *noted you.*"

"You've wondered about that too?"

She was surprised. "Have you?"

"Sure I have. Every time you dug into me in an article."

"Oh, Vance," she said gently and rested her head on his shoulder. "I was so foolish—such a little girl then. I . . ." She looked at him. "You know how they say that love and hate are alike? Maybe I fell in love with you at first sight, but I hated you because I couldn't have you."

"But you could have."

She looked at him quizzically.

"I was there on a setup," Vance explained. "A blind date. I saw you the moment I came in the room, but . . . well, I couldn't just drop her and shove my way over to you then. Though I felt like it, I thought you were going to come over and introduce yourself." He searched his memory; it was clear even after so long. "Then you didn't, and the rest of the evening you looked like the ice queen every time I cast a glance at you."

She shook her head.

"Oh, Vance, if only we . . . If only I—" She stopped.

"We wouldn't be the same people we are now," he said. "We can't regret all that; we might not have liked each other any better then even if we had met. The experiences we've had since then is part of what made us who we are, and I for one like who you are." He pulled her face toward him and kissed her.

Two hours later Vance paced the floor in the plush bedroom, as if he could chase down the thoughts, the solutions that had eluded him. Suzanne had ventured down to Como to buy clothes to replace those he had abandoned in his hotel room, and to see what else she could learn about the police who had been asking about him at the Metropole.

He'd been left with his own thoughts, and they were haunting him. His call to Kingsbury had been a waste. He was either in Spain or Italy closing a merger deal, his secretary had told him. She would try to get word, and can you leave a number? Reluctantly, he had left Suzanne's room number. It was useless; when Kingsbury was involved in that sort of business, it could be days before he'd return calls.

He sat down at the antique cherry desk and pulled out a piece of hotel stationery. Maybe he could make sense of the whole situation by committing it to paper. But even after several pages of writing, no solution emerged. He threw back the chair and began pacing again, faster and faster as his frustration mounted.

"Damn!" he said to the empty room. If only Kingsbury would call; he knew the oil tycoon could unravel the knottiest conundrum.

But Kingsbury wasn't there and couldn't help him. Just you and me, buddy, he told himself and went back to the desk and faced his notes. The chronicle of the past few days had spread to more than half a dozen sheets of the hotel stationery; the sheets covered the desk.

Taking a page from the world of journalism, he had tried listing items in columns noting "who, what, when, where, why, and how." He quickly eliminated the when and where and how as irrelevant. The murders were the big "what," and he knew when, where, and how people had been killed. He'd never forget.

That left who and why. Who, he pondered as he stared at the pages, resting his chin in the palms of his hands. A man in Amsterdam with a funny mark on his face, a bevy of lunatic priests. The thought was almost ludicrous; but the blathering religious fanatics from the Middle East to Kashmir and Northern Ireland made religious fanaticism a very real force in global violence. Who: Professor Martini, kindly Da Vinci scholars in Vienna and Strasbourg, killed; another scholar, Tosi, missing. A handful of innocent bystanders in Milan, killed. And it all followed him, a slightly erratic amateur Da Vinci scholar and exploration geologist, madly in love with a journalist who packs a pistol—or who did until they lost it. He shook his head slowly. The who was growing clearer, but the why—that was what baffled him most.

He rearranged the sheets of paper, hoping some new

juxtaposition might click. The priests and the writer, de Beatis, were Catholics. De Beatis was secretary to the Cardinal of Aragon. De Beatis was taken with Leonardo's writings, wrote of them glowingly. So what? Vance abandoned that tack.

Tosi had a degree in physics. Like me, Vance thought, he has formal training in something other than art. I am still alive, and Tosi may perhaps be. Vance made a mental note to read the copy of *Il Giorno* that had arrived with breakfast. Tosi's death would be announced if his body had been discovered. Martini and the two other Da Vinci scholars were not scientists. Why would someone save scientists—or was that just coincidence?

Damn, damn! Vance pushed the chair back and got up. Walking to the window, he stared down at the beautiful grounds and the lake, but saw neither. He walked back to the desk and sat down again. He wrote. Science; was that a connection? Maybe there was something in the Codex Kingsbury about science that . . . it covered a range of topics from shadow and perspective to thunderstorms. Thunderstorms! That was the section in which he'd found the forgery! A scientific study of thunderstorms. Vance closed his eyes and tried to remember the pages. There had been numerous drawings, references to the electrical nature of the force of lightning bolts. The drawings were magnificent. Leonardo was blessed with an amazing quickness of sight. His drawings of birds, or waves, flowing water, and lightning betrayed an almost stroboscopic, stop-action swiftness of the eye. The drawings of lightning were as accurate as modern photographs, and even more dramatic.

Science, scientists, the Catholic Church. It might have

added up to heresy. The Church had condemned Copernicus for being impudent enough to suggest that the earth revolved around the sun, rather than the other way around as the Church had decreed. But with the exception of running afoul of the Vatican over some physiological studies—dissections of cadavers—there was no record of the Pope being on Leonardo's case.

Or had there? Maybe something in the forged pages . . . Had the Church seized something which it considered heretical or dangerous and provided a forgery to cover it all up? That didn't make sense at all. And what interest did the crazy priests have in it? From what Vance had heard on his first visit to Como, they were an outcast group themselves, heretics or nearly so. Some people had gone so far as to say the entire order had been excommunicated years ago. But no one knew, and people were hesitant to talk about the monastery. "There are stories, signore," the townspeople would say, and then decline to elaborate. "Our ancestors left them alone and we shall also."

"Science, scientists, thunderstorms, de Beatis, priests, Church," Vance wrote on a separate sheet of paper.

There was a connection somewhere. But he couldn't force the idea into his conscious.

His thoughts kept coming back to the priests, to the monastery above Bellagio on the other side of the lake. Perhaps he'd find an answer there. The longer he considered this alternative, the more logical it seemed. Yes, he nodded his head definitely, he'd visit the monastery, unannounced, soon.

Vance quietly laid the pen on his pile of notes and slowly pushed back the chair.

He stood up and walked over to the window. Something nagged at him, and it wasn't so much the fear of getting caught at the monastery. For a long calm moment, he watched the sailboats slicing through the small waves on the lake. In the distance the red hull of the hydrofoil shone clearly against the deep green of the shore. Suddenly he realized that his unease came from the fear of not seeing Suzanne again. She complicated things, but oh, God, how thankful he was for the complication.

Vance turned away from the window. Then, remembering his intention to look in the paper for word about Tosi, he snatched the paper from where it lay on the bed, among mussed sheets. Settled into a comfortable chair, he perused the paper. Nothing on the first page. He fought with the thin newsprint and opened to the inside. His eyes grew wide with horror at the picture of his own face and the accompanying story.

Elliott Kimball lounged in a café chair beside a small round table for two at a fashionable sidewalk café on the fashionable Via Venuto. For the fifth time, he read the newspaper story, sipping a Chivas and soda and feeling very accomplished. Beside the small photograph of Vance Erikson was an article that was essentially the story he had directed the Milan police detective to relay to the press. Terrorista—that was what Kimball had told the detective. Erikson had used his position with Con-PacCo to cover the international travel required of a terrorist paymaster. He wasn't a religious fanatic like those he worked for. No, Erikson had only greed behind his actions: He did it for the money. But with increased scrutiny of international funds transfers after 9/11, his

secret actions were the key to helping the fanatics move
large sums of cash that funded terrorist cells around the
world. With his suspicions confirmed, the detective had
been happy to cooperate with the representative of an international organization known for its opposition to terrorism.

Kimball smiled. Genius, utter genius, he thought as he
laid the paper back on the table. In one fell swoop, he had
neutralized Erikson and his patron, Harrison Kingsbury.
The article said that Vance Erikson was wanted by Milan
police and suspected of being involved with the death of
Professor Martini in Amsterdam, and with the deaths of
Da Vinci scholars in Strasbourg and Vienna. Further, the
article alleged that Erikson was responsible for the shoot
out in Milan and for the death of the Hilton hotel maid.

As for Kingsbury, the Vance Erikson story was just the
opening stroke. Kimball's pleasure momentarily passed
into annoyance as he glanced at his watch. Where was
that damned Iranian madman? And where was Suzanne
Storm? Where had she gone? She had been such a help in
locating Vance Erikson in Como. If he could locate her,
he'd locate Erikson.

Ah, he thought, but it really didn't matter. Erikson and
Kingsbury had been neutralized, at least so they couldn't
hinder the transaction. Still . . . he hated loose ends. He'd
like Vance Erikson found, and disposed of. Now that they
had reached Kingsbury, there was no reason to keep Erikson alive.

Again, Kimball looked at his watch. Come on, you
fucking Iranian bastard! I haven't got all night.

The clothes had been no problem, Suzanne Storm thought
as she sat now in the lobby of the Metropole Hotel in a

tall wingback chair that faced away from the desk, hiding her presence from the clerk and from the police officers who gathered there on the way to and from Vance Erikson's room. She had purchased replacement clothes for Vance and paid handsomely to have them delivered to her *room—their room,* she corrected herself, then had set out to learn what she could about why the Milan police wanted Vance so badly.

It hadn't been easy. She hadn't dared approach any of them directly, for fear that they might have a description of her from the Bellagio incident the day before. So she had taken a copy of *Il Giorno* and sat in the lobby pretending to read it, using the paper to hide her face when any of the police drew near. She read the same headline for the dozenth time and found no interest in the story.

Around her, the policemen were just shooting the breeze with each other; typical Italian macho male talk, centering on women, and females and women. Such varied interests they have, she thought. She found young Italian men to be the most obnoxious in the world: They were pampered by their mothers and their sisters, and told that they were the greatest thing since sliced panini, and their wives and their mistresses told them the same thing when they grew a little older, and the crime was that they believed it all, and expected American women to treat them the same way.

Her attention wandered. She shifted her position in the chair, uncrossed and recrossed her legs, and readjusted the newspaper. Her eyes stared at the newspaper but focused somewhere a long way away. She thought of her cat, Kierkegaard, a mongrel left with her next-door neighbor. She thought of home, of the security of her apartment, and hoped that her plants wouldn't die before she got back. But mostly, she thought of Vance Erikson and the events that had brought them together.

She really had followed him to Como because of the story. At least that's what she had told herself. It hadn't been an altogether unpleasant trip; Elliott Kimball drove fast but skillfully in a Lamborghini he'd rented. She didn't know anyone rented those types of cars.

It had been a surprise, Kimball's turning up at the Da Vinci symposium in Milan. She hadn't seen him since college days. Odd that he would appear there; he didn't seem to have much background in Da Vinci. He was a cold, closed man now. There was something almost serpentine about him; he was so secretive. He gave her the impression of being . . . she drew a blank, well, dangerous.

Yes, he scared her in a veiled sort of way, made her feel uneasy; she'd put it all down to nerves. (He'd given her a number of his office in Bremen where messages could be left if she wished.) She plucked his business card from among the leaves of her reporter's notebook and looked at it once again. Perhaps he could help, she thought. Maybe she should call him. But as she had done a number of other times that day, she hesitated and then returned the card to its slot in the notebook.

A new voice had joined the policemen, and it snapped Suzanne out of her daydream. It was familiar; she recognized it from somewhere . . . Suddenly she went rigid and her mouth tasted brassy with fear. The new voice was describing a woman who'd been involved in an incident in Bellagio. She tried to swallow down the dry sticky knot of terror in her throat. It was he: the old short priest with glasses, the one who had chased them into the champagne cellar.

The man who had tried to kill them was only feet behind her! She must get out, somehow. Surely he would try again if he knew. Running would do no good; he'd see her. She would simply have to wait for him to leave. She unfolded the paper and held it up in front of her.

Skin tingling with fear, Suzanne listened as the man spoke familiarly with one of the policemen. He *knew* him. Were they helping the priest in his search? She hoped the priest would go, but it seemed to take forever. Maybe the police wouldn't recognize her. She had to get back to Vance; she wanted to be with him again.

The voices of the policemen and the priest rose as they said their good-byes. Got to move, she thought automatically; got to get out of here. She folded the copy of *Il Giorno* and hesitated, quivering like a parachutist leaping from an airplane for the first time. Move, legs, get up and go! She urged herself out of the chair. Calmly now, calmly, she told her jagged nerves.

She crossed the lobby and had gained the entrance to the hallway when a voice called after her.

"Signorina!" It was the detective who'd been talking with the priest. "Please stop," the voice said in Italian. She kept walking, behind her she heard the hurried steps of men running on a carpeted floor. Now she ran. The hallway was dark and short and ended at the dining room's reception desk. The multipaned glass doors to the left were closed. Another door led out onto the little sidewalk café where she and Vance had eaten breakfast. She pushed at the door, but it was locked. Behind her she heard the footsteps of the detectives. "Signorina!" Frantically she fumbled with the lock on the door and managed to turn the bolt. The knob yielded, and she rushed outside and down the steps. Chairs blocked the entrance to the café; she sent them sprawling as she ran through them and into the Piazza Cavour.

She looked first toward the entrance to the Metropole, and then turned to run toward the lake.

"Good afternoon, signorina." It was the priest. Behind him trotted the plainclothes detectives and two uniformed officers.

"I wouldn't advise you to try and escape," the detective said, his gun drawn.

Suzanne trembled and then regained control.

"I am an American citizen," she said formally. "I demand that I be allowed to contact the nearest embassy."

"There is no need for that, my dear," the priest said.

"But if I'm to be arrested, you owe me that right," Suzanne protested.

"But you are not being arrested," the priest said.

Suzanne turned and looked quizzically at the police detective and the two uniformed officers at his side.

"He's right," the plainclothes detective broke the confused silence.

"But . . . but what—"

"We're going to go for a short ride," the priest said to her.

"Oh, no," Suzanne said with growing horror. Being arrested was something she could handle. "Oh, no. No!" The police were turning her over to the priest. "You can't do this," she told the detective. "You can't turn me over to this man, he's a killer; he's crazy. Arrest me, take me to jail." She looked wildly from face to face and saw there was no sympathy.

"Surely you're not accusing Brother Gregory, a man of God's work, of being a killer," the detective said incredulously.

Suzanne's shriek shattered the peace of the Piazza Cavour. Heads on the park benches snapped to attention. Suddenly the men were all over her, a hand over her mouth, her arms pinned behind her, handcuffs cold and pinching on her wrists. She kicked madly; a satisfying groan came from one policeman as her toe connected with his testicles. But another took his place and pinned her legs together and as a team they manhandled her into the rear seat of a blue-and-white police car that had just stopped beside them.

Something stinging and aromatic covered her mouth and nose; blackness arose like a grid of terror and filled her head with sleep.

Chapter 15

The gloom of night matched his mood. He should never have let her go. Vance turned off the lonely farm road and headed south toward the lake, through the terraced hillside of olive trees. But Suzanne wasn't the sort of person you let do anything; she did what she wanted to do. The clothing had been delivered just after his phone conversation with Harrison Kingsbury. Vance had never heard the man sound so vague, dispirited.

"Give it up," Kingsbury had said lethargically. "You can't accomplish anything by continuing."

Vance's feet rustled softly through the tall grass. He stepped cautiously in the starlight, feeling with the toe of his right shoe for the edge of the terraced earth. Olive groves stood like giant steps up the side of a mountain—six, seven, eight feet high. Vance had things to accomplish now. He wasn't about to get hurt, stumbling off the edge of an olive-grove terrace.

Not wanting to risk using the penlight he'd bought at the fleamarket in Cernobbio, Vance felt for the edge of the terrace, sat with his legs over the side, and then eased himself as far as he could before dropping. His knee complained mildly from where he'd twisted it during the night at Castello Caizzi.

Terrace step after terrace step, Vance repeated the maneuver, approaching the monastery slowly, and from its most difficult direction. He hoped security would be lightest here.

He'd come to Varenna by ferry boat earlier, and then walked north from the town, past the only gate in the monastery's walls, and then along the twenty-foot-high wall for another mile until the road veered off, leaving the wall to cut through a section of forest. Another terrace step and then another. He walked ten feet, twenty. No edge. Finally he realized he'd left the olive grove. He walked across a narrow field that had recently been cultivated and took a sigh of relief as he plunged into the same tall trees that he'd seen at the edge of the road. His watch glowed ten o'clock in the darkness. He stared through the gloom and finally made out the outline of the top of the wall. It looked to be about thirty yards away. He took a step and for some reason looked down at his shoes. Walking back to the plowed field, Vance took handful after handful of the moist-rich soil and rubbed it over the bright white shoes until they almost blended with the rest of his clothes.

Stealthily he skulked through the thin margin of forest. He reached the wall, and felt its cool rough stone presence. It had been carefully built to leave no footholds.

Looking about him, Vance examined a thin poplar that grew very close to the wall. Too bad, he thought, there are no huge oak trees with spreading branches over the wall. No, he thought, the brothers would be too smart to let that happen.

He appraised the poplar and walked over to it and started to scale it, moving slowly, silently. A classic Lombardy poplar, the tree was about forty feet high, and slim as a pencil. He drew level with the top of the wall, and saw nothing on the other side but more poplars. They were a magnificent windscreen and served well to bar prying eyes. Vance leaned toward the wall to get a better look. There was a coil of razor-sharp barbed wire on the wall's rim. And, he thought, there must be some sort of intruder device, something hidden, pressure switches, infrared or something. It would be necessary to avoid stepping on the top of the wall.

For nearly half an hour, he sat there, his hands and legs growing fatigued. He'd seen nothing, and was ready to make his move when he smelled it first. He looked in the direction from which the wind blew and spotted a small red glow, a pinpoint in the dark. Someone had taken a drag off a cigarette. He'd smelled the smoke first. Vance watched as the glow grew larger, then disappeared, blocked by the top of the wall. Soon Vance heard the crackling of boots on dried leaves.

The sound grew louder and then diminished in the opposite direction. Vance waited ten more minutes. Now! he thought. He climbed as high as he dared in the poplar, and started leaning back and forth, setting the thin tree to swaying. The slim trunk of the young tree creaked and popped under the strain, and then abruptly bowed toward the wall, arched over it, and tossed Vance within reach of the branches of another poplar inside the wall. Vance grasped the branches and pulled himself closer to the trunk. Under him, the trunk of the smaller poplar sounded like a twig being bent to the breaking point. Vance pulled himself along a branch hoping he'd feel the trunk of the other tree before the one he rode snapped and sent him hurtling to the ground, and the trunk crashing into the alarm system. A few more inches, he thought as he reached out. Then Vance grabbed hold of the trunk of the tree inside the wall and transferred his weight to it. The tree swayed for a moment and then regained its equilibrium. No sounds of alarm reached his ears.

Looking down and through the leaves and the inky darkness, Vance spotted a faint gray path beneath him. The cool night air whispered gently down the lake, carrying with it the chill of the alpine glaciers a few miles north. Vance shivered as the breeze turned his sweaty skin to ice water.

Below him, in the approximately half mile or so between the lakeshore and the wall over which he'd just come, were half a dozen buildings. At the water's edge was a four-story villa staring grandly at the night through a score of illuminated tall windows. A lighted fountain occupied the axis of a circular drive. Two small nondescript cars waited at the curb below a set of grand steps leading to the villa. Vance noted that the driveway led both to the gate in the monastery walls that he'd walked past earlier, and to a large boathouse at the water's edge.

A long, stone dormitorylike building with rows of plain regularly spaced windows lay to his left, about a hundred yards away. Farther beyond it was a smaller building, similar in architecture, but with bars on its lighted windows. In the middle of the grounds was a chapel lighted from the outside by floodlights. A few solitary figures walked along subtly lighted walks, passing from one dim pool of light to another.

The villa, he thought, would be the main building; the dormitorylike building probably just that: living quarters for the brothers. He climbed down, then worked his way toward the main villa.

The path, flanked on either side by ornamental shrubs and flower beds, was level and easy to walk on. Cautiously Vance picked his feet up and set them down evenly, producing a sound soft enough that it barely reached his own ears. The mixed fragrances of flowers he couldn't identify came to him as he walked, and then faded as he entered a grove of evergreens with their resinous smells.

Abruptly he stopped. In the distance he heard the faint shushing of bored feet on the walk. The sounds grew gradually louder. Deftly Vance stepped over a low rail fence that ran along the uphill side of the path and into the moist earth of a narrow flower bed. From there, he made his way to a niche between two shoulder-high azalea bushes. He squatted on his haunches and waited as the footsteps grew louder.

With the footsteps growing closer by the second, Vance left his hiding place and looked for a weapon. Desperately he combed the ground with his hands, pawing the soft tilled earth and the flowers growing in it. Relief flooded over him as his fingers made out the outlines of bricks used to edge the flower bed. He pushed at one; it moved. Vance could hear the sentry softly whistling to himself. He pushed at the brick and pulled again, finally it came free from the border and Vance hefted it in his right hand. He scurried back between the two azaleas.

Seconds later, the amorphous dark form of the sentry rounded a curve in the path.

Vance froze, muscles tensed. One sound, one cry from the sentry, and it would be all over.

A short man materialized from the dark, his face and hands showing white against the night. The sound of some sort of weapon hung over his shoulder and slapping at his waist made its way softly to Vance's ears. Now! Vance lunged at the sentry, swinging the rough cool brick like a stone fist.

The brick slammed into the back of the sentry's head landing with a hollow thonk like dropping a pumpkin onto concrete. The sentry collapsed wordlessly onto the crushed gravel walk as Vance stood above him, breathing hard, legs spread wide, the brick still in his hand. His tongue was sticky and clung to the roof of his mouth. He stood there for several long moments, staring at the black form against the light pebbles.

Tossing the brick into the bushes, Vance knelt and rolled the unconscious man onto his back. A dark blotch spread over the pebbles near the man's head. Vance pulled the weapon off the sentry's shoulder and started to wrestle the short beefy man out of what felt like a cassock made from some sort of rough cloth. A monk with a machine gun, Vance thought. Friar Tuck with a new twist.

Moments later, it seemed more like an hour, Vance had concealed the sentry's body in the bushes, donned the cassock over his own clothes, and set off down the path with the sentry's boxy weapon slung over his shoulder. It was an Uzi machine gun of some sort, Vance knew, having seen pictures of the weapon in army training.

He felt more secure now with a weapon and a disguise— even if his arms and legs stuck out too far in the short sentry's garment. How long did he have before the sentry was discovered missing?

The path opened up into a broad open area, but emboldened by his disguise, Vance followed the path through the middle of it. He was nearly halfway through it before he noticed he was walking through a graveyard. Not unusual, Vance thought, particularly for a monastery. But as he continued through, he noticed a massive white marble mausoleum in a far corner of the cemetery topped with a swastika. Perhaps it was not so odd considering how silent the Catholic Church was for so long during the Nazi extermination of the Jews. Still . . . he wondered, and made a detour to have a closer look at the white edifice that stood out so ghostly bold in the darkness.

But nothing in his life could have prepared him for what he found when he reached the mausoleum. With his face but inches away from the inscription on the tomb, he read its words—inscribed in German—over and over. Stunned, he ran his finger over the letters as if by feeling the name he could change it. If he believed the inscription, which he didn't, he would have to accept that Adolf Hitler's body rested inside the tomb. And he would have to accept the notion that Hitler had lived far beyond World War II, and had died in 1957. There had been tests supposedly confirming that the Fuehrer had died in his bunker. These, he supposed, could have been faked, but he wasn't ready to accept that.

Confused, he wandered through the cemetery, examining

tombstones at random. After half an hour of wandering he realized that the cemetery was either the cruel and twisted joke of a demented mind or else it was part of a cosmic deception with the profoundest consequences for the history of modern civilization. For resting in the cemetery along with what purported to be the tomb of Adolf Hitler were grave markers claiming to stand over the bodies of a vast and varied assortment of personages from the past six hundred years who seemed to have no common thread of political or moral belief, only prominence and world acclaimed greatness in their fields—and a death that occurred under mysterious circumstances. For here he found the graves of Amelia Earhart, Martin Bormann, author Ambrose Bierce, Dag Hammarskjöld, and Glenn Miller, the orchestra leader. The names went on and on; some he recognized and others failed to ring a bell. What in hell was going on here?

But before he could ponder the question fully, he heard voices in the distance, and hurried back to the path and resumed his march.

The crushed gravel path left the cemetery, and passed over a small bluff. Vance stopped at a metal guardrail and peered over the edge. Below him he saw two men exit from a set of thick wooden doors, set into the hillside. A single mercury-vapor arc light cast a bluish glow over the scene.

Returning to the path to avoid discovery by the men below, Vance continued his rounds. The voices he'd heard grew louder, and as they approached, Vance realized they were speaking English. He rounded the crest of a steep hill and prepared to meet them. Would he be recognized?

". . . should take only another month or so," said a voice accented with Italian.

The voice that answered was clearly American. "That seems reasonable. But I would be happier with a more thorough understanding of the overall transaction."

"I'm sorry, Brother Gregory has his reasons, and I'm afraid we'll just have to go along with them."

"I think—*buona sera*." The American interrupted his sentence and greeted Vance in Italian, apparently taking him for a sentry. Vance returned the greeting and passed without stopping. The pounding in his chest subsided only gradually as the others continued on the way.

Vance kept walking, but his brain was spinning. He hadn't recognized the Italian, but the other . . . Vance shook his head as if trying to chase away a bad dream. It couldn't be. Trent Barbour, the American congressman, powerful chairman of the House Armed Forces Committee, had been killed eleven years ago in one of the 9/11 aircraft that crashed into the World Trade Center.

Although—Vance recalled more details—the man had been *reported* killed in that plane crash, but like many others, his body was never recovered. Another mysterious death, just like the ones in the cemetery. Only Trent Barbour was definitely alive. If the man he'd seen was indeed Barbour.

Vance reached a set of stairs leading down to the hillside entrance. Thoughtfully he took the first step down. What could he remember that would link them all together? Glenn Miller had mysteriously disappeared in 1944 and had never been found. Amelia Earhart had never been seen again after she set out from Burbank on her flight across the Pacific. Likewise Ambrose Bierce in 1914. But Hammarskjöld, he thought, that was different.

He took the stairs slowly, playing the details through

his mind. United Nations Secretary General Dag Hammarskjöld had been killed in an airplane crash in Africa in 1961. Just like Barbour had been killed in a plane crash? But they had found Hammarskjöld's body, hadn't they? A new thought shocked him. Suppose that Hammarskjöld never had been killed, that someone had substituted a body certified as his? Airplane crashes could render a body unrecognizable; all that was needed was one doctor on the take.

His mind reeled. Priests were trying to kill him. They'd killed the top Da Vinci scholars in the world. He was sure of that now. And these same crazy priests had a collection of people, living and dead. None of it made any sense at all.

Resisting an impulse to return to the cemetery to see who else was buried there, Vance reached the bottom of the stairs, and continued past the hillside entrance and toward the small building with the barred windows. He picked up his pace, walking purposefully but unhurriedly, so as not to attract attention in this vast open space where he felt so vulnerable. He marched steadily on, his eyes down as if on an important mission.

Approaching the small stone building with the barred windows, he cast a surreptitious glance at the entrance, which was guarded by two monks carrying Uzis like his. Was there a password? He kept his eyes lowered to avoid making eye contact. Better to appear occupied and forgetful than to say something wrong.

He passed the entrance without incident and disappeared around the corner of the building, where he stopped to listen. Silence. No alarm had been raised by his passage. Quickly he slipped into the bushes around the building and crouched quietly in the darkness and waited . . . for what he didn't know.

After several long minutes he stood up, still concealed by the tall bushes. A long narrow basement window at his feet was dark, but light spilled lavishly from a window just about seven feet from the ground. Curiosity gained the upper hand over his caution as he reached up for the cross member that secured the bars to the window. Once he raised himself up, he could be seen if anyone was watching. But he had to know what was inside.

Vance tested the bar gradually to make sure it wouldn't make noise when he trusted his full weight to it. Slowly he pulled himself up, nearly losing his grasp on the bar when his eyes cleared the windowsill. Inside, Professor Tosi sat bare-chested on the edge of a comforter-covered bed. Vance watched eyes wide with surprise as the professor held his arm out to receive an injection from a male nurse in a white jacket. Just below the professor's sternum was a sutured incision about three inches long, still red and angry from what appeared to be recent surgery.

That does it, Vance decided, lowering himself back down. I've got to get into the building. Still concealed by the bushes, he inched his way toward the entrance to the building where the two guards stood. As in many buildings of this era, the main entrance was up a set of steps and through a porticoed foyer. Beneath the steps was a secondary entrance leading to the basement. Vance slipped silently down the lower steps. At the basement door, he stopped, dismayed by the metal grill covering the door's large glass pane, and by the array of robust locks.

A more thorough survey of the building's perimeter revealed no other entrance. The only way in, other than past the guards, was by the stairs. All of the windows were barred. He rejected the idea of trying to bluff his way past the guards. Shit, shit, shit! he cursed silently as he sat down to try to figure it out.

What you ought to do, old buddy, he told himself, is get your ass out of this bizarre place in one piece. Yet he knew he couldn't leave Tosi in there. And what about the bizarre graveyard; and Trent Barbour? And priests who killed? He unslung the Uzi and laid it on the sill of the long narrow basement window beside him. As he did, his fingers brushed against the concrete in which the bars were set. It crumbled.

He grabbed a piece of the crumbly cement and brought it close to his eyes. It was old, and its proximity to the moisture of the ground had done it no good. Excitedly, Vance scrambled around on his hands and knees, prying at the concrete. The bars had obviously been an after-thought, secured in holes in the stone at the top of the window, and embedded in concrete troweled onto the sill. With changing temperatures, the stone and the concrete had apparently expanded and contracted at different rates, and over the years, the concrete had deteriorated. In less than twenty minutes, Vance had removed all of the bars.

The dirty glass window, nearly opaque from years of neglect, opened easily inward, its metal frame held by pins at the two bottom corners. Carefully Vance folded it inward until it rested flat against the interior wall. He could see nothing inside the room: It was darker than the moonless night. But without another thought, Vance shed the bulky monk's cassock and squirmed through the long narrow window feetfirst, dropping with a muffled thud onto a wooden crate. Carefully he reached for the Uzi and cassock and brought them in through the window, then tried to replace the bars as best he could. The window wouldn't stand close scrutiny, but then, he thought, it wasn't likely to get close scrutiny tonight.

In a moment Vance's tennis shoes gritted on a hard concrete floor. He stood there for a moment trying to get his bearings in the darkness, his nose filled with the musty stale odor of lifeless air shut up for long periods. Good, he thought. An unused storeroom was that much safer.

Wooden crates were stacked up higher than his head in every direction, he discovered, feeling his way gingerly between the stacks. As he came around a corner he spotted a thin sliver of light at the base of a door, and finally the room took on a shape and form around him, though no color shone in the dim illumination.

Now that he could see a little, he walked more confidently. He went to the door and inspected its knob and a deadbolt above it. The deadbolt had a thumbscrew inside! Vance fumbled around first on the right side of the door and then the left and finally located a light switch, one of the old-fashioned kinds with two push buttons. He mashed the one that protruded the farthest, and a dim glow from a dusty low-wattage bulb filled the room with yellow light and stark bottomless shadows.

Vance stared around himself at the rough wooden crates, the unfinished wood showing rough and almond-colored in the light. Again he was stunned beyond reaction, his overstressed nerves refusing to register. All of the crates were marked with the swastika and the wings of Hitler's SS. He stooped to examine a stained, cracked shipping label. The faded ink on the darkened paper was difficult to read in the dim light, but Vance managed to make out the name "Goering" on the label.

Just what on God's green and more than slightly fucked-up earth was going on here? Thoughts of Tosi temporarily submerged, Vance climbed atop the stack of wooden crates and pulled at the boards of the topmost one. The wood, dried and shrunken from years of rest, yielded easily to his prying. Through knitted eyebrows, he peered into the crate and found himself staring at the edge of a picture frame. He pulled it out, and whistled softly. The sight was breathtaking. It was a Titian, one of the thousands of priceless art treasures plundered by the Nazis in World War II and never recovered. Goering had been a notorious collector of the national art treasures purloined by the Nazis, and here was one of the most priceless.

Reverently, he lowered the Titian back into its protective crate and replaced the boards. In awe, he looked about him; a storeroom filled with crates; were their contents all as staggering as this one? He donned the monk's cassock again, hoping that no one would notice his tennis shoes sticking out of the bottom; hoping no one would notice six inches of wrist sticking out of the too-short sleeve, hoping there would be no one to notice.

He felt calm as he extinguished the light, turned the bolt back on the storeroom door, and turned the knob. He checked the Uzi to make sure it was set to fire and then stepped into the corridor.

The corridor ran the length of the building. It was empty.

Vance turned away from the end of the building guarded by the two monks and quickly reached the opposite end with an unlit stairway leading up. Purposefully, he climbed the stairs. Tosi would be on the next floor.

The stairs led to the rear of a large kitchen, dark and put to bed, with stray light from beyond a pair of swinging doors.

Cautiously, Vance pushed through the doors and walked across the dining room, his footfalls damped by deep carpeting. He faced a hallway that ran all the way to the entrance. The guards outside were out of sight, behind the dark wooden double doors. The hall was empty. Were the two guards at the entrance all there was? What a piece of cake, Vance thought. The security here has more holes than a Mafia informant in a Perth Amboy pool hall. He hoped.

He counted doorways. Tosi's would be the next to last one from the front. Vance made his way silently to the door. There were no locks, only a doorknob and a thumbscrew-operated bolt. He screwed the bolt back and twisted the knob; it turned easily.

The metal door opened outward. No one could remove the hinge pins from the inside. Vance slipped into the darkened room. Vance could see Tosi curled up under the covers. Before he shut the door, Vance ran his hand along the inside of the door. As he had expected, there was no doorknob, and no access to the bolt. Once the occupants were locked in, they were there until someone let them out. Vance pulled the door to, but not far enough for the latch to catch.

"Tosi!" Vance whispered. The figure on the bed stirred. Vance raised his voice a little. "Professor Tosi, wake up!"

"Who," the voice of a sleep-groggy man inquired. "Who are you . . . why." There was a rustle of sheets.

"I got your note too late," Vance said in Italian. The rustling stopped.

"Vance?" Tosi asked, uncertain. "Vance Erikson?"

"Right, Professor," Vance replied. "Now if you'll get dressed, I'll get you out of this place."

A silence followed, marked only by the sounds of the two men breathing. Finally Tosi spoke.

"I can't do that," he said sadly.

"What do you mean, you can't. All you have to do is walk out of here with me. Come on, we can do it together."

"You can do it, my young friend," Tosi said wearily. "But even if they hadn't fixed me, I'd never be able to keep up with you. Better you rescue your young woman friend."

"Suzanne?" Vance said breathlessly. In his excitement, he nearly closed the door completely. "She's here? Suzanne Storm? How do you know? When did she—"

"Calm down a bit, Vance," Tosi said soothingly, "and listen to me." The sheets rustled again, and Vance could see the dim outline of the old professor as he climbed out of bed, fumbled about on his dresser, and then came over to Vance. "Take this," he said. Vance found a bit of electrical tape in his hand. "I stripped it off the radio cord the day they brought me here. I thought I'd use it, and then they fixed me. It's useless to me now. But you can use it." When Vance didn't move, Tosi took the tape back from him and moved to the door. He opened the door a fraction, pushed back the latch, and taped it open.

"There," the old man said. "That'll get you back out." Then he closed the door fully.

Tosi sensed Vance's tension. "It's all right," he said. "After they lock us in at night they all go, except for the

two at the door. You see, once we've been fixed, there is
no use in leaving. Come now, sit down and talk to me for
a bit. And then you've got to leave."

Fixed? Vance thought. Suzanne was here; had they
"fixed" her too? What did it mean? The questions swam
furiously in Vance's head.

After he'd settled into the straight-backed chair offered
by Tosi, and after Tosi had returned to his bed and sat on
its edge, they stared at each other in the dark for only an
instant, and Vance spoke.

"Suzanne's here?" he asked. "You're sure of it?"

"Yes," Tosi said. "They brought her in this evening.
Caused quite a stir, actually. Seems you and she have
built up quite a legend in a very short time. Killed several
of their chaps, did you? I'd have liked that opportunity
myself. Oh, yes, there was quite a lot of talk among the
soldiers—that's how we all found out about you and her.
Didn't see her, of course, new arrivals are isolated until
they've been fixed."

"Fixed? *What* the hell does that mean?"

"Oh, yes," Tosi said woefully. "That." He paused,
painfully. "Well . . . fixed is what they do to you to make
it useless to leave. Here," he said, unbuttoning his paja-
mas. "Come over here and see if you can see this." Tosi
had unbuttoned his pajama top and was pointing to the
incision Vance had seen earlier.

"It's quite ingenious, actually," the professor said. "A
drug of some sort in synthetic membrane implanted in the
body cavity. According to Brother Gregory—"

"Brother Gregory?"

"The head of the monastery—you met him yesterday—
nearly killed him. Short fellow with glasses?"

"Yes," Vance said bitterly as he remembered the priest in the Santa Maria delle Grazie in Milan, and at the Castello Caizzi. "I remember him well. He's the head here?"

Tosi nodded. Vance settled himself back as best he could in the uncomfortable chair. "Gregory," Tosi continued, "is quite a megalomaniac. Seems he wants to be pope."

Vance cocked his head. "It's true," Tosi said. "And what's more frightening, he has the means to do it."

"That's hard to believe," Vance said skeptically. He didn't want to hear fairy tales about a bush-league religious Napoleon. "But tell me about Suzanne."

"In a moment," Tosi said calmly. Too calmly, Vance thought.

"As I was saying," Tosi resumed in a grating professorial tone. "The implants are a deadly toxin. At least Brother Gregory tells us so and the evidence supports him. It's enclosed in a semipermeable synthetic membrane whose pores stay closed as long as we consume a small amount of liquid by mouth or injection four times a day. It's an improvement on the old reverse osmosis membranes which were so popular in the 1960s."

Vance listened in rapt horror as Tosi elaborated. Everybody at the monastery had the implants, making it impossible for any person—brothers of the monastery or their "guests"—to leave without permission. To do so would mean certain death since access to the antidote was restricted to four of Gregory's highly trusted aides. "But certainly someone could rush to a hospital and have them remove the implant," Vance offered.

"They've thought of that too, my young friend," Tosi

countered. "The thin membrane is a fragile one. Gregory tells us that any attempt to remove it would inevitably result in a discharge of its contents, killing the patient. There is more he hasn't told us, I imagine."

"Maybe he's just playing on your imagination," Vance offered hopefully. "Maybe this is just a cock-and-bull story to keep you in line. How the hell could a bunch of monks have the medical sophistication required to develop this kind of implant, anyway?"

"Don't forget that many of the scientific advances, particularly in genetics, were developed by monks," Tosi corrected him. "The various orders of monks have developed a surprising degree of sophistication over the past millennium. And this order . . . this order is the pinnacle of such achievement. As a victim I detest the devices, but as a scientist, I can only admire its evil genius."

"But how do you know?" Vance persisted. "How do you really know the implants are for real? I know you wouldn't take it on faith, especially from a bunch of crazy priests."

"I'm sure that some of what Brother Gregory tells us about our implants is fiction," Tosi said. "But even if ninety percent of it is fiction, none of us knows what the ten percent truth is, and none of us is willing to risk gambling on that—none save those who grow weary enough to take their own lives. For that's what escape would be: suicide. But even that's unlikely. Death from the toxin is painful torture."

Vance sat silently, trying to absorb the implications. It explained why the security was heavy but not excessive, why there were only two guards outside this building.

"Has anyone ever escaped?" Vance asked after a while.

"According to Brother Gregory, no."

"I just . . ." Vance searched for words. "I just find this all rather hard to believe." Though after the Titian in the basement, after the cemetery—he was ripe for believing anything. "But how?" Vance asked. "Why . . . ? What's it all for?"

"That's a bit easier to answer," Tosi said. "For every 'guest' who is accepted—"

"Those who aren't accepted are killed?"

Tosi nodded in the dark. "Yes. For every guest who is accepted," he continued, "there is an indoctrination session. We're given the history, the purpose of the order; and told that we have a choice: to perform some work useful to them, or die. Few who are chosen 'guests' refuse."

"Why?"

"Because guests are chosen carefully; their life work and interests are blended with the monastery's goals and an offer is made so irresistible that . . . well, it's irresistible."

"I don't understand," Vance said stubbornly. "What could a monastery have that could induce you, or anyone else, to work for them? Especially you. Your excommunication by the Pope hasn't exactly made you an acolyte."

The old man sighed. "Let me explain completely. Let me start at the beginning and then I'll tell you why I will continue to drink my little glass of slightly bitter fluid four times a day for the rest of my life."

Tosi explained that the Elect Brothers of St. Peter had split from the Church even before the Great Schism. The Brothers saw the Catholic Church as evil, compromising, too ready to accept the conventions of the world in exchange for more church members. They were—and continued to be—very much like the Moslem fundamentalists across the Middle East who felt death was too light a penalty for infractions of their dogma. The logic at work in the minds of the Islamic fundamentalists who assassinated Egyptian president Anwar Sadat was the logic that governed the minds of the Elect Brothers.

The Elect Brothers of St. Peter found wealthy and powerful allies, who like the Brothers wanted the Pope replaced. The brothers had conspired over the centuries with one ally after another. Appointing antipopes, plotting assassinations and poisonings in the College of Cardinals; encouraging insurrections against the Church and even, in 1427, marching with the French as they sacked the Vatican. Among the relics and documents they absconded with then were the bones of St. Peter himself, replaced by the Brothers with the bones of an unknown person looted from a Roman tomb.

What's more, Tosi explained, all of the Elect Brothers were direct descendants of St. Peter himself, the offspring of a single secret and illegitimate child by the Apostle Peter.

"That's outrageous," Vance said, stunned. "And it also pretty well shoots down the doctrine of celibacy."

"True," Tosi said. "If the Catholic world found out that some unknown was lying in St. Peter's tomb, it would shake the foundations of the Catholic Church. So much would be called into question, so much which Catholics have held as holy. It's possible that the Church as it exists wouldn't survive such a revelation."

"And that's what Brother Gregory wants?"

"No. Although we weren't told this directly at the indoctrination, I gather that the Brothers must do more than just expose the fact that they have had St. Peter's bones. You see," Tosi said as he reclined on the bed, "the Brothers have had several opportunities to destroy the church. In fact, they've succeeded in removing a number of popes. But they haven't been able to accomplish it in such a way as to consolidate their power. Alliances they've formed have invariably fallen apart, so-called allies installing more manageable popes from outside the Brothers. The Brothers must manage to consolidate their power somehow. The Brotherhood attempted to build its power from within, to reduce the necessity of relying on infidels. They started their own university and scientific laboratories by collecting the finest minds available. Groups of brothers would appear suddenly at the doorstep of a prominent scientist or artist and snatch him away and bring him to the monastery. At first, the strange disappearances were accepted by a superstitious society as acts of demons. But finally, after several close calls, the Brothers started faking the deaths of its victims, burning down their houses with another person's body inside or some such thing. Those people were the monastery's first guests.

"Gradually the Brothers grew more sophisticated. They planted their own priests in other orders and used them to certify the death by disease of people actually kidnapped and brought to the order."

Vance's mind flashed to his bizarre walk earlier that night. "The cemetery . . ." he said hesitantly.

"Yes," Tosi said, reading Vance's thoughts. "It's remarkable. Galileo Galilei is buried there . . . the real one. His other grave is a fake. And beside him, a cosmic array of genius . . . Mozart, Monteverdi. Even Henry III of France, who was supposedly assassinated by a monk in 1589. You can guess what order the monk represented."

"But these people," Vance objected. "Couldn't any of them escape? They couldn't have had the implants then."

"True, true . . . but they had primitive science on their side, what with the array of genius they had amassed even then. As early as 1400, it seems, they found that the poisons in the amanita mushroom—death angel is its popular name—would be neutralized by a particular extract from plants like jasmine weed. Although it was another four hundred years before they knew that the jasmine-weed extract was actually atropine sulfate, and the mushroom's poison was muscarine, that didn't inhibit their use. The mushrooms were fed to the guests daily in their food, and then the atropine administered afterward to counteract it. They lost quite a few people before they standardized their dosages and corrected them for the size of the guest, but eventually they perfected the system, which they continued to use until the early 1950s."

Vance shook his head slowly. What genius had been wasted in pursuit of evil!

"Actually, the Brothers became collectors of the highest magnitude," Tosi said. "They gathered not only the thoughts, works, and creative results of some of the brightest minds of modern history, but the people, too. They collect human beings the way a hobbyist collects stamps or coins.

"As the Elect Brothers collected more and more people, the monastery grew. They built a barracks for the brothers, and later the 'guest' quarters. Later a more comfortable and more secure area was built into the hillside to house their allies and provide the safest place for their accumulation of treasures."

"But I saw a rare Titian in the basement storeroom," Vance interjected. "Why isn't there also?"

Tosi sat motionless in the dim light. "As hard as it may be for you to comprehend, Vance," he said after a moment, "the artwork in the basement is the least of the treasure to be found here.

"Unknown works of Mozart, original scores composed after the master was thought dead; theories from the greatest scientific minds of the world, shared only with the Brothers; works of art by masters that surpassed their known works—created long after they were thought dead and buried. Those occupied the secure space carved out in the hillside.

"As a result of all this work," Tosi went on, "the Elect Brothers developed into experts at kidnapping and assassination."

"You couldn't prove that by the way they've conducted themselves over the past couple of days," Vance said. "Not that I am sorry, but they've botched just about every attempt."

Tosi nodded. "From the scuttlebutt I've overheard from the guards, that's been a result of some conflicts of command between Brother Gregory and the Bremen Legation."

"The what!" Vance exclaimed sotto voce. Kingsbury was a member of that multinational organization!

"That's right," Tosi said. "But wait just a minute; I'll get to that. You must permit me to tell this in an organized manner, or it will be even more confusing."

With changing political situations over the centuries,

Tosi explained, despite the monastery's growing repository of genius it soon became plain that the world had simply grown too large; once again, the Brothers would have to look for an outside ally.

During most of the nineteenth century, they floundered, until finally they struck a deal with Alfred Krupp. At the mention of this familiar name, Vance sat up suddenly.

"Krupp! I'm almost afraid to find out where this is heading," he said grimly.

"Wait," said Tosi, "what I'm about to tell you will interest you especially." He continued:

"In exchange for helping them to set up the Brothers in the Vatican, Krupp would have access to several drawings and inventions by Da Vinci which had never before been seen."

That was it, then, Vance thought. The key.

"You see," Tosi went on, "the Brothers have the largest collection of Leonardo's works in the world. De Beatis was one of their people. When Leonardo died, de Beatis managed to beat the Vatican's men to Cloux by a matter of hours. Most of Leonardo's notebooks and works were carted off by monks from the Brothers and taken here. The Vatican arrived as de Beatis was loading the last of them on a wagon, incidentally including the codex your Mr. Kingsbury recently bought. Those works were taken to the Vatican and examined, and most of them given away as gifts or novelties by various popes and Vatican officials."

Vance was speechless, wide-eyed in the darkness. He knew what he was about to hear.

"You see, Vance"—Tosi's voice carried a pleading tone

that said *please understand what I've done*—"the irresistible offer Brother Gregory made to me was to spend
the rest of my life applying my scientific knowledge to a
massive body of Leonardo's works, works never seen by
modern man. You wouldn't believe what that man was
capable of. The concepts he developed long before the
technology was available to make his ideas reality are
staggering. From what I have been able to examine in
these few short days since I was brought here, many of
the concepts were so advanced that the technology still
does not exist for them." Vance was silent, unbelieving.
"Don't you see?" Tosi said. "As a physicist I have the
opportunity to see if I can develop the genius of Leonardo's
mind into modern reality."

Tosi's voice had a tinge of madness, the insanity of a
mind overwhelmed, of a man who had been forced into
an impossible decision of life or death and given too short
a time to come to complete grips with it. He was as close
to mad as a rational man could be. Brother Gregory and
his mad monks had breathed life into the Faustian bar-
gain. In exchange for access to the knowledge of the
world's most brilliant mind, Vance observed silently, Tosi
had all but sold his soul to the devil. Like some latter-day
Mephistopheles, Brother Gregory promised knowledge
and life in exchange for this man's devotion. Sadly, Vance
conceded that if placed in similar circumstances, he might
react just as Tosi had done.

Tosi was still talking, the madness gone from his voice
now as recited history. "Like alliances before," he said,
"the one with the Krupps went sour, this one because
Germany had lost the war. If they had won, I do imagine
that papal history would look quite differently. In any

event, the alliance with Krupp developed into an even stronger one with Adolf Hitler—"

"Which explains his body in the cemetery?"

"Yes, oh, yes," Tosi said. "There is an entire section of that cemetery devoted to Nazis who disappeared. And you can believe there are many more still living out their days in the quarters in the hillside. In fact, that's one reason why the Vatican took so long to denounce Hitler. Both Brother Gregory and the Pope had been trying to strike a deal with der Fuehrer; only after Hitler signed the pact with the Brothers did the Pope denounce him. The denunciation was rooted more in the pique of a scorned suitor than in moral outrage. Never forget that the Vatican is political even before it is religious. Power comes before the spirit." Tosi spoke with the bitterness of a man ousted by the Church. He had been one of the few people in modern times excommunicated for heresy. Tosi had never revealed any of the details and Vance thought it better not to ask.

Vance found himself listening to this preposterous recitation without any further disbelief. Events had grown so fantastic that if Tosi told him that Jesus Christ was living in the next room with an implant in his chest, he would believe it. The human mind is so remarkable, Vance reflected, its resilience and capacity to adapt at once its greatest asset and its most massive liability. For on the one hand, the adaptability allows the race to survive. But its tendency to adapt to the most cruel and inhuman atrocities, and to accept them as a regrettable but sometimes unavoidable part of reality, contained within it the seeds of destruction. The human mind capable of exterminating six million Jews and of putting a man on the moon could certainly create the concept and the reality over which Brother Gregory ruled.

"More Da Vinci drawings, provided to Hitler by Brother Gregory's predecessor, proved to contain key concepts which allowed the Germans to build the first rockets, and to hone their submarine warfare to such a keen edge," Tosi continued. "Understand—as I know you do—that Leonardo's drawings and studies weren't the final working drawings. But his incredible mind managed to develop concepts, unique ways of approaching a problem, which allowed modern engineers and scientists to complete and perfect their own work.

"Yes, Leonardo and the Nazis almost won World War II." Then Tosi lowered his voice and said sadly, "Leonardo would cry at this use of his inventions. But"—Tosi's "but" carried the hysteria of a man trying to convince himself of a self-created reality—"he couldn't foresee what might happen and . . . and I must continue with my work here . . . continue or die."

Tosi trailed off into a melancholy silence. The torture, Vance thought. What torture his mind must be enduring, trying to rationalize cooperating with these monsters—even if failing to do so meant death.

"The Bremen Legation," Vance prompted gently. "What do they have to do with all this?"

"Eh?" Tosi said, startled. "The Bremen Legation? Yes, of course . . . well, I'll . . . I'll get to that in just a moment." The old man's voice regained some of its vitality. "Of course, after the war—actually, just before it ended—Nazis and Fascists by the score started to show up here. The Brothers happily accepted scientists and engineers, but only the most prominent of the politicians, people like Bormann and Hitler, were accepted, but then only after surrendering their collections of art and gold. It was actually this influx of German scientists that allowed the monastery to develop the implant. It had been a Nazi invention developed through intensive testing—frequently fatal—on the Jews of the German death camps." Tosi was silent for a long moment, as if he was considering the implications of this last statement.

"But . . . where was I? I'm wandering. Yes, after the war was clearly lost they all tried to come here. Even Mussolini was headed here when they captured him just up the lake in Dongo. Hanged him there, too," Tosi said, with satisfaction.

Outside, activity on the grounds of the monastery had increased. Hundreds of lights were illuminated in the gardens and along the pathways, erasing the deep shadows through which Vance had silently slipped an hour before. Casual late-night strollers were warned inside, replaced by doubled patrols of armed sentries who walked quickly, purposefully, searching. A sentry with his head bashed in by a brick had been discovered, his body almost concealed in the shrubbery.

Suzanne pressed her face against the inch-wide crack between the shutters trying to get a better idea of what was going on. Her head still ached from the ether they had knocked her out with in Como. That was . . . who knew how long ago? They had taken her watch. Damn them! she cursed for the millionth time since awakening. They had deprived her of even her ability to know what time it was.

But, she reflected as she observed the suddenly increased activity along the network of walks, she had had her little victory: They had underdosed her with the sedative. She had regained consciousness in the back of the car even before they reached the monastery.

Faking unconsciousness, Suzanne had allowed herself to be carried into the building. From all the activity she heard around her, she deduced it was an important building. Through the fuzzy vision of barely cracked eyelids, she had risked small glances about her, and saw a grand hall filled with well-dressed visitors amid the more somberly clad priests and monks. She was taken to an office on the second floor and laid on a leather sofa.

"She's still unconscious, Brother Gregory." The peculiarly high-pitched voice had puzzled her. It was abnormally high, almost preadolescent-sounding.

Still dizzy from the injection, Suzanne had lain quietly on the sofa and listened.

"Fine." That was Gregory's voice. "When she awakens I'll question her, then we can send her to the brood quarters. Keep an eye on her now and then to see when she's up."

How long ago had that been? she wondered now. Certainly hours ago, four or five at least. She had lain motionless while Gregory conducted a meeting in his office, the subject of which appalled her: a planned assassination. She couldn't hear what everyone said; some of the voices were too low. But she learned enough from Brother Gregory's shrill, clear comments. A man named Hashami was planning to assassinate someone very important at 4 P.M. the following afternoon. Brother Gregory kept referring to "the transaction," and the assassination being a part of it all.

Below her now, Suzanne saw teams of guards leading— or more properly, being led by—huge square-jawed dogs, mastiffs, she thought. They were hunting for someone. Please God, she prayed, if it's Vance, let him get away.

Frustrated, she turned from the window and paced to the other side of the tiny eight-foot-square room with its bed, chair, sink, and chamber pot. Three steps, turn; three steps, turn; three steps, turn. Glance out the window, turn; three steps, turn. After Brother Gregory had interrogated her, she had been brought to this room. One of the eunuchs—they told her they worked in the brood quarters and had been castrated as young children in preparation for the work—led her to the room.

"Just temporary quarters," they'd said. "Until we can have you prepared for breeding."

Her anger still smoldering, Suzanne remembered her explosion at the man. Breeding? What in hell did they think she was? she demanded. A woman, the eunuch said as he slapped her. And women were good for only one thing, having babies. Terrified and still smarting from the eunuch's powerful blow (didn't their muscles go soft or something? she wondered) she said nothing more to anger the man; instead, she contritely asked him what to expect. The answer was staggering in its monstrosity. Her fear turned into horror and finally to anger.

Returning to the window, she let her attention wander back to the grounds and the furious activity. Odd that there was so little noise, no siren, no horns or alarms. Perhaps, she thought, they didn't want to wake up people. She looked at the little square building near the barracks; all of its windows were still dark, though as she watched, a group of six or eight men walked up the steps of the building, approaching the two guards there, who were now brightly illuminated by floodlights.

Again she turned from the window and, for the dozenth time, searched the room in the dark for a weapon, a tool, something to use to escape. Better to die trying to escape, then let them use her as a brood cow, she told herself. Damn! It was hideous.

According to the eunuch, the monastery had developed artificial insemination hundreds of years before as a means to keep the Brothers celibate, yet provide new monks to replace those at the monastery who died. Female babies were killed at birth. Even women from the "breeding stock" were killed as soon as they could no longer bear children, and were replaced through a variety of means, including kidnapping.

"You are a very lucky woman," the eunuch told her. "Brother Gregory could have decided to kill you. After all, you have been a trial for him."

Bless his little heart, Suzanne thought sarcastically.

"But he has determined that your genetic material is appropriate for us. You may have ten or more years of breeding. Consider yourself fortunate."

Fortunate! She scoured the room again, feeling her way in the dark. A lever, she thought, all I need is a lever to pry the padlock off the shutters. Then, once everything calms down outside, I can use a sheet rope to climb down the three stories from this room.

It had to be tonight, she knew. Tomorrow she was scheduled to be "fixed." She stood up in frustration; this search had been as fruitless as all the others. She stood at the window shaking, rage filling her eyes with bright blurred splashes. She wanted out. She wanted to stop their assassination. Most of all, she wanted Vance Erikson. "It's not fair," she sobbed softly to herself. "It's just not fair."

Vance squirmed in his seat, suddenly alarmed at the amount of time he'd spent there. Tosi was still talking: "So, after the war, the Brothers tried to recover from their disastrous alliance with the Nazis. . . ."

Certainly the guard's body had been discovered by now.

"The Brothers, I gather, initially cooperated with some of the Nazi plans for a comeback. Then as the top Nazis aged and died, those plans, too, fell by the wayside. Once again the Brothers had no ally to help them realize their plans to ascend to the Vatican. The 1950s and '60s were grim ones, for the Brothers. They went through three heads with Brother Gregory being the most recent. After he took control in 1970, it was only a year before he hooked up with the Bremen Legation. It began slowly at first, the Brothers traded or sold to the Legation inventions and industrial processes developed by the Third Reich and deposited at the monastery. That developed into a full-scale alliance and I gather something big is set to happen very soon."

"Something big?" Vance asked. "Like what?"

"I don't know," Tosi said wearily. "I've learned a great deal more than I probably ought to. But Brother Gregory has asked my help quite a bit in these past few days."

"Asked you what?"

Physics questions, Tosi said, his voice gathering enthusiasm. "Questions concerning some of Leonardo's writings. You see, in the codex Harrison Kingsbury bought, there was originally a section on storms and lightning. He began to work on a system to produce man-made lightning. That's what is contained in the missing pages you have been searching for."

"But why? Why would that codex be important enough for someone to create a forgery to cover them up? So many papers were missing, why?"

"I don't know the answer to that. I do know that the codex was among the small lot taken from de Beatis by the Vatican and stored in Rome. I also know that a member of the Brothers who worked as a spy in the Vatican managed to gain access to the codex, took its binding apart, and replaced the stolen pages with a forgery. He then started to smuggle the missing pages out of the Vatican. Roughly half managed to make it here to the monastery before he was caught and executed. The rest remains in the Vatican. Brother Gregory and his people have joined with the Bremen Legation to obtain the other half of the papers."

"It doesn't make sense," Vance protested. "Why would a powerful group of multinational corporations like the Bremen Legation cooperate with a bunch of insane priests over a set of Leonardo's drawings? Every truly major industrial corporation in the world is a member of the Bremen Legation. I can't imagine *them* needing Leonardo's drawings."

Tosi's voice was soft. "Neither could Alfred Krupp."

"What are you trying to tell me?"

"Only that . . ." Tosi hesitated. "You haven't seen all of the writings and drawings that I have. You have no idea that everything we know about Leonardo, every invention which the world currently knows about is so crude, so primitive compared to those which I have seen in the monastery's collections. It's possible—and this is just a guess but one based on my background in physics—that these drawings on the nature of lightning could provide the key concept to perfecting some large and more terrifying weapon of mass destruction. If I am right, the weapon which might emerge out of putting both halves of this Leonardo invention together could make the neutron bomb look like a Saturday-night special."

Lights were flashing suddenly around the windows, casting both men inside into stark silhouette. Vance sprang from his chair and stood carefully to one side of the window. Below him, men poured from the barracks.

"They must've found him," he said grimly. "Quick, Umberto." He turned from the window. "You said Suzanne was here. Where is she? Where are they holding her?"

"In the main villa. Somewhere on the third floor. I heard Brother Gregory talking to someone about her earlier this evening when I was summoned there to answer a question."

Vance felt the pounding under his breastbone as he retrieved the Uzi and started for the door. "Thank you, Professor." He stopped. "You won't reconsider?" Tosi's silhouette shook its head slowly: no. "Well then, I'll be back. With help." Swiftly he removed the tape from the latch, pulled the door shut behind him, and strode briskly toward the front door. He tightened the robe around the waist of his cassock as he reached the foyer. Beyond the door voices could be heard, many more than the two guards he'd seen earlier. Vance reached for the knob; he'd do no more sneaking about. It was time to attack. He jerked the door open.

"Quick! Around the side!" Vance yelled urgently in Italian as he ran through the door. Surprised, several of the guards, dressed exactly like Vance, raised their Uzis. Then they saw his uniform. Their eyes followed his out-stretched arm, which pointed to the side of the building where he had entered.

"There has been an attempt to break into the building!" Vance yelled. "Around the corner, on the side. A basement window. Hurry, we may be able to catch him."

That was all that was necessary. In the excitement, no one stopped to ask Vance why he had been in the building.

"I'll stay here to guard the entrance," Vance said. "Quickly now, don't let him escape." The band of six or eight men scrambled down the steps, save for one of the guards who had originally guarded the door.

"I'll help you here," the man said, approaching.

Wait—The man's eyes scanned his face. "I don't know you. Who?" As the man raised his gun, Vance put all his weight behind his right arm and hit the man in his Adam's apple. The guard's mouth opened to scream, but only a strangled gag came out. The guard clutched at his throat and Vance came at him swinging, pummeling. But it wasn't necessary; the first blow had crushed the carti-lage of the guard's larynx and collapsed his windpipe. He was already turning blue from suffocation when he col-lapsed against the stone pillar of the entry landing and slid to the floor, his eyes wide and unbelieving. Terrible choking, sucking noises came from his throat.

Trembling, Vance pulled the body into the shadow cast by one of the pillars. He grabbed the guard's Uzi and walked swiftly down the steps and made for the main villa. All around him people were running; he ran too. Swiftly he moved past two evil-looking mastiffs and their trainers; they were headed toward the area where Vance had left the sentry's body.

On he ran, the vision of the klieg-light-bright villa growing larger with every step. Breathing easily even after the quarter-mile sprint, Vance crossed the circular drive and ascended the steps. From the shadows flanking the ornately carved mahogany doors stepped two guards.

"State your business!" the larger of the two guards challenged him. From across the monastery compound came excited shouts; the guard he had just killed had been discovered. Shouts for help distracted the two guards momentarily. They didn't know whether to send help or examine Vance further.

"Brother Gregory," Vance said. "I have an urgent message for Brother Gregory. It has to do with them"—Vance indicated the commotion from the guest quarters—"the intruder has been spotted."

The guards looked at him disapprovingly. "Very well, I'll take you to him," the larger one said. "Follow me. Giacomo, stay here and don't move." The other guard nodded as his larger partner opened the door and stood aside to let Vance enter. Vance swallowed hard against the lump of fear that choked him. The door slammed shut behind him.

"Follow me," the guard growled again.

The hall was grand and cavernous, but decorated in a medievally spartan way. Unlike most villas, this one was devoid of religious ornamentation; there were no paintings representing the birth, baptism, or crucifixion of Christ. There was only a rough, crude cross, some thirty feet high, climbing from the dull stone floor to the ceiling. To the right a staircase rose toward the upper floors. The man led Vance past the staircase, down the main hall, and then to the left. At the end of the narrow, darkly lit corridor, they stopped. The guard knocked on the door.

"Brother Gregory," the man said respectfully to the closed door. "I beg your forgiveness for disturbing you, but there is a message." Beyond the door, Vance heard the shuffling of paper, and then the sounds of a wooden chair scraping along the floor.

"This is highly irregular!" an angry voice snapped as the door began to open. A face appeared in the partially opened door. It was angry, but it was not Brother Gregory. The face showed no recognition of Vance as he stood there. The larger guard stepped aside so the man could get a better look at Vance.

"Well?" he said impatiently to Vance, his anger growing. "Speak up! Make it quick. We have a crisis!" Vance knew he had to act before the man spotted his tennis shoes sticking out from beneath the too-short cassock. This man wouldn't overlook the shoes in the excitement as the guards outside had. Then there was loud shouting near the front door, a commotion that suddenly spilled into the hallway as the door opened. That, Vance predicted, would be the guards from the guest quarters.

A faint shout from across the yard brought Suzanne's attention to the front of the guest quarters. A knot of men in cassocks clotted at the top of the stairs, then dribbled off the landing and disappeared behind the building, leaving two men on the steps. The two struggled; one fell.

The other one came sprinting toward the villa. He was dressed oddly, Suzanne noted. He wore some sort of white shoes.

She watched as the man ran swiftly but easily, closing the distance between the main villa and the guest house in seconds. There was something familiar about him, but before she got a closer look he disappeared from her narrow field of vision.

She could hear breathless excited voices at the front door around the corner, though she couldn't make out individual words. Then she heard a familiar voice. It was Vance! He'd come!

There! That one! He's the one!" The men's footsteps clattered wildly on the stone corridor as they ran toward Vance.

The burly guard who had escorted Vance to the door glared at him and reached for his Uzi. A look of surprise and fear played across the face of the man who had opened Brother Gregory's door and who now was trying to close it against the danger in the hallway.

"No!" Vance shouted, bending low to plow into the closing door with his shoulder. He had to get inside that room; it was his only hope. Vance's lunge took the man inside by surprise and the door opened wide enough for Vance to slip in sideways before it started to close again. The burly guard had unshouldered his Uzi; another body slammed into the back of the door and suddenly Vance was pinned between the door and the jamb. The guard brought the muzzle of the Uzi to bear on Vance's head. The footsteps in the hallway grew louder, and Vance could see now that they had their weapons drawn.

Straining with all his might, Vance arched his back, forcing the door wider and dropping to his knees in the extra space as the guard fired. A buzz of angry slugs roared from the automatic weapon and chewed up the doorjamb. The shots startled the people behind the door who suddenly let go. Vance swung his right fist, which landed with a painful certainty in the guard's groin, crushing the man's testicles between his own thigh and Vance's knuckles. The man grunted and bent forward; Vance sprang to his feet, his hands locked in a double fist that caught the guard squarely on his nose. Vance watched him collapse. The Uzi clattered impotently against the stone floor.

Other Uzis cleared their throats as the clot of running guards from the guest house began to fire. Great hunks of plaster exploded from the walls; the wooden molding splintered. Vance fell to the floor and rolled into Brother Gregory's office as the band approached. Like the freeze-frame action of nightmares, Vance watched himself roll as if through a sea of glue, while a line of slugs stitched its way neatly across the room's dark slate floor, leaving tiny white smears.

Desperately, Vance sprang to his feet and lunged away from the deadly track of machine-gun fire that followed him until he was out of the line of fire.

"Shut that door," Vance ordered as he unshouldered his own Uzi and aimed it at Brother Gregory and his assistant, who crouched behind the door. They looked at him with unalloyed amazement. "Shut it now or I'll blow your fucking heads off!" Vance saw a glimmer of fear flicker in their eyes; slowly Brother Gregory rose to shut the door.

"Quick!" Vance shouted. "Tell your men to stay outside

if you want to live." Brother Gregory hesitated for an instant. Vance started to move the bolt on the Uzi.

"Stop!" Brother Gregory yelled. "In the name of God, halt." It was nearly too late. The swiftest of the band of guards crashed into the door, nearly throwing Brother Gregory off his feet. The guard looked at Vance, who had taken cover behind a small sofa, and then at Brother Gregory; again at Vance, who brandished the Uzi, and again at Brother Gregory, who had regained his poise.

"Leave us, Brother," Gregory said quickly to the confused guard, who stood there, breathing heavily, sweat pouring down his face. From under frowning, hooded brows, quick intelligent eyes inspected the room. Brother Gregory leaned over to the guard and whispered something.

"None of that!" Vance screamed, firing the Uzi above their heads. Brother Gregory jumped back in terror. In an instinctive reaction, the guard brought his weapon to bear on Vance; Vance fired. The short burst of rapid fire slammed into the guard's chest, and battered him out the half-closed door.

"Now shut it all the way and lock it," Vance commanded through clenched teeth. "And this time I don't want you saying anything, anything at all to your men."

Silently, sullenly, the monastery head complied. Once it was done, Vance came out from behind the sofa. The man who had first opened the door still crouched near a bookcase behind the door. He was a middle-aged man with thinning brown hair, watery gray eyes, and a nondescript business suit that sagged unmercifully on the man's slight frame. For several moments they stared at each other: all three surprised, needing a chance to recover, to assess, to comprehend. Finally, Vance broke the silence.

"Over by the windows," he demanded. Without speaking, the two men complied. The huge, spartanly furnished office faced Lake Como through a set of three large French doors that led out onto a small balcony.

Vance gestured with the Uzi. "Draw the curtains," he told the men brusquely. "Close them completely." But in spite of his tough act, Vance was shaking with terror and exhaustion. He drew in a long breath and exhaled slowly; it came out audible and shuddering. At the sound, Brother Gregory turned a calm, beatific smile on Vance. The sight strangely enraged Vance; suddenly he had an almost uncontrollable urge to pull the Uzi's trigger and slice this evil man in half. But he restrained himself. The brother could be his ticket out of the monastery.

"I'm afraid, too," Gregory said, taking a step toward Vance. "We're both afraid." He held out his hand. "There is a peaceful solution to all this. Give me the gun."

"Hold it, asshole," Vance said angrily. "I don't want any of your priestly horseshit." Gregory took another step. Vance flicked the Uzi's selector to single shot, and fired one bullet at Brother Gregory's feet. The priest froze immediately, his face again contorted with hatred and fury, his hands clenched into tight fists in the folds of his black robe. "That's better," Vance said. The other man in the room seemed not to have moved an inch, though his hands visibly trembled as he gripped the edge of a chair in front of him.

"Okay, take your friend over by the door there." Vance pointed to the door through which he had entered the room.

Vance lined the men up and frisked them. He pocketed the nondescript man's wallet, car keys, and loose change. He searched Brother Gregory as the monk stood, legs apart, hands high against yet another door on an adjacent wall.

"Well, what have we here," Vance said in mock surprise as he lifted a Beretta .25-caliber automatic pistol from a pocket of Brother Gregory's robes. "A new addition to mass? For performing last rites, I presume."

Leaving the two men, Vance walked to the desk and settled slowly in the chair, still holding the Uzi. The rush of blood through his ears no longer sounded like Force 10 waves battering a beach; his hands steadied.

A simple plan began to form in his mind, but he would have to act fast while the security forces were still confused.

"Brother Gregory," he began. "You and I will leave here shortly. First, however, I want you to have Suzanne brought here." Gregory made no response. "Are you listening, you bag of ecclesiastical shit!" Vance said angrily.

"There's no need for profanity." Gregory's voice was muffled as he spoke into the wall. "I heard you. But"—he paused—"I have something I feel you should listen to."

"All right," Vance said impatiently. "But make it quick."

"May I assume a more comfortable position," Gregory inquired politely. "I would like to speak with you face-to-face."

"Stay right there," Vance said. "Sorry to hurt your feelings, but I don't trust you."

"Very well," Gregory sighed. "As you know, you have had at least one chance to join us. We would really rather have you on our side than against us. You have a great deal of talent. Your scientific and technical skills are well known, and your scholarship of Leonardo is the best that exists."

"Maybe," Vance said viciously, "now that you've killed

the rest of them." He'd never forget the way Martini had been mauled. "I ought to do the same to you."

"We didn't perform the outrages about which you speak," Gregory replied indignantly. "We had far too much respect for Martini's scholarship. Those acts were performed by others."

Vance was taken aback. "Who?"

"I'll tell you if you join us."

"Why would I do that?"

"Mr. Erikson, the Elect Brothers of St. Peter have a trove of art treasures which dwarfs any other collection in the world. We have works of art and music; scientific works the world has never before seen or examined. We have here enough work and intellectual challenge to keep the true scholar happy for the rest of his life. You, Vance Erikson, are the sort of intellect we want. You can not only appreciate our collection and accomplishments, but your mind can make a grand contribution to the advancement of a new civilization—a civilization of which I will be the spiritual leader."

Vance saw in his mind the crates of art treasures and remembered Tosi's description of Leonardo's writings and drawings he'd said the monastery possessed. But then Vance also heard the desolation in Tosi's voice. Vance thought also of the hideous people the monastery had sheltered, the subhuman slime of mankind who had been allowed to hide here from justice. But most of all, he thought of Suzanne.

"Not if I can help it," Vance said suddenly.

"Excuse me?"

"You aren't going to be the spiritual leader of anything if I can help it."

"That's just the point, my young friend." Gregory's voice was unctuous. "You *can't* help it. There is no possible way you can prevent it all from happening. Destiny will not be denied."

"I can try."

"You'll die trying," Gregory responded curtly.

"So be it," Vance said. "I'd rather die trying."

Gregory sighed wearily. "How existential. And how futile. Why won't you listen to reason? I can help you. I can make you a part of all this. It would truly be a waste for you to die. Such squandered intellect. Don't you want *that* to survive?"

"Not at the cost of being your prisoner."

"Mr. Erikson, I beseech you." Gregory's voice was urgent; for the first time, he sounded frightened.

"Beseech all you want," Vance said. "But it ain't gonna do you any good. We'll both get out of here alive, or neither of us will."

Silence hung palpably in the room, broken only by the sounds of Vance rummaging through the contents of Gregory's desk. He opened drawers and shut them, pawing through their contents. "Ah!" Vance said, picking up a roll of cellophane tape. He'd tape the gun barrel to Gregory's head, and his finger to the trigger. If someone shot Vance, Brother Gregory's head would be blown to pieces.

Although Vance was by now calm, he knew the other two men in the room were not. They were sweating for their lives, because of him. Suddenly he was filled with a sense of power, and then, just as suddenly, he was nauseated. Power, he thought, does corrupt.

Tape in one hand, Uzi in the other, Vance started to stand up. There was a faint rustling, like wind, in the curtains behind him. He spun around just as a huge human form rushed at him from the other side of the curtains, grabbing at him through the cloth with powerful arms. Vance struggled to free himself and bring the Uzi to bear. But a second set of arms followed the first, pinning his arm and wrenching the machine gun out of his hands. He started to yell, but the sound tripped in his throat as a massive blow caught him on the back of his head. As blackness dropped over him, Vance chastised himself for failing to make sure the French windows were locked.

Chapter 16

He was spinning mercilessly in a black vortex, his mind and body scattered to the very edges of space. He knew he was regaining consciousness when the pain exploded, a million stars detonating in his head. He lay still, wishing for the comfort of the blackness. Then, gradually, he became aware of another sensation. There was a light pressure on his forehead, in his hair, soothing him, and soon he heard Suzanne's voice. Vance opened his eyes.

"Oh, God, you're okay!" Suzanne cried, and bent down to kiss him.

Vance was lying on a bed in a very dark room, his head in Suzanne's lap. Her movement sent poison-tipped lances burning through his head.

"Take it easy," Vance gasped. "My head feels like a major disaster area."

"Oh!" Suzanne straightened up suddenly. "I'm sorry. Is that better?"

Then Suzanne's arms were around him, and for a moment the throbbing in his head was forgotten. He turned to her and they kissed long, deep.

"Oh, I'm so happy," Suzanne said.

"Me too." Vance pulled away from her. "Suzanne," he said in a still unsteady voice, "what . . . happened to you?"

She told him how she'd been picked up by the police in Como and then turned over to Brother Gregory.

"They must be working for the good brother," Vance said. "I wonder just how powerful he is."

"But I haven't told you the worst part," Suzanne continued. "They want to keep me here to *breed*—can you imagine? They take women somewhere and artificially impregnate them like cattle to grow little monks. The whole operation is taken care of by eunuch priests."

"Eunuchs! I thought that went out of vogue a long, long time ago." He thought for a moment. "But then so did the Inquisition."

"Oh, my God." Suzanne's voice was almost a whisper. "I nearly . . . how could I have forgotten? They, the monks and somebody else, are planning an assassination . . . somebody important, tomorrow—no, *today*. This afternoon."

Suzanne's revelation cleared his head. "An assassination? Who?"

"I don't know who," she explained. "I was listening from a room next to Brother Gregory's office. They thought I was still drugged. I heard them talking about an important killing to take place this coming afternoon. It sounded like a big world figure or something."

I gather something big is set to happen very soon. Tosi's words came to Vance now, cutting through the static of pain. An alliance between the Bremen Legation and the Elect Brothers of St. Peter. Papers in the Vatican, Da Vinci drawings of a powerful weapon . . .

A weapon of mass destruction . . . could make the neutron bomb look like a Saturday-night special.

Half the papers were in the Vatican; the Brothers had the other half. An assassination this afternoon, and Tosi's words that . . . *something big is set to happen very soon.*

The outlines of a diabolical plot formed in his head. He wanted to dismiss it as nonsense, as the fantasy of a mind plucked from hell, but the thoughts could not be dismissed. For while the plot seemed evil, warped, the plan, if he was right, was the only rational, logical thing for the Brothers to do.

"They're going to kill the Pope," he said softly, not believing his own words.

"Listen," he said to Suzanne's astonished face. "I talked to Tosi for a long time, and . . ."

He related his conversation with the scholar and how the old man had told him of the impending big event, of the powerful weapon described by Da Vinci, of Tosi's decision to stay where he was, of the implants and more. As Vance talked, he saw the recognition grow in Suzanne's eyes. Even in the dark, her eyes seemed to shine.

"I just don't *believe* this is really happening! This is the twenty-first century, for Christ's sake! And we're being haunted by a bunch of psychotic priests from the Middle Ages and the invention of a man who's been dead for nearly five hundred years. It can't be happening. It—"

"But it *is* happening. And unless this is all an elaborate

hoax, then we've seen the proof. They've killed people all over Europe. They have the ability to enslave people with their implants. The police cooperate with them. They—"

"Okay, okay," Suzanne interrupted. "I can see all of that myself. I believe you . . . I believe it, but I just don't *want* to believe any of it."

They sat on the bed, with their arms around each other, savoring the warmth. "We have to do something," Suzanne said finally. "But they've done a good job of leaving us with nothing to work with." She related her many fruitless searches of the room. "The only thing I've learned is that you can remove the legs of the bed, for all the good *that* does. We could use them like a club, but the guards won't open this door for anything, not until they're ready. When that time comes, a couple of metal bedposts won't be much against automatic weapons."

"True," Vance said grimly. "Very true." He got up and examined the room himself. Over the sink, there was a small light, with the bulb missing. Tentatively, he stuck his finger in the socket and touched the two contacts. Nothing happened. He was grateful not to receive a shock, disappointed he hadn't. With his other hand he found a ball chain and pulled it.

"Ahhhh-un, goddamn it!" he exclaimed as the jolt massaged its way up his arm. He landed on his ass on the wooden floor, his feet splayed out like a child in a sandbox.

"Vance!" Suzanne cried as she leaped from the bed.

"Are you all right?" Outside, they heard the guard take a couple of steps. The doorknob rattled. Apparently satisfied the door was still locked, the man returned to his position a few feet away.

"Yeah," Vance said, taking a deep breath. "I found what I was looking for."

"And what was that?" she asked as she helped him stand up.

"Uhh!" he said painfully. "Jesus, that didn't do my head any good. I was looking," he went on, "for the same thing Ben Franklin was searching for when he flew his kites in electrical storms."

"It seems you found it," she commented sardonically. "Now what?"

"I think it may be the key to escaping from this place. Here," he said, starting to lift the mattress off the bed. "Help me with this."

Fifteen minutes later the bed was disassembled. They had worked loose several bedsprings and used the sharp points to rip open the thin mattress. Two of the bed's metal legs leaned against the wall. Next to an electrical outlet along the baseboard by the sink, they had picked and teased a mound of cotton stuffing nearly three feet high.

"Okay, now hold this carefully." Vance handed Suzanne a foot-long piece of the bed's wire grid, around which he'd wrapped strips of cloth torn from the bedsheet. Holding an identical piece, he crouched to one side of the pile of cotton facing from Suzanne.

"This has got to be perfect," he warned. "We'll probably just have one chance." Being careful not to touch the bare wire, they each inserted one end of the wire in each hole of the electrical outlet. Remembering the shock he'd received from the light socket, Vance was taking no chances.

Although it was more awkward this way, having two

people manipulate the wires decreased the chances that either would be seriously injured.

"Got the end of your wire in?" Vance asked.

"Uh-huh."

"Okay. Now poke the other end into the cotton." At the same time, Vance bent the free end of his wire to touch the free end of hers. The wires sputtered and crackled as electricity arced between them. Bluish white light illuminated the room, and they flinched involuntarily as their eyes, accustomed to the dark, took in the brightness. The short circuit lasted for only a second or two and then ceased as a fuse blew. But that instant was all they needed; sparks spat into the finely teased cotton, glowed, and then burst into flame so quickly that both Suzanne and Vance had to leap back to avoid being burned.

Outside, the guard in the hallway shouted: "Hey! What happened to the lights?" The band of warm light from the hallway no longer glowed at the bottom of the door. The lights had all been on the same circuit.

"Thank God for old wiring," Vance whispered, holding Suzanne's arm as they watched the flames grow. "Remember, don't say anything yet." They pulled the rest of the mattress over and stuck one corner into the flames. "We don't want them to discover the fire before it's going good."

It was a matter of timing. They had to wait for the fire to start eating its way into the wooden floor, but they couldn't wait too long or they'd suffocate. Waiting too long also might mean someone would replace the fuse, thus eliminating the cover of darkness in the hall.

Vance coughed. "Let's get over by the door," he said. "And keep close to the floor; the air there will be better."

With the flames greedily consuming the body of the

mattress and its coverings, the room resembled a tiny corner of an Hieronymus Bosch painting of hell: two cowering souls cast amid the billowing smoke and dancing flames.

The flames had spread to the walls by now and the heat was growing hot against their faces.

In the dark hallway, dimly lit by light that filtered up the staircase from the first floor, the guard muttered to himself as he paced up and down the corridor.

Grasping the Uzi warily, the guard paced to the end of the hall, trying to walk off his anxiety while someone located the fuse and changed it. He reached the end, and when he turned, a disturbing sight greeted him: A flickering line of yellow light poured from the bottom of the door. Impossible. There were no lightbulbs in the room; he knew because he had removed them all himself under Brother Gregory's orders.

He stepped quickly back to the room. What could be causing the light? When he heard the muffled cries from within the room his stomach dropped into his shoes.

"Fire! *Incendio!* Fire! Help! Fire!" He grabbed the doorknob; it was warm to his hand. What should he do? Brother Gregory would have his head if the Americans escaped. He removed his hand from the door and ran back toward the landing.

"Fire!" he yelled. "Fire on the second floor!"

In the room Vance and Suzanne lay trapped by their own fire, their lungs filled with the oily thick smoke. When they heard the guard outside repeat their cries, they stopped calling for help. Hope rose when they heard the doorknob rattle and then just as quickly sank when it stopped and the guard's footsteps receded.

The flames had consumed the mattress and spread to the walls steadily eroding the precious space around them.

Then they heard the running thuds of feet.

"Reinforcements," Vance said, tightening his grip on her arm.

"Vance . . ." Suzanne turned her face to his. "No matter what happens, I love you."

"I love you, too." They kissed quickly as the door handle started rattling again. "This is what's called your basic do or die." Vance stood up into the roiling smoke, clutching an iron bed leg in his hand.

"Stay low," he cautioned. "They'll rush in. Trip them up, then get out."

Frantic voices outside the door flung words in hot and furious Italian. Vance moved to the sink, his lungs bursting from the acrid smoke. With a final rattle the door flew open and slammed against the sink. Two cassock-clad men rushed into the room, Uzis drawn. Swinging the bed leg like a baseball bat, Vance caught the first man in the small of the back, across the kidneys propelling him, hands outstretched, into the flames. He never fully regained his balance.

Suzanne extended the bed leg she held, and caught the second man at midshin; he landed hard on his face. Only feet in front of him, the first man shrieked amid the flames. The fire-weakened flooring popped, groaned, and finally surrendered. In a shower of sparks, the first guard disappeared through the burning floor into the room below. The flames licked at the opening, then roared to the ceiling, fed by the air currents from below.

The rush of fresh air cleared the room of smoke for just an instant, billowing instead out into the hallway. In that instant, Vance took deadly aim at the second fallen man and brought the bed leg down on him. But the guard rolled as Vance swung at him. Instead of the man's head, the blow cracked his hand, knocking the Uzi from his grip. It clattered to the floor and landed at Suzanne's feet.

The guard jumped to his feet; outside the room, Vance heard footsteps coming up the stairway. Suzanne grabbed the Uzi but before she could shoot the guard, he leaped on Vance.

Vance felt the guard's bony knuckles slam into his breastbone. Stunned, he instinctively lashed out with his fists, landing a blow somewhere soft. The monk exhaled sharply, and then grabbed Vance around the neck. They fell to the floor, rolling against the open door. It slammed against the sink with a sharp report.

As the approaching footsteps shook the floor outside the room, a siren suddenly pierced the night air followed by the dim, disembodied voice crackling from a PA system: Everyone was to report to the main villa to put out a fire.

Suzanne stared in horror as Vance and the guard rolled toward the edge of the flaming hole in the floor. Then the sounds of excited voices in the hallway grew louder. Crouching low in the doorway, she braced her back against the doorjamb and watched as three sets of legs—their torsos vanishing into the smoke—rushed down the hall. She held her fire. She glanced behind her for an instant, just in time to see the guard throw an elbow into Vance's solar plexus. It seemed to stun him; the guard rolled out of Vance's grip and grabbed an iron bed leg.

Gasping to regain his breath, Vance painfully climbed to his knees and began to stand as the monk brought the iron bar down toward him. Vance lunged to the side as the bar arced past his head. Vaguely he heard shots.

Out in the hallway, footsteps hurried back to the open door. Suzanne brought the Uzi to bear and swept the hallway. Her gunshots roared above the inferno. First one man, then another, and finally the third fell to the floor.

With his lungs again filling with air, Vance regained his mobility. As the monk brought the iron bar up to prepare for another blow, Vance lashed out with a kick, his leg fully extended, and caught the monk on his thigh. It threw the man off balance, but as he staggered backward toward the gaping hole in the floor, he grabbed Vance's foot.

Vance felt himself start to slide, and flailed about with his arms trying to find something to hold on to as he slid toward the hole. Excited shouts erupted from the room below.

Out in the hallway, one of the three fallen guards fired wildly toward Suzanne. She heard the slugs splatter against the plaster far above her head. She saw his muzzle flash and aimed for it, squeezed the trigger, and heard the man's Uzi thud against the carpet. When she returned her attention to Vance, horror filled her as she saw him being dragged slowly toward the hole in the floor. The monk clutched tenaciously at Vance's leg. Flames licked at the guard's arms as he hung precariously, legs in the hole, only his torso still in the room. She aimed the Uzi, praying she wouldn't hit Vance. She pulled the trigger. Nothing.

God! she thought. We're the good guys; we can't run out of ammunition. With no options left, she rushed forward and threw the empty Uzi at the monk; he looked up with amazement as the heavy metal gun spun toward him and caught him full in the face. The monk screamed and plunged through the hole.

"Vance," she said, helping him to his feet, "are you all right?"

He flashed a brief smile. "That's a dumb question for a time like this. Come on!"

More steps clattered on the stairs. Vance took one of the guards' Uzis and handed it to Suzanne. "Keep track of this," he said. "It looks like you know how to make it work for you." Then he snatched up the other Uzi and sprinted down the hall, away from the stairs.

As they reached the end of the hallway, two monks suddenly emerged, running, from the thick billowy smoke. A short burst from Vance's gun stopped them. Suzanne was heading for a narrow service stairwell, and Vance followed as footsteps sounded below them. There was no place to go but up.

At the next level, they rushed past a startled guard who fired at them. Vance returned the fire, sending the man for cover. The footsteps on the stairs below were growing louder, closer. Suzanne's face was pale, and her hair clung damply to her forehead. They couldn't go much longer, Vance knew. The smoke inhalation and the fight with the guards had taken their toll. Still they climbed upward, ragged breaths echoing in the narrow stairwell.

At the top, the stairwell ended at a small, padlocked door. Wordlessly, Vance shoved Suzanne against the wall and fired at the lock. Then he ran forward and swung the door open.

"We'd better hit some good luck now," he muttered grimly. "I'm out of ammunition."

The refreshing blast of cool air revived their energy

and spirits for a moment as they surveyed a small fenced-in patio that faced the lake. It was dotted with white metal umbrellaed tables. Behind them, the brilliantly lit court-yard of the monastery was filled with running men, all converging on the villa. The faintest whiffs of smoke eddied in the breeze. The sky above the mountain had grown lighter with the approaching dawn.

Breathlessly, they made their way toward the little patio eating area. As he had expected, there was an eleva-tor and, nearby, a dumbwaiter at the serving station, used to bring food to the roof from the villa's kitchen far below. It would be large enough for them to hitch a ride on. If they could get in.

But the dumbwaiter refused to yield to his effort. A safety interlock prevented the doors from opening unless the trolley was at the station.

"The elevator's coming up," Suzanne called over to him. "I'll bet it's not filled with dinner guests."

Behind him, he heard the excited voices of their pur-suers exiting the service stairwell. It would be seconds now, Vance thought. Despair swept through him.

"I'm sorry, babe," he wearily told Suzanne who was watching him tensely. "I blew it."

She brushed the hair back from her face and looked about her determinedly.

"Don't give up yet," she said. "Come on." She grabbed his hand and pulled him to the edge of the roof. Below them a narrow frothy mustache of water foamed at the edge of the building's foundation. Like most of the villas along Como, this one had been built right to the edge of the water. Beneath the water's surface, the precipitously steep profile of the mountainside continued its plunge.

There were no beaches on Lake Como, save for those at each end; the terrain dropped off too steeply for beaches to form. Ten feet from the water's edge, it could be twenty or thirty feet deep. Or, possibly, Suzanne thought with a shiver, a whole lot less.

"Here's our exit," she said. He looked dumbly at her, then down at the water seventy or eighty feet below.

"Our exit?"

"We jump," she replied with a confidence she wasn't feeling.

"Jump?" He swallowed hard.

Shots rang out behind them. The air was suddenly alive with death.

Hand in hand, they leaped.

Chapter 17

The room was not uncomfortable; in fact, it might be described as luxurious, furnished in modern Italian designs with a lot of chrome and leather and cane. Even the original Matisse on the ivory painted walls reflected taste. Too bad, Harrison Kingsbury thought as he rose from the cane-and-leather contraption that passed for a chair, it wasn't at all to his taste.

Yet he knew, as he padded in his bare feet across the lush steel-blue carpet to the window that overlooked the old quarter of Bologna, that taste was also not the issue.

"Vance, Vance. What have I done to us both?"

The old man sighed, once again memorizing the arrangement of red-roofed buildings surrounding the Duomo, the vision sliced neatly into thin rectangles by the ornamental iron bars that had been installed to keep burglars out, but that now kept him in. For the first time in his life, he felt old. The weight of his seventy-three years seemed to hang on his bones like lead ballast.

In a few days, the company he had sacrificed to build would he worthless and the man he loved like a son would be a criminal, either dead or doomed to life as a fugitive. How had it all happened? He closed his lids against his silvery gray eyes and rubbed them with balled-up fists. He had to identify the weak link that had given the Legation what it wanted.

The talk at the villa outside Rome had been brief, but then, he knew that life's devastating blows are usually swift and merciless. That arrogant young man, Kimball, had calmly, venally, presented the Legation's ultimatum: Kingsbury would cooperate with the Legation, or he and Vance Erikson would be ruined.

Kimball outlined the clever way they had framed Vance Erikson and the girl, Suzanne Storm. Remarkable, that pair, Kingsbury thought as he turned from the window and returned to the chair he loathed. The digital clock on the table beside him read 9:53 A.M. He never would have thought that those two would utter a civil word to each other, much less become partners in crime.

On the face of it, the first part of Kimball's demand was simple: Cooperate with us, and we'll see that Vance's name is cleared, and all charges dropped. Fight us, and we'll destroy him. That had been repulsive enough, a sort of emotional terrorism that superseded the bounds of honorable warfare. Yet he could have dealt with that alone. He, too, had friends in high places; he could have given this the good fight.

No, they had known that, too, these enemies of his.

They had studied him well, as a chess master memorizes

all his opponent's moves from past tournaments. They knew him well enough to have a coup de grace waiting, a roundhouse they thought would knock him down for the count.

Somehow they had found out about his enormous oil discoveries in the Chilean Andes. That by itself would have been damaging, but not devastating. But they also knew the extent to which he had overextended ConPacCo in order to develop those resources. And that would have been devastating. Kingsbury walked to the small kitchenette to prepare himself a cup of tea. But then, he thought, taking risks that the big oil companies were too cowardly to take was what had made ConPacCo great.

He had had to mortgage virtually every penny he and ConPacCo had. Most would have called it foolhardy, but in this case, if it paid off, it would be the most financially lucrative contract ever signed in the history of the petroleum industry.

He'd gone ahead slowly, quietly. Only he and Vance Erikson, who had discovered the oil deposit, knew the entire plan. Responsibility was divided so that no other single executive at ConPacCo knew the entire plan, knew how financially dangerous it was. Kingsbury had had to move quietly too, because much of the money invested had been borrowed against the fifty-three percent of ConPacCo stock he personally owned. A drastic drop in stock prices—inevitable if other investors found out about the scheme before it started paying off—would invalidate many of the loans. If that happened, the project would have to be canceled, and cancellation meant the virtual ruin of ConPacCo. There would be nothing left then but to sell out to one of the big oil companies.

And that, Kingsbury thought as the teakettle began to sing, was what the Bremen Legation had virtually guaranteed. He poured a large English teacup full of hot water and watched the steam rise, and then plunked a bag of Twinings English Breakfast tea into it and watched the bag soak and sink to the bottom. He wished he had a proper teapot. Bags were uncivilized.

But he'd make do now as he always had, he thought, watching the golden brown liquid diffuse from the tea bag and fill the bottom of the cup. Life had been uncivilized before and he'd handle it if it became such again. He'd watched his father starve to death in the cold winter of 1916 in their pitiful home in the mountains of Wales. He had been eight years old then and had sworn he would never let that happen to him. He saw his father give up when he might have saved himself. Giving up was death. Kingsbury stirred the tea and removed the bag. Yes, it was death.

He saw the smirk, that goddamned self-assured smirk on Kimball's face as he'd revealed the Legation's plans at the Roman villa. Even now, Kingsbury's hand shook so hard with rage that he spilled three golden brown drops of tea on the steel-blue rug. There was a traitor in ConPacCo who had given the Legation what it needed.

As he drove away from the villa yesterday on his way back to Rome, Kingsbury thought he'd been checkmated. Then Vance had telephoned from Como and talked about attempts on his life. Vance hadn't given up; the boy was mad and fighting back. That got Kingsbury to thinking, and he'd nearly convinced himself he had a way to . . . if not win, then to make sure the Bremen Legation didn't win either.

But early this morning, the Legation's men came for him at his hotel. Vance was making more trouble, they said; in fact was wreaking havoc with some business the Legation was involved in. So they took Kingsbury to Bologna, to one of their houses there. Kingsbury was to serve as a hostage to make sure Vance stopped disrupting the Legation's plans.

That was the deal now, Kingsbury thought, carefully sipping his hot tea. I must stop Vance. Unless I do, Vance, ConPacCo, and I all go down the tubes. But how am I supposed to do that? How will Vance know to come to Bologna? How can he find me and what will I do when he does?

The morning sun was rising through the hazy Bologna sky. Kingsbury didn't know the answer, but he believed that Vance would come here, and would find him. A smile passed over his face. He replaced the cup in its saucer. "When you get here, my boy," he said aloud to the empty room, "we're going to have a little fun with these people. I have an idea."

Damnation!" Hashemi exclaimed in Farsi again and paced from one end to the other of the small seedy room. Who in blasphemous hell did the blond American think he was? He was no amateur who needed assistants to kill someone. This American imperialist was just like all of the rest of them, and he, Hashemi, was not about to let them stop him. He would kill the Pope his way. He no longer cared about the money. He must eliminate the Pope, the very symbol of the Christian Crusaders in his land.

Hashemi stopped and drew another heavy toke from the water pipe. The hashish coursed through his head, leaving his heart angry and ready to kill. Beside the pipe lay his nine-millimeter Browning automatic pistol and a spare cartridge clip. It was the sword of Allah. It would speak to silence the tyrant in the Vatican.

He stood at the window and stared out across the narrow alleyway at the grayish yellow stained wall. He saw in its stains a mural of his heroic deeds, and he saw himself thwarting the arrogant blond American's "contingency" plan.

The American and his "assistants" were out to rob him of his rightful goal: Only Hashemi, the sword of Allah, was destined to kill the Pope. These infidels did not deserve the glory that was rightfully his. Hashemi went to the shabby writing desk near the window and sat down. He pulled out a wrinkled piece of paper and in an erratic script wrote:

"I have killed the Pope."

Hashemi warmed to the task now, recalling his thoughts of moments ago and earnestly committing them to paper. When they buried the Pope, this letter would be his chapter in history. He wrote quickly, sealed the letter in a grease-stained envelope, and set it on the bureau under his room key, number 31.

"Allah Akbar," he said. Hashemi Rafiqdoost slipped the Browning into his coat pocket, closed the door of his room, and scurried down the creaking stairs for his appointment with destiny.

That's right: *Hashemi,*" Suzanne said into the telephone. Vance stood by her side next to the pay phone in Rome's main train station, his insides turning to dry ice every time anyone in a uniform came near. Why the devil did she have to make the call from here, possibly in full view of the police? Would there be alerts out here? He didn't know how the police worked in Italy.

"No, I don't have a last name," she was saying. The receiver was close to her ear, and Vance couldn't hear the voice on the other end of the line. "But with a name like that he's bound to be . . . what? Iranian maybe?" She listened for a moment.

"Look, Tony, I'm positive an attempt will be made on the Pope's life this afternoon . . . four o'clock . . . yes, yes I'm sure, positive."

Vance closed his eyes wearily, wanting to prolong the tiny rest to a good night's steep. The fire at the monastery's villa had gotten a good start, and spread quickly through the ancient wood interior. All the resources of the monastery were diverted to extinguishing the blaze, and even the guards who had fired at them on the roof had been pressed into service, so convinced were they that Vance and Suzanne had leaped to their deaths.

But Suzanne had been right. The water was easily thirty feet deep where they landed, and they knifed gracefully through the surface, toes first. It was an easy swim to the boathouse and, with every hand needed at the villa, a cinch to steal one of their powerboats and be gone—but not before Vance had taken a fire ax to the fiberglass hulls of the other two boats. From there they had made an uneventful trip to Como where they abandoned the boat at the pleasure boat marina near the Villa del Olmo, and stowed away on a Rome-bound train.

"Tony, would you be a real doll?"

Vance listened to the sudden change in Suzanne's voice as she talked to this mysterious Tony. She'd refused to tell Vance anything about him except that he would help them.

"Please, Tony," she crooned. "I've got no money! I look like a refugee . . . no, you have to believe me. Please . . . once you get through to the Swiss Guards at the Vatican, meet me at . . . at that little café on the Piazza della Repubblica . . . what? Of course you remember which one, silly. It was the one we sat at the afternoon you asked me to marry you . . . yes, I *know* I wouldn't be in this bind if I had said yes . . . Tony. Don't say that, we don't have time right now. Yes, yes . . . two o'clock? . . . can you make it one? . . . I know it's noon now, but it's important that I see you again. Thanks, you're a doll . . . bye."

With a loud sigh of relief, she replaced the handset back in its cradle and turned to Vance.

"I told you he'd do it!" she crowed, a radiant smile covering some of the exhaustion in her face. "He's—"

Suzanne stopped as she read the look on Vance's face.

"The delightful little café where he asked you to marry him? Just who the hell is this Tony?"

Vance Erikson be damned!" Elliott Kimball ranted as he strode furiously back across the lushly carpeted floor of the Bremen Legation's office on Rome's fashionable Via Vittorio Veneto. He paused at a corner window to glare at the American Embassy just south of him, then resumed his ranting, pacing soliloquy.

"And goddamn your soul, Brother Gregory!" Kimball reached the credenza at the other side of the office and wheeled about-face for another pass at the windows. If only that fucking crazy priest had just kept his fingers out of the pie. Why the hell had he approached Erikson in Milan, anyway? And why couldn't he have killed Erikson at the monastery?

Truly, Erikson couldn't be that important an addition to the monastery's people collection.

Trembling with anger and frustration, Kimball leaned against the smooth rosewood desk. Somehow he had to control his emotions.

If only, if only, if only. If only Brother Gregory had killed Erikson; if only Erikson hadn't escaped from the monastery; if only Carothers had let him kill Erikson weeks ago; if only—if only the Bremen Legation didn't have to work with Brother Gregory's fanatics. But, of course, Kimball thought to himself, all the "if onlys" in the world didn't change the fact that he still had to work with them.

The Iranian bothered him most. He was even more fanatical about his religion than the Brothers were about theirs. People who act on their consciences rather than on their orders are often unreliable. But then, who else would be crazy enough to storm the Pope with a handgun?

Somewhat calmer now, Kimball seated himself behind the rosewood desk and leaned back in the chrome-and-leather executive's chair he had designed himself. He took a deep breath, closed his eyes, and went over the order of the afternoon's events. His backup snipers would tie up all the loose ends. The Brothers and the Legation would have their diversion; and in another seventy-two hours, the Legation would have both halves of the most devastating scientific discovery ever discovered by modern civilization.

He slowly opened his eyes and picked up a single piece

of paper lying on the dark, reddish black grain of the rosewood desk. As he studied the words, his hand began to shake again.

Shortly before dawn, the report noted, Vance Erikson had escaped from the monastery of the Elect Brothers of St. Peter. Kimball tried to reassure himself that Erikson was no threat to the transaction, that there was no way he could know about the assassination. But doubt still nagged at him. Erikson had been able to accomplish too much; the talented amateur had succeeded against impossible odds.

One thing bothered him: Erikson had drawn Suzanne Storm into his vortex of chaos. Too bad, he thought, remembering her beautiful bottle-green eyes; he would have to kill her, too. But such, he reflected philosophically as he leaned back in the chair and smiled to himself for the first time that morning, such is life . . . and death. He flicked on the shredder.

The delightful little café consisted of two dozen tables and twice that many chairs arranged with the barest semblance of order under a sidewalk gallery fronting on the Piazza della Repubblica, about ten minutes' walk from the train station. The gallery shade was cool relief from the afternoon sun. The chill exuded from its cool checkered marble floor and the stone of the building made the open-sided establishment seem almost air-conditioned.

Traffic passed only feet away on one side of the long narrow gallery, and pedestrians heading for the shops that crowded the building on either side of the café worked their way along the gallery and among the tables.

They arrived early on purpose.

"I don't know how Tony would react to someone else besides me," Suzanne had told him. "This is one enormous favor, and I'm not sure he would do it for anyone else—I'm not even sure he will do it for me." Vance's protests were met by her firm: "I'll tell you later. It's not important right now. I'll tell you everything, but right now we've got to devote all our energy to figuring out what to do."

Any other time, and with any other person, Vance would not have settled for that. But the helplessness of being a fugitive in a foreign city with no money had eroded his usual resolve. Dependency did that to people, he thought darkly as he settled into a chair two tables away with his back toward Suzanne. He'd give Suzanne and this Tony character just one hour to do something; then, by damn, he was going to act. Do something—even if it's the wrong thing—that had always been his motto. But never remain passive. Just one hour.

An unfamiliar voice broke Vance's brooding.

"You are still as lovely as ever, Suzanne."

Jesus! Vance rolled his eyes. That's the third time he's said that.

"You know, I have not been able to get you completely out of my mind."

Muscles rippled along Vance's rigid jaw and pinched his lips together in a thin line.

"Please, Tony," Suzanne replied sweetly. "Please don't start that again. You know it would never have worked."

"That's what you said." The precisely pronounced syllables of Tony's upper-crust British accent grated on Vance's nerves. Absentmindedly, Vance picked up a fork from the next table, where he sat, unnoticed by Tony, watching the slim, immaculately dressed Englishman. The man was handsome, about forty, with dark hair starting to gray at the temples. Vance twisted one tine of the fork into a ragged circle.

"I'm afraid we don't have time to rehash ancient history today, Tony. What I'm here to talk to you about is really urgent," Suzanne reminded her companion. "This is not about the past. Going our separate ways was best for us both. You know that."

"You could be wrong, you know."

Vance bent another tine of the fork, forcing it into a tight curve.

"About us? I don't think so."

"Perhaps about us," Tony said. "Certainly about the urgency of this meeting."

"What do you mean?"

"I checked with Italian intelligence this morning just after you called. It seems that they received an anonymous message last night tipping them off to the same information you gave me: I was assured that by two o'clock this afternoon . . . a little less than an hour from now . . . all of the people involved will have been arrested and placed in custody."

"*People,*" Suzanne repeated, confused. "But . . ." She thought back to the snatches of conversation she had overheard while feigning unconsciousness. She had heard mention of only one person. "Is one of those people named Hashemi?"

"That's the odd thing," Tony replied. "I managed to get the names of them all, and not one has any sort of name like that. All are Italians, and none of them has been known to use a cover name. Are you sure of what you heard?"

"I'm positive," Suzanne said. "Completely positive that someone named Hashemi is supposed to kill the Pope."

"Do you still refuse to tell me where you got your information?"

"Look, Tony, it's just not important. And I have my reasons for keeping that to myself." Suzanne's voice was urgent and businesslike. "What is important is that the Pope's assassin is still out there somewhere."

"We don't know that," the Englishman replied stubbornly. "I believe we are facing a case of mistaken identity."

"No, damn it! No. That's not right."

"Suzanne, you don't know if you're right. And you won't give me enough information to help you appraise the facts."

"Tony"—Suzanne leaned over the table toward him— "you know I don't say things like this when I'm not sure about them. You know that." She raised a hand to silence him as he started to interrupt. "And it won't do us any good to argue about it." She tried to sound conciliatory. "But if you aren't right, if there is any chance that I am, then doesn't it make sense to reach Vatican security and have them do something: change the motorcade route, the timing, cancel it altogether?"

Tony shook his head. "I'm afraid that's out of the question. You know this Pope; he tends to his flock personally, not from behind a phalanx of aides and guards. Even if it puts his security in jeopardy, his routes are announced days beforehand. To change the timing, or the route, would be to disappoint the thousands of the faithful who had assembled to greet him. We've notified the Vatican and that's the best we can do."

"Then help me find Hashemi."

"How? Hashemi's a pretty common Iranian name. What do you want the police to do? Arrest every man named Hashemi?"

"No," Suzanne said wearily, the ordeal of the past forty-eight hours suddenly robbing her of energy. "No, you know I wouldn't think of something as unreasonable as that."

"The first thing you ought to do is to turn yourself in."

"What!" His words slapped her awake. "What do you mean, turn myself in?"

"It was on the teletype this morning." Tony reached into the inside pocket of his Savile Row suit and withdrew a sheet of paper. He watched as Suzanne scanned the words. The message was short. She had been associated with one Vance Erikson, wanted for murder in Milan and Bellagio.

"Why didn't you tell me?" Tony asked when she'd read it.

"And why did you wait to tell me about this?" she countered.

"Because I hoped it was a mistake. I really didn't want to believe it. But . . ."

"But my reaction to the message was all the confirmation you needed?" She saw the yes in his eyes.

"But I know there has to be more to it," Tony went on. "I didn't tell anyone. What I want to do is clear your name. I can help you; I can do it. I'm the director of the division in Rome now."

"I know, Tony," Suzanne said. "But you'd ruin yourself if you did. You know that, don't you?" He nodded.

"And you'd be willing to do that?" Again he nodded. She reached for his hand and took it in her own.

"Dear, sweet Tony," she said. "I could never let you do that. I couldn't. I wouldn't even if . . . if I—"

"There's someone else," Tony asked, his eyes pleading for a denial.

"There's someone else, Tony." She tightened her grip on his hand as he started to pull it away. "Can't you understand why we never worked out; why we would never work out?" Tony said nothing. "Please try to understand. Please?"

"I've tried to understand, for nearly three years now," he replied after a moment. "But somehow it just won't register. Can you understand that?"

"No, but I want to. I want to very badly."

She paused as a waiter approached their table to take an order.

"Tony," Suzanne said. "We have to put us aside for a little bit. You can't go on forever living in our past. You can't."

"I suppose this Erikson chap mentioned in the teletype is the one," he said finally.

"Yes. I want to explain all this; I want to tell you."

"I'm not really sure I really want to hear it."

"Please, Tony, listen. When I tell you, you'll understand. Just listen to me."

And without waiting for his permission, Suzanne began. She told him of Como; of the monastery, the murders in Bellagio, and the death of Count Caizzi. She related Vance's travels, the deaths of Martini and the scholars in Strasbourg and Vienna. As she talked, Tony's eyes grew more interested. He interrupted her to ask for clarification and then "Would you mind if I took notes?" Now he scribbled frantically while she talked, interrupting more frequently, asking for the spelling of a name, for a date, a time, an address.

She explained why Vance had begun the search for the missing documents; told about the documents kept in the Vatican, about Tosi being held prisoner; soon Tony no longer looked at her, concentrating instead on catching every fact, committing it to his small spiral notebook. "Jesus Christ," he muttered when she got to the leap off the top of the burning villa and the trip to Rome. When she'd finished, he asked her to go over the beginning of her story, to retell the parts he had missed, while still immersed in his pea-soup fog of self-pity. Finally, he held up his hand.

"I've got everything from there on," he said, his voice totally businesslike. "Originally I thought everything had been sewn up with the arrests of the four assassins. But what you've told me makes a lot of sense. It fits only too well with some information we have been unable to make any sense of—"

"What sort of information?"

"We keep an eye on people in some ways that some civil libertarians might find offensive," Tony explained. "We also—through our contacts with the immigration, law enforcement, and corporate intelligence services— keep a pretty close eye on important people, either those who might be targets of terrorists, and on the terrorists themselves. There is a highly technical computer model which absorbs the mass of information and gives to us on a daily basis a prognosis, a sort of handicapping sheet, if you will, listing who is likely to be the target of a terrorist attack and who is most likely to carry out the attack."

Suzanne nodded. "I hope you are having better luck with yours than the U.S. did." She had worked with the American intelligence agents who had tried to develop the U.S. equivalent. The massive computer project daily absorbed billions of pieces of information: world events and terrorist groups' reactions to them, travel itineraries of top corporate executives, government officials, military officers, and the super rich; the status and whereabouts of terrorists and suspected terrorists; and of their Swiss bank accounts; and a million other bits of information. The computer fed all the information together, hoping to predict terrorist attacks.

Unfortunately, like earthquake prediction, the system had problems. It issued as many false alarms as it did accurate ones. It "cried wolf" too frequently. And because of that, the people who should rarely paid attention to its predictions.

"Actually, we've had quite a bit of success," Tony remarked with just a hint of English superiority. "We actually enlisted the services of a well-known London bookmaker who has raised the reliability level of the program to a little better than seventy percent. At least it's accurate more than twice as often as it's wrong.

"Anyway, as I was saying," Tony continued, "something very puzzling emerged from this week's handicapping . . . selected a person, and placed him in both the terrorist category and in the terrorist victim category."

Suzanne shrugged her shoulders. "That's not so unusual. An intramural spat, different factions of the same terrorist organization fighting for power."

"Quite so. But what made this one unusual is that he was not a known member of a terrorist organization, but rather an executive with the Bremen Legation. That's why your quite incredible story shocked me."

"Who was this member of the Legation?"

"A man named Elliott Kimball. I'm inclined to . . ." He stopped as he saw Suzanne's eyes grow wide with surprise. "You know him?"

"Yes." Her mind flashed back to Milan and the ride to Como. "Yes. He . . . I met him in college. He's enormously wealthy . . . seems to have been in some trouble like many rich kids are. And I accepted a ride from Milan to Lake Como with him earlier this week."

"You seem to have stumbled into quite a fine kettle of fish."

"Elliott Kimball," she said thoughtfully. "I never would have—"

"Neither would have I. In fact, we had just chalked it up to one of those thirty percent errors which the computer makes. Had decided to ignore it until . . . well, until now."

"Tony." Suzanne's voice was excited. She leaned over the table. "Can you dig a bit deeper into the computer? Find out something more about Kimball? Something that might give us something to try and track this Hashemi?"

"You think they are connected? Elliott Kimball and this mysterious Hashemi?"

"Perhaps . . . Yes, yes, we *have* to believe it, don't we? You know as well as I that when you have only one shred of evidence, you have to assume it leads somewhere. It's better than doing nothing at all. If it turns out, we may have our killer. If it leads nowhere, at least we've tried the only shot we had. Don't you agree?"

Tony reflected, nibbling gently on his lower lip. Finally, he nodded slowly. "It's a chance. A slim chance.

But I suppose it's the only move we have left." He looked at his watch and frowned. "It's after two now," he said grimly. "If your information is accurate, we have less than two hours before the Pope is to be assassinated." He snatched their lunch bill from the table and scanned it, pulled money from his wallet to pay for it. Then he reached into his rear coat pocket and removed a white, letter-sized envelope.

"Here," he said, handing it to her. "There's about five thousand euros in here. It should hold you a while." Hesitantly Suzanne took the money from him, watching his face.

"Well, that's what you asked for on the phone," Tony said. His eyes were hard. This was a professional Tony at last.

"I'll pay you back, you know," Suzanne offered.

"There's no need. As station chief I have a not-inconsiderable fund for compensating informants and . . . I think with what you've given me this afternoon, the money has been well spent."

He stood up.

"Tony," Suzanne said. "I want you to meet Vance." She watched the look in Tony's eyes flicker a moment, the knife-sharp glare of anger that sliced for just an instant through his usual veil of cool politeness.

Vance stood up and turned to face them. For a time the two men stood silently looking at each other, sharing an ancient, unspoken communication, an assessment of power, threat, status. Suzanne looked anxiously from Tony's face to Vance's and back.

"Pleased to meet you," Vance said, making his way toward Tony, extending his hand, and mustering a smile.

The Englishman's eyes flicked briefly to Vance's out-stretched hand and then, finally, extended his.

"And I, you," Tony said, leaning forward and extending his hand. The two men held each other's gaze for a long moment. Tony blinked first and glanced away toward Suzanne.

"Well," Tony said, making a show of looking at his watch, "we haven't much time. Shall we get on about this?" Vance nodded; Suzanne smiled, then paid Vance's lunch tab with the money Tony had given her. They walked with Tony to his Fiat in an alley off the Via National, about two blocks from the café. Suzanne got in front; Vance took the empty rear seat.

"If anyone knew I had met with either of you, I'd be called on the carpet for not turning you in, although as head of this station of"—he caught himself before uttering its name—"my branch, I would have an easier time explaining you away. However, you will have to wear a hood to hide your identity. Don't worry, it's standard procedure when an informant has to be brought to headquarters—and you must remember not to say a word while the staff is about. I don't want to risk the chance that someone would recognize your voices."

Suzanne and Vance murmured their assent, and they settled back as Tony expertly maneuvered the Fiat through the traffic-clogged streets, driving like a pos-sessed Roman taxicab driver. It was 2:30 when they arrived in front of a plain doorway off a narrow twisting alley near the Forum.

Chapter 18

The soundproofed room contained three molded-plastic chairs, a Formica-topped table with cigarette burns around the edges, and a computer terminal. The air hung stiff, charged with the acrid odor of frightened human beings. It was 3:11 P.M. and every Hashemi that Tony had been able to coax from the computer's memory had turned out to be a loser: All had been listed as in jail, dead, or known to be in another country. Behind him, Vance and Suzanne watched anxiously.

"Can't you break out the data on Kimball to give us an accomp-rost?" Suzanne asked grimly.

Vance stood silently near them, watching. What the hell was an accomp-rost? And where had Suzanne learned this lingo so well? He was sure now that her relationship with Tony Fairfax had been professional as well as personal. But that meant Suzanne had been some sort of spy.

Suzanne saw the confused look in Vance's eyes. " 'Accomp-rost' is short for accomplice roster," Suzanne explained quickly, returning her attention to the screen where Tony was already punching in commands.

Tony shook his head in dismay. "Jesus, it's a long list. We'll never get through it in time." He looked at his watch: Two more minutes had passed. They had already contacted Vatican security again, but the answer was predictable: The Pope would adhere to his announced schedule and route. The faithful would not be denied.

"Wait," Suzanne said thoughtfully. "Let's do an accomp-rost by nationality: Iranian, Arabic first." Normally, Tony had an assistant pull out the information he wanted. He was rusty at using the system, and grateful for Suzanne's suggestions. The muffled clicks of his fingers sliding over the keyboard filled the room, perforating a silence alive with only the murmur of the air-conditioning and the strained notes of their anxious breathing.

The green text on the computer's screen winked and then began to display, line by line, the requested information: a name, followed by nationality, and then an alphanumeric code that would allow them to retrieve the full dossier. Seventeen names glowed in green letters on the screen.

"Shit," Suzanne said. "No Hashemi."

"There may be aliases," Tony suggested. "But we've got to go through each file one by one to find them."

"Can you suggest anything else to do?" Suzanne asked.

Tony shook his head, and punched in the first code to call up the first dossier.

They scanned first one dossier, and then the next. Vance watched helplessly as Suzanne and Tony manipulated the computer terminal. Where was the papal motorcade now? he asked himself each time they completed a dossier. Where was the assassin? Would this Hashemi, if that was really his name, succeed? Vance decided to his chagrin that he was getting an inside look at how the most sophisticated intelligence organizations in the world could let one slip through the cracks—and a pretty big one at that. More than just the life of a prominent international leader was at stake.

For if the Bremen Legation and the Elect Brothers of St. Peter did manage to put together both halves of the Da Vinci drawings, it would make possible the most awesome weapon the world had ever known, and it would be in the hands of tyrants and madmen. Vance stared down at the fuzzy photocopy in his hand, stained now from the perspiration from his nervous hands. It was a block-by-block schedule of the papal motorcade, obtained from the Vatican by Tony's people. At 3:22 P.M., the Pope's open-topped, Jeep-like vehicle would be turning onto the Corso Vittorio Emanuele II for the final stretch before arriving at St. Peter's Square. The Pope's advance people were precise, stern disciplinarians, Tony said. They stuck to their itineraries just as fiercely as the train schedules had been adhered to during Mussolini's days.

It was 3:22 now: The Pope had thirty-eight minutes to live.

Finally Vance spoke. "Isn't there *anything* else we can do?"

"What would you suggest?" Tony snapped, his cool British aplomb vanished. "Maybe you'd like to run down to St. Peter's Square and search through the tens of thousands of people who'll be there? Would you like to frisk them all?" His face was angular and hard with anger.

"Tony!" Suzanne said reproachfully. Tony looked at her, his face angular and hard with anger; his eyes burned from beneath a frown.

"I was thinking," Vance began tentatively. "Even if we came up with a picture of Hashemi, how would we find him?"

Tony looked at him. He and Suzanne started to speak at the same time.

"Go ahead, Suzanne," Tony deferred.

"Well, we have the motorcade's itinerary," Suzanne said. "We know where the Pope will be at precisely four P.M. when the assassination is scheduled to happen."

"We also know that the rooftops and buildings which might offer shelter to a sniper with a long-range rifle have all been covered," Tony added. "The Vatican has put that extra measure of security into things."

"So the killer has to be in the crowd there," Vance said. Tony and Suzanne nodded. "And he'll have to be close to the Pope since he obviously will be using a handgun, or maybe a hand grenade, something that can be concealed, right? And according to the itinerary, the motorcade is scheduled to terminate at St. Peter's Square at four P.M. where the Pope, keeping to his style, will wade into the crowd and greet the faithful personally."

Tony and Suzanne looked at him, an awareness dawning on their faces. The emotional upheaval of the afternoon, the collision of three people who were emotionally involved regardless of whether or not they wished it, had twisted and skewed the cold professional judgment that two trained intelligence officers should have brought to the situation. They had overlooked the obvious place for the killer to be.

"We know where the Pope will be at four P.M.," Vance reiterated. "And the killer knows where the Pope will be at four P.M. and Suzanne tells us that's when and where the assassination is to take place. Therefore, why don't we—you"—he looked at Tony—"take some people and search that area for suspicious people?"

"Easier said than done," Tony countered. "There are tens of thousands of people there, and—

"Look, what's the effective range of a handgun?" Suzanne said. "We're talking about a short range to be accurate. Our man has got to be within about ten yards— closer, to be really effective. So we draw a radius around the Pope's four P.M. position and start there."

"But there are so many!" Tony protested.

"Tony," Vance interrupted. "It's the only chance we've got. It's now 3:33 and unless we do something, the Pope's got less than half an hour to live." He looked at Tony, his eyes asking: Well, let's go; what's keeping you?

Tony shrugged apologetically. "I'm afraid we're not equipped to act on such short notice. As part of a foreign intelligence operation, we have a delicate relationship with the Italian government. We would have to request and receive permission to carry out such a mission. And there is no way that could be done in twenty-seven—"

"Twenty-six, now."

"—minutes. And even if it were possible to obtain permission I would have to reveal my sources of information, which would be tantamount to turning you over to the authorities, and I don't think you want that, now do you?"

Vance's frustration and anxiety had become anger now. "Well, Jesus fucking Christ! You're going to stick to your bureaucratic rules even if it means getting the Pope killed? What the hell kind of wimp are you anyway, Fairfax? Don't you have the guts to tear up your own paperwork when it means saying someone's life?" He turned halfway toward the door.

"Come on, Suzanne," he said, gesturing to her to follow. "Let's go do this one ourselves. At least I'll go down trying. I can't sit here in this nice air-conditioned room and masturbate a computer while the Pope walks into a trap!"

"Wait a minute, Mr. Erikson," Tony said finally. "I didn't say I wouldn't help at all. I can't order any of my personnel into an operation . . . but that doesn't mean that I'm not willing to do it myself."

Frantically, Vance and Suzanne slipped the hoods back over their heads, and passed through security with Tony. Once on the street, the trio ran frantically for Tony's Fiat. Boy, Vance thought as they sped away from the curb with a screaming roar of the car's tiny engine, if we get out of this alive, have I got some questions for Suzanne.

Elliott Kimball angrily stalked the perimeter of St. Peter's Square. At each station Hashemi's four backup people were missing. What the hell was going on?

The tall blond man looked like a successful business executive as he strode confidently along the edges of the vast crowd that had filled the square. Kimball's face was confident, placid, and did not betray the anger and fear that seethed just beneath its surface. This had to be that slimy Iranian's doing. Somehow Hashemi had found out about the back-up assassins, and had disposed of them. But how? While his eyes searched the crowd, Kimball ransacked his mind trying to figure out how Hashemi could possibly have done it. But one thing was clear: Kimball had underestimated the little killer.

Holding his breath, Kimball plunged into the crowd, having avoided this physical contact as long as he could. These common masses stank. Their bodies stank, their breath stank, and the thoughts that sporadically came from their minds stank. He hated having to walk among them.

But this was a job he couldn't leave to others. Just as the Schoolmaster had been his responsibility, Hashemi, too, was his alone. It was the thought of killing Hashemi Rafiqdoost that sustained him as he sidled and squirmed through the tightly packed crowd that surged and eddied like a vast tidal sea.

Kimball was a memorable sight among the crowd: His six-foot three-inch stature set him head and shoulders above most of the people in the square, and gave him a commanding view of the area around him. His blond hair and exquisitely tailored clothing set him apart from the short, stolid, mostly dark-haired people. And as he pushed his way through the crowd, toward the front tiers where the Pope was scheduled to stop, the crowd grew denser, and resistance to his progress increased. People turned to him, annoyed; then they saw his cold, unforgiving countenance, and quickly let him pass. This man, they knew instinctively, could be dangerous. Kimball pushed past stooped, fat old ladies with tattered shawls over their heads; elderly workmen dressed in dungarees; young mothers with babes in arms, whimpering in the sweltering sun. To his disgust, Kimball felt sweat begin to collect under his own armpits.

Suddenly he stopped. Ahead of him, no more than thirty feet away, stood the short, wiry Iranian assassin, swaying from one foot to the other in the very front row behind the crowd-control ropes. And just as suddenly, Kimball felt his stomach contract. It was not the idea of killing the Iranian that made him anxious; no, that he would do with pleasure. But damn it! He checked his watch again—he would have to wait almost a quarter of an hour to do it. He sighed. First the assassination of the Pope, and then the death of an assassin. The cruelly honed Sescepita tugged gently at the scabbard inside Kimball's coat. Silence was costly, he thought; and only death could assure it.

Nearby someone in the crowd had brought a transistor radio, and was playing loudly a news report of the papal motorcade's progress. Everyone talked excitedly, anticipating the Pontiff's arrival. Would *they* be the one to touch him? Many wondrous things were reported to have happened to people who touched this man, this representative of God on earth. Perhaps it would alleviate her arthritis, a stooped old woman with gnarled and twisted fingers speculated aloud. Perhaps . . . perhaps . . . perhaps. Kimball felt his anger rising. Fools! All of you are fools! He wanted to shout and wave his arms and tell them what a bunch of clowns they all were for believing in the hocus-pocus of this most visible charlatan of religion.

But Kimball's anger remained tethered, subservient to years of self-discipline. Anger was only good when you made it work for you, he knew.

Staying directly behind Hashemi, Kimball moved closer. He was now about twenty feet away. When the Iranian fired his gun, the crowd would rush forward, and Kimball with it. "Kill the assassin!" he would yell, and in the ensuing melee, the Sescepita would slip unnoticed among the flailing arms and legs, and purchase the silence of another of the world's assassins. He smiled to himself. Political assassins knew too much. And too much knowledge could get you killed. The seconds ticked away. The sounds of the crowd washed over Kimball like waves breaking on the beach, bringing memories of other days, other assassins. There had been the Schoolmaster in Pisa; a hired assassin lying in a glimmering crimson pool of his own blood in a Milan alleyway; there was a scene in a dimly lit corridor in a courthouse in Dallas. All were assassins and all had died either by Kimball's own hand or, as in the case of Lee Harvey Oswald's killer, indirectly by people who later founded the Bremen Legation.

And as he thought of the killings, he thought of one he wanted so badly the feeling was almost sexual: Vance Erikson. The man's existence was an insult. And Erikson would pay for that insult.

From beyond the entrance to St. Peter's Square, perhaps a block away, Kimball could hear the growing roars of the crowd, the waves of adulation and worship. The Pope was near.

He's supposed to stop about halfway across the square," Vance said between gasps as they sprinted desperately through a winding alley parallel to the Via Aurelia. The trio had abandoned the Fiat in a snarl of traffic on the other side of the Tiber River. They had run half a mile, at a grueling pace. Although Suzanne had been able to keep up with him, Tony had fallen behind, and they stopped now to allow him to catch up.

Sweat dripped off Vance's face and into his eyes as he stood there filling his lungs with deep gulps of the oily, polluted Roman air.

Suzanne tapped his wrist. "What time is it?" she asked.

"Three forty-six," Vance replied grimly, turning to shout to Tony as the Englishman thudded along the uneven stone alley toward them. "Come on, Tony!" Tony's breath was ragged and heavy. Twice he had tripped on the uneven surface and fallen. His was a life of computers and office work; he had people working for him who were supposed to do his running for him.

"You . . ." Tony tried to catch his breath. "You'd better press on without me." His face was ashen and drenched with sweat. "I . . . I don't think I'm in any condition to make it there in time."

"But—" Suzanne protested.

"Go on!" Tony said with a wave of his arm. He sat down heavily on a stone stoop leading to a dark, cool entryway; from within came the singsong voices of children playing. "I'll be all right; really I will. You haven't the time to—" His face twisted suddenly in pain. Crossing his right arm to his left shoulder, he clutched his chest. "Go on!" he said desperately.

Suzanne looked from Tony to Vance, her eyes frantic with uncertainty. Then the sounds of cheering crowds came softly winding around the stone buildings, and settled into the alley about them.

"He's right, Suzanne," Vance said. "We have to go on."

"We'll be back," Suzanne promised Tony as she went to him and bent to place a kiss on his cheek. "We'll be back."

"Here," Tony said, pulling a gun from his jacket pocket and handing it to her. "You may need this."

Fortified by the brief respite, Vance and Suzanne ran with renewed vigor, lunging through the crowd as it grew thicker, dodging people like broken-field runners. Finally they caught sight of the curved phalanx of mottled gray-and-brown columns that encircled two sides of St. Peter's Square.

"Near the obelisk," Vance reminded her as he ran. "He's scheduled to dismount his car near the obelisk."

"What are we going to do when we get there?"

"Something," Vance said as they ran into a wall of humanity packing the space between the columns. "We'll just have to make up something good."

Shoving through the crowds, Suzanne and Vance made their way toward the obelisk, but found the going slower and slower. Vance was slightly taller than most of the crowd, and could see above the bobbing forest of heads. In the distance were the flashing lights of the Pope's motorcycle escorts as they entered the Via della Conciliazione. They had just three more minutes, Vance thought. No, he corrected himself unhappily. If they didn't make it, the Pope had just three more minutes to live.

They reached the fountain on the south side of the square, elbowing their way forward to the fountain's edge through a crowd of rowdy young teenagers.

From a precarious perch on the stone lip of the fountain, Vance scanned the crowd. His stomach slid into his shoes: They would never spot one person in the crowd. One person out of tens of thou—

Suddenly, there in front of him, perhaps forty yards away, was a well-coiffed blond head towering over the crowd.

"Kimball!" he shouted excitedly to Suzanne. "I've spotted Elliott Kimball . . . It has to be him."

"Where?" Suzanne called up to him.

Vance pointed. "There, beyond the obelisk."

Suzanne looked where he indicated and, after a moment, saw him also.

"Come on," Vance said, jumping down from his perch, accidentally jostling a young man and his girlfriend. Suzanne and Vance shoved on through the crowd, followed by the macho bruised-ego insults hurled by the young man. "Something's up," Vance told her quickly as they went. "I think if we find our blond friend, we'll find our Hashemi." Then, raising his voice:

"Police, let us through, please; police, official business," Vance said urgently. People in the crowd reflexively made room for them.

A deafening cry of adulation roared through the square, reverberated from the circular colonnades, and rose into the sky. For a moment, swept along in the emotional maelstrom, Vance froze. There, gliding beatifically toward the obelisk, was the Pope, clad in white vestments and white skullcap, his hands and arms outstretched to the crowd in a bent-elbow cruciform. Even a hundred yards away, Vance could see the life and vitality of this man, could feel his captivating gaze.

Two minutes.

The afternoon light seemed to grow brighter and the colors deeper. Hashemi felt his heart race and flutter as he gazed at the approaching white-clothed figure. Police had cleared a space about ten feet to his left where the papal vehicle was to stop, where the Pope would step from the vehicle to plunge into the crowd. The motorcade was only fifty yards away now. Hashemi's keen eyes searched the faces of the plainclothes police who walked alongside the white vehicle, and he watched the motorcycle escort in its flying-wedge formation in front of the Pope's car. He smiled and mumbled a prayer.

One minute.

Curse the big huge American, thought Anna Marie DiSalvo as she struggled to catch sight of the Pope. She had stood there, all nearly five feet of her, for the last two hours in hopes of catching a glimpse of the Pope, when this brusque, well-dressed blond man had shoved his way past her. There he stood now, blocking her view of the Pope. Again she summoned her courage to ask him please to move. Minutes before, she'd asked him, politely and in the best English she could muster, English she had learned from the Americans who had come through her home town near Naples in World War II. He had snarled at her request then and glared down with those horrible cold eyes.

Again, she opened her mouth to speak, but her courage deserted her. Ashamed of herself, she fidgeted with the handle of the umbrella she always carried in sunny weather to keep her head cool. Actually, it kept her entire body cool such was the wide shadow it cast over her short dumpling body. The umbrella was a good one, she thought as she ran her hands nervously over the curved handle. She had bought it only last week to replace the one she had broken. She was not a wealthy woman. One didn't accumulate riches knitting sweaters for a living.

She had forsaken half a day's work on the knitting to come here today. The exclusive boutique in Milan that sold her sweaters would be by to pick them up tomorrow, and they would be disappointed to find one less sweater. And for what? she asked herself. So I can get a view of the back of this stranger's expensive suit? Her anger grew. She was going to have to do something about this, she decided. Reassembling her nerve, she drew herself to her full stature.

*T*hirty seconds.

They approached Kimball directly from behind. Vance was silent now as he wedged through the crowd. Suzanne followed him closely. In the distance, in the direction of the Via Aurelia, came the sounds of an ambulance. Neither of them noticed.

Who was Kimball watching so intently? Surrounded by solid-packed humanity, Vance stopped about five feet behind Kimball and stood up on his tiptoes, trying to catch sight of the blond man's quarry. While everyone else there was straining for a glimpse of the Pope, Kimball was looking to the left toward . . . Vance's eyes landed on a still, calm man in the crowd, a swarthy black-haired man still and calm. While the rest of the crowd jostled and chattered, grew histrionic over the arrival of the Pope, this man waited patiently. Too patiently.

"I think I see him," Vance whispered to Suzanne.

"What do we do?"

"Well, all we have to do is spoil his aim," Vance said,

his mind racing for a plan. "But Kimball's here too. Maybe he's a backup."

"I'll handle Kimball," Suzanne said. "You get to the other one."

Suzanne swallowed but nothing went down, just one dry part of her throat rubbing against the other.

Vance looked at her with dismay. She was right. "Okay, but scream bloody murder if he tries to hurt you." He kissed her quickly and plunged into the crowd toward Hashemi.

Fifteen seconds.

"Pardon me, young man," Anna Marie DiSalvo said as loudly as she could. The tall blond man failed to respond to her. "Young man!" She shouted and tugged at the hem of his coat.

The Pope's auto slowed and prepared to stop.

Ten seconds.

Hashemi removed his sunglasses and looked into the Pope's eyes. He wanted this infidel to see the eyes of Allah when he died. Hashemi slipped his hand into his coat pocket and grabbed the handle of the Browning.

Five seconds.

"What in hell do you want, old hag!" Kimball whirled about and glared at Anna Marie DiSalvo, who glared back. She was not about to let this ill-mannered puppy get away with this. But oh, precious Mary, the hatred in those eyes; they looked like a snake's—no, something more danger-ous. She opened her mouth to speak, when suddenly the blond man's head snapped up and focused somewhere behind him.

"Erikson!" Kimball hissed to himself. His hand slipped swiftly into his coat after the Sescepita.

"Young man!" Anna Marie DiSalvo tugged insistently at Kimball's coat sleeve. Kimball wheeled, slapping her backhanded across the cheek. She stumbled backward, and the crowd nearby gasped with indignation.

"Go fuck yourself, old woman!" Kimball set off toward Vance, who was still making his way toward Hashemi. He had to keep that man away from the Iranian.

"Elliott!" Suzanne's voice sailed over the crowd. "Elliott, dear!"

Kimball jerked his head toward her.

Vance glanced quickly from Hashemi to Kimball to Suzanne, and back to Hashemi. Oblivious to the drama behind him, the Iranian drew the Browning from his coat pocket. Vance's reality took on the slow-motion quality of a nightmare. Vance plunged toward Hashemi, who by then stood little more than an arm's length away.

Suzanne threw herself at Kimball. He threw a powerful backhand that caught Suzanne across the side of her head. Helpful hands caught her before she hit the pavement.

The Pope's vehicle stopped almost directly in front of Hashemi. Vance leaped toward the Iranian, but even as he moved, the Browning came up evenly and then exploded like the opening of the heavens. The Pope's hand went to his abdomen as he stiffened up and stared at Hashemi.

Relieved now after hearing the gunshot, Kimball unsheathed the Sescepita and lunged for Vance. The transaction would take place! Hashemi was a fine shot and all he needed was one shot.

But the noise and the crowd, and too much hashish, had had their effect. Hashemi had aimed for the heart, and instead shot the Pope in the abdomen. He squeezed the trigger now in rapid succession, trying to reaim as he did.

As Kimball bore down on Vance Erikson, Hashemi fired again and again, but after the first shot, Vance had jostled the Iranian and the shots went wild. One struck the Pope in his hand and the rest plunged wildly into the crowd. He heard a scream of pain, then more screams as security men leaped toward the assassin.

"I am the sword of Allah!" Hashemi shrieked. "I have killed the Pope! Allah Akbar!" Then the stunned crowd came to its senses and rushed forward, pinning the Iranian assassin to the ground.

As Hashemi fell beneath the wrath of the crowd, Vance turned toward Suzanne, and saw instead the blood-furious face of Elliott Kimball as he rushed forward, sunlight glinting off something metallic he held in his hand. Unarmed and nearly immobilized by the crush of the crowd, Vance stared in horror as Kimball came at him with the horrible knife.

"Are you all right?" bystanders asked Anna Marie Di-Salvo as they helped her stand up.

"Yes, yes," she barked furiously, cursing and jerking her elbows free of their grasp. As the blond man rushed away, she grabbed her umbrella from the pavement. "You bastard!" she shouted. She grasped the top end of her umbrella and extended the handle toward the tall blond man. The umbrella handle passed between Kimball's legs; its curved hook catching the immaculately dressed man squarely across his testicles. Kimball stopped dead in his tracks and loosed a cry of anger, pain, and surprise. The Sescepita clattered to the ground.

Like a fullback, Vance bent low and plunged through the crowd past Kimball's doubled-up figure to Suzanne.

"Did that bastard hurt you?" he asked her. She smiled weakly and shook her head. "No. I'm just a bit shaken. What . . . what happened?"

"We failed. Hashemi shot the Pope."

Book Two

Chapter 19

The Pope was still alive. Hashemi Rafiqdoost was still alive. Vance Erikson was still alive. Elliott Kimball had one testicle that had swelled up to the size of a golf ball; he wished he were dead.

Painfully, Kimball pushed himself up from the divan and hobbled over to the desk to pick up another seven-inch reel of quarter-inch magnetic tape. Pausing to look through his window down at the River Arno as it wound its way through Pisa, he carried the tape back to the divan and eased himself gently down. Gingerly, he leaned over and threaded the tape through the heads of the portable tape player sitting on the cocktail table. In a moment, Merriam Larsen's voice, caught in midsentence, filled the shabby little room.

". . . no other alternative but to use him as an example," the voice boomed. Kimball quickly adjusted the volume as another voice chimed in.

"But you can't. He's much too valuable a member of the Legation's staff. He carries more in his head than all of the other staff members combined." It was Denise Carothers, chairman of the Bremen Legation and Kimball's sometime lover.

"That's just the point," Larsen's voice continued. Kimball leaned back on the divan and closed his eyes, visualizing the room where the recording had been taped, and the faces of the people as they spoke. Larsen would be lounging at an armchair in the library of the town house in Bologna; Carothers would be pacing back and forth, gesticulating in her nervously dramatic way.

"The point is," Larsen repeated emphatically, "that we have all come to rely so heavily upon Elliott Kimball's knowledge and skills that we are dependent upon him. And through that dependence he maintains power, leverage over us, and his fortunes and success become our fortunes and success." There was a pause on the tape; Kimball imagined Carothers stopping to stare intently at the other person. Then Larsen's voice, low and sinister, once more issued from the tape recorder's speakers. It was less distinct now; the man must have walked away from the microphone.

"His failures, too, become ours, Denise," he insisted quietly. "And we can't afford failures. He has fallen past redemption."

"Now let's not take things too far," Carothers protested indignantly.

"No one is indispensable, Denise. Not you, not me, and not your Elliott Kimball! Dispensability is our *strength,* and Mr. Kimball has compromised that strength and must be dealt with." There was another silence on the tape;

Kimball could almost see Larsen lowering himself into an armchair, taking a sip of cognac.

"You know, Denise," Larsen's voice continued, "I'm disappointed that both you and Kimball seem to have missed the point of the little lesson in Pisa. After all, the Bremen Legation has functioned quite well since then—even after its treasurer found himself garrotted and impaled upon a cross."

"But that's different," Carothers protested. "The man was a traitor! He—"

"Yes, yes, that's true, Denise. But I—we—wanted also to provide a lesson that could not go unnoticed by every member of the Legation, and by every staff member who works for us. I'm truly sorry you missed that point, Denise. While I will miss Kimball, I'll regret far more the loss of your services to the board."

"My loss?" Carothers's voice rose suddenly higher than normal. "What do you mean!"

"Denise, certainly you don't think that you would be allowed to continue after the total botching of the assassination?"

"Don't be ridiculous, Merriam." Rising panic made her voice shrill. "I am the head of the Legation. This sort of matter would have to be discussed with the board . . . a vote taken."

"That has been done; the vote was unanimous."

Muffled sounds issued from the tape recorder; footsteps? Kimball opened his eyes and leaned close to the speaker, not wanting to miss a single note. There was a loud metallic rattling of a doorknob. "You had the doors locked!"

"Yes, I did, Denise." Larsen's voice was placid. "Yes, I did."

"No! No! No!" Carothers's shrieks filled Kimball's ears as the tape dispassionately played on.

"Yes," Larsen said simply. There was the *"phut"* of a silenced pistol.

"You bastard!"

"Yes," Larsen said again. Three more muffled reports came from the recorder, and there was a loud thump.

"Yes." The clinking sound of the cognac snifter came over the speaker, and another contented sigh. "Yes, my dear, you're quite right."

Kimball grimaced as he shut off the tape recorder and settled back into the overstuffed cushions of the divan. In a day or so he figured he'd be able to walk normally again. He'd recover, he thought darkly, but he'd never have another knife like the Sescepita. He closed his eyes and saw it slither to the pavement. He remembered the angry blows from men who had seen him strike the old woman—and Suzanne Storm. He remembered returning the punches and the satisfying cries of pain his powerful blows had elicited. It had been all he could do to escape. And now, he knew his biggest challenge was to stay alive.

The pronouncement by Larsen that he was to be killed had come as no surprise to him, which was why he had long maintained plans for survival. The tape was just one part of that contingency plan.

The core of his plan had been carefully crafted for more than a decade. At the epicenter of his plan lay the Glavnoye Razvedyvatelnoye Upravleniye. Better known by its acronym, the GRU, which is the Russian military's main intelligence directorate. Few people were aware that even before the collapse of the Soviet Union, the GRU operated more than six times as many intelligence agents as the better-known KGB. And while the rest of Russia had digressed into a latter-century technological disarray, the GRU operated spy satellites and communications interception technology that was equal—and sometimes superior—to America's. Much of that was thanks, in no small part, to Kimball's intervention in covertly supplying information and technology he obtained from member companies of the Bremen Legation.

This allowed Kimball to build significant relationships within the GRU on behalf of the Bremen Legation, partly for the intelligence it could provide and partly to help develop economic ties and business contracts. And on the side, he established covert personal relationships that were in his own best interests even when they conflicted with the Bremen Legation.

Through those relationships, he had learned of the GRU's desperate quest for new military technology. While part of that desperation came from the military's desire to have better, newer, and more powerful weaponry, the overriding concern was economic. In short, weapons sales were an important source of income to Russia. The official state arms trading company, Rosoboroneksport, sold nearly $20 billion a year in military arms to other companies, but was suffering because the arms it was selling were falling behind technology with the United States. No country wanted to buy arms from a country that were perceived as over the hill. For the old Soviet Union, arms had been about world domination, for the new Russia it was all about business and market share.

Painfully Kimball dragged his feet up on the divan and

stretched out, taking a few moments to arrange himself before he closed his eyes and reviewed the other elements of his survival plan.

The GRU had long operated a small but important center located in Pisa for processing and relaying information. The second in command of that operation center owed Kimball many and varied favors not the least of which was the tape he had just listened to of the murder in the Bremen Legation's Bologna town house. That intercept had come from bugs he had helped the GRU install years ago.

As he lay there, eyes closed in pain and contemplation, Kimball knew that the only thing that mattered now was snatching the Da Vinci Codex from the Brothers and trading them to the GRU. That would buy a lifetime of luxury and killing. Allegiances were not important, he thought as he drifted off, killing was. A smile spread across his face as he fell asleep.

No one in Italy makes lasagna like the Bolognese. And where others may cook some dishes as *well* as the chefs of Bologna, no one cooks them *better.* Vance thought of the nickname given to the city by the sated gourmands of the world: Bologna la *Grassa*—Bologna the Fat—in recognition of the inevitable effects of too much good food. He felt *grassa* now. He laid his fork slowly on his plate, his eyes and palate still hungry, his stomach crying for mercy.

He looked over at Suzanne as she slowly nibbled at the edge of her tortellini, sensibly pacing herself, rather than gorging as Vance had before the main course had even arrived.

Bologna la Grassa, Vance thought. It was also well known as *Bologna la Dotta*—"Bologna the Learned"—the phrase acknowledging the University of Bologna as the oldest in Europe.

La Dotta, *la Grassa.* Those phrases had drawn him and Suzanne to this city. Vance took another bite of lasagna and washed it down with a swallow of the local Sangiovese.

Vance glanced at his watch. They had managed to flee St. Peter's Square with the rest of the frightened crowd almost exactly forty-eight hours before. Using the money Tony had given Suzanne, they had bought respectable clothes and checked into a small, clean pensione on the Via Nazionale near the train station. Without eating, they had fallen asleep in each other's arms and slept until noon the next day.

The sleep had chased away their fatigue, and with it much of the hopelessness that had dogged them following the shooting of the Pope. The Pontiff would live, his doctors said. A less vigorous man, they said, would never have survived the ordeal.

Tony Fairfax, too, was surviving an ordeal. Suzanne called a mutual friend that afternoon and learned that Tony had suffered a mild coronary, and was recovering in the hospital.

But the biggest news of the day had come from the telephone call Vance had made to the Santa Monica headquarters of Continental Pacific Oil Company. Calling from the international telephones at the SIP on the Via Fossalta near the Piazza Nertun in Rome, Vance had waited, as he was told that Harrison Kingsbury could not be located directly, but that Vance should wait for a callback.

Less than ten minutes later, the clerk at the SIP directed Vance to a glassed-in soundproof phone booth. To Vance's surprise it was Merriam Larsen's harsh, cool voice that came from the earpiece.

"Harrison Kingsbury is in our custody right now," Larsen told Vance. "If you decide to interfere further with the business of the Bremen Legation, Kingsbury will be killed. Do you understand?"

"Of course." Vance swallowed the rising anger and, seconds later, was rewarded with the voice of Kingsbury.

"Vance . . . are you all right?"

"Fine, sir," Vance replied. "And you? Where are you?"

"I'm fine. And I—" Kingsbury's voice was interrupted suddenly. Through the garble of a hand placed over the mouthpiece, Vance heard someone berating Kingsbury. In a few moments Kingsbury was back.

"Vance?" he said in a quiet, tired voice.

"Still here."

"As you can surmise, my location must remain a bit of a mystery. They've warned me very sternly not to tell you. Apparently you have got them quite worried. But on to other matters: Suffice it to say that I am still fat and learned. Yes, sir, fat and learned; and they are taking quite good care of me."

The rest of the conversation terminated abruptly.

Fat and learned.

Kingsbury was elegantly slim. He had never been fat. And the oilman had never made it past high school in his formal learning, and usually made a point of it. Kingsbury was trying to tell him something, and it took no time at all for Vance to decipher the message: Bologna! Kingsbury knew that Vance's studies of Italy would make the clues obvious. So it had been that Vance and Suzanne had traveled by train to Bologna that night.

They had checked into the Hotel Milan Excelsior, a comfortable hotel across from the train station, and enjoyed the quiet, grateful lovemaking known only by those who have cheated death, but who know they must soon face it again.

"What are you thinking of?" Suzanne asked him now.

With an effort he dragged himself back to the present. "About Kingsbury, about Tosi," he told her. "And about us. About you."

"Well," she began, extending her hand to him across the small round table. "I know what you're thinking about Kingsbury and about Tosi; but what about me?"

"Oh, things," Vance said, squeezing her hand.

"What things?"

"Like why I didn't notice certain things about you sooner."

"Come on," she said exasperated. "You're being elusive. Remember, we promised no more games."

"Yeah . . . well, I'm just wondering why I didn't notice sooner all the little things that pointed to you being a . . . a—"

"Spy?" she interrupted him and laughed. "Of course you might have if we hadn't been in such danger. But then, if we hadn't been in such danger, you'd have had nothing to notice."

Vance nodded ruefully, adding: "But you never told me why you did it."

"Why did you tell the world to fuck off and become a blackjack gambler?"

"First of all, I never gambled," Vance said defensively.

"That's why they blackballed me. My system was no gamble at all."

"All right, you know what I mean," Suzanne persisted. "Why did you do it?"

"Because I had to. I needed the money."

"Uh-uh." Suzanne contradicted him. "You could have made money in other ways. You didn't take up gambling for that. You did it for another reason."

"Yeah, well . . ." Vance felt naked before Suzanne's perception. "Okay, I did it for the hell of it." He wasn't sure he liked anyone, especially a woman he was in love with, knowing his mind this well. "For the hell of it, and for the challenge."

"And the adventure. That's my point."

"And the adventure," Vance agreed. "Are you telling me that you joined the CIA for adventure?" His voice was skeptical. "Join the CIA, travel to faraway lands, meet interesting people, and kill them? I can't believe that someone who was so intent on doing things the 'right way' could be motivated by that."

"You're wrong, because I *did* do it the 'right' way," Suzanne countered. "Remember that the CIA has always been a very Ivy League sort of outfit, at least at the management level. My father served with the Office of Strategic Services, the CIA's predecessor, during World War II. And if I had told him about it, he might even have accepted it. But I didn't, not only because he might have swung his weight around to block me if he disapproved, but also because I didn't want special favors if by some slim chance he did approve."

Vance smiled at her, shaking his head slowly. "You are some woman, Suz. Some woman."

"Thank you."

The waiter arrived then with two plates of sautéed veal.

"You know," Vance said between bites, "somehow I think you know a lot more about what makes me tick than I do about you."

Suzanne just smiled conspiratorially.

It was nearly eight o'clock when they finally walked out of the restaurant into the deepening inky-blue night.

Suzanne slipped her arm through his as they walked. "Do you really think we accomplished anything today?" she asked.

"Sure," he replied. "Even in drilling for oil, a dry well tells you where not to look."

"You sound pretty sanguine about this right now."

They left the shadows of the Via Testoni and turned right to join a river of pedestrians streaming along the long arched porticoes along the Via dell'Indipendenza heading toward the Duomo.

"I have to be sanguine," he said as they blended into the throng of evening strollers. "We started with our first best bet, and we'll have to play it until we either win or bust."

"I thought you didn't gamble."

"I lied."

They walked silently for a while, enjoying the leisurely pace. Earlier that day, they had gone from one church to another, asking priests and administrators for information on the Elect Brothers of St. Peter. By the end of the afternoon, they had covered every major church and church administrative office, including the religion department at the University of Bologna. At Suzanne's request, they had taken an additional room in a hotel on the south side of town, across town from the train station—to use as their local address. The Elect Brothers had people stationed in Bologna; they wouldn't fail to notice someone snooping about asking for them, certainly not two people they had tried to kill only a few nights before. So, all messages left at the hotel on the south side of Bologna would be called for by telephone; payment for the room would arrive by messenger. Suzanne and Vance would not walk inside the hotel again, for fear they'd be followed.

"What'll we do if they don't leave us a message?" Vance asked after a while.

"Well," Suzanne said in a businesslike voice, "that would mean that they decided to watch the hotel and wait for us to appear. If we don't get a message, then we either have to identify the people they have staked out or one of us has to walk into the hotel, and draw them out."

"Not a fun alternative," Vance remarked.

"Nope. No fun at all. Let's hope we don't have to walk that route."

All his instincts told Vance to hide Suzanne away somewhere, to protect her. What kept shocking him was the realization that it was she, not he, who was the professional and that very likely she would be able to survive all this alone better than he would. He didn't know what to make of his confusion.

"Want to try our second-best shot now?" Suzanne asked, pulling Vance's thoughts back to their mission.

"Now?" he asked, confused. "Tonight? But I thought we decided—"

"We did. But I thought that if we really stirred things up as hot and heavy as we could, maybe the Brothers might react faster."

"I don't know," Vance said. "I suppose we could. I was thinking more about—"

"Something recreational?" She looked coyly up at his face, seeing the answer in his eyes. He grinned at her. What a little boy, Suzanne thought. How had he ever managed to keep the truth from leaping from his eyes when he'd played blackjack? She shook her head and returned his smile. "Later," she said, stopping to plant a kiss on his cheek.

Nearby, a waiter serving espresso to an old man at a sidewalk table watched them, smiling. The old man also smiled; no one loves lovers more than Italians.

"That can wait until later," she whispered to Vance when they had resumed their walk. If there is a later, she thought suddenly. Stepping off the curb, she led Vance across the Via Ugo Bassi toward a phalanx of taxis idling near the statue of Neptune. The driver of the lead taxi leaped from his conversation with four other drivers, and pulled himself up to his full five feet six inches, beaming at the beautiful woman and her escort. Ten minutes later, he dropped them off on a quiet, middle-class, residential street near the Sports arena.

They're not staying here," Brother Gregory announced bitterly to his aide. "This is just a decoy, probably used for picking up messages."

He should have expected this, Gregory told himself. Erikson and the woman had been a bit too open and much too industrious in their visits to church organizations. Clearly their actions had been meant as a message to the Elect Brothers of St. Peter, a challenge to him, as head of that order. By six o'clock, Gregory had received three telephone calls from priests who had been alerted by the Brothers to look for Erikson. Erikson had left the same hotel telephone number with them all.

Angrily, Brother Gregory strode to the window and, throwing wide the curtains, glared down at the street. Are you down there, Vance Erikson? How is it that you have managed to accomplish so much? Gregory struggled with his grudging admiration for the talented amateur.

Below his window, a battered Fiat with no muffler popped and banged its way along the street, but Brother Gregory barely heard it. Vance Erikson had been there in St. Peter's Square; a snapshot taken by a tourist, and subsequently run in the newspapers, showed him leaping for the Iranian. How, in the midst of tens of thousands of people who crowded the square that afternoon, had Erikson managed to find him? It was a shame, Gregory thought, shaking his head slowly, that they would have to kill the American. Although it would certainly be a waste, they just couldn't afford to have him alive. You've had your chance, my son, Gregory thought as he turned from the window to face the two tall, solidly built men who stood respectfully silent in the middle of the room. It was like destroying a work of art, killing the quick facile mind of this American, but then God presents us with challenges that must be met.

"All right." The men snapped to attention. They were both in their mid-twenties with the lean muscularity that comes only with harsh disciplined physical training. "I want a man in here, and enough men to watch the entrances. Not that it will do any good, for I doubt Vance Erikson will ever return here.

"Vincent." Brother Gregory turned to the taller of the

two men. He was a bit over six feet tall, dressed in casual clothes, and the generous muscles of his chest and arms strained at the knit of his shirt.

"Yes, sir."

"Vincent, I want you to contact this man at the office of the mayor." Gregory handed the tall man a piece of foolscap on which he had hastily scrawled a name. "This man works for the mayor, but he also owes us favors. Like the rest of the Bologna government, he is a member of the Communist Party. For our purposes, you are to tell him that Vance Erikson is an American CIA agent, an *agent provocateur* here to meet with fascist elements in an attempt to destabilize the Communist government here. Ask him to have the police circulate his photograph at all the hotels and pensiones in Bologna, but tell him they must do it quietly. Use the photograph from the cover of *Il Giorno*. Make sure this man understands that no alarm must be raised."

"In all respect, Father Gregory," the monk called Vincent ventured hesitantly. "But could we not just ask the innkeepers for a list of passport numbers and compare them with this man's?"

"Good thinking, Vincent," Gregory said graciously. The monk was visibly relieved. Brother Gregory could be unpredictable; he might have interpreted such advice as reflecting on his judgment. "While it's true that a passport is required to register at a hotel, I am taking no chance that our resourceful adversary managed to obtain another passport under a false name."

"The Holy Father is wise," Vincent said sincerely. "Please forgive me for being presumptuous."

"You are forgiven, my son. Now go."

Without a further word, the man whirled on his heel and left the room, his back ramrod-straight and his walk distinctly military. He had been sent by the monastery to receive military training in the Italian army and, like his companion, had progressed to an elite commando unit before going AWOL and returning to the monastery.

"You, Peter, will remain with me. We shall return to our quarters and wait for word on the whereabouts of our elusive prey. Then"—Brother Gregory smiled beatifically—"our work truly begins."

Gregory took a few moments to write a note on the hotel's stationery and then carefully folded it and sealed it in an envelope on which he inscribed Vance Erikson's name. On the way out he would leave it at the front desk. In a second envelope, he placed 250 euros and after sealing it wrote the hotel's assistant manager's name on the front. It had been an expensive key to purchase. But, he reflected, it would ultimately be even more costly for Vance Erikson.

Night had fallen completely by the time Vance and Suzanne had alighted from the cab, but the thinnest fingernail of a moon shed just enough light to forestall the long spaces of gloom between streetlights. The buckled, uneven concrete sidewalk snaked its way uphill along a narrow, uneven asphalt street. The sounds of children at play mixed with the lower, more subdued notes of older, mostly male voices speaking rapid-fire Italian as they stood about in huddles that spilled off the sidewalk and into the nearly trafficless street. Suzanne and Vance greeted the neighbors in Italian as they passed, with Vance taking the lead, since his Italian was better.

While the men talked endlessly outside, the women could be heard in kitchens, laughing, rattling pans, and conjuring up aromas that drifted from yellow-lit open windows into the street.

About halfway up the street on the left, they came to a modest three-story house. Like most of the other middle-class dwellings on the street, it had a head-high fence around its two gates—one for the driveway and another for people—and a small patch of front lawn with flowers. But unlike the other houses on the street, no lights shone warmly from the windows here, no sounds of gaiety, no aromas of impending supper wafted through its closed kitchen windows.

"He's been gone for several days now," a kindly voice said from behind them. Vance and Suzanne turned, startled, but saw no one. Then they looked down, and in the dim light left by a distant streetlight, they found a short man with a white shirt, dark trousers held up by suspenders, a fringe of gray hair crowning a pate that shined in the dark, and an infectious smile that beamed out from among the vast river system of wrinkles that decorated his face.

"I'm sorry," the old man said. "I didn't mean to startle you."

"That's all right," Vance said. "We're two of his students and we were thinking of dropping in on the professor."

"Yes," the old man said, and then peered closely at Vance's face. "You look familiar, young man. Do you live nearby? I seem to remember your face."

"No, I—"

"It's the tricks of an old mind," the man said. "Professor Tosi frequently leaves. Gives his housekeeper a vacation and then shows up a few weeks later. He is a brilliant man, Tosi," he added proudly. "A real fixture in the neighborhood. We're going to miss him."

"I don't understand," Vance said. "I thought you said he was away often."

"Yes, yes, I said that, didn't I? Well, I don't mean to mislead you. I mean I wasn't trying to mislead you, for he did leave just as always, but"—the old man lowered his voice and leaned toward Vance conspiratorially—"his housekeeper, Angela, she talks to me. You see, since I retired, I sit a lot on my porch over there"—he pointed across the street—"or I walk a lot. And a lot I walk to see Angela. She is quite a sight. She's—" He glanced quickly at Suzanne, and then grabbed Vance by the arm and dragged him a few paces away. "She's quite well built, young, nice legs, and big—" He stretched his hands out from his chest. The old man grinned, one man to another. Vance couldn't help laughing along with him.

"But Angela tells me only two days ago that she received a letter from the professor containing six months' salary— six months, can you imagine?—and informing her that he will no longer require her services. I can imagine what services he might require." The old man grinned, another joke between men.

"I see, then—"

"No, no, that's not all," the old man continued. "Every day since the professor left, a priest comes to the house. He has a key to the gate, and to the house. He walks through the gate, picks up the mail, and leaves. Then yesterday, a truck comes, a truck with license plates from north of Milan somewhere, and removes boxes. No furniture, just boxes."

Tosi's files probably, Vance thought. "When does the priest come?" Vance asked.

"All times. Day, night. But he's a mean priest; a man of the devil, if you ask me." The old man crossed himself. "He never pauses to talk with me and once when I walked over to him to say hello, he *cursed* at me!" The man's voice dripped with indignation.

So Tosi's household had been taken over by the Brothers, Vance thought, his mind racing. What else should he expect?

He tried to piece it all together, while he pretended to listen to the old man, who was talking rapidly on, gossiping about his neighbors like a washerwoman. The house wasn't watched, but a priest appeared every day to pick up the mail. If they could follow the priest, they'd find their way back to the Brothers' organization. And if they did that—Vance's heart leaped with anticipation—then they might have a chance at snatching the Da Vinci papers. With the papers, Vance felt sure be could negotiate Kingsbury's release. Either that, or he would destroy the documents: rare papers drawn by the hand of a man Vance had spent a lifetime studying, revering.

They'd need a car, but without a driver's license, no one would rent them one. Steal another one, Vance my boy, he told himself. You're already dug in up to your eyebrows.

And they couldn't loiter on the sidewalk, or sit watching from the car: Strangers parked on the narrow street would attract more than just the attentions of a little old retired grandfather. The quiet residential street with its unbroken facade of houses, fences, and gates offered no concealment. There was only one solution: They'd have to break into the house and wait for the priest. Vance Erikson, criminal par excellence: murderer, thief, burglar. A great resumé. Suzanne made her way to Vance's side, getting a reluctant nod of acceptance from the old man.

"That man, the priest I was telling you about before. I said that I was so angry at this man that I wrote down his license number. Pietro's son: Pietro is the baker who lives next door to me, his son Renato is a policeman and I asked him, as a favor to an old man—you see I have known Renato since he was a bambino—I asked Renato to do a favor for an old man and I explained about the priest and that I wanted to write a letter to protest the man's demeanor, so I asked Renato—did I tell you I've known him since he was a . . . but of course I did." The old man chuckled. Vance fought back a rising flood of impatience and smiled understandingly, nodding.

"Oh, dear, where was I?" The man looked about him in confusion.

"Renato?" Suzanne prompted kindly.

"Yes, thank you. You are a very beautiful woman," he said and smiled broadly at Suzanne. "Yes, Renato did a favor for this old man and checked the files for the license number of the priest's car, and just yesterday gave me the address. And I wrote the letter to the rector, oh, yes, I did! That priest, whoever he is, is in for it now."

"The rector?" Vance said, trying not to sound too interested.

"Yes. The rector at the Santuario di San Luca. He will be a most angry man, I tell you now, to have one of his priests acting so with devoted parishioners. And to think the Santuario is but a couple of miles from here. Why, if I weren't such an old man, I'd walk up there and tell the rector face-to-face. Why, I—"

"Signore," Vance interrupted as politely as he could. "It has been a great pleasure talking to you. More pleasure than you could ever know." The old man beamed at the compliment. "But we really must be going. We had intended to spend only a few minutes with the professor, and we have overstayed even that time. We—"

"Don't worry," the old man once again took Vance by the arm and said to him in a hushed voice, "If I were escorting a beautiful woman like her, I too would not waste my time listening to an old man like me either." He winked.

"I didn't mean—" Vance tried to protest.

The old man held up his hand. "Of course you did. But it's all tight. I already appreciate the time you've allowed me to bend your ear. Go with God, young man." With that, he offered another wink and turned away. They stared after his back as he disappeared through a gate across the street.

Suzanne walked over to Vance's side. "It seems our luck has picked up," she said, slipping an arm around his waist.

He pulled her close. "And about time, too."

"Yeah," she said quietly. "About time."

Chapter 20

The mayor's assistant was not happy about being called upon during his evening meal. But the prospect of thwarting a fascist plot sent his blood surging and so it was that he went with the casually dressed stranger to the main Bologna police station. The mayor's assistant entered the police station alone, spoke to the assistant chief who was on duty that night, and issued the orders. The muscular stranger then drove the mayor's assistant home to finish his dinner. At the midnight shift change, duplicate pictures of Vance Erikson were handed to every officer on duty.

Checking hotels for fugitives, criminals, and missing persons was a routine task. But this night, the officers were more zealous in their tasks than usual. They all wanted to be the policeman who located this prominent murderer.

＊　＊　＊

He came to her gently through a dream, delicately brushing away the bloom of soft sleep. She felt his lips on her cheeks, her neck, her breasts. Suzanne stirred, wanting to hang on to the weightless pleasure of sleep, yet yearning for what the kisses promised. She rolled over on her side, and without opening her eyes, found his lips. Her tongue found his and she murmured a moan of pleasure as Vance took her in his arms.

When his lips left hers and began lightly caressing the soft sensitive skin behind her ears, Suzanne opened her eyes. The room was still dark.

"What are you doing?" she asked with mock seriousness. "It's the middle of the night."

"No, it's not," Vance said, interrupting his tongue's exploration of her earlobe. "It's just after six; I looked. Half the morning's already gone."

"Uhmmm," she replied as she pressed her breasts against his warm, hard-muscled chest and rolled over on top of him. "Then let's don't waste the day." She slid down to kiss his neck and rolled her tongue down the middle of his washboard stomach. He groaned with pleasure as she moved lower.

Enrico Carducci pulled the blue and white Alfa squad car to the curb across the street from the train station and looked at his watch. It was already 6:11. He yawned. His partner was slumped against the window snoring like a broken muffler dragging over a gravel road.

Let him be, Carducci thought, stifling another yawn. He straightened his blue policeman's hat on his head and opened the door. All night they had been stopping, showing a copy of a newspaper photograph to the night managers of every hotel in their precinct of Bologna. No luck, none at all. The photo, duplicated on cheap thin paper, was getting smudged and cracked by now, but the picture of the man they sought was still clear. Carducci got out of the Alfa, closed the door gently so as not to awaken his partner, adjusted his gun in its white leather case, and walked into the first hotel. There were three commercial hotels here across the train station. Perhaps the killer was here, Carducci thought optimistically as he pushed through the glass door.

What am I doing with this man? Suzanne Storm asked herself as she lounged on the bed, her eyes half closed with the afterglow of their lovemaking. She watched Vance standing by the dresser toweling his hair dry. A small perlexed frown passed over her face while she wondered how she could ever have overlooked his good qualities. No other man she'd been involved with had ever taken her so seriously, she realized; really taken her seriously as anything other than a . . . well, as a woman.

Of course, some of her employers had; she was an excellent writer and a more than competent intelligence agent until . . . Beirut. But none of the men she had dated or taken as a lover had ever taken her seriously.

Beirut had been a nightmare. She had gone in as a journalist for a French news picture magazine and been set up for ambush what her superiors at the CIA told her was a vicious branch of the Hezbollah. When it was all over, she had walked stunned among the maimed and mutilated bodies of children—teenagers. They carried Kalishnikov automatic rifles given to them by the Syrians and Iranians, and their fingers on those triggers killed as surely as did adults. It was true that these child soldiers had been guilty of heinous acts against helpless civilians, women, children, and teenagers like themselves. But when Suzanne wandered among the lifeless fragments, looking at the smooth young faces, she cried and wondered what sort of world sends its children to be killed. She grew angry at parents who would send their offspring out to do their fighting for them; and in sadness she turned in her resignation as soon as she returned to Paris.

The retreat into the rarified world of art, as a writer for *Haute Culture,* had not satisfied her; neither had a steady string of forgettable lovers.

But now, she smiled lazily, watching Vance towel off his back, she felt like someone; she felt free. It was more than the adrenaline of danger that can make people who survive together think they're in love. No, she decided, it was the way he looked at things, the way he did things rather than *what* he did. She liked Vance's disregard for outside authority. Maybe, if she was lucky, some of it would rub off on her.

The night managers at all three commercial hotels across from the train station failed to recognize the photograph of Vance Erikson.

"Of course, he might have checked in during the day," they all explained. At Carducci's request, they'd also checked Erikson's passport number—to no avail. Carducci, mindful of his superior's admonition that the man might be traveling under an illegal passport, put more stock in the photo. He returned to his partner and gently roused him.

"You take the car back to headquarters," Carducci told his groggy car mate. "I'm going to wait around until the day managers get here at seven. I'll take the bus home." Irritated at having been awakened from an erotic dream, his partner sullenly agreed; the car moved jerkily away from the curb and down the street.

It was not that Carducci really expected to find their man here, but he lived only ten minutes away by a bus he could catch right in front of the hotels. Besides, he disliked the sergeant at the station who was such an asshole at the mustering out. He'd just as soon miss that, especially when he could doze for a few moments in one of the comfortable chairs in the lobby. He settled down in a soft chair by the front doors of the Milan Excelsior, and at a quarter of seven, dropped off to fitful dreams.

What a great hotel this was, Vance thought as he padded out of the marble-floored bathroom and reached down to open the small refrigerator next to the television in the bedroom.

"Orange juice?" he asked Suzanne, who was sitting up in bed watching television.

"Sure," she agreed. "A little exercise always makes me thirsty. Listen, Vance, it's after seven and we've got—" She broke off abruptly as a news item concerning the Pope's condition played across the television screen.

The Pope was doing well. The assassin's bullets had damaged his intestines, and he had been given a temporary colostomy to give the wounds time to heal. The announcer said the Pope was conscious, and had said his prayers, begging forgiveness for the assassin.

The assassin, an Iranian named Hashemi Rafiqdoost,

had been taken into custody by Rome police and was being held for trial. Rafiqdoost, said the announcer with evident disgust, was wanted in Germany for murder; had apparently been a suspect in the shootings of Iranian dissidents there and was suspected of being well financed by Hezbollah although the man himself professed to be working alone.

The television screen showed the man being transferred from a paddy wagon to the Rome city jail. His eyes were mesmerizing, wild. "I am the sword of Allah!" he shrieked maniacally in Italian, then in English and Farsi. "Allah Akbar! I have killed the Pope!"

Vance sat on the edge of the bed next to Suzanne and sipped his orange juice absently as he watched the news. The film clip of Rafiqdoost was followed by a recently released snapshot of the assassin and the Pope taken from somewhere behind the Pope right before the shooting. The snapshot showed Rafiqdoost with his gun raised. Vance looked at the picture and suddenly almost lost his grip on his glass: At the left side of the picture, clearly identifiable, was his own face, contorted with effort as he lunged to prevent Rafiqdoost from firing.

"Oh, my God!" Suzanne said slowly. "Oh, my God. Vance."

The name of the tourist who had taken the photograph was given. White circles superimposed on the screen highlighted first the gun, raised for firing; then Rafiqdoost; and finally came to rest like a noose around Vance's head.

"Authorities have been unable to contact this man," the announcer said. "But they believe he is the same one wanted in connection with several recent terrorist attacks in Milan and the countryside around Lake Como. Authorities also said they were unsure if the man was trying to assist the gunman or attempting to prevent him from shooting the Pope."

The hyperactive news quickly shifted its limited attention span onto other stories, international outrage over the shooting, calls for the death penalty, and on and on. But Vance heard none of it. I'm sinking deeper and deeper and deeper, he thought darkly. His beloved Italy had turned to quicksand beneath his feet.

What! Uh, yes. Good morning!" Bologna police officer Enrico Carducci leaped to his feet. The day manager had arrived. It was six minutes after seven. It took Carducci a few moments to clear his head, and then he produced the picture of Vance Erikson.

The day manager stared at the photo, looked up at the ceiling, licked his lower lip thoughtfully, mumbled a sort of pensive murmur, and said, "Yes, I remember the man."

Carducci's spirits leaped. This could be the promotion that got him off nights. He had found their man and he'd done it by working above and beyond the call of duty. He imagined what his mother would say.

"Well," the day manager continued. "I actually remember the woman he was with—a beautiful woman, beautiful. I probably wouldn't have remembered the man had it not been for the exceptional woman who accompanied him. They registered as . . ." He squinted as he tried to recall the name, and then headed toward the front desk. Carducci followed him, his feet barely touching the lobby's polished marble floor.

While the day manager searched for the correct name

on the register ("We had only twelve people register yesterday," he said, turning the register pages), Carducci struggled to remember what they had been taught at the police academy. He had to struggle, not because he was a poor student—indeed, he had graduated second in his class—but because he could hardly stifle the images of himself kicking in the door to the room and arresting the man singlehandedly. He could imagine the headlines, maybe even a picture.

But he also remembered the training and he remembered his sergeant who would make sure, after all of the headlines and the public approval had passed, that Carducci would be busted and made an example for disregarding procedure. Reluctantly, Carducci decided to call headquarters and ask for assistance. The manager let Carducci use the telephone while he finished searching the registry.

"Damn!" Vance said. "Why does everything have to happen all at once?" He was fully dressed now in Levi's and a light blue polo shirt. He paced back and forth in the room while Suzanne finished dressing, also in jeans but with a blue chambray work shirt turned up at the sleeves.

"Our big advantage is that nobody knows we're here," Vance thought aloud as he walked back and forth. "Nobody except the Brothers, and we'll deal with them separately."

"Unless they have an agreement with the police here like they did in Milan and Como," Suzanne interdicted.

Vance stopped short. "Well, I'm gambling on Bologna being too far away from the monastery. I can't imagine them having that much influence down here. But we've got to be wary of people spotting us . . . me. That means keeping out of sight as much as possible until tonight when we visit the Santuario di San Luca."

They could steal a car and drive into the countryside; the roads up in the hills got little traffic. They would buy some bread, cheese, wine, and mineral water and have a picnic. Yes, a picnic. Only . . . a car would be hard to conceal. A motorcycle, then. He missed his powerful classic bike, which rested securely in its allotted space underneath the ConPacCo Building in Santa Monica. How far away that life seemed now.

Ten minutes later, they shut the door behind them and walked toward the elevator. They had not heard the approaching motorcade of police squad cars, motorcycles, and vans, because the police had come silently, using only their flashing lights.

At the end of the hall, Vance punched the call button for the elevator.

"Um, just a thought," Suzanne said.

"Yeah?"

"Suppose the night manager recognizes us?"

Vance shook his head. "I doubt it. Those guys don't really pay attention to customers in hotels this size. All they want to know is if we're going to pay our bill, and we left money in advance to keep him from worrying."

"Still . . ." Suzanne worried.

The elevator arrived; the door slid open.

Nervously playing with the holster flap that covered his revolver, Enrico fretted as he paced back and forth in the lobby. He had his suspects' room number. But his backup had not arrived. What was taking them so long? The station was just off the Piazza Maggiore, a straight shot from the Via dell'Indipendenza. It didn't matter to his pounding heart that less than ten minutes had passed since the day manager retrieved the proper name. Carducci watched the elevator indicator swing to the third floor and stop. Maybe that would be him, he fantasized. *Then they'd walk right into my hands and I would get credit for capturing them singlehandedly.*

All right," Vance said, letting the elevator doors close without getting on. "You could be right."

"Well, it won't hurt anything," Suzanne said. "At the least, we'll get a bit of exercise."

Vance followed her to the enclosed stairway at the opposite end of the hallway. The echoes of their unhurried footsteps followed them down five flights of concrete steps to the hotel's basement. At the bottom, they walked halfway down a short corridor swarming with housekeeping staff, and climbed to ground level into the littered lot Vance had seen from the room.

They walked across the dusty lot, picking a path through the haphazardly parked cars and motor scooters. The lot was bounded by buildings on three sides, and by a tall wooden fence on the fourth. As they approached the gate, the sounds of racing engines and screeching tires reached their ears.

The engine sounds grew louder. As Vance and Suzanne reached the gate, a police van, its blue light winking desperately, charged through the gate and raised a smokescreen of fine dust. Two squad cars and a motorcycle plunged into the dust cloud after the van, filling the lot with dust.

"Down!" Vance shouted and pulled Suzanne down

with him behind a rumpled red Fiat, its fenders already turning to rust.

Vance peered around the rear of the car and watched as the van disgorged a squad of men who ran into the building followed by the motorcyclist and those in the squad cars.

"This doesn't look like a practice exercise," Vance said fearfully. "Let's get out of here." They stood up and started for the gate when a third squad car roared through and slammed on its brakes blocking their exit.

"Halt!" said one of the policemen as he drew his sidearm. "You're under arrest!"

"Not if I can help it," Vance said as he reversed his course and headed back among the jumble of parked cars pushing Suzanne before him.

Behind them a shot exploded; the windshield on the red Fiat exploded next to them. The squad car's engine revved; they could hear its rear wheels throwing gravel as it sped forward. More shots echoed through the fine Italian morning.

"Keep your head down!" Vance shouted.

A burst of automatic weapons fire stitched the earth in front of them as Vance grabbed Suzanne and pulled her back. The squad car stopped about halfway between the gate and the hotel's rear entrance. There were excited shouts as the doors opened and footsteps pounded the earth.

"Do you still have Tony's gun?" Vance asked. He looked down to find that Suzanne already had it out. "Cover me," he told her. "I'm going after the cop's bike."

Vance sprinted across the opening between two cars and as the policemen with the machine gun stopped to fire at him, Suzanne squeezed off a shot that tore up the dirt at his feet, sending him diving for cover. She quickly scrambled to the shelter of another car, one closer to the gate, as a hail of bullets descended on her former position.

Vance leaped from the cover of one car to the next as Suzanne drew the bulk of the police fire.

One of the three remaining men from the squad car ran to drag his fallen comrade to safety while the other two concentrated on Suzanne, trying to keep her pinned down with their sidearms.

Vance reached the motorcycle—a powerful Moto Guzzi—and noted with satisfaction that the key was still in the ignition. He leaped on the bike and turned the key. Behind him, the policemen clattered up the steps from the basement of the hotel, shouting excitedly. The engine caught and leaped forward as Vance twisted the throttle.

Suzanne had worked her way to the gate, pursued by two groups of police. She heard the roar of the motorcycle and fired one more shot as she ran for the gate.

The bike was screaming in second gear when Vance headed for the exit and began to slow so he could pick up Suzanne. The men who had been chasing Suzanne whirled and brought their guns to bear. One man followed Vance, leading the bike like a hunter draws a head on a fleeing deer. The other man braced his elbows on the top of the red Fiat and aimed carefully at Suzanne. Vance watched as the windshield of the bike turned suddenly into a spiderweb of cracks when the slug exploded through it. Amazed, he watched Suzanne leap behind the safety of the wooden wall just as another shot rang out. Behind him he heard other gunshots.

Weaving an erratic course to foil the aim of the men behind him, Vance brought the bike to a rolling halt. Even before the bike had come to a complete stop, Suzanne leaped behind him onto the passenger seat. The rear wheel spun on the dirt, then squealed as it finally caught pavement. Shots sounded behind them but the slugs splattered blindly against the stone pavement.

They sped west on the Via Boldrini. The bike careened through the crowds of pedestrians strolling through the gardens by the Porta Galliera, and then headed south along the Via dell'Indipendenza. The blinding acceleration of the bike's engine had let them quickly outdistance the squad cars.

But all over Bologna, they knew, calls would be going out by radio; police would descend with a vengeance on the stolen motorbike. When you hurt one of their own, don't expect mercy from the police.

Vance accelerated through the light morning traffic. He was splitting the white line in the middle of the street when blue flashing lights appeared ahead. Behind him, the first car in the caravan from the hotel had turned the corner.

If you can't beat 'em, join 'em, Vance thought as he freed one hand to fumble with the array of switches on the bike's compact dashboard. First the emergency lights started to flash on the bike and then its siren. Left and right cars and trucks pulled to the side of the avenue until at last it was just the motorcycle and its pursuers, racing headlong with reinforcements from the police station.

Vance could almost see the expressions on the faces of the two men in the lead squad car as it hurtled toward them when at the last moment he whipped the bike left across its path and diagonally into the Piazza dell'Otto Agosto.

Suzanne watched the onrushing vehicles with rising terror, gripping Vance's waist with one hand and clinging to her purse, which contained Tony's pistol and all their money.

The two onrushing columns of police cars nearly collided with each other as they both frantically attempted to enter the Piazza dell'Otto Agosto at the same time.

Vance headed for the winding narrow streets of the old town; the motorcycle had speed, but it also had maneuverability, and he knew he'd have to put every advantage they had to work for them.

The sunlight had barely climbed high enough to illuminate the top story of the houses along the Via Venturini as the bike plunged from the brightly lit piazza into the deep shadows of morning. While the upper stories glowed red from their paint and from the warm rays of the morning sun, the bike hurtled through the chill gray shadows hurling an angry bellowing roar at the walls of an alleyway barely wide enough for a single Fiat and a pedestrian to pass side by side.

The bike shot across the Via Righi and back into the shadows of the alleys. At the intersection with the Via Marsala, he turned left, and caught a glimpse of a squad car coming from the right. He gunned the bike. Less than a block away, another squad car emerged. He turned right again and found himself in a winding alley that threaded its way south. He recalled walking this alley several years ago, and a cold hand clutched his gut as he remembered there was no outlet for more than a quarter of a mile. If there was a cop at the other end, it was all over.

With the Moto Guzzi's tires barely gripping the rough pavement through the torturous turns, Vance coaxed the bike to the end. They were in a small piazza opening onto the Via Zamboni. He wheeled the bike to the left, toward the university, and gave the throttle a brutal twist as another police car burst around the corner from the direction of the police station.

It was a faster car, this Alfa, and despite the Moto Guzzi's acceleration, the Alfa had a running start on them. Vance weaved as one of the policemen in the car began to shoot at them. The bike and its two terrified passengers screamed past the old buildings and the endless porticoes, past the Piazza Verdi where the wider two-way street turned to one way, against them. The Alfa pulled closer and Vance saw one slug smash into the wall just in front of his head.

The narrow slot of the one-way street was bounded, like many Bolognese streets, by a long porticoed walk on one side, and the stone wall of a building on the other. It looked clear, but just as Vance gave the bike more throttle, a Volkswagen bus pulled out from the Via del Gusto and neatly plugged the gap.

Suzanne closed her eyes and hung on to Vance. Vance wanted to close his eyes as he realized there was no space to stop. He banked the bike left, nearly lost it as it leaped a shallow curb, and then steered it through two upright steep posts designed to keep vehicles out of the pedestrian porticoes. The bike plunged into the shadows of the pedestrian walk. The columns wooshed by.

Behind them they heard the frantic horns and screeches of imminent collision and then the sounds of tinkling glass behind them as the police car collided with the

Volkswagen. Vance slowed the bike to bring it once again to the street. They left the sounds of angry voices and the wails of sirens behind them as they sped to the end of Via Zamboni and out through the Porta San Donato heading for open country.

They reached the A14 Autostrada without further pursuit. Breathing a bit easier, Vance flicked off the lights and siren, and opened up the throttle, eating up the superhighway as they headed west. At the airport, Vance swung south on the Autostrada, then took the first exit he could find.

They had come 180 degrees around the city and headed up into the hills to the southwest.

The road twisted higher and higher. Above and below them on the steep slopes, vineyards ran their orderly ways around the hills. There was first one type of farm and then another. Cattle, vegetables, but mostly fields filled with the filigreed white flowers of Queen Anne's lace. Then they rounded a switchback and she saw it: a massive round brick building with a weathered green onion-shaped dome and a host of supporting spikes and towers. It squatted on the summit of the tallest hill around and looked, for all guesses, like an alien spaceship reconnoitering the landscape.

Vance pulled the bike over to the side.

"What in the world is that?" she asked breathlessly.

"Santuario di San Luca," he said, then motioned to Suzanne to dismount. "Somewhere inside there—or maybe down the hill from it in the support buildings—I'm betting we'll find the Elect Brothers of St. Peter and, with any luck at all, the Da Vinci drawings." He turned the ignition off. "It's either our salvation or . . ."

"It'll be our salvation," Suzanne said as she got off and helped him wheel the bike off the road and conceal it in a stand of locust trees and underbrush. Then they moved a half mile down the road and hunkered down in the brush to wait for night.

Down in Bologna, Enrico Carducci was still trying to explain to the sergeant why he had commandeered a Volkswagen bus to join in the chase rather than remain at the hotel without transportation. In his own defense, Carducci kept insisting, "It was you, Sergeant, who was traveling the wrong way down a one-way street, not I."

Chapter 21

From across the valley, the Santuario di San Luca looked almost like a fantasy toy for children. But as they approached it in the gathering darkness, its imposing bulk silhouetted against the sky grew to awesome proportions. The Santuario was famous for drawing tourists in the daytime, and for its two-and-a-half-mile-long portico stretching from Bologna's southwest city gate, the Porta Saragozza, up the steep slope of the Monte Della Guardia to the Santuario.

Along the top one-third of the porticoed walk, one wall was solid and punctuated periodically with paintings, sculpture, and anonymous doors. The doors, some with numbers, some without, led to offices and residences of the church officials responsible for or connected with the Santuario. The address the loquacious little old man had given them during their chat in front of Tosi's home corresponded to one of these anonymous doors with a number.

Vance had been driving slowly and steadily in order to minimize the noise of the bike's powerful engine. At the top of a demi-summit, he decided to cut the engine entirely and coast the rest of the way.

After the endless rumble of the engine, the sudden night silence was audible, broken by the humming of the tires on the pavement and the whine of lubricated bearings turning faster and faster as the bike gathered speed. Then, before the bike completely stopped on the uphill slope, Vance and Suzanne leaped off, pulled it over to the side, and left it there.

They walked in silence on the pavement, hand-in-hand. Somewhere over the hill a single-engine airplane droned through the night; the muted surf of traffic on the Autostrada rose and fell as the air currents vacillated. Vance stopped and looked at Suzanne, kissed her gently. "No matter what happens," he said, "I love you." He stood there looking into her face in the dark, wondering if it wouldn't be better to just run. But he couldn't. There was Kingsbury, and there were scores to settle for Martini, for Tosi, and for dead people who should be living.

"Come on," she said, sensing his indecision. "Let's get this over with."

They went on, passing a small driveway on the right that led up to the front of the Santuario, and continued on up the hill. They had nearly reached the top when they heard the sounds of a powerful engine and a screech of tires as a car accelerated down the hill on the other side. They ran for the top.

"I see it," Vance said. "You?"

"No. But it sounded familiar . . . like—"

"Like Elliott Kimball's Lamborghini?"

"Well, like a Lamborghini, anyway."

Vance wrinkled his brow. "That's what I was afraid you'd say."

"Of course, Italy has a lot of Lamborghini's," Suzanne offered. "They make them here."

"I know, but how many would you expect to find after dark here?"

She shrugged.

"It squares," Vance said, talking quickly. "Kimball was working for the Bremen Legation. He was their go-between. Damn it! We just missed the transaction. In a few minutes the Legation will have their papers, and I'll have no hope of freeing Kingsbury."

He turned away from her, suddenly awash in hopelessness. Not only had their luck soured, but they had failed at every turn. Never before had Vance felt so empty, so devoid of hope. But loathing can be a powerful stimulant, and the urge to take revenge, no matter how small, grew within him. If Brother Gregory was at the address the little old man had given him . . . Vance's anger grew, and his emotions found a new use for the adrenaline circulating in his system.

"They're going to pay for this," he said decisively. "Give me Tony's pistol."

Suzanne handed it to him. She had been stingy with the ammunition that morning: there were still five shots left in the automatic's magazine.

They rounded the top of the hill and ran along the road outside the porticoes, slowing as they approached the address. There was no window, but a slat of light shone at the base of the door. Waiting in the dark shadows of the road, they strained to catch any sounds of activity, but heard nothing but their own breathing.

Cautiously, first Vance, then Suzanne stepped over the low wall and crossed the portico in three steps. Backs flattened against the wall on either side of the door, again they listened; still the night was silent. Vance sidled to the door, careful not to lean against it, lest it give him away with a rattle. The automatic hung heavy in his right hand; his finger itched to pull the trigger on Brother Gregory.

A faint guttural noise reached his ears from the other side of the door. Vance leaned gently on the door to try to hear better when suddenly it swung gently open.

Quickly he sprang back and pressed himself against the wall again. But no one appeared, and the door was only open a crack. He waited, trying to summon the courage to enter. His eyes met Suzanne's. She smiled. Christ, Vance thought, the woman has nerves like a battleship! Taking a deep breath, Vance kicked the door open and leaped back to safety as the door swung inward and slammed against the wall. He waited. There were still no sounds save for a gagging whimper. Suzanne stuck her hand across the open doorway and pulled it back quickly. It drew no gunfire. She looked at him with raised eyebrows.

He boldly stepped into the doorway, followed close behind by Suzanne. But nothing could have prepared them for the sight that greeted them. It was a slaughter-house. Bodies were strewn about the room like castoff clothes. A bloody trail on the floor tracked the dead men's last movements. Blood ran along the uneven floor, pooling in a far corner. The men had been dead for only minutes. They had all been mutilated and slashed with some sort of blade. Sitting in the middle of the room, gagged and bound to a chair, was Brother Gregory, naked save for his shoes and socks. A jagged scar, like the one Vance had seen on Tosi, ran along the priest's chest.

The only thing Vance could think of was the Manson murders.

"Sweet Jesus," Vance whispered with parched lips when he'd recovered his voice. Suzanne turned aside and vomited. She saw Beirut again and the monstrous vile acts of violence human beings are capable of performing on each other.

Numbly, Vance crammed the pistol in the rear pocket of his jeans and approached Brother Gregory. The air was redolent with death, with the smell of secret places of the human body that should never see daylight. It reminded Vance of Iraq and he supposed he would have thrown up if he hadn't already done it a million times over there.

As Vance approached him, Brother Gregory's gags and whimpers grew steadily more agitated. Fear burned in his eyes, but it wasn't a fear of Vance.

"What . . ." Words came reluctantly from Vance's parched throat. "What happened?"

Vance stopped in front of the dying man and leaned over to untie the rag that bound Gregory's mouth. Behind him, Suzanne coughed and sniffled.

"Kimball," Brother Gregory gasped when Vance had removed the gag. "He did this. He did all of this, the bastard!" Brother Gregory bowed his head and grimaced with pain.

"He . . . he came here, and took the . . ."

The priest grimaced again.

"The papers?"

"Yes. Those too, but he took the antidote!" The words came out in a vicious hiss; then the man was racked with a convulsion.

A curious mélange of pity and exultation filled Vance. He had no further desire for revenge against this helpless, naked man. Yet there had to be justice somewhere in the universe for a man to be so appropriately dying from the devices he had used to enslave others.

"Use that gun," Brother Gregory said. "Please." Then Vance understood the fear he had seen in the priest's eyes: it was a fear of the pain and horrible death the poison produced. The evil inside Vance, that evil that lives in every heart, flared for an instant as Vance imagined himself turning away and letting the poison take its toll.

Suzanne watched with increasing detachment, her mind trying to cope with the hideous play that was entering its final moments before her eyes. She leaned against the doorjamb for support. She wanted something to do; she wouldn't be sick any more then.

"You have every reason to kill me," Brother Gregory pleaded pitifully as pain wracked his body in increasingly frequent waves. "You must hate me . . . you must, you must!" Tears began to well up in the man's eyes. "Please, please for the love of God," he screamed, "pull the trigger!"

"Maybe," Vance said. "I'll make you a deal."

"What do you want? I have nothing to give you. I am a *dead* man and all I want is to die quickly!"

"Yes," Vance said flatly, "I'll bet you do. I suppose you've watched some of your victims die slowly, haven't you?" Gregory managed to nod his assent before another tremor seized him.

"I'll do as you say if you'll tell me why Kimball did all this."

Gregory gave him a grateful look. "Gladly, gladly," he said.

"I thought you had a deal with the Bremen Legation. You were to share power. Why did Kimball kill you? Was there a double-cross?"

"No . . . No, that's not it at all," Gregory began. "Kimball found out that he was to be killed . . . that his failure to stop you had been the final straw."

"So, knowing where the papers were to be kept, he decided to preempt the Legation and *steal* them himself," Vance guessed.

Gregory nodded.

"But why did he . . ." Vance struggled for the appropriate words. "Why didn't he just steal them and leave. Was all this"—he waved his hand around the carnage—"necessary?"

"He's an evil man," Brother Gregory said, bowing his head. "He has taken every opportunity to belittle the Church, to ridicule our religion." Indignation gave Gregory's voice strength. "He wanted us to suffer; he taunted me as he killed my brothers; he humiliated me and through us our Lord and . . ."

Sanctimonious to the end, Vance thought as the priest finished his diatribe. Aloud he asked, "So he uses the papers to negotiate his way back to the Legation?"

"No! That's just it," Gregory hissed, his breath coming in short pants. "After he had killed my brothers, after he had humiliated me, he bragged to me . . . he knew I was a dead man. He bragged and taunted me about taking the documents to the Russians. 'That will ruin your little plans, won't it?' he said as he strutted back and forth in front of me." Unconsciously, Vance found himself staring down at Kimball's bloody footprints that colored a path on the floor. He did not even notice the reddish streaks that had smeared on his own white tennis shoes.

"He told me, 'The Russians have the stomach to stand up to your kind,'" the priest continued. "He is a proud, vain man and he told me how much more the Russians would appreciate him and how much better they would treat him than the Bremen Legation. He knew . . . he *knew* how much it meant to me to finally restore the sanctity of the seat of St. Peter. He *knew,* and he's made sure that in my dying moments that I would realize that my life had been . . . less than worthless." Brother Gregory was racked with sobs, interrupted only by the spasms of pain. Vance untied the man's hands, which lay limply now in his lap.

"When he was bragging, did he say where, when he would give the documents to the Russians?"

Brother Gregory looked up blankly.

"Where would he be going now?" Vance said, louder.

"Pisa," Brother Gregory answered obediently. "He has a place he stays in Pisa. I've visited him there. It's near the tower; he's supposed to meet the Russian there tomorrow morning, two tourists on the tower; an exchange of an envelope. Ahhh-h-h!" A convulsion twisted the priest's body. "Now will you kill me, please kill me now. Please, I beg of you!"

Vance pulled the pistol from his back pocket.

"One more question," Vance said.

"Please."

"What kind of weapon can be made from the Da Vinci papers?"

Gregory seemed to summon his reserves for one last effort of coherence. "The papers alone could not be used to make a weapon," he began. "What the papers contain is a unique way of *looking* at a weapon, a unique concept which will allow scientists to perfect a charged-particle beam weapon."

A charged-particle beam weapon! That was the ultimate death ray. From the sketchy reports published in scientific journals about this ultra-secret weapon, Vance knew it was like a giant atom smasher that accelerated beams of charged particles to near the speed of light, and then beamed them at a target. The target, assaulted by an energy that dwarfed even nuclear blasts, would simply disintegrate, vanish in a cataclysm of pure energy. The weapon left no fallout; it was precise and surgical and acted with the speed of light. It could vaporize a nuclear missile and its warheads before they had a chance to explode, or be used to attack cities and enemy forces. The ultimate, in offensive and defensive weapons, it would relegate nuclear weapons to a niche in museums alongside bows and arrows.

Both the United States and Russia had struggled for years to perfect their weapons. But both countries were also struggling with the same problem: the atmosphere. While the prototype weapons already built were awesome in space, they were incapacitated by the atmosphere. The swiftly traveling particles from the weapon collided with the molecules in the air, and dissipated their energy in gigantic thunderbolts with a limited power and range.

"Leonardo dreamed up the answer to perfecting the weapon in his studies of lightning," Gregory continued. "In a set of drawings, he conceived of using the earth as a giant charged electrode which would pull as well as push the beam of particles. He conceived of a two-staged beam, the first blasting a tunnel through the air, and the second following seconds later. But his real genius was to make the target an electrode. He—" The priest's cry of pain was deep and guttural. Vance feared he would get no more information from him. But what more was there to know? His hand shaking, Vance raised the gun. More than the life of Harrison Kingsbury was at stake now. It was incredible, Vance thought as he walked behind the priest and placed the muzzle of the gun against the base of the man's head. What Leonardo had done for Krupp more than a hundred years ago, he was about to do again for the twenty-first century. And all from a man who considered war a most beastly madness.

What would Leonardo think if he were to walk into this room now? Vance wondered. Would he see what he expected of men? Knee-deep in the blood of their own kind, reduced to animal urgencies, bound to their animal instincts? Or would Leonardo somehow find something that transcended the reality? Was he an artist *because* he could find the transcendent beauty amid the blood and the filth?

Suzanne had turned away and jammed her fingers in her ears. What would you think, Leonardo? Vance thought and then pulled the trigger.

Chapter 22

The red Lamborghini was parked with its wheels up on the sidewalk in a narrow street just off the Piazza Garibaldi, near the Ponte di Mezzo, the middle bridge in the old section of Pisa. The house had been easy to find. They would have found it even if Brother Gregory's instructions hadn't been so detailed.

Slumping in fatigue on the rear seat of the cramped Fiat taxi, Suzanne and Vance stared red-eyed through the steadily dawning morning, watching the Lamborghini and the front door to Elliott Kimball's building. The Fiat rested near a collection of parked cars scattered pell-mell in front of the shuttered arches of a café. The angle of the car gave them a clear view of Kimball's car and front door twenty yards away. Vance looked at his watch: It said 6:11. He thought wistfully of what he and Suzanne had been doing just twenty-four hours previously. But before he could linger on the memory, the torrent of events of that day flooded through his mind.

The killings, the chases, the brutal massacre at the Santuario di San Luca—that was what replayed in his head. They had wrenched off the police motorcycle's lights or obliterated its markings with dirt and ridden it south from Bologna away from Brother Gregory, avoiding all the main highways. They had traveled the hills toward Florence, staying west of that grand old Renaissance city and driving instead through the hill towns of Rioveggio, Vernio, and a dozen other collections of old stone dwellings huddled close to the road with names that appeared on no one's maps.

Shortly before eleven P.M. they had ditched the bike in deep brush outside of Pistoia and walked into town, where they took a bus to Empoli and from there a train to Pisa. At 4:39 A.M. the train finally arrived at the Central Station in Pisa. They roused a slumbering taxi driver at the curb, and negotiated a fare for the day. By 5:30 they had located Kimball's apartment and settled down to wait for his next move. With the dawn, the piazza and the streets that led into it grew busier. Shopkeepers arrived to wash down their sidewalks and take delivery of goods from suppliers. Workers who had gotten off shifts at the textile and glass factories straggled by, on their way home to sleep. With the day came more people to blend with, to hide within from the penetrating gaze of Elliott Kimball. Vance rubbed his face with both hands and then shook his head and blinked. Suzanne had dropped off into a light slumber against his shoulder. He decided to let her sleep for a bit. There was no need for both of them to be bleary-eyed. He looked down at the gently falling cascades of her auburn hair, and enjoyed the scent from her body. He had never loved anyone in the world this much . . . and he had no idea if either of them would live long enough to savor it.

Elliott Kimball had tossed fitfully in his bed all night.

With the dawn he gave it up altogether and sprang out of bed, tingling with anticipation.

Why didn't I think of this before? he wondered as he stretched methodically and then raced through his morning routine of calisthenics, whipping through fifty pushups, twice that many sit-ups, and an analogous number of a dozen other exercises. The pain in his groin was manageable now. The old wooden floor creaked with the vigorous activity.

Sweat dripping from his nude body, Kimball walked to the windows of the room and threw them wide, drinking in the early-morning freshness.

"Why haven't I done this before now?" he asked aloud. Clearly, the Bremen Legation held him in much lower esteem than he deserved. He'd reviewed the events of the past year, picking out one incident after the other that should have told him that his stock was slipping in their eyes.

"Fucking peasants!" he cursed. Merriam Larsen had come to wealth and power not by right or by birth, but by being a suitable manipulator—a modern-day Machiavelli who, while a valuable servant to a prince, did not deserve to rule. A frown passed over the tall blond man's face as he stood gazing at the languid water of the Arno;

he was ashamed to have let Larsen manipulate him into playing their game. His foolish acquiescence in their low-bred machinations had simply pulled him down to their level.

"Pigs!" he nearly shouted.

But then, and here he smiled, he had outwitted them all! *He* had all of the Da Vinci papers: the winning hand. No one else had any cards of value, and they would all have to deal with him, to dance to his tune.

In the hours since eliminating that cross-bearing slug Gregory, Kimball had contemplated a dozen maneuvers, most of them ways to use the Da Vinci papers, and the dossier he had been keeping on the Legation's activities, to regain his standing with the Legation and to force them to recognize his superiority.

But in the end, he decided it was beneath his dignity to deal with the Legation, to allow them a recognition they did not deserve. No, he would destroy them. And the GRU would help him.

Not only did he have the key to the most powerful military technology on the planet, but no one knew the workings of the largest multinational corporations in the world as he did. Kimball was privy to more embarrassing corporate weak spots, their Falstaffian appetite for corruption that made Enron and WorldCom look like Mother Teresa. And no one else in the world had the ammunition, the detailed files and dossiers that Elliott did—dossiers that detailed not only corporate evil, but the systematic corruption of government leaders that spanned the globe.

In the proper hands, these dossiers could unravel the mainstays of global business and government or be used as blackmail to manipulate decisions that governed the lives of billions of people. The Russians would help him. Oh, yes! He smiled broadly. *They* would recognize his worth.

Elliott stood transfixed: It was destiny, he knew it now. From the very first person he'd killed, from his first act of disobedience against society, it had been his destiny. Always he had wanted to break free of the smothering blanket of wealthy anonymity cast over him by his rich and famous father. He had bided his time, and bided it well. Now Elliott Kimball would have his fame; it could not be denied.

This apartment had been his father's, a remnant of the days when the old man had owned a textile business in Pisa. The factory had long been sold, but the apartment remained as a vacation villa. As a boy, Kimball had come here with his father, and had taken a liking to the city of Pisa. The young Elliott Kimball spent hours upon hours trying to figure out how he could shove someone off the Leaning Tower without getting caught.

He'd never had occasion to work that one out completely, but the old emotional bonds brought him back to Pisa frequently, especially when he needed a rest, time to think, or a place to hide.

He turned away from the window and walked to the bathroom, past the tall four-drawer filing cabinet with its fire insulated walls and combination lock. He'd put years into compiling its contents, thousands of pages of ultra-confidential documents, memos, tapes—all gathered from the most secret reaches of the largest corporations in the world—the Bremen Legation. Oh, it was all there, he thought with satisfaction: assassinations, successful and unsuccessful; tax evasion; price fixing; schemes against every major, and most minor, governments of the world;

the poisoning of the environment for the sake of profits, and their endless attempts to destroy free enterprise and capitalism with their oligarchic practices. He turned on the shower and stepped in. Elliott Kimball would be famous, for ever and ever.

A shaft of sunlight made its lazy way from the tops of the ochre-colored buildings and splashed over the rear of the Fiat. In the glare it was hard to see the Lamborghini, and impossible to make out details near the front door of Kimball's building, itself still steeped in early-morning shadow.

Vance rolled the grimy rear window of the taxi down halfway, and blinked as the bright light hit them full in the face.

"I see him!" Suzanne said shortly after seven A.M. Vance snapped his head around and peered through the window. The sunlight had reached the red Lamborghini now, and Vance got a solid glimpse of Kimball as he walked from the shadows of his front door into the wedge of sunlight. He was carrying a black briefcase. The growl of the Lamborghini's engine echoed down the narrow street and filled the morning.

As Kimball pulled cautiously off the curb and made his way down the street toward the Piazza Garibaldi, Vance shook the cabdriver awake. The taxi driver snapped out of his light sleep and cranked the Fiat. Kimball turned right, heading north into a maze of narrow winding streets. The cabdriver pulled the Fiat out into traffic and followed.

A scoundrel, Vance had explained. The man driving the Lamborghini had proposed marriage to Vance's sister, even though he was secretly married to another woman.

The taxi driver was all too eager to help Vance and his other sister protect the honor of their foolish younger sibling. Affairs of the heart move Italians more than any other people in the world, and this man was thrilled to have an opportunity to delve into this affair. Oh, what fun he'd have relating it to his Anna when he got home. Besides, the two strangers had paid him well. And just think, they had come all the way from America to protect their sister.

At the Piazza Donato, Kimball bore off to the left, turning left again at the Piazza Cavalieri toward the Duomo and the Leaning Tower. The Fiat had no trouble keeping up with Kimball's leisurely pace. He was obviously unconcerned with being followed.

The cab pursued Kimball's car right along the Via Santa Maria as it emptied into the Piazza Duomo. Kimball paused for a moment and turned right and took a parking place in the Piazza Archivescovado. Vance directed the cab driver into a taxi stand to the left.

Holding the black briefcase in his hand, Kimball emerged from his car and walked briskly toward the tower. The souvenir stands cluttering the piazza were being readied by their chattering proprietors for the onslaught of tourists that would descend upon them within the hour. The tower opened at eight; and a line would have formed by 8:30.

"Wait here," Vance told the cabdriver. "We won't be long . . . I hope." As Kimball disappeared down the steps to the Leaning Tower's entrance, Vance and Suzanne followed at a trot.

They covered the hundred yards from the taxi to the tower in half a minute. A very puzzled taxi driver wondered after them as he watched their bodies grow smaller and finally disappear down the steps toward the tower's entrance. He was growing uneasy. The tall blond man with the black briefcase looked like an unkind man, dangerous. The cabdriver hadn't survived for thirty years without developing a sense of danger, a feel for people. He pondered briefly the idea of using his radio to call the police, then thought better of it. But, just in case, he left the engine running.

At the bottom of the short set of steps that led to the tower's entrance, Vance hesitated, his chest racked with fear. Suzanne paused behind him. Two voices could be heard from within. Then there was silence. Vance stared at the rough wooden door with its heavy iron hinges and straps, and then took a deep breath. He reached out and tried the door. It was locked.

Hands tense, Vance rapped on the door. There were shuffling footsteps, then the rattling of a bolt inside. The door opened wide enough for an old man to stick his head through.

"Good morn—" Suddenly the friendly look on the old man's face turned to fright as he tried to slam the door. Clearly, he had expected someone else. Vance stepped forward and wedged himself in the door. "I'm sorry, but we're not open yet, signore," the man protested. "Please come back later."

"But you've just let in another man."

"Oh, him. He . . . works here."

"Well," Vance said, shoving the door open and stepping through, "we're here to transact a little business with him." He whipped the pistol out of his jeans pocket and pointed it at the man's face. "Don't say a word, my friend." A look at Vance's eyes, and the old man decided to comply. He'd take his chances with the tall blond man and his Russian friends later. He nodded.

"That's intelligent," Vance said. "Now back there behind your desk . . . move!" Vance walked with the old man to his desk and checked to be sure there were no weapons within the old man's reach. Suzanne shut the door and locked it as Vance accompanied the old man to his desk. "Now I want you to take off all your clothes," Vance told the man. The old man's eyes grew wide.

"That's right," Vance said, responding to the man's look of surprise. "But you can sit down to do it . . . she won't watch." Reluctantly, the old man complied. Vance gathered the clothes up, and with a box of matches found in the trousers, set the heap in the middle of the room and set them afire. The old man looked on the strange scene with an expression that oscillated between anger, embarrassment, and sheer incredulity. He was even more stunned when Vance gave him a hundred euro note. "When this is all over, old man, go buy yourself some new clothes."

Turning to Suzanne, he smiled. "I don't think he'll be too much bother to you now," Vance said. It was remarkable how compliant people became when you took their clothes away.

Vance took a step toward the circular stairway, and then walked quickly over to Suzanne and handed her the gun. "You'll probably need this more than I will." And oblivious to the stare of the naked skinny old man hiding behind the desk, Vance started up the stairs.

Around and around, the narrow steps climbed a topsy-turvy corkscrew upward, fifty-seven meters high, about

190 feet. He took the steps two-by-two, pausing on every landing to listen. When he reached the fourth landing, he heard steps above him. Kimball, too, heard Vance's steps.

"Mikhail?" Kimball's voice drifted down the spiral staircase. "You are early." Kimball spoke in Russian. Vance didn't speak Russian. Suddenly there was only silence as Kimball received no reply.

Vance stood there, listening: for Kimball to make a move; listening to the sound of blood rushing through his ears, listening to the lively shouts and greetings of people far below on the ground.

Still, Kimball didn't move. Impatient, Vance resumed his climb.

Vance reached the fifth level. He saw only the portal full of sunshine opening up onto the loggia. Where was Kimball? Vance walked to the portal and peeked about both ways.

Perplexed, Vance walked out on the platform—the last one before the top. He had been amazed as a student coming up here to find there were no guardrails. He'd wondered how many people had been killed as a result.

Now Vance found himself shaking with fright at the open height as he edged his way around the loggia, trying to stay as close to the wall as possible.

So hard was Vance concentrating on his fears of the height that he failed to hear Kimball until it was too late. He turned to see Kimball's six-foot three-inch frame rushing at him.

"Kimball!" It was all he managed to say before the huge man, four inches taller and twenty pounds heavier, was all over him.

*   *   *

This is too good to be true, Kimball was thinking joyously. The only loose end he hadn't tied up was killing that asshole Vance Erikson. The gods are with me today, Kimball thought as he lunged.

The tall blond man's first blow caught Vance squarely on the side of his head and sent him sprawling across the narrow platform. Vance looked down, and instead of seeing the stone platform, stared straight down at the morning grass far below, still sparkling wet with dew. He tried to roll back to safety when suddenly Kimball picked up his feet and started toward the edge with them. Vance grabbed the base of one of the loggia pillars and kicked. The first smacked against the blond man's face, and the second found soft tissue. Vance heard Kimball exhale sharply as his grip on Vance's feet loosened. Vance rolled to safety and stood up unsteadily as he watched Kimball massaging his solar plexus, his face a twisted mask of crimson fury.

"That was a lucky blow, Erikson," Kimball said angrily as he moved slowly toward Vance. "But it's all the luck you're going to get."

Kimball had the blinding speed of a man who trains to fight, and the quickness of a predator, used to winning. He came at Vance in a crouch, barefoot, bare-handed. Vance suddenly wished he'd brought the gun with him.

Miraculously Vance dodged Kimball's first blow, and parried the second, but the follow-up kick landed solidly.

Vance doubled over and rolled to try to defend himself against the skilled killer's expertly aimed blows. But to no avail. Kimball had studied killing as well as Vance had studied Leonardo, and it was no contest. This game didn't have rules like rugby did.

Kimball used his hands and feet like bludgeons; sweat dripped from his face with the exertion and he smiled at the almost sexual fulfillment of beating an enemy to a bloody pulp. Finally, the blows stopped. Kimball stood back and watched his victim struggle to stand.

Blinded by the blood in his eyes, Vance felt the blows stop. He scrambled up on his hands and knees but fell back down on all fours when he tried to stand up. The world was spinning too fast to let him stand. Why had Kimball stopped? Vance crawled about until he bumped into a pillar. Steeling himself against the pain, Vance clung to the pillar and pulled himself up. He stood there hugging the stone column with his eyes tightly shut against the blood; he felt his strength return. He was in good shape and his body could take the punishment and come back. If Kimball were gone, he speculated with his eyes closed, then he could make his way down the stairs.

Vance opened his eyes. The vertiginous drop from the next-to-top story made his head spin more. Cautiously, he brought one hand up to his eyes and wiped away the blood that was obscuring his vision. Kimball was grinning at him.

"I was afraid you'd fall off," the blond man said amiably. "I didn't want you to deprive me of that ultimate pleasure." He took a step toward Vance, smiling broadly. In slow motion, Vance saw Kimball's foot arc toward him. Clinging with both hands to the pillar, Vance tried to dodge the only way he could: by swinging out over the edge of the tower. Kimball's blow missed, but Vance had traded one peril for a worse one. He felt his legs swinging into the vertical nothingness of empty space, his hands slipping along the pillar.

Was this how it all would end? Sweat flowed with the blood on Vance's face. Would it hurt much? He wondered if he'd die immediately, or whether he'd be in pain for a long time. He heard himself scream, as if the noise were coming from the throat of another. But the scream ended suddenly. His body had slammed against the stone tower. He hung on to the pillar, his feet dangling over the edge, an exquisite pain radiating through his fingers as Kimball hammered against them with his fists.

With each blow, Vance cried out in pain. And with each blow, his grip on the pillars loosened. Finally, flesh pounded between stone and hard knuckles could stand the punishment no longer. Vance let go.

Take everything off," Suzanne ordered, her voice hard and businesslike. "The socks, the briefs . . . everything!" The stolid GRU man with the heavy jowls and poorly cut suit was more unhappy about having to disrobe in front of a woman than he was at having a gun pointed at him. Mikhail had had plenty of guns pointed at him in his lifetime, and he'd had women point guns at him, but this was something new. Burning with shame, he slipped the cheap cotton briefs off his pudgy waist.

"Throw them here with the rest," Suzanne ordered, and the man meekly complied.

Warily, clutching the automatic, Suzanne struck a match against the stone floor and held it to the pile of cheap Russian clothing. She wouldn't give this man money to replace his things; let Mother Russia do it.

She had just straightened up and stepped back from the small pyre when she heard Vance scream. Forgetting her naked charges, she rushed outside, following the sound of his voice. At the north side of the tower, she looked up in horror to see Vance hanging over the edge, his legs dangling helplessly. Above him, the tall figure of Elliott Kimball hovered menacingly. She tried to aim the weapon at the tall blond man, but he stepped quickly back from the edge. Moments later, she saw Vance start to fall.

The Leaning Tower of Pisa leans toward the south. And even though the tower's increasing lean has been stabilized by a series of heroic engineering efforts, an object dropped from the exact edge of the top story will strike the earth 4.3 meters from the base—about fourteen feet. The tower has seven stories; every story on the south side is about two feet farther out than the one below it; conversely, on the north side, each successive story sticks out some two feet less than the one below.

Suzanne caught her breath as Vance dropped. But after only six inches, his feet caught the outcrop of the ornamental capitals on the top of the column directly below him. It would have been only a minor bump on the way toward hitting the ground had the tower not inclined enough in his favor to let him lean inward, close to it, a reprieve that could never happen on any other part of the tower.

Despite the trembling in his body, Vance managed to firm up his precarious foothold, carefully planting the front half of each foot on the protruding section of the column capital. Leaning in close to the stone, Vance could feel gravity pressing him lightly against the inclined stone. Relief flooded through him. He'd survived. So far.

Kimball again appeared at the edge of the sixth story to examine his handiwork. But instead of the satisfying sight of Vance Erikson's maimed body crumpled up on the ground, he found himself staring at a woman, her body diminished with the height, her legs braced and spread. Perplexed, Kimball leaned farther out, hanging on to the column for support as he looked for Vance. The big blond assassin's mouth dropped when he spotted Vance clinging to a narrow perch just below him. If they hadn't happened to have fought on this side, if Erikson had fallen outward rather than slid down, the man would be dead. Kimball was outraged. How could this have occurred? In his amazement, he had discounted the woman on the ground, but suddenly something in his trained killer's mind broke through to him. He rarely considered women a threat, but when he looked back at her he saw a muzzle flash and the faintest wisp of discharge from the barrel of what had to be a pistol. Reflexively, Kimball turned to duck.

Pain burned through Kimball's right thigh, and the leg collapsed under him. Blinded by pain, he clutched the wound with his right hand, shifting the rest of his weight onto his left leg. The maneuver only unbalanced him. The sharp report of another shot reached his ears, and then a second slug ripped through his body and smashed through the masses of nerves in his lower back. The muscles in his slightly bent left leg involuntarily flexed and straightened for the last time in response to the blizzard of commands from the damaged nerves. The powerful jerk of his leg broke his grip on the column entirely and propelled him in an arc that took him out over Vance's head.

Thank God for good grades on the range, Suzanne thought. She saw the look of amazement on Kimball's face as the first slug struck him in the inside of his right thigh. A fountain of blood gushed immediately from the wound; she had hit the femoral artery.

Suzanne watched the second shot slam into his lower back when he tried to turn and leap out of the way. Her third and fourth shots missed. But the first two were enough. Suzanne held the pistol limply at her side and watched the tall blond man plunge backward, headfirst off the next to highest level of the tower.

The horizontal push from Kimball's left leg propelled him outward far enough so that he cleared three levels before his body slammed into the inclined tower again.

No-o-o-o-o!" Kimball screamed. "They can't do this to me! I must live!" he insisted while the sky and earth spun crazily about his head like a berserk merry-go-round. The severed artery in Kimball's leg sprayed blood into the air and on the tower's marble as he caterwauled downward. The last thought Elliott Kimball had before his head smashed into the marble ledge of the third level was the humiliating realization that he had been defeated by an amateur and a woman.

Suzanne ran for the tower; she had to get to Vance. Now she heard anxious shouts and, from the corner of her eye, saw people running toward the tower.

Inside the tower she found a set of ropes that were used on crowded days to keep tourists in line. She unhooked the metal clasps on either end of a twenty-foot segment of rope, coiled it up, and sprinted up the stairs.

Vance's calf muscles were beginning to ache as he perched with only his toes on the column's decorative crown. He looked upward at columns only a couple of feet away from his hands. If only he could reach it and pull himself up. He felt the strength in his arms and the rest of his body returning, and only the cramps in his calves remained to remind him of how sapped his body had been from Kimball's beating.

"Vance!"

He looked up and saw Suzanne standing above him. She looked like an angel.

"Just hold on a few more seconds," she said, anxiously looking at his bloody face, not knowing which was his blood and which was Kimball's.

Quickly Suzanne looped the rope around the pillar half a dozen times and passed one loose end to Vance. She held the other end firmly. The friction would keep it secure so she could control his descent to the next level.

He passed the rope around his waist and tied it in a bowline. His cheeks tingled with relief. Never had anything in the world felt so good.

He pulled himself up slightly to let Suzanne test her friction-belaying system, and then gamely stepped off the perch.

When Vance stepped safely onto the platform, Suzanne dropped her end of the rope and ran down the stairs to him. Halfway down she stumbled over a black briefcase, Kimball's. Briefcase in hand, she ran to Vance.

"I thought it was all over," she cried, burying her face in his chest.

"Me too," Vance replied, enjoying her warmth. "So did I." She looked up at his face, her eyes brimming with joyful tears.

"Oh!" she cried, startled. "Your face. It looks . . ."

"Like hamburger, I'll bet," Vance said, gingerly exploring his face with his fingertips. "But I'll be okay in a couple of weeks."

Suzanne looked closely at his face, and despite its bloodied and battered appearance, she found the same tropical blue water eyes and the familiar sparkle in them. "I love you so much!"

"I love you, too," he said, then broke their brief embrace. "But we'd better get out of here, don't you think?"

"Yeah," she said, her thoughts returning to reality. They turned for the stairs. Suzanne stopped abruptly and reached for the briefcase, lying forgotten on the platform in a moment of grateful reunion. "Here's something you may be interested in."

He took the case with trembling fingers and snapped open the latches. Vance examined first one sheet and then another and another, all clearly drawn by Leonardo, all clearly the papers they had been searching for.

"It's here," he said exultantly. "It's all here."

"We got it?"

"We got it.

"And now," he said, snapping the briefcase shut and handing it back to her, "we've got to get out of here." In the distance, police sirens wailed their seesaw sounds.

Down in the anteroom the two nude men fended off a crowd of onlookers trying to enter the tower.

"Good work, gentlemen," Vance said, smiling. Both men turned sharply, frowns on their faces. "It's okay. We'll be leaving now."

Vance opened the door, and plunged into the small crowd of about twenty people, clearing a path for Suzanne who followed with the briefcase. To their right, a larger crowd had gathered about Elliott Kimball's body.

Vance's bloody face presented a grotesque mask that literally frightened people out of his path as he and Suzanne bounded from the tower. At the edge of the crowd, they paused to get their bearings when two tall men suddenly blocked their path.

"We'll take that briefcase, Ms. Storm," a man with a bland accountant's face said in English. He would have looked harmless had it not been for a vague reptilian glint in his eyes and a .357 Magnum revolver in his hand. His companion, a square-jawed chunky man with mirror sunglasses, also carried a Magnum.

Vance felt the heavy weariness of despair drop onto shoulders. It was too much, too much.

"I said, give me the briefcase," the accountant said.

Suzanne hesitated, and the man cocked the hammer of the revolver. "I don't want to kill you . . . at least not here." The man smiled. "But I will unless you give me the briefcase."

She wanted to scream. She looked at Vance and he nodded. Without speaking, she dropped the case at the man's feet. The chunky man stepped back a pace to cover his buddy who quickly retrieved the case. The police sirens grew louder.

"Let's go!" The accountant pointed with the barrel of his gun toward the square. Vance noticed their taxi had left; in its place was a Mercedes limo. With no choice other than to follow or die, Suzanne and Vance headed for the limo at a jog, followed closely by the two guards. As they approached, the limo's driver leaped to the doors on the passenger side of the limo and opened them both.

Vance and Suzanne were motioned into the rear of the car. Two police squad cars and an ambulance screamed into the piazza with a riot of sirens. Startled, the chunky guard shoved Vance and Suzanne into the back of the car and climbed in after them. The accountant slammed the door and jumped into the front of the limo, which shot away from its parking place and sped west.

Vance and Suzanne had tumbled into the backseat and were thrown against the back cushions by the surge of the limo's powerful engine.

Suddenly Vance froze. There, sitting on the other side of the seat, was Harrison Kingsbury. Kingsbury opened his mouth to speak when the limo screamed violently into a right turn and accelerated northeast along the Via Piestrasantina toward the A12 Autostrada.

The guards barked instructions at each other and then fell silent as they watched their charges. The accountant sat beside the driver in the front seat, and pointed his gun at Vance who sat in the backseat facing him. Between Vance and the accountant, on the trundle seat, was a distinguished man in a pin-striped suit. Squatting on the other trundle seat, beside the businessman and directly behind the driver, the chunky guard held his revolver warily, his eyes flickering among the faces of his prisoners. Harrison Kingsbury sat at the left side of the backseat facing the chunky guard, Suzanne sat between him and Vance on the backseat.

As his eyes adjusted to the light, Vance recognized the man in the pin-striped as Merriam Larsen, oil company president, Bremen Legation member, and longstanding enemy of Harrison Kingsbury. Vance noticed how the guards deferred to him, positioned themselves to protect him.

"Good morning," Larsen broke the silence as the limo blew past slower traffic. "You have had a most interesting morning . . . indeed a unique set of days." He took the briefcase from the accountant and placed it over his knees and snapped it open.

"Although I must admit that you've proved to be persistently troublesome for us." Larsen plucked a sheet of the Da Vinci papers from the briefcase, and turned on a reading light and examined it cursorily. He smiled faintly. "You have done us quite a favor this morning." He looked again at the sheet and replaced it. "We had quite lost sight of Mr. Kimball and were dismayed that he might avoid not only the justice which we had prepared for him, but that he might also do something rash with these treasured papers."

Vance shifted in his seat; the accountant's pistol came quickly up.

"Relax, trigger-happy," Vance said. "I'm just trying to get comfortable. Something you and your friend aren't helping."

"My, such a temper, Mr. Erikson," Larsen said with a smirk.

Kingsbury shifted in his seat and Vance watched with alarm as the chunky guard raised his gun reflexively.

"Easy, easy, son," Kingsbury said to the guard, using an unfamiliar old man's voice. Vance looked at Kingsbury and asked with his eyes: "What have they done to you?" But when Kingsbury returned the look, there was fire and cunning burning just as brilliantly as ever. What was going on? Vance wondered. "I'm just an old man," Kingsbury explained to the guard, "trying to get comfortable. All of this sitting cramped up here is not doing my arthritis any good. I'm just trying to get comfortable."

Arthritis? Kingsbury had never suffered from arthritis. So startled was Vance that he failed to catch Larsen's last sentence.

"I said, I am prepared to offer you a position with the Legation, Mr. Erikson. Both you and Ms. Storm here."

"A job?" Vance repeated dumbly. "Why . . . why would you want us?"

"Because you're good. That's why," Larsen said succinctly. "You accomplished what the CIA and all the resources of the Legation could not."

"The CIA?" Vance echoed.

Suzanne knew what was coming. It had been one of the reasons she'd quit the Company.

"Surely, Mr. Erikson, you know the CIA frequently works for us," Larsen said. "We have . . . how shall I put it . . . many objectives in common with theirs. In addition, the gentlemen at the Company are intelligent enough to recognize that we, not the U.S. Government, are their future. The brightest of the CIA's management and staff have cast their lot with us, but I must admit," Larsen continued, "they sometimes disappoint me. They had been charged with locating Elliott Kimball, and they failed."

Vance watched out of the corner of his eye as Kingsbury rearranged himself again. This time the chunky guard didn't move.

"You found Kimball; you found his apartment." Larsen sounded as if he were leading a child through a fairy tale for the first time. "And you recovered the documents."

"But you found us," Vance reminded him.

Larsen nodded. "Yes, fortunately for us. However, you're probably wondering how we did it." So enamored was Larsen with the sound of his own voice that he did not notice Kingsbury squirm in his seat once again. Nor did he notice that Kingsbury was moving closer and closer each time to the chunky guard.

"Well, it's quite simple," Larsen continued. "The only thing the CIA did do right was to maintain surveillance over a number of Kimball's former associates, ones to which he might likely turn after a break with the Legation. One of those happened to be an obscure major in the GRU stationed in Pisa—"

"Mikhail—"

"Alexandrovich," Larsen completed the name. "Yes, quite right. A bit of extra sleuthing indicated that he might be meeting Kimball this morning. We followed. But of course by the time we got here, you were . . . hanging for your life and had done all our work for us."

"What makes you think that Suzanne and I would work for the Legation?" Vance asked defiantly.

"Life. Yours, and Mr. Kingsbury's. You've fought so hard to keep it today . . . in the past weeks. You've killed, you've stolen, you've lied and cheated to stay alive. With all that, I scarcely think you've a mind to let Rudi—" he looked at the chunky guard—"or Steven, behind me, end it all with a bullet. Now, are you?"

"I don't think you understand people very well, Larsen," Vance said angrily. "I don't suppose that you understand dignity, freedom. People die for dignity. I'm not sure life is worth hanging around without—"

"Oh, come now, Mr. Erikson. *Dignity?* Who do you

think I am, some soldier, a piece of cannon fodder ready to be ground into dog food? Nobody dies for dignity anymore. People just want to *live,* to have things. If you give people enough to keep their bellies fed and a roof over their heads, give them a shiny new car and the bread and circus of television, they won't care about dignity."

"Is that how you see people?" Vance said.

"Of course," Larsen said. "Look at the abuse people will put up with in the demeaning little slots they are fed into when they work for a corporation. They do it because we pay them; they know if they don't, they'll be fired. A corporation can't tolerate disruption, and that's just what dignity becomes. People have to be broken of dignity before they work for us; and believe me, they *have* been broken. So don't talk to me about dignity. You and everybody else in this world will do anything—"

Larsen's words were cut short by the movement of a body flying suddenly across the small space inside the limousine. It was Harrison Kingsbury, who had hurled himself at Rudi, the chunky guard. A shot exploded in the backseat; Kingsbury stiffened but refused to loosen his grip on the chunky man's gun.

Vance leaped to help Kingsbury; Larsen ducked to the floor and covered his head, giving the accountant on the front seat a clear shot at Vance's back. But Suzanne lunged over Larsen's body and deflected the gunman's hand with an uppercut to his wrist. The slug slammed harmlessly into the roof. With both her hands, Suzanne grabbed the man's wrist and slammed it into the half-open Plexiglas partition behind the driver's head. Another shot plowed into the ceiling.

Vance punched Rudi in the nose and was rewarded with a satisfying crunch as it broke, and a split second later, a burning arrow of pain shafted through his injured hand. Kingsbury had managed to pin the man's hands, and Vance took advantage, throwing one punishing punch after the other at the guard's face and head.

But the big man was hearty, and Kingsbury's grip was weakening. With a guttural grunt, Rudi heaved the older man's body away. Vance leaped in to take Kingsbury's place, grabbing the hand with the gun, smashing it against the window. Still the guard would not relinquish his grip.

Suzanne flailed at the guard named Steven. She scratched and clawed, her fingernails raking blood from Steven's head and face. The gun wavered. Somehow she managed to keep his arm straight and pointed away from her. The driver's eyes darted anxiously from the road to the fight taking place beside him, as the muzzle of the powerful .357 Magnum passed back and forth over his head.

The confinement also prevented Steven from bringing his left hand into full use; it was all he could do to protect himself from Suzanne's clawings.

Finally, he managed to get his fingers around a hunk of her long hair. Suzanne yelled when he jerked her head down, striking the back of the seat. Stunned, she narrowly missed being struck by the pistol as it descended like a club toward her head. She twisted away and grabbed the fist with the gun with both hands, sinking her teeth into the tendon at the base of his thumb. He screamed in agony and tried to shake his hand free, but the harder he tried, the deeper her teeth went. Suzanne snatched at his face with her right hand, plunging her index finger and middle finger in his eye sockets. She felt the pliable wet gelatinous balls of his eyes and heard him shriek with exquisite pain as she tried to get a grip amid the slick tissues.

Beside her, Vance continued his struggle with the big chunky guard, his replenished strength rapidly fading. The guard shook his left hand lose from Vance's grasp and cocked the arm to throw a killing punch, but the hand slammed into the window. Vance took advantage of the hesitation, braced his legs against the floor, and loosed a punch with all his strength, concentrated in the hard powerful end of his right elbow. The punch landed just behind the chunky guard's ear; the gun dropped from the man's hand and he fell unconscious.

An inhuman shriek filled the limo as Suzanne's probing fingers stabbed repeatedly at the accountant's eyes. He dropped the revolver as he brought his hands up to his face to protect his eyes. The .357 fell to the floor in the rear of the car. Larsen grabbed it and fired at Vance, but Suzanne's movement jostled him and the slug went awry. Vance felt it whiz past his neck.

Larsen brought the gun to bear again; Vance plucked the revolver from underneath the guard's fallen body, ducked as Larsen fired again, and then aimed and fired at Larsen. Vance watched as a gaping red hole appeared in the oil company president's forehead like a ruby on an Indian rajah's. The pistol slipped from Larsen's hands; he collapsed and lay still, as the limo rolled to a stop on the shoulder of the Autostrada.

Vance leaped up, over Larsen's fallen body.

"Don't anybody do anything stupid!" he ordered,

pointing the revolver first at the guard, who still swayed back and forth, moaning and clutching his right eye, and then at the driver. "Take the keys out of the ignition and give them to me." Sullenly the driver complied. "Here," Vance said, handing the revolver to Suzanne, "keep an eye on them." He moved quickly to Kingsbury, whose labored breathing filled the now-silent limo.

The old oil man lay sprawled over the backseat where the chunky guard named Rudi had thrown him. A massive wet red stain covered the front of his white shirt. Tears welled up in Vance's eyes as be cradled Kingsbury in his arms.

"The Larsens of this world are wrong, Vance. You've always understood that," Kingsbury said, blinking his lids over the silvery gray eyes and managing a smile. "That's why you are my son more than any natural offspring could ever be. I . . ." Kingsbury coughed violently, trying to clear the blood that was filling his lungs.

"Please rest," Vance said. "We'll get you to a hospital."

"Vance," the older man pleaded, his voice a strained whisper. "Just listen." Vance bent low to hear Kingsbury's weakening voice.

Though Suzanne kept a cautious eye on her two charges, her attention was inexorably drawn to Harrison Kingsbury and Vance Erikson as they whispered face-to-face. She saw Vance turn aside for a moment to wipe away his tears and then resume the whispered conversation. She watched as Vance used his fingers to gently comb the older man's long silver locks from his face, and to stroke his forehead.

Suzanne watched, awestruck by the depth of the love

between these two. Her throat caught and she bit her lower lip when Vance let out a sob and clutched Kingsbury's head to his chest. After a few minutes, Vance finally looked up, and their eyes met.

When he spoke, there was reverence in his voice.

"He said it was a death worth dying," Vance told her, and his eyes filled again with tears.

Epilogue

What do you mean, you don't remember?" yelled the spokesman for the group of three men—one from the FBI, one from the CIA, and one from the Joint Chiefs of Staff. They all looked about the same: dark business suits, shoes gleaming, hair cut just so, late thirties in age. The man from the Joint Chiefs served as spokesman.

"Just what I told you, gentlemen," Vance Erikson responded as he got up from his desk and walked to the huge window of his office in the ConPacCo Building in Santa Monica. Down below him, a solitary sailboat glided by on this Wednesday in late March. Just wait, Vance told the sloop, I'll give you some company.

"We heard what you said," the Joint Chiefs' man said again, wondering whether or not to get up so he could be on an equal standing with Erikson. "But I—we—find it hard to believe that the chairman of the board, the owner if you will, of one of the largest independent oil companies in the world would not remember what he did with those documents."

Vance turned from the window. "You must realize," he said patiently, "I haven't been chairman long. In fact, I still haven't recovered from the shock of finding out that I inherited it from its founder." Vance smiled. "Perhaps it was the shock which makes me unable to remember."

"I'm warning you, Mr. Erikson." The man from the FBI found his voice. "Those papers are of the highest priority and we are—"

"No!" shouted Vance. "I'm warning you, that if you don't stop harassing me and my employees, you and your bosses are going to be out of a job! Is that clear to you?" Vance walked over to where the three men sat in front of his desk and glared down at them.

"I hardly think that you're in a position to threaten us in this manner," the man from the CIA said sarcastically.

"No?" Vance fixed him with a cold hard stare. "Do you remember how your boss got his job?"

"He was promoted to deputy director upon the resignation of his predecessor."

"I'm glad to see you've done your homework," Vance said. "But do you know why he resigned?" The CIA man looked at him blankly, a growing unease in his eyes. "Well, I'll tell you. It was because he took a bundle of cash from a very, very large conglomerate. And do you know what he took that cash for?" The man shook his head. "He took that cash as payment for an assassination." Anger and indignation grew in Vance's voice. "Not just any assassination, but the assassination of an American politician. And do you know what? That makes me angry as hell, just like all of you and all of your bosses make me angry as hell.

"But let me tell you what prompted that man's resignation. He resigned because I confronted him with incontrovertible evidence of his guilt and told him that he either resigned or I turned it over to the networks and the three big papers."

"Why didn't you?" the man asked, genuinely curious.

"Because by God this country doesn't need anything else to shake its faith in itself," Vance said. "It just needs to have the slime and the filthy crawling creatures cut out like the tumors they are." Vance was breathing hard; ever since he'd gone through the files Elliott Kimball had kept in his flat in Pisa, his insides tightened up like a snarled anchor line every time he thought of their contents.

In his dying words, Harrison Kingsbury had told Vance the name of a top-ranking official in the Italian national police intelligence service who could be trusted.

After Kingsbury died, Suzanne and Vance had bound and gagged the three surviving Legation employees, thrown them by the side of the road, and called the police at a pay phone just outside of Via Reggio. There they also called Kingsbury's man. He arranged for Suzanne and Vance to turn themselves in.

The trials were short and ended in acquittals. A police raid on the monastery had turned up witness after witness who rightfully placed the blame on the Elect Brothers of St. Peter for the murder of Count Caizzi, and the hotel maid in the Milan fashion district shoot-out.

One of the chief witnesses was Professor Umberto Tosi; now back at the University of Bologna after extensive microsurgery had freed him from the Brothers' poison module. He had been one of the lucky ones. Nearly half of those who underwent the surgery died under the knife when the poison released suddenly.

But Tosi went home a free man. Not so the Legation's chauffeur and the two guards, who drew light jail sentences in exchange for turning state's evidence. Their testimony cleared Suzanne and Vance in the deaths of Kimball, Larsen, and Kingsbury. They also identified the man who killed Professor Geoffrey Martini and the Da Vinci scholars in Vienna and Strasbourg as an employee of the Bremen Legation. He was never apprehended.

When the trials ended, Vance, Suzanne, Kingsbury's man from the Italian national police, and Tony Fairfax, who was now recovered from his mild heart attack, forced their way into Elliott Kimball's apartment and broke into the files. The contents were monstrous: staggering indictments of government officials and multinational corporate executives, all solidly documented. They split the files among them, with Vance taking custody of all the files relating to the United States.

"It seems that your boss's predecessor sort of forgot whose side he was on." Vance refocused his attention to the representative of the CIA who sat quietly before him. "And you two gentlemen"—he nodded in their direction—"have plenty of examples within your own departments; there's more, much, much more.

"You, Atkinson," Vance spoke to the man from the Joint Chiefs' office. "Would you like your wife to know that you enjoy an occasional fling with the boys?"

"That's hardly unusual—"

"Between the sheets?" Vance asked. "With nine-year-old

boys?" The man's face turned pale. His two companions tried not to look at him, but cast him furtive sideways glances all the same.

"That's right, Atkinson," Vance continued. "The Bremen Legation was thorough. Pictures and affidavits from the little boys. For shame, Mister Warhawk.

"But the point is," Vance continued, "that the Bremen Legation was far more thorough at spying on the lives of government officials than the CIA ever was at spying on U.S. citizens, and the files I have in my possession are a substantial part of the Legation's files."

"That's blackmail!" the FBI agent protested indignantly.

"Maybe," Vance responded. "But this country can no longer afford to live with that sort of corruption and incompetence in its government and military. And since the corporations in the Bremen Legation used these dossiers to blackmail public and military officials into doing things which weren't in the public interest, I intend to use them to remove every last one of them. Yes," Vance said, looking at the military attaché. "That includes you, Mr. Atkinson. If I were you, I'd start composing my resignation letter. Unless, that is, you want to see the story complete with pictures in the paper.

"What was the name of that society you belonged to?" Vance paused. "You know, Atkinson, the one with the motto 'Sex by eight or it's too late.' Come on, Atkinson, you can remember."

The military aide gave a cry of anguish and leaped from his chair and fled the room.

"Gentlemen, the contents of those dossiers are duplicated and well guarded. They will all be made public if something should happen to me. The evidence is so widespread and so pervasive within the government that I'm afraid the crisis is something the republic might not survive. That's why I'm using the dossiers gradually and quietly. What we really need is a government which works for the people, not the other way around."

"But . . . but the president—" stuttered the man from the FBI.

"You are naive, aren't you? That man's ham-fisted supply-side economics did nothing more than turn the government over to the big multinational corporations. He isn't helping capitalism. He's helping the fucking corporate oligarchies, and those guys are more dangerous to free enterprise than a billion clones of Marx and Engels marching in lockstep. Capitalism and free enterprise made this country great; not a legion of octopus corporate kingdoms with more bureaucrats than the Social Security system."

The buzzer on Vance's desk sounded. "Excuse me," he said, reaching for the receiver. "Oh, all right, fine. Put him on." He paused a moment and then spoke. "Yes, yes they're here right now. Yes, thank you for calling: I can give you my answer directly. What? No, I don't want government money and I don't want a legion of government bureaucrats and readers-over-the-shoulder. As I've said time and again in public and in my letters to you, America will have its particle-beam weapon because I am going to build it and give it to you. I'm tired of all the money we pour down the rat hole of the Defense Department because half of it goes to retreading the lard on the asses of bureaucrats. This is one weapon that I'm not going to allow the government to fuck up and I'm not going to have some gold-plated corporation double the price of it.

"And no, I will not tell you where it's being made. The

components are being assembled at more than a dozen places, and government interference in any one of them will mean no weapon, no documents. I'm not turning over the Da Vinci drawings to you or to anyone else, I'll build your weapons and America will have them for free and we'll have them decades before the Ruskies get theirs, although by God that's no fault of our own bloated military establishment.

"Yes, sir. Yes, I intend to continue using the information I obtained. I will use it to see that for the first time in more than a century, Americans will get the government and the military protection they paid for and need . . . No, sir. I don't enjoy this one little bit. In fact, I'd much rather be sailing." Vance listened and smiled. "Thank you." Vance said good-bye and hung up.

"That was the president," Vance said. "You can all go home now, and he says to call off your dogs and get the hell out of here."

In late March, sailing can be chilly in southern California, and while it's no real challenge to the experienced sailor, it does keep most of the amateurs off the water. It was nearly midnight, Vance had come home late from Con-PacCo, and they'd cast off from the slip at Marina del Rey and headed for Catalina.

"But that's the point," Vance said as he leaned lightly on the wheel to keep them on course. "I don't want to do all this. I'm sick of having to beat people over the head with their sins. I don't like to tell the president once a week that I'm not going to turn over the charged particle-beam weapons program to him. I don't want to be in charge!" He yelled into the wind to vent his frustration.

"But you are," Suzanne said. She could see the light of Ship Rock clearly now. They'd made good time despite the weak wind, and despite having to detour around a huge barge and tow. "What are you going to do?" she asked him. "Run away and let someone else do it?"

"That would be super."

"Let's see now," Suzanne said slowly. "There's Bill Macintosh."

"Too young."

". . . or Philip Carter."

"Too bureaucratic."

". . . or Tony Adams."

"Lacks nerve."

"Lee Tyler . . ."

"Give her a few years and she'll be able to run the company."

"There!" Suzanne said enthusiastically, as if this hadn't been the hundredth time they'd had this discussion. "You'll just have to hang on a few years, then you can wander back off into the boonies on your bike."

"Life was a lot simpler then," Vance said wistfully.

"We didn't know each other then."

"Yeah. But why did I have to take the company and the Da Vinci drawings . . . and the blackmail documents to get you?"

"Are you having doubts?" she teased him.

"Well . . ." he said in mock consideration. "Can I think about it?"

Suzanne punched him in the ribs, and he immediately lost his course.

"You're dangerous," he said.

"I know."

"That makes you even more dangerous."

"I know."

"This could go on forever."

"I hope so," Suzanne said, leaning over to kiss him. The forty-two-foot ketch drifted off course until the sails were luffing wildly.

Vance leaned away from her for a moment. "The captain says the first mate shouldn't distract him when he's sailing," he said.

"Are you complaining?"

"Nope. Not on your life," Vance replied as he struggled to find the wind again. It could never be the same, Vance thought. But life was never the same. It kept on changing. He supposed it was all for the best. But enjoying it meant learning to like the journey, not just the destination.

"What are you thinking?" Suzanne asked.

"Oh, about something Leonardo wrote."

"Tell me."

"It was somewhere in the Condice Trivulziano. He wrote: 'In rivers, the water that you touch is the last of what has passed and the first of that which comes: so with time present.' Life is a lot like that."

"Hmmm. Well, lets just you and me keep our heads above water," she said cheerfully and then kissed him again.

TOR

Award-winning authors
Compelling stories

Please join us at the website
below for more information
about this author and other great
Tor selections, and to sign up for
our monthly newsletter!

www.tor-forge.com